HER *Rough Ride*

BOOKS BY HEATHER VAN FLEET

Her Wild Ride

HEATHER VAN FLEET

HER
Rough Ride

bookouture

Published by Bookouture in 2019

An imprint of StoryFire Ltd.

Carmelite House
50 Victoria Embankment
London EC4Y 0DZ

www.bookouture.com

ISBN: 978-1-78681-945-1
eBook ISBN: 978-1-78681-944-4

PROLOGUE

Sebastian

"Tell me about another god, Story Boy." She rolled over on her side to face me, and the bed shifted beneath us. Every time I inhaled I smelled her vanilla-scented skin. I think I was addicted to the lotion she wore or something because it's all I thought about.

"Which one?"

"Poseidon."

I stared up at the ceiling and frowned. "You know about him already. He's the god of the sea."

"I love the ocean. Especially the Pacific."

I heard the smile in her words, then quickly glanced at her mouth just long enough to torture myself. I shut my eyes and exhaled a second later, wishing I hadn't bothered. Now all I'd thinking about tonight was that lip gloss she was wearing—and whether or not it tasted as sweet as it smelled.

"I'm gonna live near there someday. Guarantee it," she added.

"Where?"

"California." She sighed. "Not Malibu, but maybe San Diego. I hear they have some pretty great beaches."

"I wouldn't know."

"You could visit me there if I do move."

I wondered how that would work, seeing as how the girl barely talked to me during the day. Would she make an exception to that rule when she lived by the beach? That seemed unlikely, but what did I know about the opposite sex anyway?

"Maybe." I shrugged then started in about Poseidon again. It was safer for me to talk about mythology and Greek gods. Why? The past is documented, not to mention definable, but the future is undetermined, which scared the hell out of me.

"So, Poseidon's the god of the sea, earthquakes, and horses. His siblings are Hades, Demeter, Hestia, Zeus…" I went on, throwing facts out there like I always did. Flick, my guardian and the vice president of the Red Dragon MC, said I had a brain most would kill for, but I wasn't so sure.

"Have you always been this smart?" she asked when I finished.

I shrugged, not liking compliments. They made me feel weird.

"I've never known anyone who can spout stuff off like you. It's… cool."

My face got hot, and I looked the other way, hoping my cheeks weren't red. Being smart was good and all, but that meant nothing in the world I lived in if I didn't know how to kill a man—least that's what my uncle, Pops, told me.

The thought of the Red Dragon club president had my gut squeezing. The guy scared the hell out of me because I regularly saw what his fists could do. My cousin, Niyol—his son—usually got the worst of it, but I'd seen him raise a hand at some of the others before. The younger ones, mostly. Flick tried to keep me away from Pops's wrath, but now that I was a few months from turning eighteen, I was pretty sure I'd have to run from the club for good, or join up as a prospect.

I lifted my arms and put both hands behind my head, not wanting to waste time thinking about that tonight. My nights were hers, and only hers. Nothing else mattered when we were together like this.

"You ever think about getting a tattoo?" she asked out of the blue.

I shook my head, letting it drop to the side to look at her again.

"You should." A tiny line formed between her eyebrows as she studied me. "I'd totally draw something if you wanted. A design template right here with a black Sharpie." She leaned closer and placed her hand over my heart.

I froze.

Delicate fingers spread over my pec. She lifted her gaze again, and I swear to Christ, her eyes sparkled as she searched my face. Beneath her soft palm, my skin started tingling too. Warm and electric, kind of like static, but hotter. It made me wonder if she had magic powers or something—a goddess in disguise, hiding behind her perfect, human skin.

"Maybe." I cleared my throat, staring ahead at my dresser, nearly losing the last of my control.

"Tell me about another one." She kept her hand on my chest. "How about a goddess this time?"

I blew out a slow breath. "What about Persephone? You want to hear about her?"

"Who's that?"

"You've never heard of Persephone?" I narrowed my eyes.

"Nope. What are her strengths?"

I sighed, prepping for an all-nighter. Before she and her mom, June, had come to stay with me and Flick a few weeks ago, I used to sleep like a baby. Now, I was lucky if I got two hours a night. Not that I cared. Every time I told her a different mythological fact, she got all excited, her pretty eyes sparkling like stars.

The best part of our nights together, when I wasn't talking to her, were when she'd lay her head on my chest without asking and tell me that the sound of my heartbeat kept her bad dreams away. Seeing as how I liked smelling her lotion, liked her close to my body even more, I figured it worked out for both of us.

"Okay. Persephone's greatest strengths..." I dug into my memory, coming up with the first two things I could think of. "She's good at compromising and she's adaptable to situations."

"Her weaknesses?"

"Wanting to please everyone."

She hummed and shut her eyes. The second they were closed, I missed them. All hazel and wide… sometimes they looked green in the sun. Golden when she was riled up about something. Then when it was rainy out, or she was sad, they seemed to turn brown. One thing I knew for sure: I'd never seen eyes as beautiful as hers before.

I always wondered what she'd do if I tried to kiss her. Taste that lip gloss and the mint on her breath from her toothpaste. If I did try, I'd probably screw up somehow, ruin whatever we were. Secret friends in the night—is that what she called us?

It was stupid. I didn't know why she couldn't talk to me during the day. But at the same time, I never asked because I was worried she'd stop letting me come lie with her in my bed if I did. She'd taken over my room, made it her own, while I crashed on the couch… well, up until a few weeks ago, that is.

"Persephone sounds a lot like me," she whispered.

"Why do you say that?"

"Because…" She paused. "All I've ever wanted to do was please people."

"You don't need to try to please me." I liked her just how she was.

Her lips ticked up on one side, but then she leaned in, distracting me from saying anything else.

My body grew rigid, and I waited, not knowing what to expect—this was the closest she'd ever been to my mouth. She pressed her forehead to my chin, and because I couldn't help it, my dick got all hard, throbbing against the zipper of my jeans. I shut my eyes, waiting, feeling the heat of her mouth against my throat…

Then she used her fingers and started tracing the pulse at my neck, and every nerve inside my body started humming. *Begging.*

Back and forth.

Up and down.

Over and over and over…

I licked my dry lips, breath heavy, waiting for something.

Anything.

Everything.

God, I wanted to kiss her. Lift her chin up, press my mouth to hers, and just… do it.

But then she sighed, breaking the silence. "See, that's the thing about you, Sebastian. Unlike everyone else I know, you always make me feel like I'm worth something."

I swallowed hard, not expecting her to get so serious. It didn't match with our position—how our thighs were pressed together, how my hard-on was shoved against her stomach. I knew she had to feel it, but she didn't comment—didn't make a move to touch me anywhere but my neck and chest either. Not that she ever would.

We were friends, that was all. I knew better than to think anything else. Still, that didn't stop me from saying what I said next.

Why? Because I was pretty damn sure I was in love with this woman.

"You're worth everything to me."

She didn't speak, but she did urge me onto my back. Not bothering to look at my face, she laid on my chest, settling her ear against my heart like every other night.

My throat ached when I tried to swallow. Disappointment I didn't want to feel made it almost too hard to breathe. Still, I wouldn't ask her what she was thinking because I was scared of what her answer would be. When she finally did reply, her words… they hurt. A heart-throbbing, burning kind of hurt that I'd never get over.

Or forget.

"You're incredibly stupid for thinking that, Story Boy."

CHAPTER ONE

Eight years later

Slade

In all my years of being a Red Dragon, there was one rule I followed religiously: be the best brother I could be.

If being the best meant riding an hour through the suburbs to get Hawk some expensive-ass Nicotine gum to curb his cravings, then I'd do it. If being the best meant slicing a fucker across the neck because he messed with my club pres, Flick, or going to the pen just to keep my oldest friend, Archer, out of trouble, then I wouldn't hesitate to do either of those things.

But there was one thing I refused to do. One thing I *could not* manage, even if it meant life or death. And that was flying to California to pack up Flick's niece and bring her back to the club without a single hair missing from her head. Why was that? Because I hated Maya Davenport more than anyone else in this world.

"Ain't gonna happen," I told my pres. "Get Chop to do it. Or what about *Hawk*?" Seeing as how he'd been her damn fuck buddy once.

I glared at my cousin, Niyol—Hawk—Lattimore, for good measure. Dark eyes like my own narrowed back at me from his seat across the table in Church. Did he know what I was thinking?

I sure as hell hoped he did. Wasn't exactly in the mood to say more than I had to.

His feet were kicked up on the edge of the chair and his hand rubbed furiously at his jaw. If I hadn't known Hawk my entire life, I probably would've pissed my pants at the sight. Lucky for my boxers, I was immune.

People said we looked more like brothers than cousins. Same dark hair, dark eyes, forever tanned skin. I didn't put too much stock in it myself because the two of us couldn't be more different on the inside.

"Summer and I are just getting our shit together," Hawk argued. "I'm not leaving her for longer than I already have."

Last July, Hawk went on a little road trip of his own, running from the club after getting out of prison. Summer, his sister's best friend, was the one who took him. He'd been heading to see Maya, as he planned on hiding out with her in San Diego—away from the club that he thought was out to get him. But an attack from Pops, along with the fact that he'd fallen for his blonde escort, had him changing his mind, and coming back home to Rockford—for good this time.

Still. Did they really need more fucking time to get their shit together? Hell no. "It's been seven months. How much more time do you need?"

"You got no idea what it's like," Hawk sneered, his right eye twitching. "And unless you find someone permanent to warm your bed at night, then I'm pretty sure you'll never know."

Having an old lady tie me down? Screw that. Up until last year, Hawk would've agreed with me.

No matter. The bottom line was the two of them had plenty of time to get back into the game. Hawk and Summer were just too busy fucking like bunnies, living out their happy-go-lucky lives up the road from the club in their new, perfect house, to do anything important club-wise.

Flick leaned forward in his chair, elbows on the table. He was the picture of calm today, surprisingly. "You're the road captain, Slade. It's your job to go on runs."

"Runs are one thing, but babysitting? Hell no." Especially not when it came to *her*.

"My niece doesn't need a babysitter." He laughed. "She's a big girl who just so happens to need a bodyguard, and *you're* the only one who's free right now to make it happen."

"And who's going to protect everyone else while I'm away, huh?" I should've been the guy leading the charge when it came to protecting the RDs. Especially now. A prospect had just been killed. *My* prospect. I should've been the one finding the guy responsible for taking down Carlos's killer, damn it.

Young, eighteen, eyes wide and ready to see the world as an RD brother. Carlos had wanted to be the one to go on our run about two weeks ago. That was proof he'd been ready to patch in. He'd told me to stay behind, that he was fine on his own, and because I'd been too busy having relations with a bottle of Jack, I'd waved him off. Given him the keys to my bike, too, because I liked the kid. Trusted him. Knew he had a hard-on for my Harley. It went against club rules to let him leave on his own, but even Flick hadn't seen the harm in him taking parts into town.

When he hadn't shown that night for a party at the club, though, me and Arch had gone off looking for him, thinking he'd gone to visit his girl or some shit. I'd been pissed—he was on my bike, for fuck's sake. But a couple miles outside the compound, we'd seen him in a ditch, bloodied body thrown off my bike. At first, we'd thought it was an accident—it'd been raining all day. Then when we'd got close enough to see the three bullet holes in the back of his head, we'd known that wasn't the case.

He'd been picked off.

Since then, I'd been making it my duty to protect anyone and everyone at the club. Old ladies, groupies, hang-abouts, my brothers… Flick told me I had a hero complex, to get over whatever was bugging me. But what my pres didn't know was that I'd never forgive myself for what happened to Carlos. So to leave for California like he was asking of me? That shit wasn't gonna happen.

"We're fine here." Flick shrugged. "Golden, really."

"Golden? Carlos was just picked off two weeks ago, damn it. And you don't even know who did it."

He sighed, a hand in the air, placating. "This shit's personal for you, I get that. But you need to let it go for a while. Give yourself some time to relax. Go to California, get Maya." A shrug. "Call it a vacation, if you wanna."

"I don't need a damn vacation. I need to be here so I can make sure nobody else gets offed."

"There's nothing you can do for us that we can't do for ourselves, am I right, boys?" Flick looked around, gaining nods of approval from a few other brothers in the room: Chop, Hawk, Crazy…

"Flick's right," Hawk added. "Go get Maya. It's only a couple days anyway."

Ignoring my cousin again, I kept my gaze locked on Flick's. He may have taken care of me after my old man was murdered when I was kid, but things were different now. I wasn't a kid anymore. And at this point in time, I was willing to pull every last string I had left just to keep shit around here safe. To not let what happened to Carlos happen to anyone else.

And to avoid this damn trip, most of all.

So, I tried a different angle right then, pulling the card I'd sworn I'd never use.

"You really want me, a guy who's seconds from losing his shit, to go play bodyguard to your niece? Cause I can guarantee you that my head is not in the right place."

Flick rose from his seat, still too calm for my liking. If he didn't have a beard down to the middle of his chest and newly buzzed hair with tats all over his head, he would've looked regal.

He cocked his head to one side, moving to stand in front of me. "You telling me no then, *Sebastian?*"

I flinched, knowing I'd walked right into that one. That son of a bitch was long gone, tucked away in the pit fires of my own, current hell. Sebastian was nothing more than a pain-in-the-ass wimp who felt too much and loved too damn hard. I'd given up on being him when I'd prospected. He didn't belong in this world. Slade did.

I stood and took a step back dragging both hands down my face. Holding them there, I took a heavy breath, knowing I was running out of options—fast. Seeing Maya again? It'd wreck me. But going against Flick's orders? Nobody did that.

A door creaked open, heavy footfalls sounding behind me. I knew who it was before I could face him, the low Irish lilt of his voice keying me in. "You're running too hard. Seconds from falling apart. You need a break, brother."

"I'm fine." I dropped my hands and curled them into fists, nails digging into my skin.

"You're not fine," Archer growled at my back, smelling like the foreign whiskey he loved to indulge in, even this early in the morning. "You're dead on your feet, seconds from collapsing. And as the VP of this club, I'm siding with Flick."

"Fuck you," I hissed, turning to face him. Archer never pulled the VP card.

Hawk stood to his left though—my two best friends, a force against me.

Sons of bitches.

"Archer's right." My cousin lifted his chin. "You need a breather, Slade."

"You're both assholes, you know that?" I scrubbed a hand over my mouth, done with the nightmare that was today.

Neither of them understood what this trip could do to me. Neither of them knew what the fuck would happen if Maya got under my skin again. This wasn't just about the club's protection.

It was about protecting myself from the one woman who'd always had the power to ruin me.

Before I could say anything other than no, I had one question for my pres. "Why the rush, huh?"

Flick tugged at his beard, jaw twitching. Right then and there I saw the secret in his eyes. Something big was going down. I narrowed my eyes in suspicion, waiting for whatever bomb to drop.

"I got reason to believe Pops is behind Carlos's death."

And just like that, *everything* changed. My world, my motivation, my desire to protect. I switched gears. The bags were already being packed in my mind, strategies developing in my brain at the same time. This was big—huge. As MCs we fought every day, but if Pops had something to do with Carlos's death, everyone associated with us was at risk. And that included Maya.

"How long have you known about this?" Hawk asked what I couldn't. I may have been smart, but speaking coherently was always a struggle for me when I was worked up.

"About an hour ago." Flick folded his arms. "It's why I called Church."

"Maya will fight me on this," was the only thing I could say.

Flick picked up a pack of smokes and started packing them against his palm. "She won't fight you."

Maya had left this town for a reason eight years ago, wanting to get away from the lifestyle that came with the RD world. I respected that, even though I hated her for it at the same time.

If anything, I barely thought about her most days… but nights were different. She was always there in my room when it got dark, even all these years later. A ghost in my dreams that never let me go—I both hated and lusted after the memory of her.

I was living with Flick when Maya and June had come to live with us. Poor orphaned Sebastian, with the dead dad and the mom who'd run off just a week after she'd had me, never looking back as far as I knew.

The night they'd got there, I'd been out late at the library a few towns over. Didn't even know they'd shown until it was too late. As the young, skinny dork with the glasses, nobody bothered updating me on anything club-related, not even Flick. Back then, before I was patched in, I preferred it that way.

It wasn't until I'd opened my bedroom door, and found a girl standing at my dresser nearly naked, that I'd realized Maya was there. Had I been Hawk or Archer, I probably would've made a joke about her taking me to dinner before giving me dessert. But I wasn't like my brothers back then. Still wasn't when it came to certain things.

The second I'd seen her taking off her bra, I probably should've walked away. But I'd never seen a naked girl before, least not in real life, so I'd stayed rooted to the hall floor like some sort of creep, watching as she stripped the black lace off her chest and ass.

Slow motion—that's what it had felt like seeing her. Maya was all soft skin, not a freckle or scar in sight, with short, shoulder-length black hair and the most perfect tits I'd ever seen reflecting in the moonlit mirror. I fell in lust with her body before I fell in love with her mind. At the time, she was what I'd thought of as a gift from Eros, the god of love.

When she'd lifted her gaze and caught me staring in the mirror, I instantly hated myself for perving on her. But even as I apologized, explained who I was, she never yelled at me to go. Didn't tell Flick either. Instead, she'd walked to the door, looked me in the eyes, and cocked her head, as if she'd been waiting for my idiot self all along.

Neither of us had moved, but something had passed between us right then at the same time. A charge. An instant connection. Something both heated and serious. Primal. If I could have, I would've leaned in and kissed her, but I'd been too shy. And, in the end, she'd shut the door in my face with a soft click.

For a long moment, I'd thought—hell, I'm pretty sure I'd *prayed*—that maybe, for the first time in my life, someone was going to pay attention to me. Like me for me. A hot girl at that. But then Hawk had shown up the next day, taking what I'd wanted so badly for himself. The second the two of them met, I was long forgotten. At least during the day.

The nights though… they'd been for us.

"Slade, you hear me?" Flick asked.

I blinked, pulled out of the memories. "Yeah. I hear you."

"Good. And Maya *will* go with you because I haven't given her a choice."

"What all does she know?"

"That she needs to come home," he said.

I nodded.

"And you're not gonna tell her anything else either. No point in scaring her," he added.

Of course he didn't want me to say anything. If I told her, I'd fuck it all up somehow. It's what I did. Smart brain, powerful killer, but my communication skills sucked ass. Even back when I was Sebastian, before Maya took off, I couldn't get shit straight. The only thing I was good for was being Maya's pillow, and therapist, in the middle of the night.

I remembered the first time I'd heard her crying. I'd been lying on the couch, unable to sleep, thinking about her body in my bed. Then I'd heard her muffled cries, taken a chance, and knocked on the door. When I'd gone in, I'd found her on the floor in the corner of the room. Not knowing what to do, I'd walked over and sat down next to her. Neither of us had talked but she'd fallen asleep on my shoulder.

Then the next day, when I'd tried to say hi in the kitchen, ask her if she was okay, she'd ignored me. Not gonna lie. That shit hurt. Bad. But I was stupid enough to pretend it was okay because, to me, Maya was the most beautiful thing I'd ever seen.

The following night, I'd heard her crying again. Went into the room, found her in bed this time, and asked her if she needed anything. Instead of answering, she'd patted the space next to her and asked me to lie down, only for her to fall asleep against my chest.

That's how our summer had gone. I'd become her secret at night, then a stranger during the day. Every time Hawk would run off with her, I'd grow angrier, more bitter, and by the end of the summer, on the night before she was supposed to leave town, I'd had enough. I was done being her whipping boy. Her fucking secret. So I'd gone to the club with Archer, who'd been bugging me for as long as I could remember to hang out with him and the other brothers.

I'd gotten drunk that night for the first time in my life.

Had a couple of women for the first time too.

Then I'd gone to sleep feeling worse than before.

When I'd driven back to Flick's place the next morning, the only sign left of Maya had been the scent of her vanilla lotion still lingering in the air. She'd left without a goodbye, and Slade was born from the ashes of Sebastian's incinerated heart.

"So, that's it, then. You'll do it?" Flick's gray brows lifted mid-forehead.

Regardless of the fact that I was absolutely fucking terrified of seeing Maya again, I knew I had to go.

"Guess so." I frowned.

Flick smirked then slapped my shoulder. "Good. Because your flight leaves in three hours."

CHAPTER TWO

Maya

Waking up on my bedroom floor at five in the morning with an empty bottle of fruit-flavored vodka tucked under my armpit and an eviction notice stuck to the bottom of my foot was a low I'd never expected to experience. But fate was a bitch, and life as I knew it was over.

Was I being overly dramatic? Possibly. But when you'd gone through the sort of hellfire I had within the course of forty-eight hours—fired from your job *and* evicted from your apartment—a little extra theatrics was understandable.

A door slammed in my face and a metaphorical kick in the ass. That's all I had to show for the last year of my life. I'd put my soul into working at San Diego Ink, only allowed to tattoo college girls who were usually looking to ink their skin more to piss off their daddy than to appreciate the art of what I could do with my tattoo gun. But now I couldn't even do that.

Would things have ended up differently had I been a guy? No doubt in my mind. But being a female tattoo artist in a male-run business had never been easy for me.

It'd started and ended with a scuzzy boss who'd touched me one too many times for my liking. And when it wasn't his touching, it was his dirty innuendos.

It had all come to a head on Wednesday night, though, when Micha—said disgusting, scuzzy boss—had asked me to stay behind after hours to talk shop. Thinking he was finally going to give me a permanent chair, I hadn't thought twice about his proposed meeting.

At least not at first.

He'd poured some drinks, downing them like water, and the next thing I knew, I was on the desk in his office beneath him. His mouth on my neck, his hands up my skirt… I'd known it was wrong, wasn't feeling it in the least, and when I'd tried to pull away he'd gotten pissed. Called me a dick tease.

In turn, I'd broken his nose and left.

Naively enough, I'd thought maybe he'd forget it all. Blame it on the alcohol or something. But when I'd shown up Thursday at the parlor, ready to work, everything had fallen apart. And Micha? He hadn't forgotten.

Just inside the front entrance of the parlor, he'd stopped me, throwing two lame and completely bullshit excuses in my face for why it was time for me to move on: *Your tats don't pick up enough business for us to give you a permanent spot. You're too distracting and the guys just don't like you here.*

"Good riddance." I flipped the ceiling my middle finger and rolled over onto my back, shaking out my foot to loosen the dread-worthy pink sheet from my toes. Another hell coursed through me right then. I pulled the paper closer to my face and immediately cringed.

Crap. I'd been praying this portion of my hell had well and truly been just a nightmare.

Department of Housing
Eviction Notice: All occupiers
Effective: Immediately
Building scheduled for demolition in one week

"Ugh." I squeezed the paper into a ball.

God, what I wouldn't give to have the floor open up and suck me into the pits of hell where I belonged. Mom would have a field day with this one. I could hear her voice already: *I told you so.*

When I'd mentioned I was moving to San Diego from Rockford, Illinois, eight years ago, Mom had nearly had a conniption.

Girls like you aren't meant to be on your own like that. Stay here, marry an RD. Let them take care of you. This is where you belong.

I rolled my eyes at the thought, disgusted by her lack of backbone.

After I left Illinois, I stopped speaking to her. Had no interest in any kind of relationship with her anymore. I wanted more out of life than she wanted for me. A change from the MC world as a whole, especially since I'd grown up in it. Bikers and motorcycle clubs only led to heartache; she knew that better than I did.

Of course, when the seventh week of cutting her off had come along, Mom had shown up at my apartment door, frantic and sobbing out her apology, all while three men stood behind her in the hallway, beefy arms folded across their chests—her biker bodyguards.

Even then, I'd refused to come home. And I'd stuck to my guns about that decision for years.

The way I looked at it, I had two options: find a new place and a new job, or run back to my mom and uncle in Rockford. They'd both take me in, no doubt, but they'd be so smug about my return. That's exactly why I was done with my one-night pity party. Job-hunting would commence today.

No way would I go back to Illinois.

No. Flipping. Way.

With painstaking slowness, I rolled over onto my knees, closing my right eye when the room began to spin. I was seventy-five percent sure it was the hangover, twenty-five percent worried I'd gotten a concussion from hitting my head on the corner of my bedframe when I'd tripped over my rug.

I wasn't puking, so that was a good sign. But the nausea was bad. *So* bad.

"Stupid liquor." When I managed to get to my feet, I bent over and picked up the bottle, intending to throw it away. That's when the pounding on my front door started.

Who in the hell is that? It's five in the morning on a Friday, for God's sake.

Curling my lip, I opened my top dresser drawer and pulled out my can of Mace. Of course, I wasn't planning on using it, but growing up around the Forsaken, and spending a summer with the RDs, had left me constantly on edge and always expecting the worst. I stuffed the can into the front pocket of my hoodie, keeping one hand on it as I stumbled through my tiny apartment.

The knocking grew incessant. Louder. Annoyingly so. I inhaled, starting to wonder if there was a fire or an earthquake; something life-threatening that I'd been too out of it to notice. The ground wasn't shaking, and I didn't smell smoke, but by the constant thud of a fist against the door, you'd think it was life or death.

"Hold on!" I yelled, slipping on a pair of leggings that were neatly folded in a laundry basket by my couch.

Once I was dressed, I pushed my hair from my face and peeked through the peephole, frowning, blinking, pulling back, then looking again.

"Hawk?" I whispered. I knew better than to think he was here. Seven months ago, my oldest friend had been on his way to see me. Live with me. Shack up with me—without the actually *shacking* part. But then he'd fallen hard for his peppy blonde escort and gone back home to the Red Dragons. Last I knew, he was crazy in love, happy—everything I currently was not. *Lucky asshole.*

Still, there was no denying his similarities to the man in the hallway. My morning stranger wasn't quite as tall as his doppel-gänger, but he had everything else going on—things that I'd never even noticed about Hawk before. Or *chosen* to notice, seeing as how he was more of a brother than a one-night stand. Sure, there were the obvious similarities, like the large muscles and dark eyes with ashy lashes that fanned over tanned cheeks when he blinked. The high cheekbones and the forever broody glare were there too, which I'd once thought Hawk had trademarked. Until now.

The biggest difference between the two men that I could see was the deep ridge of the dimple on the stranger's face. Even without a smile, I could make it out. Paired with his *I'm gonna eat you alive if you don't open this door* expression, this man had me biting my lip with both curiosity and lust.

Messy hair settled over his forehead, covering one of those sinfully brown eyes. And though I knew he couldn't see me ogling him through the peephole, I still felt stripped bare by the intensity of his gaze.

I swallowed a sigh, thinking of how long it had been since I'd been with a man. Too long, apparently. Because everything about this bad boy had my belly doing flips and my thighs squeezing together with anticipation. My own personal sex toy, minus the batteries—that's what I imagined him to be.

This guy was a complete stranger. He could've very well been here to off me. But there was something about him that seemed impossibly familiar, to the point where I wasn't worried like I should have been by his presence.

"Open up," he growled. "I know you're in there. I can see your shadow under the door."

My shoulders fell at his order. *Sigh.* All the cute ones were assholes.

Slowly, I unlocked the deadbolt but left the chain in place, cracking the door just enough for him to see me. Sensationally sexy, familiar or not, I wasn't ready to trust him yet.

"Can I help you?"

"You gonna let me in or what?" He frowned.

"Depends. Are you here to kill me?"

His full lips slanted into an even harder line, and his fingers tightened into fists at his side. He looked disgusted… with me. *Interesting.*

Had we hooked up once? Was he pissed I couldn't remember it? It'd be a sad day if that were the case, because the thought of not having a recollection of his gorgeousness seemed impossible. And tragic. Regardless, I'd never in my life be able to forget the rugged, painful-looking scar that slid from his temple to his chin. It said vulnerable and badass all in one long swoop.

"No. Not kill you. But your neighbor might if you don't open the door and let me in."

Ah, yes. Mrs. Brinkman. She was seventy, bitter, and grumpy. Her Pomeranian was the tiniest, most evil dog in the history of canines. I could hear him yipping now.

"Give me your jacket, your shirt, your pants, and your bag first. Then I'll decide if you're okay to come in."

He looked back at me like I'd told him unicorns were evil and put on this planet to murder us all with their horns. "You're kidding."

"Nope. It's the only way you're getting in here." I smiled, opening the door a tiny bit wider, unabashed as I took him in. He was big. Muscular big, like I'd first thought. Even closer like this, without the door blocking him, I noticed the slight layer of stubble on his chin and cheeks, covering what could only be described as a drop-dead gorgeous baby face. He looked no more than twenty-four, or five. Young. Not that I was old, but twenty-seven was still older than whatever he was. No matter. My 5 a.m. guest had me a little bit breathless.

"I'm not stripping in the fucking hallway." He dropped his bag though, and did push it toward the door with his foot. I unlocked the chain, a hand back on the Mace in my hoodie pocket as I reached into the hall to grab his bag and tug it inside.

"Nobody will see," I said, reattaching the chain. "Everyone's asleep at this time of the day. Any *normal* person, that is."

He rubbed a hand over his mouth, seeming to weigh his options. He was wearing a T-shirt, so it wasn't like he could pack anything under there, weapons-wise. And his jeans were really tight too—tighter than most men's. He wore a pair of black motorcycle boots though, a little scuffed, but he could have something in there. That was enough to justify my reasoning for the strip-search.

"Jesus Christ. I'll kill him," he mumbled to himself.

I narrowed my eyes. "Kill who?"

He blew out a heavy sigh and looked at me again. "Nobody. Turn around."

"Are you embarrassed?" My lips twitched at that.

His neck turned pink, drifting up to his cheeks. "No, but…"

I lifted my brows, disregarding the pounding in my temples and my need to pee. "But?"

"Fuck it." He reached for the end of his shirt.

"You use that word a lot, don't you?"

He stopped with the striptease, his fingers curled under the hem of his tee. My heart raced a little harder than it had a few seconds before, as the anticipation of what I might see beneath the cotton was doing lots of things to my underworked libido.

"What word's that?" he asked, completely stoic. Serious. Not to mention clueless as hell. *Is this guy for real?* Vulnerable and badass, all rolled up into one giant package? Maybe my luck was changing after all. *Thank you, Jesus.*

I licked my lips again, waiting still, imagining belly lines and a dabble of dark hair that may or may not travel beneath the button of his jeans.

Oh, what a happy trail that would be.

"*Fuck*," I answered, feeling my mouth dry for some reason. "The word I was referring to… is *fuck*."

His gaze swept to my lips, something flashing there for a beat. My chest grew hot in turn, and that swooping in my belly intensified. I gripped the doorframe a little harder, knees wobbling, thighs clenched. Holy hell. Who would have thought that a Friday-morning interlude with a random man in my apartment hallway would lead to me feeling the need to ditch my own clothes and touch myself.

He's gorgeous.

It's been a while since you've had decent sex.

Imagine what all that muscle would feel like pinning you down on a bed.

Like he couldn't believe what I was saying, the stranger with the dark demeanor shook his head and finally gave in, giving me the slowest striptease of my life, starting with his threadbare tee.

My breath caught at what I saw beneath: tattoos for days, lines and lines of muscles on his belly and chest, and yep… there was that happy trail that led to…

Sweet God in heaven. I bit my lip, but kept my gaze on his chest and abdomen. Words and phrases in foreign languages lingered under his pecs, and tribal tattoos wrapped around his belly, down his arms, across the lines of his hips that were barely covered by the waistband of his jeans. As much as I loved a man with ink, it was almost a shame for there to be so much of it this time because they covered the beauty of his gorgeous chest and abs.

Looking my fill, I watched as he went for his pants next, his thumb and forefinger lingering on the button. I swear the air thickened when he slid them down his thick thighs to his ankles, but… *Hangover. Stranger.*

Despite the voice in my head begging me to step back, I leaned forward a little more with *way* too much interest and watched as he lifted a foot to untie one boot. He shook it off then did the same with the other before flinging it toward me. They both landed with a thump, hitting the wall to my left in front of Mrs. Brinkman's door, and of course her tiny dog yipped even louder.

Swallowing hard, I continued to look, unashamed, tempted to look lower again. But then I saw it.

The red tail on his shoulder. Scaled.

I froze.

Crap. I knew that tail. Knew what it meant, too. This guy was a Red Dragon. A Red Dragon who looked oddly like Hawk. Hawk didn't have a brother, at least not that I was aware of. The only blood relative he did have, besides his parents, was…

I stopped, blinking as I stared into the man's eyes again.

No. This couldn't be *him*.

Little Lattimore was skinny, wore glasses, and had hair to his shoulder. I shook my head, laughing, minus the humor. My Sebastian was long gone from the world of the Red Dragons, leaving just days after I did, according to my mom. I wasn't sure where he'd gone, because I hadn't asked. If I had, it would have meant I still cared, and after what had happened the night before I left, after what I'd seen, I'd told myself I was done caring for men, harboring *real* feelings that went beyond attraction.

I kept up that M.O. too. And until I could figure out how to love another person like that again—like I'd once done Sebastian—I would continue to be who I was. The empty woman with the sad, unintentionally false promises.

"You happy now?" He held his hands up in front of him.

"Turn around," I ordered, swirling my finger in the air, *so* done playing. What I needed now was full proof when it came to this stranger and his scaly, red tat.

He quirked an eyebrow at me. "You wanna see my ass?"

"No," I huffed, trying not to appear tempted by his suggestion. Asses were asses, right? "I want to see the tattoo on your back."

His gaze hardened at my request. But, without further prompting or questions, he did as I asked, his hands lowering to his thick thighs.

The second I saw it, I cringed. That stupid, *beautiful* tattoo which marked him as taken. Owned. Because once you were an RD, you lost not only your will but your semblance of a soul. Such was the price of being a member of a motorcycle club.

"Did my uncle send you?" I gritted my teeth at the thought. "Or are you a rogue?" Not that he'd admit it if that were the case. Regardless, the thought had me tightening my hand around the Mace then slowly pulling it out.

Unlocking the door, I aimed it at him when he turned to face me and crouched down to pick up his pants so I could search them. If this was some freak of a rogue, like the ones who'd attacked Hawk last summer, then I refused to let them do whatever it was they wanted to do to me without a fight on my end.

Surprisingly, the stranger barely spared my can a glance before leaning back against the wall and folding his arms. He didn't look the least bit perturbed. If anything, he looked… confused.

"Flick sent me." He cocked his head to one side. "Didn't you know?"

"Of course I don't know," I growled, Mace raised higher as I searched one-handed inside his bag. Nothing was there. Not a gun or a knife. No form of protection, which was odd. RDs, or bikers in general, were rarely unarmed.

The guy rolled his eyes. "Figures."

I was pretty sure I was either dreaming or still drunk, because there's no way my uncle would know about my homeless, jobless dilemma already. He was nosy, yes, but he'd grown more respectful over the years—him and Mom both giving me the space I'd craved.

Yet, this was all too convenient.

"Why are you here?" After searching through his pants and finding nothing, I tossed them back his way. His shirt was still in my hands and, selfishly, I kind of wanted to continue my ogling now that I knew he wasn't here to murder me.

He swallowed and looked away, and the movement of his Adam's apple pulled my gaze toward his throat. "There's been an issue at home. Flick wants me to take you back to Rockford for a few weeks."

I folded my arms, mirroring his position, suddenly aware that I wasn't wearing a bra. My boobs were fine without one. Even so, I felt stark naked standing before him like I was.

"What kind of issue? And why didn't I get any kind of warning?"

The guy looked from one end of the hall to the other, that dimple on the opposite cheek of his scar popping even more with his deeper scowl. I frowned, studying the indent again. It looked so… familiar.

"It's club business," he said. "Just let me in so I can help you get your shit together. Our flight leaves at midnight."

"Oh my God, no." I tossed my head back and laughed. "There is absolutely no way I'm going with a virtual stranger on some plane right back to the last freaking place I want to be." With that, I slammed the door in his face.

Leaning back against the wood, his shirt still in my hands, I waited to see if I'd wake up from a nightmare. I even squeezed my eyes shut then blinked a good three or four times to help matters along. Unfortunately, everything stayed as it was. My dark, lonely apartment with one small loveseat. The rug under my two-person table that sat in my tiny, galley kitchen across the way. To my left sat my lonely washer and dryer, stacked on top of each other. Everything was neat and orderly. Tidy. Nothing out of place. I wasn't a freak about things staying clean, but I wasn't a fan of dirt and grime either. It's why I rarely had anyone over. I'd been paying for this apartment on my own, with a job that I'd loved so hard… before it had all ended in disaster because of some guy's need to get his dick wet.

Knock. Knock. Knock. Knock.

Four slow and consecutive raps rattled the other side of the door.

"Maya," the man's voice growled from the other side. "Open up."

"No." I wiped at my cheeks, pulling away when I felt the wetness on my fingertips. Jesus, I was crying. *Why?* What was wrong with me?

The hallway grew quiet. For a second, I thought maybe my escort had left, but seconds later, I heard him growling and huffing and talking a mile a minute. It was too soft for me to hear exactly what he was saying, but I overheard the name he spoke, clear as daylight: *Flick.*

He'd called my uncle. Lovely.

CHAPTER THREE

Slade

"You didn't tell her I was coming," I said to Flick on the phone, pacing the hall outside Maya's apartment. The worst, and best, part about it was she also clearly didn't have a clue who I was.

Flick sighed. "Yeah, sorry about that. Figured it was easier this way."

"You're not sorry," I grumbled. "And easier my ass. She slammed the door in my face and left me in the hall." Not to mention stole my T-shirt after making me strip down to my briefs.

It'd been a lot of years since I'd last seen this woman, and my body had gone through a hell of a lot to get to where it was today. Endless training and bulking up, hours under a tattoo gun, and a scar I wasn't necessarily proud of but wore with pride as a reminder that perfection was over-fucking-rated. The surgery on my eyes, courtesy of Flick so I didn't have to be blind without glasses, was more so for my ability to be the best RD. And keeping my hair cut short? That's because the long length annoyed the piss out of me when I got on a bike.

Slade was born out of bitterness and heartbreak, yeah. But at the core, I'd done it mostly because of the woman behind that door. The one who had run away from me.

I didn't miss the way she'd looked at my near-naked body. Eyes flaring, red cheeks, nipples hard against her tee… She was just as superficial as she'd been way back in the day, only now it was me, not Hawk, she was into. Go fucking figure.

Though I still hated her, maybe even more now than before, there was still this stupid part of me buried deep inside that wanted nothing more than to go all caveman on the woman—and show her exactly what she'd been missing out on.

"Yeah, not really surprised. She's always been a firecracker, that one." I heard Flick inhale, the spark from his cigarette crackling over the other end of the line.

"She's not interested in letting me into her apartment, let alone coming with me." I leaned back against the wall opposite her door again. "Hell, Flick, she pulled a can of Mace on my ass." Not gonna lie… the Mace bit was kinda hot. Not that I wanted to get sprayed, but it was hot that she still knew how to protect herself: a pint-sized badass that looked every bit as sexy as I remembered.

My dick still wanted her. Reminded me of that the second I saw her. He'd twitched when I'd first looked into her sparkling star eyes, then when I got a look at all her long hair? He went full-on steel, painfully pressing against my zipper. Still shiny and inky, blacker than the night, other than the sweetheart-looking braid that settled in the front with a slash of blood-red running through it. God, it was stunning, and as I shut my eyes I could easily imagine what it'd be like to wrap my fist around the length, then bend her over the bed, one hand holding it against her spine, the other yanking her panties to the side so I could easily slide right between her pretty, naked thighs.

"Mace, huh?" Flick's reply had me shaking my head and getting back to what mattered. There was worry in his words, that's what I noticed first. In a way, I couldn't blame the guy. Whether I liked Maya or not, my natural instinct to protect her had gone into overdrive.

Why *did* she need the Mace? Simple self-defense? Or was there something going on in her life that Flick didn't know about? A crazy stalker, an ex who wanted more than she was willing to give… Both thoughts had me clenching my teeth in uninvited jealousy, not to mention unwelcome concern.

"Yeah. And she looks like shit, too." That was, if shit could be drop-dead gorgeous, with a tight little body that was the stuff of wet dreams and nightmares combined.

Flick blew out another breath, this one sounding weighted with guilt. "I'll call her. Might take me a day or so to convince her to go, but she will."

"A day or two? Are you shitting me right now? Our flight leaves tonight."

"Plans change."

"Yeah, well, not mine. I'm gonna get her on that plane tonight if it's the last thing I ever do."

"Calm down, boy. Ain't nothing happening here that we can't handle."

Back and forth I paced the hall again, so much so I started sweating. Beads of it dripped down my temple, and I was sure I smelled like ass, but fuck. *Fuck.* The last thing I wanted was to spend more time with her than I had to.

Hell no.

Next to the door, I eventually slid to the ground, the phone staying pressed to my ear as Flick kept up with his bullshit excuses.

"You're the only one I trust with her." His words were almost a whisper, tortured even.

I squeezed my eyes shut and hit the back of my head against the wall. Deep down, I knew he was right. I *was* the most trustworthy brother in the Red Dragons. The other brothers would've gotten the job done, no problem, especially Hawk and Archer. But none of them would lay their life down to make it happen.

Not like me.

Carlos dying… I'd never forgive myself for letting it happen. And because of that, I was pretty damn sure Flick was playing my vulnerabilities against me because he loved his niece like his own kid.

I sighed. "Just sort through the mess. The woman won't even let me inside her apartment, for Christ's sake." The Mace was one thing, but telling Flick that she'd made me strip down in her hall? No way. He'd laugh his ass off then tell Hawk and Arch, likely every other brother in the club too.

I'd be the laughing stock of the damn compound if they found out.

"I will." He cleared his throat. "I owe you."

"You owe me a hell of a lot, I'd say."

Flick was a good leader. Did what he had to, to get shit done. But when it came to his family, the guy didn't care who he hurt to keep the ones he loved safe.

"Do me a favor though," I added last-minute. Not real sure why.

"What's that?"

I leaned my head back, studying her door again. "She doesn't recognize me. I'm Slade now, remember? Don't…" I rubbed a hand over my forehead. "Don't tell her who I am." If he did, then all hell would break loose—on my end, likely, not hers. I might call her out on what she'd done to me, just like I should've done eight years ago.

For now, for the sake of getting her home with my balls attached and my head on straight, I would stay Slade: the hard-ass who hated too many questions, never second-guessed a kill, and *never* let a woman get too close.

Not since her.

Not since she tore me to shreds by leaving, pretending what we shared that summer wasn't worthy of a goodbye.

Yes. Skinny, dorky, glasses-wearing Sebastian with the brain would stay long gone until the time I was ready to admit the truth.

If that time ever came.

No question asked, Flick replied, "Yeah. I got it."

*

Twenty minutes later, when I was damn near asleep in the hall, Maya finally opened her door and tossed my shirt out. I waited for her to come out next, either to tell me to leave or invite me in, but her door stayed half opened and she never bothered to show her face. If I hadn't heard her footsteps, I would've thought it was a ghost letting me in.

Reaching forward, I grabbed my shirt and threw it on, not bothering to put on my boots as I headed into her apartment. I started looking around the second the door shut after me. But Maya wasn't in her small kitchen ahead, not in the laundry room to my left, or the little living area with the one sofa either. So she'd either jumped out a window or gone to her room or the bathroom. Either way, I knew what it meant.

She'd talked to Flick.

Instead of sitting, I took a stroll around, studying a few framed pictures on the wall. Pictures of her and a bunch of tatted-looking dudes who could've easily passed as bikers without their cuts. I'd have to check in on that, make sure she wasn't associated with another club out here. Archer could do some digging back home and find out. I'd shoot him a text soon.

There were also pictures of her alone too. Dressed in long skirts and cropped shirts that barely covered her tits. I shook my head, fighting against a smile when I saw one of her doing a backflip in the sand along the beach, one short leg kicked up in the air, the ocean waves behind her. It was an action shot. Her face was red, probably from the blood rushing to it, but she looked happy, and yeah... un-fucking-believably gorgeous too. Question was, who was taking the shot? A boyfriend?

The thought had me gritting my teeth and looking away.

In the kitchen, I spotted a half-filled coffee mug. Next to it was a bottle of Baileys. I picked up the cup, inhaling, then shook my head when I set it back down. Apparently Maya liked to spike her morning drinks.

I walked to a glass sliding door and looked outside. The sun was barely coming up, but I could make out the water in the distance.

Footsteps sounded behind me a few minutes later, but I didn't turn to look, not even when she started talking. "It's prettier up close." I knew she was smiling, I could hear it in her voice, but refused to look at her. "The ocean is half the reason I moved here."

Her shoulder brushed against mine. I looked down at her hand for some reason then, swallowing hard at the view of her forearm. She was inked with a bird tat, drawn to look like wire. Black and tiny. Perfect against her skin.

Before I could respond to her comment, ask her what the other half of her reason was, she walked away, leaving behind the scent of lemon. Apparently, she'd grown out of vanilla.

Because I couldn't help myself, I turned, watching her movements, the sway of her hips at first, then her hair, which was dripping like she hadn't bothered to rub a towel through it. Following the length of her body, I noted her form, how much it had changed over the years. All womanly curves, short legs with tight calf muscles, and a thick ass that was just barely covered by her dress. A dress that was bright yellow, like the sun. Thin, too. So much so, I could see the outline of her panties.

A skinny thong, white lace…

Jesus Christ, if she dressed like that now instead of jeans and old band tees like she'd done at nineteen, then I was in a hell of a lot more trouble than I'd assumed.

"I talked to my uncle." She sat on the arm of her couch, head down, hands playing with the hem of her dress.

I pushed away the image of her lifting that dress up and over her head, then tossing it at my feet with a lazy smirk.

"What'd he say?"

"He told me we fly out tonight for Illinois," she finished.

I cleared my throat. "That gonna be enough time for you to get your shit ready?"

She crossed her feet at her ankles. "Do I even have a choice?"

I walked her way, fisting my hands so I didn't reach out and pull her against me. "It's temporary. You can come back when shit settles down."

"Suuuure. I mean, it's not like I have anything keeping me here at the moment." She snorted, wiping something from her cheek before turning away.

Jesus, was she crying? What was going on with her?

Like I was thrown into the past, all I wanted was to tug her against my chest. Hold her there until she stopped, or fell asleep. But asking what was wrong, comforting her? It wasn't a good idea. The last time I'd done so, I'd gotten my fucking heart ripped apart. I'd learned my lesson.

Getting her back to Illinois had to be like a business transaction. Get the goods, keep them safe, take them where they need to go, then be on my way. Nothing less, nothing more.

"You got a suitcase somewhere?" I changed the subject, pushing down the old me.

She blew out a slow breath, and pieces of her hair flew up and down, sticking to her damp cheek. "Yeah. I've got to see about getting a storage unit or something first."

"Why?" It's not like she was gonna be gone all that long. "Can't you just keep paying rent?"

She opened her hand, revealing a balled-up piece of pink paper. "Nope."

Reaching over, careful not to touch skin, I grabbed the paper from her palm, unfolded it, and winced at what was written there. "You're being evicted?"

"Looks that way." She shrugged one shoulder. "Apparently the building is getting demolished."

"How long have you known about this?"

"Since yesterday morning when I got home from work." She held up a finger. "Wait, scratch that. When I got home after being *fired* from work."

She'd been fired and evicted in one day? *Damn.*

"Least that means you don't have to take time off," I offered.

She lifted her head and narrowed both eyes. "Really tactful there…" She paused as if to say my name. "You haven't told me what to call you."

"Name's Slade."

Rolling her eyes, she stood and headed into the kitchen. "Club names are *not* names."

"It's the only one I go by."

She dumped out her mug then refilled it with fresh coffee, only to pour more Baileys inside. "Then I guess I'll just have to name you myself." She winked at me, but nothing about it was flirty or sweet. If anything, she looked bitter. Pissed.

Good. It was better that way. For both of us.

"Be my guest," I told her.

She looked me over, her gaze lingering on my lips. I bit on the bottom one, giving her a show, when deep down, I hated how much I liked her eyes on me.

"You remind me of someone," she said.

I tensed.

She chewed on the inside of her cheek like she was waiting for her memory to kick in. Thankfully, her coffee seemed more important because she reached for it and took a long drink.

Tension hung in the air, making my skin crawl. So, I pulled out a cup without asking and helped myself to some coffee, minus the Baileys. Then I walked back to the screen door again. Now, more than ever, I was determined to make this as quick and painless as I could.

For me though, not her.

CHAPTER FOUR

Maya

When the majority of my worldly possessions were packed away in garbage bags, I kicked my feet up on my bare mattress for the last time and reveled in the final hours of peace I had before relocating to the last place I wanted to be. Or should I say the *second* to last place I wanted to be.

I might have hated the Red Dragons— I stayed at their compound with my mother and uncle for that one summer when I'd turned nineteen—but our home prior to those few months I'd stayed in Rockford had been ten times worse.

The Forsaken MC, located in Arizona, was the only place I'd known from birth until the age of eighteen. An outlaw club where every single member lived a felony life, including my father: the Forsaken club vice president. Mom and I had been trapped under that man's control for far too long, and the simple thought of it still, to this day, continued to rob me of a good night's sleep.

A knock sounded on my bedroom doorframe and I stiffened, nearly forgetting I'd left it open.

"You need help?" Slade asked, eyeing my small bedroom.

"No, thanks. I've got everything in order." I sat up and pulled both knees to my chest, sparing him a glance before I looked out the window. Exhaustion was heavy in my chest and droopy eyes, and I knew no amount of sleep could curb it at this point.

It was sunny now—bright-blue skies lit with rays. Not a winter wonderland like I was sure it was back in Illinois. Mid-January wasn't the best time to relocate to the dark and dreary Midwest when you'd been so used to the warm and sunny West Coast. But it would seem I no longer had a choice.

"Can I?"

I looked to Slade, watching as he waved a hand into my room.

"You wanna come in?"

He tucked his hands into his jean pockets and nodded.

"Go for it."

Taking a few steps through the door, he proceeded to look everywhere but at me. Did I look that hideous? I frowned at the thought, also wondering what planet this dude hailed from. Most of the MC members I'd known in my life were cocky assholes who cared little about women or their privacy, other than Hawk and my uncle. So, the fact that he'd asked permission to come in *and* offered to help me was… different. Odd different, but *good* different.

Wordless, he leaned a hip against the dresser and stared out the same window I'd been looking out of. Like that, he was the picture of calm as his messy, dark hair flopped over one of his eyes. Even the hard line of his jaw had relaxed for the first time since he'd arrived, though the scar on his cheek gave him a dangerous air.

"What are you staring at?" I asked, setting my chin on my knees.

His lips twitched just barely as he peered at me from the corner of his eye. "Whatever *you* were staring at."

A smart-ass ass then. I could deal with that.

I slid off the bed and stepped around the bags piled high in my room, thankful my equilibrium was better now than it had been this morning. For some reason, I needed to get a closer look at this guy. My entire life, I'd always been too curious for my own good, which wasn't the best news for my secretive new escort. But he'd have to get used to my nosy ways for the next few hours.

Standing in front of his muscular frame, I mirrored his position and gave him a slow once-over while I was at it. What was God thinking when he invented so much gorgeous in one man? Oh, how I wish I knew. My need to invade his personal space was overwhelming. I barely knew the guy. But dang, he was hot, to the point where I tingled just by looking at him. Plus, that bad-boy appeal never failed to sucker me in.

Imagine what it'd be like to be naked with him.

"Wanna tell me why you're in my room?" I quirked a brow.

I didn't miss the flash of his eyes as they zeroed in on my lips, but it didn't last long. His stoic annoyance returned like a cloak of invisibility he couldn't seem to part with.

"We need to leave soon if you're looking to get all your shit into a storage unit." He folded his arms. "I just wanted to see what was taking you so long."

"Yeah, about that…" I cringed, looking down at my feet, a flash of heated embarrassment squeezing my chest. "I kinda can't afford a unit at the moment."

The price the lady had spouted off to me just twenty minutes before would take every last penny of my savings. And then some. Which meant, when I came back home, I'd have nothing left to get a new place with. Or live off of until I got a new job.

"It's fine. I'll pay for it," he told me.

I shook my head. "Thanks, Mr. Virtual Stranger, but I don't take handouts."

"Then consider it a loan." He frowned, like he couldn't figure out what the big deal was. This man apparently didn't know what it was like to suffer financially. *Must be nice.*

"That would still be considered a handout, and I have no idea when I'd be able to pay you back. I'll just call someone. See if they can keep my stuff for me." I fidgeted with my thumb ring, regretting the words the second they left my mouth. In the eight years I'd lived here, the only friends I seemed to make were work acquaintances. Even then, any job I'd held didn't last long enough for me to make friends who I felt comfortable enough to call on out of the blue for help.

Slade's brows furrowed. "I've got the money and you need the help. Don't make this complicated."

I winced but didn't immediately turn him down this time. It made sense, I suppose, him helping me. But that didn't mean my stupid pride wouldn't take a hit because of it.

"Fine. But I'll pay you back. *With* interest."

"Whatever you need." His voice stayed emotionless as he studied me; not even a hint of kindness could be seen behind his angry façade. God, he hated me. So much. But for the life of me, I couldn't figure out why.

Regardless, he *had* to have some sort of heart in that bulky chest of his since he'd come all this way to help me out.

I looked up at him again. "You're not like the other bikers I've known."

"How so?" His eyes turned into slits. It seemed my compliment had offended him. *Typical.*

"You're nicer."

"I'm not nice," he snapped.

"You are." I smiled, ignoring his bark. "*Which* I appreciate. It's kind of refreshing." I hadn't dealt with a nice guy who wasn't looking at me for the sole purpose of getting me into bed for a very long time. Although with *this* gentleman, I wouldn't mind messing around naked underneath the sheets, that was for sure.

"You don't know me." His jaw clenched as he looked toward the window again.

"You're right, I don't. But at the same time, I kind of feel like I do." Head tipped to the side, I took a step closer, drawn to him once again for reasons I didn't yet understand. The heat of his body was nearly nuclear, and when my thighs grazed his, I lost all semblance of the word "space."

What was it about this man that drew me in so deep?

"What are you doing?" His gaze shot to my mouth first, then lifted and stopped at my eyes. He blinked, then blinked again.

I dipped my gaze down to look at his hands, which were both balled into fists. Apparently, he was as affected by me as I was by him.

"What's your real name?" I asked again, in no way willing to call him Slade.

"If I wanted to tell you, I would."

I grinned, liking his snark, testing it. "Are you afraid of me? Did I hurt your feelings back in the—"

"Enough."

Before I could take another breath, he grabbed me by the hips and pushed me against the dresser. I gasped, but not because it hurt. His arm shot around my back, keeping my spine from digging into the edge, in fact. A gentleman, even when he was trying his hand at dominance. I should have been scared of his sudden movement, but it felt familiar somehow. And the worst part was, I freaking loved it. Every bit of his hardness. Every bit of his loss of control.

"What are you doing?" I whispered, eyes to his mouth, chest heaving. An ache formed in the pit of my belly, sliding even lower when the heat of his ragged breath grazed my forehead.

His lips pressed into a harder line as he lifted me up and set me up on the dresser. We were eye to eye then, and before I could protest, let alone blink, he spread my legs and settled between them.

"Let's get one thing straight here. I am *not* afraid of anything. Especially little runaways like you."

Lifting both brows this time, I couldn't help but ask, "You got a lot of anger in there, don't you?"

"Stop talking," he snarled.

"Why? You afraid of what I might ask?"

He stiffened at my question, gaze zipping from my forehead to my chin, all while his fingers dug a little deeper into my waist. The heat of his giant palms scorched me through my dress while his upper lip curled into a deep, angry scowl. I shivered, wondering what was going through his mind. Anger, to me, burned as hot as lust, and damn did I like the look of it on this man.

"I'm afraid of nothing. I told you."

I arched a brow at that, lips twitching, heart racing…

Don't do it, I told myself. *You're asking for trouble.*

But that dire need to know what was going on behind those dark eyes of his was doing me in, and I had *no* idea why.

Leaning forward, I lifted my hand, running a finger across his neck-pulse, crossing lines I had no business crossing. "You're just like the rest of them, aren't you? Getting off on the untouchable. Flick has told you I'm off limits."

Maliciousness washed over me, and I couldn't help but grin. Bikers had been the bane of my existence for as long as I could remember, yet my unyielding attraction to them was never far behind that hatred. With this man, it was like touching the flames of an unstoppable fire—so pretty you'd be willing to get burned just to run your hands over the surface a little.

Swallowing hard, I lifted my other hand and set it on his pec, surprised by how much I was shaking. His erection jumped against my leg, proving he wasn't unfazed by my touch one single bit.

"Maya," he warned, but made no move to push me away.

"Hmm?"

"Stop…" But his plea was lost on a breath as I continued to explore.

Sliding the hand higher up against his neck, I studied his face while I tangled my fingers into the back of his hair, fascinated when I felt him shudder against me. He was like a block of ice, fighting against my melting touch. I felt almost guilty for doing what I did.

Almost.

That tug of contrition didn't stop me, of course. And instead, I kept going, greedy for things I couldn't comprehend. The softness of his waves curling through my fingers like layers of silk, the feeling of his hot breath grazing my lips... I blinked at the familiarity of it all, head dipping to the side as I watched his once unmovable presence crack with every passing second of my touch.

Maybe it was the Baileys from my morning coffee, or the remainder of last night's drink still coursing through my body, but touching this man, burrowing deep under his skin, was all I wanted in that moment. And I had no idea why.

He lifted his chin, nuzzling against my palm as I brought my fingers to his cheek—the familiar intimacy of this all taking me by surprise. I found myself smiling through it along the way, the sight of him reminding me of an animal, needy of my affectionate touches.

The scar along his cheek was even more weathered and pink up close. Staring at it, I couldn't help but drop my inhibitions, running one finger down the puckered mark.

I had a problem with impulsiveness when it came to touching others, and with this man, my problem was no different. If anything, it was worse. He made me want to touch him all over—and often—which showed that my intimacy-starved body needed to be nourished, pronto.

His breath caught as I ran my thumb down the center of his throat, and the power I felt from that alone sent my head spinning with more thoughts than I dared express. I did have *some* restraint.

Other than the awful scar, the rest of his skin was unblemished but for a day's worth of stubble on his chin—which only added to his appeal.

Who are you, Slade?

Before I could ask that question out loud again, he grabbed my wrist and yanked my hand off his face, ending my explorations.

"That's enough."

I stiffened at his growly tone, his dark eyes rising to meet mine. The rough bark of his voice sent another shiver down my spine, enough so that I finally snapped out of my stupor.

You dumb, impulsive girl, what were you thinking?

"Sorry," I whispered, settling my hands at my side once more.

"We need to leave in ten minutes." Emotionless again, and not acknowledging my apology, Slade took another step back and looked the other way. "Be ready."

"Okay." I tried for a smile, but he slipped out of the room before I could even begin to garner his reaction.

The moment he was gone, I released a heavy sigh, my tight lungs freed of the breath I'd been holding. I didn't move away from the dresser right away and instead just stared at the spot he'd abandoned, wondering to myself for the millionth time in the last five minutes, *What in the hell was that?*

CHAPTER FIVE

Slade

One thing I'd always prided myself on when it came to women was my ability to control myself around them. I wasn't a horny bastard like Archer, getting between the legs of any blonde or redhead I could. And I sure as hell wasn't Hawk, who lost his shit and lived only for *one* woman. Yet thirteen hours after Maya jumped back into my life, I was already forgetting how to be Slade. Why was that? It couldn't be the fact that I was still in love with the woman, that's for damn sure. She'd messed with me—teased me like a little kid. And all I could do was take it all in, savor her touch like it was a lifeline I'd been missing my entire life.

Maya held up one finger across from me in the passenger seat of the car I'd rented, making an X over her heart. Her mischievous hazel eyes were loaded with more danger now than they had been in her room.

"Just *one* more question about the club. That's it."

"Doubt it," I muttered under my breath. "You haven't stopped asking questions since we left that stupid storage unit."

"Do you really hate my voice that much?" She batted her lashes, an innocent hand pressed to her chest.

I groaned and slammed on the gas, pulling through the stoplight like zombies were on my ass. It'd be a damn dream if I could hate her voice. That way I wouldn't have spent countless hours jerking off to the memory of it when I was seventeen. Raspy and low, devious with an underlying sweetness that suckered a man right in…

Maya had always been full of questions back then and, somedays, it seemed like her mind was as wild and inquisitive as mine had been.

Admitting any of that bullshit out loud would be a death wish for me. It'd leave me vulnerable, which was something I refused to be from here on out—for her safety, not to mention my sanity. So, instead of answering her, I cranked up the radio and concentrated on getting us to the airport, even rolling the window down a crack to inhale some good old-fashioned car exhaust. It was a hell of a lot easier to concentrate when her lemon-flavored skin wasn't all I could smell. Lemon-flavored skin that left me wondering if it tasted just as sweet as it smelled.

Since I'd slid between her tiny legs in her bedroom, my body was hypersensitive to everything she said, did, even *whispered* for fuck's sake. Which meant she just needed to stop talking and everything would be fine.

"I haven't been that bad, have I?" she asked, turning down the volume of the radio.

"Yeah. You have." I shook my head, stopped at yet another light. And because I was an idiot, I looked at her again.

One side of her mouth was pulled higher than the other. I sucked in a breath through my nose at the view, eyes narrowing when she smiled full on. The woman looked like an evil seductress sent from the depths of hell just to torture me with her beauty. Maya was Medusa, minus the snakes; I was dead stone around her with the heat of Hades burning within my gut at the same time.

"Don't be grumpy. It's not attractive." She kicked her short, toned legs up on the dashboard, nearly causing me to run off the side of the road.

She wore heels. Mother. Fucking. *Heels*.

Since when did the Maya I know wear heels instead of sneakers or boots? Not to mention pretty, yellow, see-through dresses. We were getting ready to travel on a plane, back to the Midwest, in the middle of January, yet she looked like we were heading to a beach in the tropics instead.

"I'm not *grumpy*," I growled, refocusing ahead. And even if I *was* grumpy, I sure as hell didn't give two shits if it made me attractive or not.

"You sure? Because for the last hour, every word coming out of your mouth has either been snappy or grunty."

"Grunty's not even a word."

"And what are you, the English language police?" She laughed, pushing my shoulder this time. *Always with the damn touching.* That much about her hadn't changed.

"No. I'm a guy who wants to get to the airport, get on the plane, and go the fuck home." I needed to get away from this woman. If I didn't, then I'm pretty sure I'd pull her onto my lap, hike up that tiny dress, then kiss her until she shut the hell up and could only moan my name instead.

"*Anyways*," she huffed. "My question for you is this…"

"I didn't say you could ask anything."

"And I'm pretty sure that you're not in charge of my voice."

Groaning, I dropped my head back against the seat, clinging tighter to the wheel. My head was starting to hurt from scowling so much, yet Maya was like a damn lawyer, throwing question after question at me about the club. *Has it changed since Pops left and my uncle took over? What is going on that I have to come back?* Stuff she'd find out soon enough, if she just waited until we got there.

I got it. It'd been a while since she'd been to Rockford, so she was probably nervous. But it was her fault at the same time for *not* knowing. She was the one who'd chosen to ignore everyone who ever cared about her, only so she could run to California and build a life that didn't seem a hell of a lot better than the one she'd left in the first place.

"Are Hawk and Summer getting hitched?"

At the mention of my cousin, I rolled my eyes. Of course that'd be her last question. "Don't know, don't care."

"Aren't you friends with him?"

"Sure."

"You don't sound too convincing."

I rubbed a hand over my mouth, trying to tame my reaction. "We're friends. Yes."

"Then you should know if they're getting married or not. I haven't talked to him for a few months now. Last I knew, he was thinking of asking her, then he just stopped answering my texts."

"What the hell does it matter if they are?" My control slipped with her words. "You still want him or something? That why you care so much?"

I heard her quick intake of breath. If I looked at her again, I bet she'd looked wounded. But the sad part was, I didn't feel bad. If that made me a dickhead, so be it.

All these years later, though, Maya's obsession with my cousin still rubbed me raw. At least now that I was Slade, I could call her out on it. And if she wasn't over him, then she was in for one hell of a treat because Summer had my cousin so tightly wrapped around her little finger it wasn't even funny.

"Why would you ask me that?" she questioned, her voice low. Accusing. Hurt.

I hesitated. For a hot second, I'd forgotten that she didn't know who I was.

"You guys have history, don't you?" Hopefully that was convincing enough. What I needed to do was tap down my outbursts and keep my emotions in check. Work through whatever was bothering me the most here.

"Well, yeah, but we're friends. That's all."

"Sure." I snorted. I'd believe it when I saw it.

Every second that passed between us pushed all my old insecurities right back into play, even though I had nothing to be ashamed of. Least not in how I looked.

It wouldn't take much for me to admit the truth to her. And part of me wanted to throw it in her face that I wasn't who she thought I was. That the boy she'd abandoned was now a man with a fired-up hatred of her. But she was obviously attracted to the guy I was now. And I wanted nothing more than to screw her senseless too.

"Seriously. Hawk and I were never actually like that."

"He said you two fucked." That wasn't a complete lie. Days after she left, when I was too numb to even think, let alone talk, I'd found out from Archer, who'd gotten it out of my cousin when they were drunk. At the time, Archer didn't know I'd been in love with her. But the second he saw my reaction, he asked me what was up, and I'd told him the truth about everything that had happened between Maya and me. Pretty sure he hated her more than I did after that.

"He told people that?" she whispered.

"Course he did," I sneered. "Said you were a damn good lay too." The lie was bitter on my tongue. Least the latter half was.

Hate me. Hate me so I can keep hating you right back.

But my mental mantra didn't work. And instead, Maya gave me back an emotion that had my gut squeezing in regret.

"What an asshole," she whispered, leaning against the door. "This is why I hate that place." Then she finally gave me the silence I'd been craving.

Refusing to feel bad, I dropped my head back against the seat and tried to relax. I had every right to be an ass to her—or that's what Slade told me. But over the next fifteen minutes, the quiet between us tested me, and the longer it held, the harder that guilt knocked against my chest, demanding repentance. As much as I'd complained about her question game earlier, I realized I didn't like her silence even more. It left me with too much time to think… not to mention regret.

I cleared my throat, attempting to be selfish when deep down I knew that wasn't the case at all. "Why'd you get fired?"

At first, I didn't think she'd answer me, but then the flash of her phone lit up the car, and she shoved it closer to me, a picture of some douchebag with a Mohawk on her screen. He looked like Hawk, but uglier.

"Because of this guy."

"Who's that?" I frowned, pulling down the road that led us to the airport parking lot.

"My ex-boss." She shrugged then shut off the screen, pocketing her phone. "He runs the tattoo parlor I'd been working for. When I refused to sleep with him, he fired me."

I slammed on the brakes, sending us jerking forward in our seats. I was ready to turn the damn car back around and show the asshole what the bottom of my boot looked like.

"It's fine. I broke his nose, so we're even."

Even though she could easily defend herself, I didn't like the thought of her doing it. Call me a chauvinistic asshat, but it was the biker inside of me, wanting nothing more than to look after the people he cared about.

Not that I *cared* about Maya anymore.

Our eyes held for more seconds than I could count. She looked so damn sad, even though she claimed she was good. But feeling sorry for her wasn't in the cards for me. It couldn't be. I'd protect her. Get her home. Then be done with her once and for all.

I cleared my throat and looked away first, pushing the gas pedal again.

"Why does it matter to you?" she asked.

It doesn't. "You're my charge right now." I stuck with that. "Flick's niece."

My throat squeezed tight at the half-lie, but I let the words go anyway, keeping them somehow casual, concise.

"I'm a job then."

I nodded.

As I parked in the rental-car return, I leaned back in the seat and scrubbed both hands over my face. I didn't like being a dick, especially when it came to women, but there I was, being exactly the kind of man I hated for the sole reason of wanting to hear her voice. Her voice that drove me *wild*. Add to it the way she licked her lips and laughed, those star eyes twinkling the entire time, and I was seconds from spilling the truth she didn't deserve to know.

Still, when I looked over at her before opening the door, my gaze found its way to her mouth, watching as she nibbled on her bottom lip and stared out the windshield. That pull was back again. The one that urged my body closer. She was sexy as hell all grown up. Soft curves, wild eyes, perfection. Forbidden.

Get your shit together, Slade, I growled to myself, wishing for a break, a reprieve.

Lucky for me, Maya got out of the car first, the door slamming behind her. I sighed, gathering my thoughts. I'd be away from this woman soon. Just like I wanted.

CHAPTER SIX

Maya

We checked our bags inside the airport and found a spot to wait outside our gate until boarding. Slade was back to his overly broody self, and it kind of made my head spin. I wasn't a talkative person by nature either, but this man's silence was unnerving, which is why I'd played the question game in the car.

But there was something about one of his comments that had rubbed me the wrong way. He'd called me a job. Something he was doing for the club. And though I'd only met him this morning, that admission stung.

I just wish I knew why.

No matter. This guy had zero right to be mad at me at the moment. I hadn't done anything wrong, other than talk to him. The thing was, he didn't know who I was, yet he sure seemed to have a vendetta against me for some reason. Because of that, I found myself more curious than hurt over what he'd admitted in the car about Hawk.

Big deal if the entire club was aware that I'd screwed the guy the night before I skipped town. None of them knew the real me, anyway. And, because of that, nothing anyone could say mattered. My heart had been broken back then. And the entire time Hawk and I were together, I'd cried, claiming it hurt because it was my first time instead of admitting that the majority of the pain I was experiencing stemmed from my shattered emotions.

My soul and heart had belonged to another man, but I'd given my body freely to another. It was just one of the many mistakes I'd made in life.

When I couldn't take the forced quiet between us any longer, I finally got the guts to ask Slade a few questions about himself this time—safe and unassuming. Nothing that led back to me and *my* history with the club. My experience with men led me to believe that they were all about talking when it meant they could boast about themselves. Hopefully Slade was no different.

"How did you become part of the club?" I asked.

He stiffened, elbows on his knees, eyes focused on his phone. "Happenstance."

His big word made me grin a little, despite my mood. Not all men who wore cuts on their backs were idiots.

"Did you know the second you met the guys that it was where you belonged?"

He dipped his chin, hesitating. "Yes."

His answer disappointed me for some reason. I'd only known one person who was born into that life and he chose another path in the end. According to my mom, he was long gone.

Still to this day, I regretted what had happened between me and Sebastian Lattimore. I'd ignore him during the day, but he'd still be free for whatever I wanted of him at night. Hawk was fun and wild, we had a blast together, sure. But nobody made me feel as real as that seventeen-year-old boy had.

The one who had told me about Zeus, Hades, Poseidon… The boy with the long hair he often hid behind. Those thick, Coke-bottle glasses, and his skinny frame that looked more sick than healthy. The boy who made me feel as if I was a goddess, when really I was nothing more than a selfish demon in disguise.

Before I met Sebastian, I'd hated stories, myths, and legends. Then again, I'd never really heard them before, courtesy of my lovely upbringing. But Story Boy? He'd changed my mind, and my world, by teaching me about those things. Worlds I'd never known of but eventually couldn't stop learning about. He encouraged me to ask questions, be curious.

The night before I was set to leave for California, something had clicked into place for me when it came to Sebastian. For months, I'd lived two lives with two different boys, but the one I wanted the most, the one I craved deep in my heart, was never Hawk.

Sebastian had been so very right to me from the beginning. I didn't have to be someone different with him by my side. The badass girl with the hard soul who'd lived through more hell than most of the RDs had—Sebastian had accepted me for me. In turn, he was the one I'd originally wanted to give myself to before I left Rockford. At one point, up until the last few hours before I'd left, I'd even considered staying put because of him. But unlike every other night that summer, Sebastian didn't show up to his room to see me. Nor did he come to me and call me beautiful, or tell me stories, or let me lie on his chest to fall asleep.

In his bed, I'd lain there for hours, crying one minute, growing angrier at him the next. He'd known it was my last night there, yet he'd done the exact thing I did to him during the day, giving me a taste of my own medicine: he'd ignored me.

Done with waiting, and feeling like trash for my own constant denial of him in the first place, I'd left to find him, determined to make things real between us once and for all. I'd even enlisted help from Hawk, not admitting that I wanted Sebastian outright, but admitting that I needed to talk to him, that we'd grown to be friends over the months, yet nobody knew it except for us.

But then I saw what I did and it rocked me to my core: Sebastian through the window at the club on the compound… two women in front of him, on top of him, both doing very dirty and upsetting things to his body.

My eyes burned with unwelcome tears at the memory. For so long I'd refused to look back on my past and regret the things that were out of my control. But there I was, rehashing the pain like I was currently living through it all over again.

I looked away and wiped my eyes, hoping Slade didn't notice I was crying. Unfortunately, he was more perceptive than I gave him credit for.

"What's wrong?" he asked.

I blinked, refocusing on his profile, offering him what I hoped was a real smile. "Nothing. Just tired."

He rubbed his palms over his jeans, seeming nervous about something. "Bullshit. You're crying."

I lifted my chin high, determined not to let him see how right he was. "No, I'm not."

"Then what's this?" He raised his hand to touch my face. Slowly, he grazed his thumb across a tear I'd missed by my chin.

Lips parted, I let him calm me, selfishly needing this stranger's hands. I welcomed the chill on my skin his touch provided, and the odd warmth in my belly that went along with it. Finger lingering long after the tear was dried away, Slade searched my face with an uncanny expression of familiarity.

But then our flight announcement came over the speakers. And just like that, the spell between us was broken.

CHAPTER SEVEN

Slade

Through the window of the airplane, I couldn't see much, other than the occasional snowflake. Yet even knowing we were safe for a few hours, I couldn't let myself fall asleep. Why? Because there was a gorgeous woman pressed up against me, her temple on my shoulder, fucking sound asleep.

Maya wasn't making it easy to ignore her. Not with her snarky comments, endless questions, her sweet little voice, those color-changing star eyes, and her tight little body I wanted to rub my hands all over. Getting beneath the hem of her yellow dress, sliding my fingers between her warm thighs, and finding that she was one fantasy I couldn't curb. The image my mind created had me groaning: Maya against a wall, dress lifted as I rocked against her, lips to hers, hips slapping.

My cock loved the idea, apparently, pushing hard against my zipper again.

Fuck, shit, damn it. Now I needed to jerk one out. Dealing with a hard-on for the rest of this ride would not be cool.

Maya murmured something in her sleep that sounded dangerously like a moan. I tensed, both hating and loving that sound. Knowing this might be my only chance at escaping to the bathroom for a little while, I set my hands on the armrest and went to stand, only for the pilot to come over the speakers.

"Ladies and gentlemen, this is your captain speaking. Due to an unexpected weather system moving slowly across the country, we will be landing in Denver…"

The rest of the announcement droned on, pissing me off more with every word that came out of the man's mouth.

"Mmm, what's going on?" Maya roused, lines on her cheek from being pressed against my shirt.

"Bad weather. We're landing in Denver." I moved away from her, an elbow on the window.

"Oh." She yawned. "That sucks."

I nodded, lips pressed into a hard line. Sucks wasn't what I'd call it. This was fast turning into a damn nightmare.

She kicked her legs out, parting them lazily, her calf brushing against mine. Eyes narrowing, I noticed the wider gap forming between her thighs, which sent me over the edge once more.

"Fuck me," I mumbled and unbuckled my seat, ignoring Maya's questioning gaze as I stood.

The flight attendant yelled after me down the aisle, "Sir you need to sit—"

"Gotta piss." I pushed my way through then stepped into the tiny stall before slamming the door shut behind me. Against the sink, I dropped my hands and lowered my chin to my chest.

Deep breath in, deep breath out.

When I finally looked up at myself in the mirror, I couldn't help but cringe. I looked like a caged animal on the verge of snapping the second a pair of fingers slipped through the wires. Face red, hair a mess, lips curled in a snarl…

"Focus, you son of a bitch," I told my reflection.

The asshole didn't look convinced.

A couple of minutes later, when I thought I had my shit contained, there was a light rap on the door. "Slade? Open up, it's Maya."

I shut my eyes, inhaling, exhaling once more… knowing, most of all, that I was better than this. Letting her get to me was the worst thing that could happen, and I was struggling so damn hard. In her bedroom, just now in the seat…

One more night was all I needed to endure. Then we'd be fine. *I'd* be fine. Back in Rockford, she'd stay at Flick's place, and I'd stay in the dorm on the compound until she went back home whenever the danger ended. We wouldn't even have to see each other. I could deal. I had to. There wasn't another option.

I splashed some cold water on my face then opened the door.

"I'm fine. Just got a headache," I told her.

She blinked up at me in concern, all innocent doe eyes looking more green than brown now. "Are you sure?"

"Yeah. I'm fine."

Maya nodded, still not looking convinced. Wasn't her place to worry about it anyway. She was a job to me. And I'd do it the best I could, keeping my distance from her without actually leaving her alone. I was good at shutting out people. I was even better at ignoring them.

Forty minutes later, we were walking off the plane and heading into Denver airport, Maya at my side, half asleep, while my mind swam with too many thoughts. The first thing I noticed was how full the airport was at three in the morning. Second thing I noticed was how all the faces seemed to blur together, making them hard to decipher, to identify. I stuck a hand in my coat pocket, coming up empty as I unconsciously looked for a gun that wouldn't be there.

Apparently they'd taken care of Carlos's killer. Archer found him hauled up in a downtown Chicago warehouse just a couple minutes before midnight. Some dipshit drugged out on meth who wasn't even part of Pops's inner circle. Apparently, the guy had been wired money to do the job, never even had direct contact with Pops—not that we doubted Pops being behind it.

No matter if the guy was dead or not, the news had put me in an even pissier mood than before. Sure, there was one less killer on the streets, but the fact that I hadn't been the one to avenge my prospect's death made me feel like a shit brother.

To top it off, there was no sign of Pops anywhere. That's the shit that made our delay in Denver so tricky, what set me even more on edge.

It'd been almost six months since we'd gotten word about the former RD pres's location, and that was due to a lone text from Hawk's mom, Lisa—Pops's ex-wife, who'd taken off with the guy last June to keep her daughter, Emily, and son, Hawk, safe.

Lisa had gotten word out privately, away from Pops, saying she was alive and safe, and that they'd crossed the border into Mexico and planned on staying a while. We didn't get specific whereabouts, but it was incentive enough for Flick to send a crew there to hunt for them.

Chop and a set of brothers who were newly patched in, Mute and Talker, looked for them for a solid month, but came up short in the end. Pops was a son of a bitch with more ties to people than the president of the United States, so likely someone had hidden the guy away.

Maya didn't speak much as I led her toward our bags. And regardless of my self-promised distance, I kept a hand along her lower back the entire time. The protector in me just wouldn't stand down.

I felt her exhaustion, so I put her in a seat where I could keep an eye on her, then headed to talk to one of the airport personnel, my gaze never straying far from her as I waited in line.

"We're sorry, sir. But all flights out of Denver are cancelled until further notice due to the incoming snowstorm," the guy behind the counter said.

"What snowstorm?" I growled, dragging a hand through my hair.

He frowned at his computer screen, barely sparing me a glance. "The blizzard, sir. It's stretched across the entire central United States and is incredibly slow-moving."

I remembered seeing barely anything when I walked off the plane, let alone snow. Then again, I'd been too focused on the way Maya had been pressed against my side, as if she needed my body to hold her upright.

"Why not cancel flights out of California first then?" I argued. "Why herd us all here like animals when you knew it was going to be this way?" I pounded a fist against the top of the counter, on edge, frustrated, and needing this nightmare to end.

"There a problem?" A police officer approached my side. I didn't miss the way he stared at the tats on my neck.

"Yeah, there's a problem. I'm trapped here in this damn airport, with no place to go, no ride home, and I've got…" I stopped myself from finishing. Obviously the cop didn't need to know I was on edge about potential threats toward my MC, and finding myself unable to resist my teenage crush. "I've got places to be." I blew out a breath, shoulders falling, stomach tight.

"We can set you up in one of our local hotels if there are any availabilities, sir," the airport dude said, unfazed by my shitty attitude.

"Yeah, no thanks." Because being in a hotel with Maya was a really good idea right now. One bed and two bodies… I could see clearly what would happen if we wound up in some room together. I knew how this shit worked. And as a man with a hard heart, I wouldn't let that little asshole called fate get the better of me like it had at seventeen.

"You got a car-rental place anywhere?" I asked.

Seeming satisfied that I wasn't gonna go ballistic, the cop gave me and the worker a nod before taking off.

"We do," the airport dude said, pointing at a few different places. "Unfortunately, from what I just heard, there are no more cars available to rent at the moment."

"Of course there aren't." I rubbed a hand over my mouth then turned back toward Maya, eyes narrowing when I saw what she was doing: on the ground, ass in the air, her yellow dress showing the world all her goods as she searched through her suitcase, tossing things out beside her, left and right.

"Christ, woman, what're you doing?" I muttered before refocusing on the worker. "You got a waiting list or something?"

"Not sure. But you're more than welcome to check with the agencies, if you'd like." Then he pointed me in the direction of a couple rental places.

I walked over there and jotted down my name and was told they'd call if anything became available. Then I headed back toward Maya, wishing I could have a stiff drink right now. Something strong enough to burn the back of my throat and make me dizzy enough to pass out so I didn't have to watch the show play out in front of me. Maya was bent over on all fours, on the ground, inspiring more unwanted fantasies in my head.

As I took a seat, I stretched my arm over the back of the chair and continued looking, thankful her ass wasn't the first thing I saw from this angle. If that'd been the case, I'm pretty sure my resistance would have been completely fucked.

She tossed even more shit out of her bag: leggings, a couple of tees, a few more short dresses, and a pair of socks.

"Have you seen my phone?" She sat back on her heels, hands on her thighs. "I could have sworn I had it on the plane."

Scraps of tiny lace and silk littered the floor when she started hunting around again. A couple of the panties fell over the end of my boots, and my eyes narrowed at the sight, making me almost forget about the fact that I'd pocketed her phone when she'd fallen asleep with it on her lap on the plane. I could tell her the truth, hand it over, and be done with it. Or I could hold onto the lie until we got home. Last thing I needed was her calling Flick and complaining about me.

In the end, my decision was easy. "Don't have a clue where your phone is."

My own phone buzzed in my pocket. It was a text from Archer.

Just wait it out. Snow is shit to drive in.

I snorted.

You're just as bad as Flick.

Three sets of high heels later and Maya had emptied her suit-case completely. Where were her damn sneakers? A pair of boots even? It was gonna be negative below negative back home, likely with snow on the ground too. No way could she walk around in nothing but high heels.

Just send us a text when your flight's back on.

Screw that. I wasn't waiting for a flight.
Hawk jumped in then, and I frowned. Seemed Archer had added him to the messages.

Flick know what's happening?

I rolled my eyes as another fucking shoe hit my shit. Flip-flops this time. Christ, where'd those come from?
I typed out another text to my cousin and friend.

No. Don't plan on telling him either.
You're asking for trouble not communicating like that.
Dumbass.

Annoyed with them both, I powered off my phone and leaned over to put it in my bag, forgetting Maya's was in my pocket. It fell, crashing screen-side down against the chair next to me, hitting the ground, shattering.

"What the hell?" she screeched, eyes wide. "You had it all along?"

I picked it back up, wincing when I saw the now-shattered screen.

"You idiot!" She slapped my gut when she sat beside me and swiped it from my hand. "I don't have insurance on the thing."

"Should've bought a case then." I smirked, well aware that I was being a dick.

"This had all of my contacts in it. Pictures I'd taken, appointments."

"It's just a screen." I frowned. "You can get it replaced, a hundred bucks at the most."

"A hundred bucks that I don't *have* at the moment." She growled and plopped herself back against the seat. "This is all your fault."

Yeah. It kind of was. But she was making a huge deal out of it. "I'll pay for it."

"No." She jutted out her chin. "I've already taken enough of your money. I'll figure something out on my own."

So stubborn. "Yeah, well, I broke it, so I'll be the one to fix it. Don't fight me on this."

Thankfully, she didn't.

"Why did you take it in the first place?" She whipped her head back my way, her eyes like heat-seeking missiles as she searched my face. "Were you spying on me or something?"

"You got secrets I should know about?" I fired back, which earned me a bigger glare.

I looked at the broken phone again when she didn't reply, rubbing my thumb over the cracks. Sighing, I decided there was no harm in this truth. "I took the phone because I didn't want it to fall off your lap while we were on the plane." Oh, the damn irony of this all.

"Why didn't you give it back when I asked for it?"

I shrugged. "I'm a dick sometimes."

She kicked her feet out ahead of us and muttered under her breath, "Certified dick is more like it." Apparently, my answer was good enough, though, because she didn't comment anymore—though I could tell she was still pissed.

Her short legs twisted together at the ankles, and every so often they shook from her bouncing knee. Compared to mine stretched out, it looked like she was a kid, not a woman older than me by two years.

Even at nineteen, she'd been short. But that didn't take away from how fierce she was. The spicy attitude she showed off for the world was one of the things that had drawn me to her. And as much as her unfiltered mouth got to me, I also found it refreshing, weirdly enough. At least at seventeen. Now, I found it annoying as hell because, well, I was a douchebag and would rather not hear her talk. Why? Because her voice was the thing of porn stars on 1-800 lines, and damn if it didn't make me hard all the time.

"Look, I think we should just lie low until the airport reopens," she finally said. "Flights won't be delayed forever. And I'm sure I can find a place to fix my screen here."

"Not happening. I need to get back. I'll drive us the rest of the way once a rental comes in." I needed to get my ass home. The club needed me, my guidance, my protection, my dedication most of all. Plus, the longer I was with Maya, the more I wanted to test the waters between us that'd been muddied since our reunion the day before.

"I think it's dumb to drive." She rolled her eyes. "But what do I know, right?"

"Look. We don't have another option here. From what I've heard, the snow's only gonna get worse, which means the airport's probably gonna close. It's better if we jump ahead of the storm while we can, don't you think?" Not that she had much of a choice.

Her shoulders slumped. But instead of arguing with me, she got back down on the floor and started picking up her stuff. I watched as she started putting it all back into her suitcase, then decided the least I could do was help. So, I did.

"I'm gonna go get a drink," she told me once we were done.

"Not a good idea." I zipped her bag and set it upright by my feet. Last thing I needed was for her to be alone with Pops and God knows who else running wild. And who's to say she wouldn't take off on me?

"You're not my keeper."

Technically, I fucking was.

I stood and went after her the second she took a step, grabbing the tie on the back of her dress. "Maya," I warned.

Against me she stopped, which pushed her ass directly against my cock. I pulled in a sharp breath at the feel of her tiny body so close, eyes shutting at possibilities laid before me. God, I wanted to lean over and bury my nose against her hair, rub it alongside her neck after that. It'd been a long, long time since someone had made me feel the way this woman did.

Hell, who was I kidding, she was the *only* one who'd ever made me feel like this.

Angry.

Frustrated.

Needy as hell.

"If I'm gonna be riding in a car during a blizzard without a phone," she lowered her voice, the sound husky, breathy, "then I need to be drunk in order to do it."

I pressed my lips to her ear, mouth curving when I felt her shiver. "You sure do like your liquor nowadays, don't you?"

She stiffened. "Nowadays?"

Shit. Not again.

Think, bastard, think.

I cleared my throat. "Yeah. According to Flick, you were always a good girl way back."

She whirled around to face me, eyes narrowed. "Exactly how long have you been a part of the Red Dragons?"

"Long enough."

"Not an answer." She folded her arms and lifted her brows, challenging me.

I counted back the years in my head, heart thudding in my chest as I scrambled for an answer that was two years off. "Ten years."

Frowning, she turned back around and took off. "I'll be back in five."

"Maya, wait—"

"You follow me, I'll cut your balls off when you sleep."

"Brutal." I cringed, staying put, but kept watch as she headed into a gift shop. Never once did I let her out of my sight though. She could try to hide all she wanted, but I wouldn't let her run.

CHAPTER EIGHT

Maya

Sadly, I was unable to get drunk. Not for lack of trying, though. All the places that served or even *sold* alcohol in the airport were closed. But I did settle on a bottle of water and my vice: a bag of Cheez-Its. Slade said they tasted like ass. I didn't bother asking how he knew what ass tasted like, mostly because I didn't want to get into another pissing match with him.

The thought of driving unfamiliar, dark highways at night during a snowstorm was not pairing well with my anxiety over what was to come once we got to Rockford. Slade, though, was almost giddy when he got the call about a rental car being available in an hour.

To ease the strain of my sudden batch of nerves, I yanked out my sketchbook as an idea hit me for a new tattoo. One, lone snowflake, black not white, with swatches of gray highlighting the edges and intricate lines in the middle. White was too traditional, and other than when it first fell, snow didn't always stay untainted. Kind of like people.

Before I knew it, I was finished and tracing a thumb around the edges, wishing like crazy I could put it onto my own skin. Unfortunately, I'd got blood poisoning from the ink in my one and only tattoo, so I couldn't get myself what I'd given to others in the form of my art. But that didn't mean I stopped drawing and creating and, most importantly, tattooing.

"I'm gonna go pick up the car keys." Slade stood from his chair and hovered over me. "Stay here."

I saluted the back of his head with my water bottle and said, "Sure thing, *honey*." Then I slid him the middle finger when he turned his back to me.

Whoever this guy was, I hated how intrigued I was by him. And I hated even more that he had such a fantastic ass, especially wearing those tight, faded jeans. One thing that stood out to me about him, surprised me more so, was that he didn't wear his cut in public. All club members wore those stupid leather vests, proving that their bodies and souls belonged to whatever club had suckered them in. I'd seen Slade tuck his away inside his bag at the airport in San Diego before we got on the plane, though. It was yet another mystery about this man I couldn't figure out. Maybe he didn't want us to be sitting ducks if there was some sort of crazed danger out there.

Ten minutes later, he was back, grabbing our bags. "Let's go."

Slade snuck his hand around my wrist and attempted to pull me up, but I shook him off. "I still think we should wait here. I don't want to ride in a car if the roads are shitty." Especially at—I looked at a clock across the way—five in the morning.

"Yeah, well, I'll swing by a gas station. Get you some OJ and champagne. You can mimosa your ass to sleep." He winked.

I rolled my eyes but couldn't help but snicker at the same time. *Mimosa my ass to sleep?* That was actually quite… funny. It would seem Mr. Doom and Gloom had a personality beyond broody after all.

"I'm not gonna kill us if that's what you're thinking," he continued, losing some of his edge. "We're gonna head south and out of the storm anyway." Then he shrugged off his leather coat and tossed it my way. "Now, put this on. It's cold out there and you're wearing a dress."

No shit. I had the chattering teeth to prove it already, but I wouldn't admit my fault in clothing at the moment. Instead, I frowned, staring down at the coat in my hands, wondering if the warm leather smelled like him. I really would have preferred to wait for a plan, but I had to admit, sitting in this airport had left me uneasy, especially not knowing the extent of what was going on in the Red Dragon world.

I grabbed my carry-on bag while he tugged my suitcase behind him, slipped on his warm coat, and followed him like a good little puppy dog.

Slade strolled with purpose across the floor, his gaze alert and his head on a constant swivel, it seemed. I did the same, looking left and right as thoughts of my past hit me in the belly like a hammer.

Those memories, even all these years later, never failed to eat me alive.

Mom's broken cheekbone, her frail body sitting in the passenger seat of the car I'd stolen from a guy at a gas station after we'd escaped the Forsaken compound.

From the time I was born until I was eighteen, my father had basically cut us off from the outside world. In turn, Mom didn't have numbers to call when we managed our escape, only names—the main one being her brother. A guy she'd never told me about and, apparently, hadn't talked to for over fifteen years.

During our car ride, she'd told me all about him. How Flick had been the one to raise her after their parents died. How he'd worked his ass off and sent her to college. Sadly, after she met my father, she'd been forced to abandon him. I asked why he'd never come to find her. She told me he had, but that she'd been forced to say she wanted nothing more to do with him and the RDs if she ever wanted to see me again. Even then, my father had made me a pawn.

It wasn't until Mom and I had made it to Texas that I'd finally taken a real breath… that was until I'd found out that my mystery uncle was *also* part of yet another huge motorcycle club. This one in Illinois.

I'd nearly driven us to Mexico just to get out of the stupid country and away from any and all MCs for good. But Mom had begged me to get in touch with Flick, promising that things would be okay if we stayed with him. She said he'd take care of us, give us a place to stay. The idea didn't sit well with me at first, especially since I'd gotten used to taking care of Mom on my own for years. But if it meant we were finally going to be out of my father's clutches, then I would deal with it.

Within seven hours after my initial phone call with my uncle, he'd sent guys to where we were, disposed of the car I'd stolen, then flown us all back to Illinois. There, he'd welcomed Mom and me into his home and given us everything we'd never had: constant food, stable shelter, and—best of all—protection from my father.

A month after being there, Mom had grown stronger, formed a *real* backbone too, promising she'd stay away from my old man for good this time. And I'd believed her, which was how I'd been able to leave her by the end of the summer.

For one reason or another, which I didn't understand, good ol' daddy dearest never came after us. He spent a few years in prison or something, according to Mom. But even so, he was a powerful man with powerful connections that were never used.

Still, that didn't mean I'd forgotten him and what he'd done to us… to Mom, mostly. To this day, I woke up screaming with fear in the middle of the night, worried he'd found us, that he was there to finish us off this time.

I shuddered when we stepped outside—the memories and the wind both causes. Snow stuck to my lashes and cheeks, only adding to the freezing temperatures. I pulled Slade's jacket tighter around my chest, wishing I'd have thought to buy a pair of tennis shoes for moments like these. I'm not sure what I was thinking wearing this dress either, other than the fact that the weather was gorgeous in San Diego. In all honesty, teenage me would have laughed at how high-maintenance and prissy I'd become. But twenty-seven-year-old me loved to look pretty, what could I say?

My teeth chattered as we walked toward a car parked near the curb. Beside it stood a guy in a sweater, smoking a cigarette. I stopped, grabbed Slade's arm, and whispered, "I am *not* riding with a random stranger."

"He's not a stranger. That's Avis."

I groaned, tossing my head back as Slade took off toward the smoking dude. "Who names their kid Avis?" I asked myself, struggling to stay upright in my heels on the ice.

"Thanks again, man. Appreciate it." Slade shook the guy's hand then turned and grabbed our bags, tossing them into the backseat.

"Wait, so we're *not* riding with him?" I frowned.

"No. He was the rental-car guy from Avis. Gave me the keys and shit."

My cheeks burned. Of course the guy's name wasn't Avis.

Slade opened my door, not looking at me. "Let's go."

Taking a heavy breath, I stepped forward and slid inside, failing to ignore the way he touched my arm and helped me down into the car. He shut the door behind me—a gentleman, actually. It made me want to look at him again when he got into the driver's seat, study his strong, angular face in the dark, and try again to figure out why he looked so familiar.

"You cold?" he asked.

Thankfully, it was fairly warm in the car. But seeing as how I was not a winter person, I still asked him to turn up the heat more. He blasted it then put on his seatbelt while I shut my eyes and placed my hands in front of the vents. It felt amazing, like burrowing my fingers in sand amazing.

When Slade didn't pull away from the curb right away, I reopened my eyes and found him on his phone again.

"You're a bit addicted to that thing." I tipped my chin toward his device, still bitter about my own phone.

He shrugged one shoulder, but his scowl grew darker with every tap of his thumb against the screen.

Feeling my irritation growing thicker with each minute that passed, I frowned and looked at the clock, then out the window at the snow, realizing that it wasn't lightening up in the least, even with the sunrise imminent.

"Are we going to leave sometime in the next century?" I asked. "Because if we sit here any longer, we'll get snowed in."

He scowled at the screen again, distracted still. "Yeah."

I shook my head, needing music. Something to fill the deadness inside of this car. So, I settled on 80s on 8, thankful the car had Sirius XM Radio. "Jack & Diane" by John Mellencamp poured through the speakers. I knew every single word of that song. Maybe if I showcased my amazing vocal skills, then I'd get this guy to lighten up a little.

I leaned back in my seat, ready to belt out the chorus.

Slade had other plans.

"No music." He tapped the button on the speaker, muting the radio.

I scowled, watching as he finally tucked the cell down underneath his thigh. Who had he been texting? Did he have a girlfriend? An old lady?

"Why not?" I folded my arms and kicked off my heels as he pulled out of the parking lot.

"Loud music will make it harder for me to hear directions." As if mocking me, the GPS told him to turn right out of the lot, which he did.

"Then I'll turn it down a little so I can help you listen."

"No. You'll sleep, and I'll drive in silence."

"What if you fall asleep at the wheel?"

"I'll be fine."

"Suuuure."

Ignoring my smart mouth, he reached up and rubbed the scar alongside his face, still frowning.

"What happened there? On your cheek, I mean," I asked.

"Broken bottle to the face in a bar fight."

"A broken bottle?" My brows rose.

His answer was a shrug and another glare. I hated how I couldn't even get a rise out of him now. What was his issue? *So many mood swings.*

"Did someone hit you with it? Another club member?"

"A guy."

I groaned in annoyance. We had a long trip ahead of us, which meant I wouldn't be happy until my stupid curiosity was sated.

"I told you, I'll find out everything there is to know about you once we get to Rockford, so you might as well spill all your sordid details now." The lovely Northern Illinois city that held all the mysteries of the RDs; I was still in denial that we were headed there.

"Not if I have anything to do with it," he mumbled.

I leaned my temple against the window and stared outside. The second I did, though, my heart hammered a few thousand beats a second at what I was seeing. The conditions were now whiteout-worthy. Not good at all for this little car. If I closed my eyes, the anxiety might lessen. But at the same time, if I was going crash and burn into a fiery death, I'd rather see it coming.

My stomach tightened even more as we came upon the bumper of a pick-up truck a few minutes later. I gripped the seat console, the oh-shit bar above my window too. In and out I breathed through my nose as my foot slammed down on an invisible brake.

"Maybe you should slow down a little."

"I'm going fifteen in a sixty," Slade said, leaning over the wheel, his elbows bent as he squinted through the windshield. It was not a very encouraging view.

"We should just pull over. Sleep in a hotel or something."

He sighed, sounding bored. "No."

I chewed on my bottom lip, hating that the flick of the car's wipers ticked with the slamming of my heart in my chest. God, we hadn't been driving for very long, and I was already regretting that I hadn't taken him up on his mimosa offer.

A half hour later, the tense silence between us had grown twofold. We continued to ride in the shadow of the truck's brake lights, probably so Slade could see the center line better. There was a reason I preferred the West Coast and this was it. To me, driving in the snow was akin to driving in hell—an ice version of it.

Every once in a while, cars would zoom past us, disregarding the slick roads like complete idiots. And with every one that did, I found myself breathing a little faster and, yes, eventually shutting my eyes.

"You good over there?" Slade asked, only slightly knocking me out of my panicked state.

Swallowing around the lump in my throat, I licked my lips and attempted to regroup as I opened my eyes again. "I don't like driving in snow."

There was no huge issue why. No tragedies in my past to support my fear. Nothing like that. Heck, I barely even liked driving during the driest peaks of summer, preferring public transportation to owning a car.

"It's not so bad," he told me.

"Do not try and downplay my anxiety." I huffed. "We can barely see five feet ahead of us. Who knows when these tires were last changed?"

Slade snorted under his breath.

"Don't laugh, damn it. This is a legitimate fear."

"For fuck's sake, Maya. I'm not laughing at you. Just…"

For the first time since we'd gotten on the highway, I managed to look his way. "Just what?"

"Just realizing that you're different than what I thought you'd be is all."

I'd said the exact same thing to him. "What, because I'm scared of night-driving on the nasty Colorado highways in the middle of a blizzard?" I grumbled. "Any normal person would be."

Slade was quiet for a moment, his words barely a whisper when he finally did speak. "I'll never be normal. Guess that's why I don't mind it."

I frowned. Those words… They were so sad. Filled with pain that made me want to disregard all of my own issues just to try and help with whatever seemed to plague him.

Could I have pushed to get to know him? Maybe. But what was the point? Not only would I annoy him, but once he dropped me off at my uncle's place, I didn't plan on seeing anyone from the club except for Flick and my mom. Maybe Hawk, not that I was excited about that, seeing as how he'd apparently told everyone our little secret.

"Shit." Slade looked in the mirror, his eyes narrowing.

"What is it?" I glanced over my shoulder then looked at him again, stomach churning with a different kind of anxiety.

Still eying something behind us occasionally in the rearview, all he did was shake his head. I turned to look too but saw nothing. Nobody.

"Slade, what is it? Are we being followed or something?"

"I don't think so."

"You don't *think* so?" I looked behind us again, and there it was. One single light about a mile or so behind us flickering in and out of the snow. "Crap."

"Type in alternate routes, would you?" He motioned his chin toward the GPS.

Deciding it was better to trust him than argue, I leaned forward to do so, but the screen wouldn't adjust while the vehicle was in motion. Stupid GPS.

"It won't let me."

His lips flattened into a straight line, and soon the car was slowing.

"What are you doing?" I stiffened as he slid off to the right side of the road.

We skidded to a stop and he flicked off the car lights. "Give it a minute."

Nodding, I followed his lead as he urged me down lower in the seat, a hand on my shoulder the entire time.

"What is it?" I whispered on instinct—not that anyone could hear me besides him.

He sat up just enough to look at the side mirror. I looked there as well, holding my breath as the single light grew closer and closer…

We waited, watching out the back, and soon the front, windshields as an old junker of some sort went on its way around us. The single light did not, in fact, signify a bike, like I'm sure he was probably thinking, but a car with only one headlight.

"Is this what it's going be like the entire drive?" I huffed, rubbing my hands together as I sat up straighter. He'd turned off the car and the inside was already turning into an icebox. I *really* should've put on pants.

"What?" Slade frowned, restarted the vehicle, then punched in a new route once the GPS was running again.

"Constantly on edge, thinking someone's after us, I mean."

He glared ahead when we pulled back out onto the interstate. "There's a lot of bad shit going down right now, so yeah, likely. I'm not taking any chances."

"I know what happened to Hawk last summer. If this is about him and his father, then it's not some huge secret. So, tell me. What is it? I'd like to know exactly what I'm up against." I folded my arms, rubbing them to try and warm up. Even with the heat blasting, I could feel the cold air slipping through the seals of the door and window. This tiny Civic had zero insulation.

"You don't need to know. It's club business."

He was using the club-business excuse again? *Great.*

Things had been so calm in my life, up until this week. I'd thought all of my troubles would be long gone by now. At least that's what I'd hoped.

"Well, seeing as how I am in this car, being forced to go to Rockford, I have a freaking right to know what I should be on the lookout for, don't you think?"

"Did Flick tell you anything?" Slade asked.

"Other than Hawk's father has been stirring up trouble again, he didn't say a thing."

Charles Lattimore—Pops—was evil to the point of no return. Framing and attempting to assassinate your own child? Not ideal parenting in the least. Yet who was I to judge when it came to parental units? My own father nearly killed my mom and threatened to marry me off at the age of eighteen just to settle a score with some drug lord he'd gotten into debt with. And that was just one of his many parental fails.

"Figured you'd say that." Slade shook his head.

"What's that supposed to mean?"

He sighed, taking a hand off the wheel to run it through his messy hair. If it wasn't so damn sexy, I would've yelled at him for it. Who had time to muss their hair while driving through a blizzard?

"Nothing. Just you thinking this is all because of Hawk."

I jerked my head back. What was his deal with me and Hawk? He almost sounded jealous, which was stupid seeing as how we'd only just met.

"I didn't say that."

Instead of defending his ridiculous accusation, the jerk spat out something else entirely. "You and Hawk, by the way? It's not gonna happen. He and Summer are gonna get married."

"Ahh, of course you knew that." I pointed an accusing finger at him. "I should've kept pressing you about it before."

It was kind of hilarious how this guy, who didn't even *know* me, thought I wanted to *be* with Hawk like that.

"And for your information, I have zero feelings for Hawk. Just like I told you earlier." If anything, he had been like a brother to me over the years. Whatever Hawk and Summer had was the real deal. And I sure as hell wasn't some homewrecker. Summer was a really good person, a light in Hawk's dark storm. I was happy that my oldest friend had found the stuff of fairy tales, even if I didn't believe in them myself.

Yet, at the same time, I'd be lying if I said I wasn't secretly jealous. Not because I wanted Hawk like that, but because I wanted to know what it felt like to be so completely enamored with someone that you couldn't breathe unless they were beside you.

Love was something I was never taught to feel or experience. Something I wasn't sure if I even wanted to live out. Mom did her best to show me how love went down—back when she wasn't always hiding in fear from my father. But it hadn't been enough to make me believe that everyone out there had someone who was considered their other half.

In a world filled with billions, how was I supposed to find my light when I wasn't even sure how to look for it?

Though at nineteen, for a moment, I'd honestly believed I'd found it.

What a sad girl I'd been back then.

A few minutes passed before Slade finally replied. "You met her, didn't you."

It wasn't a question. "Summer?"

"Yeah."

"I did. In the hospital in Nevada." After the assassination attempt on Hawk when he was on his way to see me in San Diego, Summer had phoned me out of the blue, telling me what had happened, *begging* me to come. Because she wouldn't stop crying, and because I was worried sick about Hawk, I'd taken the first flight out to Nevada.

She'd been so sweet in the waiting room that I couldn't help but instantly like her. All too easily, I could see the love in her eyes for my old friend, even though she'd insisted at the time that there was nothing going on between them. It was unlike anything I'd ever witnessed, honestly.

Then when Hawk had talked about her to me in that hospital room, I knew for certain the feeling between them was mutual, and that there was no way he'd let her go back to Rockford without him.

Honestly, though? Knowing they were content kind of gave me hope that maybe even in the ugliest of hours you could find the happiest of moments.

"She's different, that chick."

I frowned, gaze slipping from the dark road to Slade's profile. He was all over the place with his thoughts.

"I like her. Hawk needs a steady person after everything he's been through, don't you think?" I twirled the end of my braid and pushed my seat back, kicking one foot in front of the heater to warm my toes and legs this time.

My gaze never left Slade's face, especially when I saw him staring at my legs. Granted, they were short and thick around the thighs, nothing worthy of a double-take. Yet the way he studied them before refocusing on the road ahead? It wasn't normal. Nor was it unwelcome.

My lips twitched. The fact that he was affected by me in other ways than just being annoyed changed things.

A lot.

"So, you're pretty close with Hawk, then."

"Yeah." He paused. "He's my brother."

Brothers, brothers, brothers. That word was losing its punch, in my opinion. It was an idea that had been nailed into my skull since the time I first learned to talk. *Club brothers are forever. Club brothers are life. Brothers before anything else.* My father had been the same way about his brothers.

"You still cold?" he asked.

"Maybe a little. Mostly my feet." I curled my knees up to my chest. Perpetually cold was going to be my new name at this rate.

"I got socks in my bag if you wanna reach back and grab them."

It was tempting, and sweet, but way too personal. Not that it was a bad thing for this man to be sweet. It was far better than him being an ass.

"It's fine." I reached over and patted his arm. "I'll live."

We continued to drive at a snail's pace for over an hour, barely making it fifteen miles. This was a two-lane highway, darker than our last one; without a streetlight to be seen, I felt as though we were soon-to-be victims in a horror movie. Slade, though, appeared calmer than ever, even mentioning how the snow was supposed to be lightening up the further away from Denver we drove. If anything, in my opinion, it seemed to be growing heavier, to the point where he had to turn on the brights.

"We'll stop at the first town I see. Get some breakfast," he told me after a while, my guess noticing how badly my knee was bouncing with nerves. At least he wasn't making fun of me.

I pulled one foot up on the seat and set my chin on my knee. My belly wobbled with anxiousness, and I was not in the least bit hungry. Still, I was down for stopping until the sun rose at least.

"Okay."

After a while, my eyes grew heavy, but going to sleep wasn't possible. Slade may not have looked tired, but he had to be feeling it. Driving like this was ridiculously draining.

"Do you need to pull—"

The car swerved before I could get the sentence out. Slade cussed loudly, only for something huge and loud to smash into the front bumper. I screeched, a hand to the roof, the other to the window, my heart in my throat, burning.

Down we went to the right, into a ditch, the ride endless, my life all but flashing before my eyes. Slade's words were barely audible over the crunching of the tires, but I heard them anyway.

"Hold on."

Then, just like that, it was done. And other than the shaking of my body, we stopped moving. Stalled out. The front bumper down, the back of the car on a hill.

"Fuck!" he yelled, punching the steering wheel. "*Fuck!*"

I opened my mouth to speak but couldn't when I saw what was in front of us: the biggest pile of snow I had ever seen in my life. One that our front end was currently buried beneath.

"Shit, shit, shit." Slade turned over the ignition but the car wouldn't start. He pounded on the wheel again, even harder this time. I was sure he'd bloodied his knuckles. We needed to be smart about this, and him hurting himself was not the way to go about it.

"Slade, stop." I reached over and grabbed his wrist, stopping him.

The tenseness he emitted at my touch was even scarier than the downhill ride into the ditch. I was anxious, yes, but not for the reason one might think. A shot of vulnerability had punched its way through this hardened man, showing me that behind his darkness stood someone who felt things, real things, just like any other person. And that, to me, was dangerous because it meant he was hiding who he really was.

I could barely see his face through the dark, but I heard his breathing increase with every passing moment. Heavy panting, over and over… until he asked the one thing I least expected.

"Are you okay?"

"I'm fine." I reached down and rubbed my throbbing right knee. There was a bump forming on the outside from hitting the door handle, but I'd live.

Without warning, he unbuckled his belt, pushed the console up between us, and tugged me onto his lap.

I stiffened, somehow fitting between him and the steering wheel, my legs dangling over the side of his thighs. "What are you doing?"

With no rhyme or reason for his behavior, Slade wrapped both of his arms around my waist and pulled me tighter against him, placing his chin on top of my head. "You're gonna get cold," he grumbled.

I bit down on my bottom lip, not buying his excuse in the least. Something had triggered his reaction, and I was *going* to figure out what that something was.

"You're upset," I told him. "Why is that?"

"It's nothing," he griped. "I'm fine."

"It doesn't feel like nothing."

It took a few more heartbeats for him to relax. To breathe again. For sure, I thought he'd drop the subject, but he surprised me again, his soft words barely above a whisper. "I'm just… I'm pissed that I messed up."

I blinked, taken aback by the admission, wondering why him being upset would cause him to yank me onto his lap like this. Leaning away from his chest, I looked him in the eyes and asked, "What do you mean 'messed up'? I'm fine. You're fine. The car's not fine, but that doesn't matter in the grand scheme of things."

He frowned, dark brows pressed together into a V. "Sure as hell matters when we're stuck in a ditch in a blizzard."

"But—"

"Maya. Fucking drop it, would you?"

"But—"

"I said, let it go."

I winced at the bark in his words, noting the broken pieces of his soul right then and there, without even seeing him clearly. Every day of my life I saw that same haunted expression he wore on his face whenever I stood in front of a mirror. Because I struggled to help myself most days, I decided that, at least for now, I could maybe help someone else battle their demons instead of fighting off the ones I'd never defeated myself.

"You can talk to me, ya know." I shrugged.

"A deer," he muttered. "I hit a damn deer."

That made sense. I'd felt the thud against the bumper, seen a shadow out the window too. Thankfully it wasn't a human or some sort of Sasquatch. But it didn't give me the answer that I wanted. At least I didn't think it did. "So, what, are you like some huge animal lover or something?"

He groaned. "No. It's just…" One deep breath later, he finally finished. "I'm supposed to be keeping you safe."

His admission made my heart squeeze. "It was an accident."

"And I was being fucking careless when I should've been more in control."

"You were driving in sn—"

"You don't gotta make excuses for me, alright?" He scrubbed a hand over his face. "I messed up. Let me live with it."

I took a moment to let his words sink in. I had a tendency to try and make excuses when it came to other people's issues. Their mistakes, most of all. It was a flaw I didn't always recognize.

"I'm sorry," I whispered, taking in a breath through my nose. He smelled like winter: pine mixed with the undertone of sweat. Intoxicating. Mesmerizing, even. I shut my eyes, wondering what might happen if it were another time, another place. He wanted to keep me safe, protected, warm… That was the only reason I was on his lap. Nothing more.

"Wouldn't have happened if I was on a bike," he muttered.

Because a bike on icy roads in a blizzard was *really* smart. Regardless, I decided to poke fun at him a little. The heavy was too much right now. "Yeah. I'm undoubtedly better on a bike than you are, just so you know."

He stiffened. "Huh?"

"Not the *Harley* kind of bike, just to clarify." I toyed with the zipper of his coat, the leather one still wrapped around my body. Not owning a car, and having an expired license, meant I relied a lot on public transportation and my bicycle back in California. "Sad to say, I *have* been the cause of road kill—ten-speed-style though."

"What?" He laughed, and the rough, unexpected timber of it against my back had me grinning, despite the humor being at my expense. "You made road kill with a ten-speed?"

I gave his arm a playful smack. "Don't laugh. It was really traumatizing."

"How so?" Fingers grazed my hip as he squeezed my dress between his fingers.

I shifted closer.

"I was nine years old and riding my bike with a friend. We were near the back fence, where there were a lot of trees and stuff, and came across this, *monster*-sized raccoon."

He groaned, as though he didn't believe me. "Monster-sized? Really?"

"Seriously. The thing was huge. Like… a small tiger." I shuddered at the memory. "Anyways, it was all wobbly and drooling, kept snapping at us too. Plus, it was daylight, so we knew right away what was wrong with it."

"Rabies?" he asked.

I nodded. "It was awful. I had to slam my bike on the thing's head just so we could get past it. Hence the road kill."

"Jesus." He set his chin on top of my head as he said, "You were a little badass, weren't you?"

"A survivor was more like it." In all walks of life. There was no other choice when your father was the VP of the Forsaken.

The things I remembered most about that day were the animal's screech, its beady eyes, and two front claws as it struggled under my tire. I wasn't that scared, but my friend was crying.

"You gotta point to this story, My?"

I smiled a little at his nickname for me. Maybe he was finally starting to let his guard down. "Just that fear is ingrained in us all, but it's mostly an illusion, ya know? We handle it in different ways, and in that moment, my defense mechanism against my fear had been to trap the raccoon with my bike while my friend stood by watching and crying." I paused, letting that set in with him before I continued. "Yours, when we crashed into this ditch, was to yell." I found one of his hands, stroking my fingers over his open palm, my chest warming in surprise when he intertwined our fingers a second later. "Any of those responses are fine, is what I'm trying to say here. There's no shame in how we react to things."

"I'm not ashamed of anything," he grumbled. "Wasn't scared either. Just pissed at myself, like I told you."

I squeezed his hand a little harder, tipping my head back to look up at him. "But you were scared, and I don't want you to think that it's bad to show your fear." I shrugged. "What we went through just a second ago was scary. But we're both okay." I winced, looking out the windshield. "A little snowed in, and in my case freezing, but we're both breathing and kicking and good to go." When I extended out my right leg, though, I realized that the *kicking* part wasn't going to be possible for a day or two. Still, if I told him that, he'd freak out even more, so it was best to keep that little detail under wraps. I was sure it was just bruised anyhow.

He released another sigh, and the word that followed proved the conversation was done. "Whatever."

My fingers were like icicles—greedy little bastards too—so with his hand still clasped in mine, I pulled the sleeve of his jacket down and over our intertwined fingers, then stuck my free hand beneath my thigh.

"Aren't you cold?" I asked.

Voice empty once more, he said, "I'm fine."

"Well, I'm still freezing." My teeth began to chatter. "I really wish I'd worn pants."

Slade reached out from behind and began to rummage for something on the seat beneath us. "Lookin' for my phone," he stated, his voice a growly whisper. "Need to call someone to get us outta here."

"Hmm." I nodded, though the selfish part of me didn't want him to let me go. Not just because I loved the way it felt to be held in his arms, but because his nearness, the oddly possessive hold he had on me, was comforting. Familiar. Every touch was like a reignition of memories I'd never actually experienced before. It was clearly the cold causing me to hallucinate, but I couldn't get enough of this man.

Still, I knew he was right. Driving out of here would be impossible. And if we didn't call for help soon, we'd likely freeze.

I attempted to sit up to give him some room, but Slade surprised me by tugging me back against his chest. "Don't move. You'll just get colder."

So, I didn't move. Instead, I laid my cheek over his heartbeat, relaxing when I shouldn't have been, all while watching as he tried to dial 911 on his phone.

There was something about a heartbeat that calmed me. Especially his.

"Damn, I don't have a signal," he said, pulling the phone from his ear.

"It could be our location." Not to mention the huge pile of snow we were currently burrowed under.

He nodded. "Gonna have to climb up the hill. See if I can flag someone down or get a signal."

"What? No." I sat up and shook my head. "It's freezing out there and cars won't be able to see you anyway. Let's just wait until the sun rises."

Fingers touched my chin, urging my face toward his. "I'll be fine."

Suckered into his gaze like this, I was a woman lost, needing his reassurance, his strength, his promises, though I was very much capable of taking care of myself.

He didn't make a move to get out, nor did he drop his hand from my chin. My skin tingled where he touched me, shooting a direct message to the space between my thighs: *Kiss him. Kiss. Him.*

I attempted to tell my libido to stand down—it sure as hell wasn't the time—but her curiosity was getting the best of her when it came to this gorgeous man.

"I'm coming with you," I said.

"No."

Determined to strive for survival, I ignored that terrible word, *no*, and reached into the backseat, rummaging through the bags like he was. I found the camouflaged duffel he used and yanked out a pair of flannel pajama pants before asking, "Do you have boots or something in here I can use? I didn't pack for a winter hike."

"You're not gonna need them, because you're *not* getting out of this car."

"The hell I'm not." I gritted my teeth together and went back to looking.

"Don't be stubborn," he said. "Just let me go up there, see if I can get a signal or try to flag someone down. If not, I'll come back and we'll figure out what to do together."

Thoughts of him getting run over by a random car had me gripping the neck of his shirt. "I'm not the stubborn one here. *You* are."

"Christ, Maya. You're unbelievable."

"Unbelievably *awesome* is more like it." I smirked, resuming my hunt.

He groaned. "Please. Just give me ten minutes, alright? That's all I'm asking. If I'm not back, then you can come find me, and I won't even be pissed about it."

"Oh, how generous of you." I rolled my eyes.

Did I want to get out of this car in the first place? No. Mostly because I knew it would take forever to warm up again if I did. But the other half of me that didn't like to be rescued without putting forth an effort of my own wasn't having this.

Yet sitting here and arguing wasn't doing either of us a favor. So, if all he was asking of me was ten minutes, I could give him that.

"Fine. Go." I tapped my temple. "But my mental alarm clock is set and starting now."

One half of his mouth tipped up into a small, yet very real, smile. Wow. Slade-whoever-he-is was off the charts sexy when he didn't smile. But when he did, the guy was well on his way to perfection.

"You need to do that more." I slid back into my seat and pulled his flannel pants up and over my hips, wearing them beneath my dress.

"What's that?" He frowned and that smile I already adored fell away as he threw on another hoodie over his long-sleeved thermal.

"Smile. It looks good on you."

He didn't reply. Not that I was surprised. I felt his gaze on me all the same, searching for something I probably didn't have. When he leaned a little closer, for whatever reason, the heat of his breath washed over me and I instantly noticed the smell of cheese.

He'd snuck some of my Cheez-Its, apparently. *Sneaky.*

"There's a bunch of socks in my bag in the back, along with a hoodie." He moved away and reached for the door handle. "If you have to come looking for me, put them on, along with my coat. Last thing you need is to get hypothermia or frostbite."

"Will do." I smiled, saluting him.

He didn't smile back, of course. But he did nod. Then a few seconds later, he was out of the car.

I could barely see him as he made his way up the hill, which sent my nerves skyrocketing. Before he was even out of sight, my hands started to shake against my thighs.

"He'll be fine, stop worrying," I told myself.

To bide my time, I decided to prep a little, reaching in the back for Slade's bag once more. After pulling it out from the backseat and setting it onto my lap, I searched for his socks, instantly finding a wooly pair that would work perfectly. I put them on then found his hoodie, pulling it on over the top of my dress. Any extra layers would help keep me warm. Afterward, I grabbed my ballet flats, foregoing my heels, and wore them on top of my new wooly socks. The tightness squeezed my toes, and I could barely get my feet inside, but at least it would provide a little protection from the elements.

Minutes passed, and I continued to count down in the back of my head. Six went by, followed by seven, then eight. At the nine-minute mark, I noticed the car windows had begun to freeze up. The glass was also covered with a fresh layer of snow. Then at ten minutes, when my eyes were welling with tears and I was thinking the absolute worst, that he'd been abducted by rogues along the side of the road, or ran over by a stray car even, I tried to open the door to get out.

The problem? The stupid thing was frozen shut.

"Damn it." Over and over I kicked, managing to inch it open enough to wedge a foot through. Going out Slade's door would have been a much wiser option, but the trek up the hill would be easier from my side. From what I could tell, the snow seemed less pronounced over there.

"Come on, come on!" I kicked so hard it sent a shot of pain up my calf, but I powered through, only for the snowdrift to sneak in when I finally managed to get the door unstuck. Shivering, shaking, and wearing a tiny smile, I gave my inner self a high five.

I slid out of the car, my cockiness short-lived when I stepped into a huge pile of snow. "So much for less pronounced." Three big footsteps later, and I could already feel ice forming on my damp lashes. My fingers tingled and burned as I struggled to grab the side of the car to stay upright, and just when I thought I was in the clear, the ground seemed to fall out from beneath me and I was down, sliding, too panicked to scream for help.

My knee twisted, turned, popped.

"Oh God," I finally managed, losing my balance and falling head first into the corner of the back bumper.

CHAPTER NINE

Slade

Damn that woman for getting shit out of me like that. Damn my emotions for tangling up with my wits. But the second we'd landed in the ditch, an image of Carlos's dead body had flashed through my head, and all I could think about when the car came to a stop was, *It could've been Maya.*

Staying focused was more than important now, so I shook the unwanted thoughts from my head and continued my climb to the top of the hill through the snowdrifts. Even though the wind was damn near brutal, and I couldn't feel my fingers, sweat still managed to form across my temples under my hoodie. Once I reached the top of the hill, panic started setting in when I realized just how screwed we were.

"Motherfucker," I mumbled to myself, eyeing the expanse of the highway.

Even if the deer hadn't come along, there was no doubt the ice beneath the snow would've kicked our asses. There wasn't a car for miles. I held an arm over my head to try and fight the sting of blowing snow, but it still hit me from every angle—face, cheeks, legs, top of my head, back of my jeans. I had no gloves, no hat. Only the sweatshirt on my back. The one thing I did have, thank Christ, was a signal on my phone.

"911, what's your emergency?" the guy on the other end of the line asked.

I covered the ear not pressed to my phone to block the wind and told him where we were and what happened.

"Sir, that road has been closed for over an hour. It's unpassable."

"The hell you mean, *unpassable*?" I yelled. "We're stuck right here in a ditch."

"I'm sorry, sir. We'll try and get someone out there to assist you as soon as we can. Just please stay in your car and leave it running if you have gas. The temperatures are dropping—"

"My car's in a goddamn ditch. How the hell am I—"

A noise sounded somewhere behind me. I froze, thinking it was an animal, something in the wind getting closer. When I turned to look, I didn't see nothing. But that didn't mean there wasn't anything there.

"Are you there? Sir, are you okay?"

"Yeah, fine, just hurry."

"I'll send a patrol your way as soon as I can."

Done with the guy's bullshit, I hung up and decided to call Arch. Didn't exactly feel like listening to Hawk's know-it-all attitude, but I needed to keep someone in the know. Problem was, Archer didn't pick up. The line rang and rang…

"Shit." I hit end then looked at the time. I'd been up along the road for fifteen minutes. Maya would be getting out soon if I didn't head back. Still, I had to keep someone from the club updated, and I decided Chop was the second-best person to get a hold of.

Got stuck in a ditch in snow. Waiting for help. Let Arch know. What about Hawk?

I rolled my eyes and typed.

He doesn't need to know.

After sending my GPS locale, I pocketed my phone again. Then I pulled my shirt up and over my nose and mouth and took off down the hill, careful to keep my feet flat.

The snow wasn't all that high, up to mid-calf, but it was drifting. I'd need to keep my foot on the brake inside the car until someone got there, and continuously get out of the car to wipe off the brake lights too. Otherwise, they wouldn't be able to find us. Maybe I'd rig something up to hold the brake in place. Leave the lights on too. The battery was probably fine.

Least I hoped it was.

When I spotted the car, I noticed the interior lights were on. The other thing I noticed was Maya wasn't inside.

"Shit."

I ran faster, slipping on my ass twice. My tailbone would be bruised, but that'd be nothing compared to what Flick would do to me if something happened to his niece.

"Maya?" I yelled, reaching the bumper. That's when I saw her door was open.

Circling around to her side, careful to keep a hand on the bumper, I spotted a body on the ground by the tire.

Maya. She was face down in the snow, not moving.

"Fuck, fuck, *fuck*."

I rolled her over, checking her pulse, her breathing. When I found both, I yanked her up into my arms, thankful when I heard her moan.

"Hey, hey, wake up." I patted her cheek, trying to rouse her.

When she didn't respond with words, I rushed toward the back door, unable to ignore how cold she was. Once we were settled in the small backseat, I held Maya against my chest, arms around her as tightly as I could. "Maya, wake up. Wake up."

"Mmm," came her reply.

"Come on, that's it. Open those pretty eyes for me." Against me, her soaked clothes seeped into mine, making me shiver. I needed to change her, get some dry ones on her right away.

"Slade?"

I blew out a relieved breath when her eyes met mine. "It's okay, I gotcha. Keep your eyes open for me, okay?"

She nodded.

"Good girl." I held her face between my hands, heart racing wickedly.

"What happened?" she managed, slowly reaching up to touch her head, wincing when she touched the bump along the side.

"You fell. Hit your head on the bumper."

She laughed weakly. "I-I told you I hated the snow."

I wanted to laugh with her, but my hands were shaking too hard to let it happen. Cold, nerves, and fear were making it hard to function. Still, I kept my gaze glued to her face, staying as stoic and in control as I could. As the road captain, I was a strategic thinker, forever a man who made things happen and stayed in control.

"We gotta get you out of these wet clothes, My. You good with me taking them off?"

Her eyes began to shut again, but before I could yell at her about it, she whispered, "If I'd known you wanted to see me naked, then I would've worn sexier panties."

I yanked off the coat first, then reached for the end of the hoodie she was wearing, pulling it up and over her head. "I'm pretty sure you could wear a garbage bag and still be gorgeous."

The back of my knuckles skimmed her bare skin, and she hissed through her teeth. Still, she managed, "Y-you think I'm gorgeous?"

I cleared my throat, heart racing for a whole other reason right then. "Thinking you might be the most beautiful woman I know."

Her lips lifted in a smile even though her eyes stayed shut. "You're the second sweetest man I've ever known, Slade."

"You're delusional. Must've hit your head harder than I thought." I pulled a new hoodie over her, then reached up to touch the bump on her forehead.

"More like a decent judge of character." She sighed, snuggling closer to me.

"We gotta get you into a new pair of pants."

"K," she whispered, barely moving.

I grabbed more dry clothes from my duffel. A pair of old jeans were all I could find. They were too long for her tiny legs, but they'd have to do.

I tugged one of her legs out of the flannel pants she wore, making sure to move slowly in case she was hurting anywhere I couldn't see. Along the way, my hands warmed a little as I glided them across her goosebump-covered leg. Maya worked with me, even when her eyes were shut, lips parting in a way that I refused to think of as enjoyment. She was hurting, shivering, could fucking die here. But the way her breathing echoed around us, the way her thumb suddenly traced the pulse along my wrist, made me think she was loving the hell out of my care.

When I tried to reach down for the other leg, though, she yipped, yanking my hand away. "My knee."

"Shit, I'm sorry."

"I must've twisted it or something."

In the dark, I couldn't see shit, but I knew it wasn't a good idea to keep her wet leg uncovered. So I covered her body with anything and everything I could find that was dry, praying it was enough: jackets, bags, pajamas.

On my lap, I settled her ear against my chest again, directly over my heart, while stroking the back of her hair. I alternated that movement with brisk strokes of my other hand over any piece of exposed skin she had left.

I kissed her temple and shut my eyes, then told her something I didn't wholly believe. "I'll get us out of here soon."

*

A few hours later the bright sun woke me, reflecting off the white shit piled high outside the doors. I hadn't meant to fall asleep, but my adrenaline had crashed in a heap soon after Maya was out. Slowly, I opened one eye, wincing at the reflection of the white snow against the light. I could barely feel my fingers or toes, and my teeth started chattering the second my eyes opened.

The first thing I did was look at Maya—all warm and tucked away on my lap. Her pink cheeks proved that she was way better off than I was.

We'd made it through the early morning and the worst of the snow, but I wasn't sure how much longer we had. Rescue hadn't shown yet, and the longer we were down here, the worse off we'd get. It took me five seconds of looking at Maya's sleepy face to know why we hadn't been found yet, though, and I rubbed a hand over my mouth to keep my groan inside. I'd been so damn busy trying to keep her warm that I'd forgotten to turn the lights on for a signal.

Fuck.

"Slade?" My name on her lips was soft—the best sound I'd heard in a long time. I squeezed her closer again, hands wrapping around her waist. Had she not woken up after I'd found her, I don't know what I would've done.

"You okay?" I asked, voice cracking.

She groaned and rubbed the bump on her head. It looked worse in the light, but not something that required a hospital.

"Told you I should've gone with you," she sassed.

"And I told you to stay in the car, didn't I?"

She leaned away from me, and her mouthy-ness soon turned into painful moans. "It hurts…"

My stomach churned. "What does? Your head?"

"A little. But my knee mostly."

Slowly, she leaned over and pulled away the clothing I'd piled on top of it to get a better look. The second it was exposed, I cringed. Bruised and swollen: not good. It looked as if someone had stuck a balloon inside her damn knee.

"Has anyone…" She bit her bottom lip and looked outside, then behind us.

I shook my head. "No. We're gonna have to hoof it."

"I'm not sure I can make it out of the car, let alone up the hill."

"I'll carry you." I shrugged.

"No, you won't. It's God-only-knows how snowy and cold out there right now. You'll never be able to carry me."

"You don't know what I can and can't do."

"Oh, but I *do* know what the human body is physically capable of. So unless you're Clark Kent, I'm afraid you carrying me a long distance is just not going to be possible."

"Already back to being a smart-ass." I shook my head, pretending to be pissed, when I was anything but.

The last few hours on my lap like she was had nearly sent me to an early grave, and for the first time in a long time, the most important thing on my mind wasn't the club.

It was almost like we were back in my bed, eight years ago. Holding each other in a way that felt like friends, but always should've been more. Twenty-four hours in, and she'd started burrowing under my skin. If I wasn't careful, she'd be making a home inside me again.

"Just go alone. I'll be fine here."

It was messed up how quickly the roles had turned in a matter of hours. "Not happening."

She frowned. All dark sinful and sparkly star eyes made for rolling in the back of her head in pleasure. I knew what those eyes were capable of doing to a man. Which was why I looked out the window.

When her argument never came, I put my plan into action. "We'll need to put as many layers on you as we can."

"You are *not* carrying me, Slade."

I set her on the seat beside me, watching her profile as she winced. Her knee was worse than just a sprain, I could tell.

"We can both stay here and freeze to death, or you can let me play hero and carry your ass, because there's no way in hell I'm leaving you alone."

Groaning, she tossed her head back and looked upward. "If we would've just stayed at the airport like I said, then none of this would have happened."

Christ, not the blame game again.

"Well, we didn't. I fucked up. Sue me." And Flick would no doubt let me know about it too. I reached onto the floor and found the flannel pants she'd worn earlier. They were practically ice, but I needed the layers, so I tugged them on over my jeans.

"What are you doing?" she asked.

"Layering." I tried to ignore the fact that my legs were getting numb, but it was a struggle.

Once I was finished, I searched for more things to layer Maya in, but a knock at her window sounded before I could find anything useful.

"Shit." She jerked back against me, a hand flat over her chest. I saw the flash of red through the glass before I heard the growly voice asking if we were okay.

Rescue was here.

"Looks like we won't be walking after all." I opened my door, or tried to, but it was stuck. Frozen, I think. I kicked it once, but it didn't budge.

"Here, I'll try mine," Maya said, doing the same—using her good leg. It opened with a slow creak, making way to some guy wearing a huge, red jacket with a fire logo on the front.

"You two alright down here?" The dude crouched beside the car, looking between us before focusing solely on Maya.

"Yeah." She shivered again. "We're just cold and tired."

"And she's got a bum knee," I added.

"I'm the fifth person who's been up and down this road, but the only one to see you. Looks like you both got lucky." He smiled and held a hand out for Maya.

"I can't walk. I hurt my knee." She cringed.

"Like I said," I growled.

He scowled my way with accusing eyes as he said, "Alright then. Let me help ya."

I got a better look at the dude when he tucked his arms under Maya's body. Mid-thirties, tall. Bulging muscles and a good-guy badge on his coat, compared to the patch on my cut. Mr. All American Hero already rubbed me the wrong way.

"On three?" he asked, focused on her in a way that had me gritting my teeth.

"Let me help." I grabbed her beneath the arms and helped her scoot closer to the door. She cried out in pain, and another pair of pants fell off her knee, exposing it. "Hold up, let me grab something to put over her leg."

"I'll be fine." She waved me off with a hiss.

"No, it's cold." My coat wasn't all that wet anymore, so I set it over her thigh.

Our eyes met, hers softening as she said, "Thank you."

I nodded, having no idea why she was thanking me. I was the one who'd got us in this mess. If anything, she should hate me.

Seconds later, the guy hoisted her up into his arms before settling her against his chest, doing exactly what I'd intended to do. The view pissed me off to the point where I was jumping out right behind them, more than ready to take her from his arms.

I had no right to feel jealous. Hell, I should've been thankful he was even there, seeing as how he was saving our asses. But there was no denying the fact that this man holding Maya, rescuing her… I didn't like it.

I jumped ahead of them, arms outstretched in between me and the guy. "I'll carry her."

"It's fine, sir. She weighs next to nothing." He smiled down at Maya, the sight making my left eye twitch.

"And I *said*, I've got her."

Our gazes held in a staredown, with Maya glancing in between. No doubt she'd call me out on my dick-headed behavior later, but I had a hero complex. When it came to rescuing people I cared about—or in Maya's case, people I didn't *want* to care about—I refused to share the responsibility.

I barely spared the guy a glance as I pushed my arms beneath Maya's body and stole her from his arms. She hissed at me, her cheeks flushing in embarrassment as the jacket on her bare leg slid down onto the snow. *Fuck.*

"What the hell, Slade?"

I swiped it up, shook it out, and re-covered her exposed skin with the side that hadn't hit the snow. Ignoring her question, I took off up the hill, calling out behind me to say, "We got bags in the backseat. Grab them for me, would ya *pal?*"

I followed the hollows of the guy's boot prints on the way to the road.

"Seriously. You're doing that… that *thing* all bikers do," Maya huffed, slapping at my chest. It didn't hurt. Felt more like a love pat than anything, really.

The cold wind smacked against my face, and I winced, barely able to get my question out. "What *thing* is that?"

"That *controlling* thing." She nuzzled her nose against my neck, despite her attitude. "It's not cool."

I smirked. "The thing where I take care of what's mine?"

Her lips grazed my skin, and I shivered for another reason than being cold.

"The last I checked, I was nobody's *anything*." Maya sighed, finally relaxing against me once I found my stride up the hill.

"Don't worry. I'll be done with you in a few days."

"Asshole," she grumbled. "And maybe I *wanted* that hottie to save me. Did you ever think of that?"

"Did you?" I arched an eyebrow. "Because by all means, I'll take you right back down there and drop you into the snow if that's the case." No, I wouldn't. She was mine to protect, not his. And there wasn't a chance in hell I'd ever put her in harm's way again.

"You wouldn't dare," she growled.

I stopped at the top of the hill, eying her through a wayward strand of my hair. Despite my shitty mood, I couldn't help but smirk. "Try me, Davenport."

Her eyes filled with mirth, a little bit of fear, as well as annoyance. But there was also a playfulness to her twisted lips, proof that she knew I was only halfway teasing. She liked what we were doing. Foreplay, back and forth—the best and the worst kind. The worst because it was my favorite, the best because it meant something beyond just wanting to roll around with her, naked, in the sheets. All these years later, and this woman still challenged me. And from the feel of the tension between us, I thought that she liked how I challenged her back.

She yanked on the string of my hoody. "That a warning, or a dare?"

"Depends on how far you're willing to go."

"I'm willing to do a lot more than you think" She flattened her other palm over my chest near my heart, squeezing the cotton. I watched her tongue dart out over her lips, wetting them.

At the view, I swallowed hard, taming my rapid-fire emotions. Then, somehow or another, I continued my way toward the guy's truck, only responding with, "You're asking for trouble."

She sighed, the sound riddled with what could only be disappointment. "And here I thought you might be different than all the others."

"Never assume anything about a wolf," I grumbled. "We'll eat you alive when you least expect it."

She laughed, dropping her head back, her hair spilling over my arms, looking almost blue in spots against the bright sun and white snow. "Oh, trust me, sweetheart. I know there's nothing more than a tiny little puppy inside of your big old body, yipping away. Because a wolf would've let me stay in that man's arms."

"Bullshit."

Before she could get another word in, the fire dude approached the cab of the truck, throwing our bags in there with a thud. Then he stood beside us, narrowed eyes on me. "She's gonna need to see a doctor."

"Then take us to one."

He opened the door and I set her inside, not sparing the dude another glance.

"Could you *please* take us to one, is what he means." Maya pulled my hoodie strings even tighter, not letting them go once she was seated.

"The nearest hospital is an hour away, I'm afraid," he admitted. "But there is a small family clinic up the road about ten miles. Doc Mitchell. He'll see you."

I looked to Maya. "You good with that?"

She dropped my hoodie strings and stared out the windshield, scowling. "Probably don't have much of a choice, do I?"

"It's not looking that way, I'm afraid," he told us both.

The view of her puffy, lower lip was so damn cute I wanted nothing more than to bend over and kiss it.

The hell, Slade? Knock it off.

My brain was warped and twisted.

I couldn't think shit like that.

Mushy and sweet and… relationship-y.

Yeah, no. I needed to keep my distance. I was supposed to hate her, for fuck's sake.

I looked back at the fire dude for the sake of my sanity, throat tightening.

Getting trapped in a car with a hot girl could've had its merits. Just so happened that now wasn't one of those times.

CHAPTER TEN

Maya

The interstates out of the little town we were approaching had been deemed unfit for travel by our rescuer, Fireman Jake. Thankfully he'd get our car towed out of the ditch and looked at as soon as possible, though with the city practically shut down, he wasn't guaranteeing it would be any time soon. Slade had been pissed off when I'd told him about yet another delay, but at the moment, I wasn't too bothered—I needed the time to rest.

"It's just a sprain," I told the two men when I walked into the waiting room on a pair of crutches. The doctor, though, had stated otherwise.

You're going to need an MRI, miss. I'm certain you've torn something.

I told him I would do exactly that… when I got to Illinois. He wasn't too thrilled with the idea, but he did give me a prescription for painkillers and a laundry list of things to do to help with the swelling.

Slade rose to his feet before Jake at the sight of me, rushing toward me, then stopping when our bodies were just a foot apart. For a second, he looked torn about something. Cringing, his hands lingering in the air between us… Before I could ask what was wrong, he settled both hands at my hips under my new crutches and released a sigh.

I, on the other hand, couldn't help but stiffen. If this was some macho display of dominance or something, then he had another thing coming.

But then he pulled me closer, our chests touching, and when I felt him relax against me and release yet another heavy sigh, I couldn't help but shut my eyes.

Something about this moment felt so oddly right, though I had no idea why.

"What about your head?" he asked, pulling back a bit to search my face, my hairline. He lifted a hand and, using his thumb, he slid a slow circle around what he now proclaimed to be my "unicorn bump."

"It's just a goose egg." I smiled, leaning into him again, drawn to his hulking nearness and warm body like a beacon I apparently couldn't steer clear of.

Not even if I tried.

I wasn't sure what to make of Slade's tender behavior, but I knew one thing for certain: I liked it. A lot.

"I'm glad you're okay," he told me, and the smallest smile prickled his lips.

"I'm alive," I mumbled against his chest, feeling more alive than I'd felt in months. Maybe even years. "Just banged up."

He hugged me tighter, an anguished noise sounding from his throat. I didn't question it. He wouldn't tell me if I did. Instead, I just let myself enjoy it.

And as much as I didn't like that Slade was adamant about being my bodyguard, I couldn't deny the fact that secretly I liked his protective ways. It'd been a long time since someone wanted to be there for me like this—take care of me like he was. And holding me like I meant the world to him, with a reverence that felt... saintly? It stirred countless emotions inside of me, from peace to comfort, familiarity once more, to... lust.

That last part hit me the hardest, sending a shockwave throughout my body. Even at this clinic, in the middle of nowhere, I felt it in ways I'd never felt before. It confused me, sent warning bells through my head. I did not get involved with bikers, yet there I was, wanting one all the same.

Spoiling myself for once, I inhaled his shirt, smelling the coldness of the air, car exhaust, sweat. It was strangely intoxicating.

Fingers danced through my hair, grazing down the bare skin of my neck, my spine, then back up again. Never once did he stop touching my hair, but his fingers were so big, they seemed to spread everywhere on me, making me feel *too much,* but still not enough.

Jake cleared his throat from behind Slade, and I stiffened, almost forgetting we weren't alone. As the first to break away, Slade barely looked into my eyes when he turned around to face Jake, his arm pressing against my lower back as I resettled onto my crutches.

Right. We had an audience.

With that, I took a step forward, ignoring Slade's broody gaze on my profile as I approached Jake. Jake, the handsome firefighter who would make any girl lucky with his baby-blue eyes and blond hair. His pretty white teeth too. Too bad for him, I liked men with bad attitudes, lots of tattoos, and dark eyes that promised to do devilish things to your body if you let them.

I smiled. Politeness came easy to me with strangers who were kind. "Thank you so much for all your help today."

Jake dipped his head and a blush covered his cheeks. "Sure. Just doing my job, miss." He nodded and took off his hat, glancing between me and Slade. "My sister's got a little cottage you all can stay at overnight until the storm settles, if you'd like. Free of charge."

"That's really—"

"We'll be fine in a hotel."

I frowned back at Slade, no words. If he would've let me finish, that would have been *my* answer. But oh no. Like every other asshole biker, he wanted to jump right in and take control.

"You sure?" Jake asked, his gaze locked only on me.

I lifted my chin, wondering what Slade would do if I ignored his plans and went with Jake after all. Would he pick me up? Throw me in the back of a cab, tie me to a bed, and then…

Nope. Do not go there, girl.

I patted my inner self on the back for keeping her calm, though her ulterior motives were about as ugly as mine.

Slade stepped up beside me once more, his hand pressed to the small of my back. Again. This time I knew he was staking some sort of claim—a claim that was not his to take freely.

"We'll be fine at a hotel." Then I added, just to spite my bodyguard, "But would you mind giving us a lift to one?"

Jake smiled. "Absolutely." Then he gave Slade a small nod, with a clear warning in his gaze that said, *I'm watching you.*

I rolled my eyes. Men and their big, giant egos.

"The next round of snow is coming through this afternoon," Jake continued. "So we better get you settled. They're talking another foot of snow. Maybe more. The wind won't be as bad, but it'll still make for some troublesome spots on the road."

"Shit," Slade growled under his breath, taking a step toward the door of the clinic.

"Are you sure everything's okay?" Jake startled me as he set a soft hand on the back of my arm just thirty seconds after Slade was out the door. I stiffened, not welcoming the touch. He was handsome and kind but really did nothing for me in that way.

"Yeah. He's just frustrated." I looked out the glass door, watching as Slade dropped his head back and stared up at the sky. I could tell his eyes were shut, like he was praying. Or maybe he was begging for patience, possibly a way to get out of being my bodyguard. Suddenly, the idea that we were so close to being friends, only to have my snark push us apart, didn't settle well in my chest.

*

The only hotel in town that wasn't booked did not give me Holiday Inn or Hilton feels. If anything, it was like we'd stepped into a time warp, seventies style. The lobby was very retro— *everything* was neon-green or plum-purple—and it didn't get much better in the room itself.

"You can take the bed," Slade said, apparently unaffected by our accommodation as he dropped our bags onto a maple-colored dresser in the room.

Mouth slightly agape, I looked around the tiny space, wincing at the sight of the double bed. Eighties floral design, purple and green, like everything else in this place. I half expected Barney the Dinosaur to come flying out of the bathroom with a joint hanging from his mouth, but even that seemed classier than what I expected of this place. In no way had I turned into a diva since leaving California, but come the hell on. This room—this hotel in general—screamed murder in the daylight by the décor alone, with a little meth cooking on the side.

The two lone pillows atop the mattress were mismatched and banana-yellow. Rusty-brown stains covered the wall, in between long scratches that looked to have been put there on purpose. The green shag carpet was more matted in places than it was shaggy, and if it wasn't matted, it was missing.

I shuddered. A person didn't have to use too much imagination to wonder what kinds of things went down in this room.

Slade sat down at a small table that matched the dresser, then kicked his big boots and socks off. I'd be sleeping in my socks, thank you very much.

"Gotta make a call," he mumbled from over his shoulder. "Why don't you go shower or something."

I narrowed my eyes, wondering if his dismissal of me was because that's how he treated all the women in his life, or because he was hiding something and didn't want me listening. Either way, the temptation to take a bath was too much to pass up on.

"Fine, I will then."

Surprisingly, the bathroom seemed to be in better shape than anything else in this hotel. The tub was neon-green, of course, but it looked clean enough. I bent over the best that I could on crutches, inspecting for pubic hair or something ten times worse, thankfully coming up with nothing.

In the end, I settled on a shower instead of sinking into a bath full of bubbles. I still had to get in the tub, which proved to be difficult, unfortunately. But I worked through it, determination leading the charge.

Using my crutches, I pulled myself upright. Somehow, I managed to land flat on my feet, albeit a little wobbly, before finally making my way inside the tub. Yet the second I turned on the shower, all hell broke loose. The kind of hell that could only be remedied by a biker that I was fairly certain hated my guts.

Crap.

CHAPTER ELEVEN

Slade

"Where are you?" Flick barked on the other end of the line.

"Small Colorado town. A hotel."

"Jesus, Slade. Ya got her mom all fucking worried."

If I smoked, now would be the time to pull one out. Instead, I tapped the notepad against the table. "Shit happened. But we're okay."

"You run into anyone suspicious? Rogue RDs that might be affiliated with Pops?"

"Nope." Unless you wanted to call the fire dude *suspicious*.

I couldn't get the image of him eye-fucking Maya out of my head when we were at the doctor's office. A man in lust at first sight was the most dangerous kind there was. Plus, he wouldn't stop dropping hints that he was into her. The guy's constant line of questioning about her rubbed me all wrong while we waited for her to get out of the exam room.

Where's she from?

You two together?

She's real pretty. I'd love to take her out, if that's alright with you.

It wasn't alright with me, damn it. The second the words were out of his mouth, I shut that shit down, telling him she was mine. He didn't look convinced, but I had a way with words, and one hell of a death glare, so he soon gave up and kept his distance.

"When are you two gonna get outta there?" Flick asked.

"Roads are all closed, can't go anywhere for today. Rental car's screwed, so we need to wait for a new one. Hopefully tomorrow."

"You should've just waited at the airport, damn it."

Like niece like uncle.

His words pissed me off to the point where I almost claimed a bad signal and hung up on his ass. That was until he tossed his confession at me.

"We got problems, boy. Bigger than you can imagine."

I stiffened. "The hell you mean, *problems*? Pops?"

"Yeah." He cleared his throat, finishing with, "He's not working alone no more. Fucker's got help."

"Who?" I rubbed a hand over my mouth, expecting him to say more rogues, more young kids he'd initiated into his little harem of bikers for the sole purpose of taking us down. The last thing I ever expected, though, was for him to tell me what he did.

"Maya's old man."

My heart stopped—swear to Christ it did. Because Maya's old man was VP of the Forsaken MC in Arizona. Satan was his name. A man who was even worse than Pops.

"Where'd you learn this?" My gaze automatically went to the door of the bathroom, and a blind rage shot through me. The one that said *protect, protect, protect* at any and all costs.

"I gotta guy in south Texas. Runs an MC there. Apparently he's heard some shit. Don't know the full details, but just know something's up."

I dropped my chin to my chest with a sigh. "Do I tell her?"

"No. I'll do that shit. You worry about keeping her safe. Getting her here."

"Yeah, alright." I sighed. If getting her fucking safe meant getting stuck in a damn ditch, only for her to mess her knee up, then sign me up for a medal of honor.

Once the call ended, I stood from the chair and started to pace. My gut twisted with every step I took, fear making it hard to think straight. Wasn't scared for myself, but for My. Which was a whole other thing in itself.

She's a job. No different than anyone else.

But my subconscious had this shit wrong.

"Um, Slade?" Maya said from the bathroom a minute later, stopping me just outside the door.

"What?" My hand went around the knob, ready to twist it open. Until I remembered she was probably naked and wet and…

Don't go there, you piece of shit.

A minute passed, testing my patience.

"I kind of need some help."

"What is it?"

"I can't get out of the shower."

I knocked my forehead against the door. Of all the fucking things to deal with right now…

"It's my knee," she continued. "I overestimated my ability to stand in the shower and now I can't get up."

"Alright." I sucked in a sharp breath and turned the handle. "I'm coming in."

She didn't reply, but I heard her cussing. Something clinked, plastic upon metal, and the second I peeked inside I saw what it was. A neon-green shower curtain was half off the rod, covering Maya's naked body in the tub. I blinked, taking it all in. Water still poured from the spout, raining down on her legs and the plastic lining, more than half of it running to the floor.

"Jesus," I mumbled under my breath, then rushed over and shut it off, shaking out my wet hands then turning to look for a towel. "Where're the towels at?"

Her cheeks grew pink when she shrugged. Soaked, black hair stuck to her face, and I noted right away she'd taken out that red braid. Before I could make a move to help her, the shower curtain slipped lower, exposing the curve of her breast. As quickly as I could, I looked to the ceiling, praying for some sort of strength.

This shit wasn't fair. None of it. I was already finding it hard to resist her clothed, so how the hell was I supposed to resist her *naked?*

"I didn't think this through." A frustrated sigh slipped through her mouth.

I rubbed a hand over my mouth, then let it fall. "Obviously."

"You don't have to be a dick about it. I was cold and sore, and *you're* the one who told me to shower."

"You're pruny and the water's like ice." I looked at her face, thankful she'd covered herself up. "Why didn't you yell for me earlier?"

"I didn't want to." Her lips were set in a stubborn line, but her cheeks were even pinker than before. "And getting *into* the shower was alright, but I couldn't take the crutches with me, so I let them go, and when I got too weak to stand, I had to sit and, well… here I am." She dropped her chin to her chest, looking about as exhausted as I felt.

"Fine. How we doing this then? You want me to just pick you up? Maybe get your crutches?"

She chewed on her bottom lip for a minute. "Can you get behind me? Help me stand that way? I'll try to keep the curtain wrapped around my body, seeing as how the only towel in here is that one." She pointed at the floor. I looked, spotting a white thing that could barely be passed as usable. It looked like it'd been dipped into a pile of hot glue.

I heard her splashing around in the water again, then heard her hiss in pain. That noise was enough to push me out of my head, away from being selfish because I was too weak not to want her body.

"I won't look at you," I said, voice cracking. "Grab my hand."

She stared at the back of my fingers, all cracked and scarred, stained with oil and grease. They were hands that belonged to someone who'd done some terrible things in life. Things I'd once thought I wasn't capable of.

When she didn't take hold right away, I lost my patience, shaking it at her. "Grab my damn hand, would you? I won't bite."

She frowned but eventually did what I asked, using my arm and shoulder as leverage to stand until I could get behind her. Water dripped onto my clothes, onto the floor by my feet, but I kept my eyes glued to the side of her face.

"God, this hurts." A tear dripped out of eye, but she looked away before I could see where it landed.

I grinded my teeth together, hating to see her in pain. "Just a sprain, huh?"

Impatient, I slid one arm under her thighs and used the other to hold her upper body. Surprisingly, she didn't argue. Any pain she felt must've had her "save herself" side tapped down real good. I knew what that was like, which was exactly why I was determined to tame down the asshole and be the man she needed until we got her home. Because if she was hurting, I hurt too. Why? Had no explanation for it, other than the fact that it came with the territory of having a heart that was warm yet locked up inside a block of ice most days.

Ignoring the way her soft skin felt—the way she fit so perfectly in my arms—I held her as close to my chest as I could and pulled the shower curtain further up her body. Water dripped down my jeans, soaking through my shirt, but I didn't mind if it meant keeping her body covered.

"You cold?" She giggled, setting her hand over one of my pecs, patting it. My protruded nip was hard against my shirt when I looked down.

I grunted, lip curling as I walked her into the room.

"Aww, don't be so grumpy," she teased. "You know what they say about a man with hard nipples, don't you?"

"We're not discussing my nipples, you hear me? That shit's just weird."

She giggled. "Well, would you rather we discuss your shoe size?" Then she winked, and even though I didn't want to, I felt my lips twitch.

"You're crazy." I walked her toward the bed.

"I've been told that a time or two."

Me too, I wanted to say, but didn't.

By the time I got her to the edge of the mattress, my dick was hard as fuck—even with her jokester side coming through. Before I set her down, I glanced at her face, finding those star eyes I'd dreamed of for so damn long locked on me again.

The space between her brows pinched, like she was trying to figure me out, unpuzzle me.

Not liking it, I set her down and turned away. "I'll get you clothes."

I squeezed my hands into fists, trying to keep from turning back around, grabbing her face, and kissing those lips that called to me like fireflies in a summer night's sky. No way did I need the complication of a woman right now. Especially not a woman who would no doubt leave me even more broken than the last time she'd left my ass.

In her suitcase, the first thing I found was a pair of leggings—I must've missed those in the car. Then came an old-tee and a black bra, followed by the laciest midnight-black panties I'd ever seen.

Slowly, I rubbed a thumb over the edge as I walked them back to her. "Here."

Our fingers grazed as she reached out and grabbed her stuff. "Thank you."

I nodded and cleared my throat. "I'll give you a few minutes."

"Wait." She grabbed my wrist before I could turn away.

I stared down at her hand, perfectly manicured fingers, soft skin… Her tat was the only thing marring her body, but instead of looking out of place, it fit. A little darkness on untouched flesh, likely mirroring her past.

"Why the bird?" I asked, my thumb grazing its wired wing. "Why the wire?"

Goosebumps formed under my finger as she spoke. "It means being trapped in freedom."

I scowled at her. "That doesn't make sense."

She shrugged and frowned at the same time. "I'm free but never fully feel like I can live without guilt."

"You got things to feel guilty about?"

One nod later, she said, "A lot, actually."

She tipped her head back, gaze locking with mine again. Quiet. Patient. Curious. Three more dangers I couldn't let get to me.

"What?" I asked, trying not to squirm. I hated how raw everything was now that we were together again, even if she didn't know who I was.

She shook her head, deciding against whatever she was thinking and said, "I might need some help getting dressed."

I tensed.

"It's hard for me to move my knee, and getting underwear and leggings on might be an issue."

I dropped my head back and looked up at the ceiling again like I'd done in the bathroom. Was she doing this on purpose? "Least put your bra on first."

"I can do that."

The rustle of the shower curtain sounded when I turned around to wait. Then a few seconds later, she cleared her throat.

"You decent?" I asked.

"Uh huh."

Inhaling through my nose, I turned back around, eyes widening as I zeroed in on her tits. "That's not a damn bra, Maya. Jesus."

She frowned at the see-through torture device. And I say torture because that was exactly what it did to my dick. Black and devilish. Meant to seduce, not cover. I'd been so damn worried about her underwear, that I'd not even bothered to check the bra.

"You're the one who picked it out." Her eyes narrowed, likely waiting for my rebuttal that never came. Instead, I let out my dangerous side, deciding it was time to play with fire. The kind of fire a man couldn't steer clear of when it came to a body like hers.

It was the kind of fire that made me want to get burned.

Licking my lips, forgetting the fact that I didn't want nothing to do with her anymore, I let myself look at that bra and everything she showcased beneath it. With wickedness in my veins, I threw Sebastian the middle finger and enjoyed every single second of my perusal. Pink nipples hardened against the material as I stared. Lush, cream skin surrounded the centers too.

I grinned, deciding to toy with her a little. "Who's the cold one now?"

She folded her arms beneath her tits, pushing them up to attention. I nearly groaned at the sight, losing my smirk, wanting nothing more than to pull those nipples out and suck them until they popped.

"Are you gonna help me dress or ogle me all night?" she toyed right back, one eyebrow lifting higher than the other.

Lips pressed in a flat line, I waited and waited… not really sure *what* I was even waiting for.

Rolling her eyes, Maya grabbed her shirt and slid it on, thank fuck, but the thin, cotton material did next to nothing to cover her hard nipples.

"This better?"

I grunted my answer.

When I didn't take a step forward, she frowned. "You're… different than all the other biker assholes I've dealt with."

"You said that already," I told her.

Reaching over, she grabbed her panties, sliding them up her good leg. "It's the truth."

"I'm not different." Least not in a way she needed to know about.

The part that Maya got from me so long ago, this different part she was talking about. That'd been all hers. I'd given her more chances than *anyone* in my life to have me as Sebastian, but she'd pushed me aside.

"You are. You're good, Slade. I see it when I look at you." She lowered her voice, one half of her mouth sliding up. "I feel it when you look at me, too."

I dropped to the floor in front of her, grabbing the other side her panties to help her put them on over her bad leg. "You've got no idea who I am."

"See, I think that's where you're wrong." She snapped the band out of my hand and attempted to get them on herself again—huffing then ultimately failing. "I'm a good judge of character. And you? You're hiding everything. Why is that?"

Because you made me this way! I screamed inside.

"I am different than other bikers you've met, but for one reason: I don't put up with bullshit from people, especially runaways who think the world owes them a favor."

My hands shook as I finally slid her panties over her knee. Then without asking, I grabbed her leggings and started yanking them on right after, not preparing her for my jerky movements.

"Stop. My knee!" she yelled so loud I fell back onto my ass.

"Shit. I-I'm sorry." I tugged her pants right off, guilt eating me up. She let me, no hesitation as she lay back on the bed, sniffling loudly.

God, I was an asshole.

No longer thinking about half-naked tits and hidden pasts, I took in the swollen flesh of her knee, trailing my fingers over the huge bruise that colored her skin. It didn't look much different than it had before, but I wasn't a doctor.

"I'm gonna get you some ice." I stood back up.

She didn't even nod.

*

Fifteen minutes later, I'd managed to scrounge up a baggie from the front desk and got some ice. The room was quiet when I returned, no more sobs or sniffs, but she was still awake and staring at the ceiling, lying in the same position I'd left her in.

I sat beside her and placed the ice bag on her bare knee.

She hissed and slapped my hand away. "Towel. Please."

"Sorry," I said again, flustered.

I grabbed the glue-coated towel from the bathroom then set it on her knee before placing the ice on top of it. I held it there, not sure what to say. And Maya didn't bother to break the silence either.

"We gotta leave first thing tomorrow. You need a second opinion," I finally managed to spit out. Unthinking, I rubbed my fingertips across the side of her kneecap, back and forth, up and down.

"What about the roads and the car?" she whispered, shivering a little.

"I'll figure it out. Just know we can't keep staying here and fucking around."

"Fucking around?" She laughed bitterly. "You think that's what we're doing?"

"Well, no. But the bath thing—"

"Just because *you* don't clean yourself up doesn't mean I can't." Her eyes grew red, as did her cheeks.

I dropped my head. God, I didn't know how to talk tonight, apparently. "I'm sorry."

"Yeah. Sure. Whatever you say."

I winced at her sarcasm but stayed quiet. I wasn't a man of many words anymore. My stories and thoughts were lost somewhere in my head, along with my ability to be a decent human being, apparently.

The bedframe squeaked as she put her back to me, legs hanging over the opposite side of the bed. Huffs followed puffs as she struggled to reach for her crutches, and I almost asked to help her but knew she'd likely rip me to pieces if I did.

The thump-click of her crutches hit the floor as she made her way around the foot of the bed. More hisses sounded out, which had me cringing and wishing I could ignore my emotions and let all this shit go. My bitterness. My anger. And most of all, any lingering feelings I had for her that were not as hidden as I'd hoped.

"Seriously," she started in again. "You don't get to be an arrogant asshole and then expect me to ignore it. I've dealt with enough bikers and selfish men in my life to know how to—"

She screeched, losing her balance before falling forward against me. With an arm around her waist, I caught her, pulling us both back onto the bed.

She lowered her forehead to my chest and let out a low groan.

For a second, neither of us moved let alone breathed. Like this, it'd be so damn easy to forget everything and let go, just for a night. Take her and make her mine like I'd wanted to so long ago. But mistakes weren't meant to be made twice, and I sure as hell wasn't going to be the person who fought against fate again. That shit was powerful and knew what it was doing. Wasn't my place to ignore it for the sake of my dick.

I rolled her off of me and onto her side, but before I could put distance between us, she gripped the front of my shirt and burrowed her face against my chest, cussing about my *stupid, hard muscles*, my *stupid dimple*, and my *stupid, pretty-boy lips*.

My mouth curved into a half-smile, my heart skipping—liking the fact that my body affected her. "Nice vocabulary there."

She pulled back to look at me, stopping short with whatever she was about to say. Instead, she found some sort of solace in my mouth and lips, looked down at them like they held all the answers to her prayers. "You're smiling again." She blinked, her voice awed.

Our bodies stayed pressed together from the waist down, but with those star eyes widening, flashing from gold to green, I nearly forgot my own name, let alone how close we were.

Surprising even myself, I slowly inched forward and did what I hadn't allowed myself to do for a long time.

I pressed my forehead against hers.

"Maya," I breathed. "You're..." *Beautiful.* I wanted nothing more than to say that word. Because she was. So damn beautiful. But doing so would lead us down the wrong road—a road that would only get bumpy for the both of us.

Regardless, my fingers—too curious for their own good—slid up and over her waist. I allowed myself to do what I shouldn't, loving the sound of her heavy breaths. I slid my palm around her back, beneath her shirt, and against her spine. If I kept her close like this, acted on the chemistry we shared, it'd be explosive. Epic. *Everything.*

But then she'd find out who I was, and, well... what kind of asshole would I be if I pretended to be one man who'd fucked her, then decided to come clean later as the man she'd been too *embarrassed* to fuck once upon a time?

"I'm sorry for being an asshole." I sighed, settling with that. "I just gotta lot on my mind."

"I'm sorry too," she whispered, her fingers sliding into the back of my hair. "I've just been through a lot lately, and, well, you were an easy target."

"Yeah," I said, licking my lips. "But I'm no angel myself."

She sighed, her eyes drooping sleepily. "You can make up for it by getting me under these covers, because I'm pretty sure if I don't sleep soon, I'll turn zombie on you."

Throat tight, I nodded and pulled away, helping her get under the sheets. I set the towel and ice back on her knee then covered her. But before I could stand, she grabbed my hand again.

"Slade?"

"Yeah, My?"

Her eyes softened at my nickname for her, and she waited a second before asking the last thing I expected her to. "Will you... lie with me?"

I stiffened, brought back to a time I didn't want to revisit. To a time I never thought I'd find again. Yet the longer I stared down at her, watched her cheeks turn pinker with my silence, the more my resolve slipped.

"I have some pretty crappy nightmares sometimes," she continued, fidgeting with the end of the blanket. "Especially when I'm in a new place, and…" She covered her face. "Ugh. Never mind. It was stupid of me to ask."

My throat burned, the memories eating me up and telling me what a screwed-up idea it was to even consider doing this. But just like when I was seventeen and clueless, I couldn't tell her no.

Only this time when I lay beside her, the distance between us couldn't have been any wider.

CHAPTER TWELVE

Slade

We rolled out of the small town around noon the next day. The rental car was shot to shit, thanks to my stellar driving skills. I'd been ready to hike it to the next town over for a new one, but while I'd been in the shower, Maya had called her dear little friend Jakey, who'd been all too eager to give us a ride back to Denver. When I'd asked why we needed to go there, Maya'd told me she'd booked train tickets for us, via the hotel phone, insisting that the only way we'd get back to Illinois was by Amtrak.

I wasn't thrilled with the idea. Being on a train left us vulnerable. Hell, anyone could've gotten a ticket and followed our asses. There again, we'd been good in the ditch—good, as in protected from enemies, but not the elements.

I wasn't especially fond of the idea of riding with My's new little *friend*, either. But at this point, we were kinda screwed as far as transportation went, especially with the airports shut down, and the fact that I wasn't looking to get behind the wheel again anytime soon.

The main highway wasn't too bad, but *Jake* said the side roads and exits were still mostly covered. In the guy's big truck it took us an hour and a half to get back, when normally it was supposedly just a forty-minute drive. Maya slept the majority of the time, thank God. No way did I want to sit there and listen to her and Mr. Pretty Boy flirting the whole way.

I didn't bother talking to the guy myself, and he wasn't much for talking to me either, it seemed. But that was fine. I wasn't looking to make any new friends.

By the time we got to the train station, it was close to two. Our train left at three, so we had an hour to kill. Maya sat, still half asleep, in a row of chairs close by, while I went to the counter and got our tickets.

"Picking up two tickets east under the last name Davenport," I told the attendant, looking back over my shoulder as I waited for the lady to print them out. I spotted Maya where I'd left her… but she wasn't alone. Jake had come inside too, his body damn near hovering over hers as he sat beside her. Thankfully she didn't look as enthused.

"Would you like to upgrade to an overnight room, sir?" the attendant asked.

Whipping my head back toward the lady, I grunted out, "Yeah, whatever." Then I handed over some cash, not giving a shit how much any of this cost anymore.

We'd stop in Osceola, Iowa, which was close to where Hawk's woman's grandparents lived. They'd said we could crash with them for a night. Then in the morning, we'd finish our drive to Illinois in another rental car, seeing as how the snow had shifted south and wouldn't be headed toward home.

Once the tickets were in my hand, I turned to go back and meet up with Maya and her new Prince Charming. Maya was grinning at the guy, her face damn near glowing as he said something. I watched through narrowed eyes as he took one of her hands in his, then felt my gut harden when he brought her fingers to his lips.

Motherfucker, I muttered under my breath, then made my way over, done with whatever game this guy was playing. The entire time, my heart thudded in my ears like a drum, a repetitive boom that said, *Mine, mine, mine…* Though she'd never be that.

To the left of Maya, I dropped my bag on the floor. It landed with a thud, which had Jakey Boy shooting to his feet. A snicker left my mouth, and Maya gave me a dirty look.

"It was good to meet you," Jake said to me, reaching out a hand.

I lifted my chin. It was best he remembered this moment, because if I ever saw him with his lips on Maya's skin again, I'd…

Shut it down, dipshit.

Breathing in through my nose, I stared at his fingers, despite my inner voice. Respectable and good. Clean-cut. Was this the type of guy Maya was into now?

Not wanting to know whether my thoughts were true, I sneered at the guy's trembling fingers, more than ready to tell him to go to hell, until Maya kicked my shin. I rolled my eyes but shut down my pride and shoved my hand into the dude's, staying quiet.

"Good riddance," I muttered under my breath once he'd left, sitting next to Maya.

"Did you wake up on the wrong side of the bed today, or what?" She rolled her eyes.

It was on the tip of my tongue to say, *Any morning with you in my bed is a bad morning*, but I wasn't in the mood to argue so I shrugged instead.

Lips pressed together, Maya stared hard at her hands, probably mad that I wasn't taking the bait and arguing with her.

"You hungry?" I asked, trying my hand at being nice.

"A little." Still with her eyes on her hands.

Leaning back in my seat, I settled an arm around her chair, careful not to touch her. "You want something outta the vending machine?"

She shrugged and looked toward the window.

Not asking what she wanted, I headed to the vending machine, searching until I found what I was looking for. Two dollars later, I set a bag of Cheez-Its on her lap, not missing the way her lips lifted higher on one side.

"Thanks," she whispered, peering at me from around her red braid.

I chewed on the inside of my cheek then looked away with a grunt.

Golden, that's what color her eyes were today. They were midnight-brown when she looked like she wanted to cry, green when she was angry, like a dragon, even. And the gold sparkle there meant she was happy. I hated liking that color most of all because it only made my heart thaw out. Hated how I liked knowing, too, that regardless of me not being a pretty boy with good morals, I could make her light up with a simple bag of crackers. And though the idea was stupid, there I was thinking what I'd have to do just to get a lifetime supply of Cheez-Its for her, all so I could see those star eyes light up for the rest of my life.

God, I was so fucked.

I wasn't sure how long I'd been nursing my whiskey. A while, I guessed. Getting drunk wasn't a good plan, seeing as how I was on bodyguard duty. Still, sitting in that train, watching the late-day sun fly by out the window, had me feeling like I was choking on air.

Maya was in the room, resting. I'd left her there, telling her I needed a drink, and that I'd grab her some ice for her knee on my way back. But one drink had turned into two, then four, and the thought of going back to the room and sharing the tight space with her had become the last thing I wanted to do.

It was hell to feel so lost when, for a long time, I'd been living a life I'd created out of a desperation to escape. But knowing that the person who could turn that upside down was just a train car away had me clawing my way back into the darkness for dear life.

For some reason, my thoughts went to my old man. I could barely remember what he looked like anymore. But I could remember his voice, and all the shit he'd told me. That life wasn't for losers, but winners. And if I wanted to be something, then I needed to be the opposite of what he'd become.

I thought he liked being a Red Dragon, but at the same time, I wondered why he'd never pushed the life on me more. Granted, I was ten when he was killed…

I didn't cry at his funeral. Mainly 'cause I didn't want anyone to make fun of me. But in my room that night, the one I'd moved into at Flick's place, I'd cried to the point where I'd stopped breathing. Where I didn't want to breathe anymore, was more like it. At ten, no kid should think that, but my old man was all I had. And dying seemed a hell of a lot easier than living in the shit world my father had left me in.

Still, I took his words to heart and demanded to Flick that I continue to learn and go to school and shit. The man didn't bat an eyelash at my request. Just nodded and drove me there every damn day. Unlike some of the other club brothers, he was the only one who didn't make fun of me when I went to the library instead of the compound. Most nights, he'd take me there too. Told me he was just honoring my dad's wishes. I never asked what those wishes were exactly, but I'm pretty sure he followed through with them.

I wondered what my old man would say right now if he were here, watching me fight against all the things I'd sworn to never feel again when it came to Maya.

Buck up, boy, he'd tell me. *She's just tits and ass.*

I laughed to myself at the thought, pretty sure my father never had a real old lady in his life. Hell, even my mom wasn't nobody special, just a one-nighter who'd gotten too much out of the thrill of sleeping with a biker.

Rubbing both hands over my face, I leaned back on the stool, wishing all this mush and madness in my chest made sense. Maya left me, for God's sake. She *ran*. Didn't even say goodbye either. How could I even consider letting her back into my life?

Why the hell was that thought even crossing my mind?

You know why, asshole.

You never stopped loving her.

You never. Fucking. Will.

I growled, wishing I could slap myself upside the head, get those thoughts to go away forever. Instead, I got them out in other ways… by downing the rest of my drink, then motioning to the bartender for another glass.

"Hey." Someone nudged my shoulder. I blinked, thinking it was morning, and I'd be in my room at Flick's place. Head falling to the side, I found a window instead, blurring in and out of focus. It was still light out there when I'd fallen asleep, but from what I could not see, it was pitch black.

"Yeah?" I cleared my throat and turned, finding an employee in a blue suit. A woman. Tall and beautiful. Red hair and brown eyes.

"I'm sorry, but you can't sleep in here, sir. I'm going to have to ask you to return to your seat."

I waved her off and stood, stumbling along the way. Going back to my room meant seeing Maya, and I wasn't ready for that. At least I was still drunk enough that it wouldn't matter. Numb like I wanted to be, which meant I'd sleep away the temptation of crawling into bed with her the second I hit a chair or the floor.

My steps were slow as I made my way from the car to our room, knees smacking together as the train rushed over the tracks.

Though I wasn't proud of how shitfaced I'd gotten, I also wasn't disappointed in myself either. This was who I was now.

The train blurred, my hands holding each seat I passed to keep me upright. Once I made it to the door of our room, I took a breath and held a hand against the knob, slowly twisting it open.

The small space was pitch-black, except for the light shining through the window by the lower bunk. The first thing I noticed was that Maya wasn't in bed. The second? She was still sitting in the same chair I'd left her in when I went to get some ice for her knee.

Ice that I'd forgotten hours ago. *Fuck.*

I sighed, moving until I stood over her body, the movement of the train rocking me again. Somehow, I managed to stay upright, watching her sleep for minutes when I should've just left well enough alone. It made me restless being so close to her like this; my skin itched and crawled with sensations I hadn't let myself feel for years. Why did she have to come back into my life when I'd finally forced her out?

"Maya," I managed.

She stirred a little, but her eyes didn't open. Instead she winced in pain, and *God*, did I feel like a dick because of it.

"Maya." I crouched down in front of her, landing on my knees.

Beautiful, sweet Maya. My secret girl in the night and my stranger in the day. At seventeen, I would've been content to live that way. At twenty-five, I wasn't having it.

She moved a little more, moaning, her face pinched in pain. Drunk or not, I needed to get her on an actual bed. Her protection and safety were my priority until I got her home. I had to remember that.

I tripped over her crutches as I stood, kicking them aside with a grunt.

"Slade?" she whispered.

"Let's get you in bed."

She nodded a little, not a single fight in her as I scooped her against my chest and carried her to the lower bunk.

"I didn't get you ice," I told her as I propped her knee up on a pillow.

"It's okay," she murmured. "Doesn't hurt much."

"Liar," I mumbled, then crouched down next to her and pulled the covers over her chest. She was still wearing that old tee and leggings from the hotel, but it was cold in here and I knew she was likely freezing.

The room spun when I tried to stand, but Maya reached out, keeping me steady as she touched my fingers. "Lie with me?"

My chest grew tight. I blew out a breath, reliving those years once more.

Lie with me.

Sleep with me.

Tell me one of your stories.

Every night she'd have a different excuse: nightmares, sadness, emptiness, fear.

I related to her excuses so fucking much. Which was why telling her no wasn't something I ever did. Probably never would.

Instead of saying yes with words, I unbuttoned my jeans, let them fall to the floor, then took off my shirt and tossed it somewhere. I climbed over her body on the bed, careful of her knee, and did what she asked. Somehow my drunk-self thought this was okay. So did Sebastian, who was fighting his way out every additional second he was with her.

Stand down, fucker, I tried telling him. *You don't belong.* But the more I fought with that guy, the less control I seemed to have.

"Get some sleep," I said. I wouldn't touch her or hold her, just like last night. I'd just sleep next to her. Not let her lay her head on my chest and listen to my heart. Not hold her hand. And most importantly, I wouldn't tell her any stories.

CHAPTER THIRTEEN

Maya

Two hours. That's how long I lay awake, snuggling against Slade's chest as he softly snored against the top of my head. His arm was draped around my waist in a protective manner. And though his breath and skin smelled of liquor, he still felt warm and right and completely unexpected. It was obvious he was struggling with something internally, and the more time we spent together, the more I realized I wanted to know what that struggle was about.

I fell back asleep sometime when the sun was starting to peek through the curtains, and stayed asleep for several hours. A train whistle woke me up. Not the nose in my hair or the fingers against my belly, mindlessly stroking just above my waistband.

Sighing to myself, I willed myself to relax against him, pretend that the two of us weren't strangers now bound together by everything I hated in life, but instead, two lovers on a cross-country journey, no end goal in sight, with nothing but time to revel in being close.

I was incredibly attracted to Slade, that was a given. He was exactly my type. Tall, dark, handsome, with hints of vulnerability burrowed inside of him. I hadn't found someone like that in years. Not since… *him*.

I frowned at the thought of Sebastian Lattimore, feeling oddly guilty for some reason. I owed nothing to that man and our memories, seeing as how he'd abandoned me as much as I'd abandoned him.

Mood falling, I finally sat up, barely rousing Slade. He moved to the pillow I'd been lying on, now flat on his back, arms spread out like he was waiting for me. For a moment, I watched him sleep. His full, pink lips parted, and another soft snore echoed from his nose. Every inch of him captivated me. The dimple indenting his cheek, that awful scar, and the way his dark lashes lay almost carelessly over the top of his cheeks.

God, he was gorgeous. Truly. Soft and hard edges all fighting for control on his face. So young-looking too. Familiar in a way that made me frown once more.

There was nothing wrong with him wanting to keep things from me. But I had an undying need to figure him out at the same time.

Looking around the room, I spotted his pants discarded messily on the floor. Coins and dollars lay next to them, as well as a wallet.

A wallet…

Oh, hell yes, a wallet. His ID. Where in the hell had that been hiding all this time?

I bit my lip to curb the giddy squeal in my throat and grabbed my crutch. As quietly as I could, I pushed it out ahead of me then tugged his wallet toward my feet. He stirred then, a finger grazing my back. I froze, waiting for him to catch me. But then I heard his snores once more.

As slowly as I could, I reached down to grab his wallet, careful not to move my knee much. Something pinched and pulled, a pain running down my shin this time, but I was able to capture a rising hiss in my throat as I pushed through the hurt and finally got the wallet in my hands.

I studied the dark leather, the scuffs, and the scratches. He'd had it for a while.

Stop while you're ahead, the angel inside of me begged, while the devilish, curious one told me to keep going, that I had a right to know who this man was.

So, I opened it.

I gasped at what I found inside. Through my tears, I blinked and read then reread the name I was seeing, a hand pressed against my mouth. This had to be a mistake. A joke. Karma wouldn't do this. Fate wasn't that cruel.

Yet there it was, in blank ink, permanently real and everything I never expected to find.

Sebastian Lattimore.

Oh my God.

Slade was *my* Sebastian.

Sniffling, I quickly wiped at my wet cheeks, sticking the ID back inside his wallet. Then I tossed it on top of his jeans once more, feeling both betrayed and angry, and… relieved, if that made sense. I kept my hand over my mouth when I turned to look at him, everything rushing through me like a tidal wave. The memories, the pain… They were like hurricanes. Tsunamis. Earthquakes. Every terrible force of the environment known to man.

Same dark hair, dark eyes, the dimple, that mouth. It really was him.

My Story Boy.

For that entire summer when I was nineteen and living with Flick, Sebastian Lattimore had been my emotional support system. Why? Because I'd fallen in love with him but had been too selfish to admit it to anyone, for fear they'd say I wasn't good enough for the smart boy, two years my junior.

My heart throbbed then shattered at the thought of the boy-turned-man beside me becoming the last person he wanted to be. Something had happened to him to make him the way he was today, and I wanted to know what that something was.

This also meant mom had lied to me about what had happened to him. It's not as though she knew my feelings… right?

I squeezed my eyes shut, exhaling a heavy, shaky breath. My movements, or maybe my noises, made him stir, and too soon I could feel him waking as the mattress shifted beneath us.

"Maya?" His voice was gravelly. Not like I remembered it to be. Not soft and kind, but a hardened man's voice. "You okay?" He laid a hand against my shoulder as he sat up. "Are you in pain?"

Only my heart, I wanted to say.

I shook my head and covered my face with both hands, embarrassed. Ashamed. *Angry.* Suddenly *so* angry I couldn't see straight.

He moved to sit next to me, our thighs grazing. "What is it?"

"Why…" I hissed, gathering my thoughts as I pressed a palm to my bad knee. "Why didn't you tell me who you were?"

He froze. Even his breathing seemed to stop. Slowly, I shook my head, eyes narrowed into slits.

"Tell me the truth, *Sebastian.*"

A sigh left his mouth. Unsettled. Sad. Maybe a little bitter, too. "Would it have made a difference if I did?"

"For one, I wouldn't have fought with you about coming. And—"

"I can't do this right now." He threw on his jeans, body stiff. Angry, jerky movements of his arms and shoulders confused me and hurt me and made me want to fall to my knees and wrap my arms around his legs.

"Don't walk away," I said to his back, reaching down to grab both of my crutches. "Don't you dare pretend that this doesn't change things."

By the time he had his shoes on and was reaching for the door, I was on my feet, following him.

"Slade, stop." He did stop. But he also didn't look at me. "Don't run away."

He laughed, but nothing about the sound was funny. "Why the hell not? That's what you do. *Run.*"

I winced with every small step I took, each one hurting worse than the next. But I needed to say this. Reaching out, I grabbed his upper arm, holding it tight. "Let's just talk about this, alright? Please?"

"Nothing you can say or do will change what happened," he hissed, his gaze still locked on the door, even as I stood at his side. "It's over and done, the past was shit, and now I wanna continue forgetting about it. You should do the same."

"Sebastian, I…"

He swirled around, seething, eyes red. Wild with rage. I sucked in a breath, fear running through my veins, but not because of him. No. My Sebastian wouldn't hurt a fly, and behind those dark eyes he was there. I could see him. *Feel him.* But if I wasn't careful, I could lose him again. Something I refused to let happen. Not when I'd just got him back. And not when everything between us was so electric and real and right. Full circle. We'd come full circle. This was fate. Our time.

Feel it, Sebastian. Feel it, please.

I lifted a hand, touched his shoulder. He flinched and I watched as his right eye twitched. It was like he was on the verge of losing something himself, something I was pretty sure I couldn't save, even if I tried my hardest to do so.

"Do not call me that," he hissed. "I'm Slade now. Sebastian died the second you walked out of my life."

I gasped, blinked my eyes, unable to stop the tears from falling this time. Then before I could say anything else, he left me alone in my misery. Alone in my regrets, most of all.

CHAPTER FOURTEEN

Slade

Twenty minutes later, I somehow managed to shove my balls back into place and go back to the room. Now there I was, standing just outside the door in the hall, hand on the knob, hesitating again. I'd been a pussy—an asshole too. Running away like I did was about as fucked-up as I could get. Slade didn't run because he was scared. And that's who I was now. She needed to know that. I needed to remind Sebastian of that.

What the hell did I have to lose by pretending we weren't the same two people who'd shared something that summer in my room anyway? I needed to get over myself, get over the past, and just be done with her and these feelings once and for all.

Taking a breath, armed with another bag of Cheez-Its, I twisted the knob, hoping my cracker offering would be a good "I'm-sorry-for-being-a-dick" gift. Wasn't used to apologizing to anyone, tending to steer clear of any emotional BS. But I needed to. Why? Because I wanted to show her I wasn't still affected by her, especially since she knew who I was now.

I opened the door, stepped inside, but stopped short when I found her on the floor next to the bed. One hand was on her bad knee and she was crying, head bowed.

"What happened?" I dropped the crackers and raced the three feet to get to her.

"I was coming back from the bathroom and slipped." She sniffled.

"Come on. I got you." I scooped her up and laid her on the bed, propping a pillow beneath her knee, then behind her neck. She shut her eyes the second her head was down, and I couldn't help but reach over and wipe at her tears with my thumb when I sat beside her.

"I'm so sorry, Slade," she whispered. "I was awful back then. I—"

"Not now, alright?"

"Please. Just let me get this out."

At this point in time, I was pretty sure I'd do whatever she wanted. Because facts are facts and truths are truths… no matter how hard a person tries to shove that shit out of their head. I didn't just want Maya's hot little body. I wanted her mind and her soul, maybe even her heart most of all. I just wouldn't allow myself to have it. *Any* of it. Who knew how badly she'd screw me up if I gave it to her again?

"Fine. Say what you gotta say."

She nodded, sniffling again as she sat up straighter. "I wanted more out of life than being a woman whose world revolved around an MC."

I nodded, all along thinking to myself, *But you could've at least said goodbye.*

"But the thing is…" She paused, exhaling. "I would've stayed, in Rockford I mean. If it meant being with you."

"You never told me that."

"I was going to." She reached for my hand. "That night, I tried to find you. Hawk even drove me around. But you were… preoccupied."

"Preoccupied how?" I frowned, remembering everything about that night. The pain I'd felt, knowing she was with Hawk. The pain I'd felt so fucking deep in my gut that I wasn't sure if I'd ever recover. It's why I'd left with Archer. I'd needed to feel something else—anything else but my gut wrenching.

"That night before I left, I… I saw you."

"Where'd you see me?" My jaw clenched.

"At the club."

"The hell you mean at the club?" My eyes narrowed while my chest gaped open, drowning my heart.

Holy shit.

I didn't know she'd come to the clubhouse that night.

"You see, I didn't intend to leave the way I did," Maya continued, messing with the edge of the blanket. "Because when I finally realized how stupid I'd been all that summer, I wanted to make up for it."

"How so?" I scowled, waiting for her to look at me. To tell me the truth on her tongue. To make me believe in what she might be saying here. Not that it would change the past.

When her eyes met mine this time, it was like a sinkhole formed beneath the bed, sucking us both in, arms around each other, holding on for dear life as we fell into the pits of all our darkest memories. Our pasts. Our pains. Our hell.

"My feelings? My heart?" She took a breath then let it go in a rush. "They belonged to you. They've *always* belonged to you." She dropped her head to the side, settling her hand against my cheek as she finished with, "I was just three months too late to realize it that summer."

I dropped to my knees on the floor beside the bed, too weak to sit up. "What the hell do you mean? I thought you loved Hawk? He was all you talked about."

This wasn't right. This wasn't how it was supposed to be. She didn't want me. She wanted Hawk. *She left me. She didn't even say goodbye.*

But she'd tried. She'd come to the club, for fuck's sake.

"Not true." She scowled. "And it wouldn't have worked anyways." She shook her head, eyes flashing darker, angrier.

"You don't know that," I growled. "You ran before you even bothered asking me what I wanted."

"It doesn't matter anymore, isn't that what you said?"

"The hell it doesn't." I took her chin in my hand, holding it there. "This changes everything." Then I did what I'd always wanted, the word "finally" running through my head the entire time.

I kissed her.

CHAPTER FIFTEEN

Maya

I was captured by the mouth and hands of Slade—Sebastian Lattimore—and there was nothing on earth that could pull me away, even if I wanted to stop.

Slade urged me onto my back, frantic as he crawled over my body. His huge frame pressed so close to me it felt like we were one. Still, it wasn't close enough. And as our lips touched, an all-consuming desire to have this man inside of me was like nothing I'd ever experienced before.

It was fire, and smoke, and ice, and lust, and *greed*, all rolled into one.

Fingers grabbed the bottom of my shirt, pulling, yanking. He cupped my waistline, scraping his fingers across my belly, while his other hand kept him propped up by my head. I moaned against his mouth, needing more as I slid my tongue over his bottom lip. Then I tugged on the back of his hair, yanking him closer, terrified this was some sort of dream I'd soon wake up from.

He parted his lips, a low groan echoing in the depths of his throat as I pushed my greedy tongue inside. Even though my knee throbbed, I still managed to roll him onto his back, guiding my good leg up and over his thighs at the same time. The need to control the situation, to finally take what I'd been too scared of eight years ago, was dire, desperate, *everything*.

His hands continued to work their magic, but never to the point where I needed them to be. "Touch me," I groaned, nipping at his bottom lip. "Please. Put your hands on me."

He shuddered, and I could tell he was just barely hanging onto the last morsels of his restraint. The power that consumed me, knowing I could drive this man wild, was intoxicating.

Taking matters into my own hands, I grabbed my shirt and lifted it up and over my head. I was so done with the delayed gratification. We'd missed way too much to play slow, and I wanted full speed ahead.

Baring myself to him, bottom lip tugged between my teeth, I waited impatiently for his touch, any sort of growly reaction that I'd come to expect from a man like Slade. But he didn't move, didn't even speak. Instead, he sucked in a breath and simply studied my breasts, like they were million-dollar pieces of art.

I couldn't help but smile as I watched him. "You okay?"

His pulse jumped at the side of his neck, gaze flitting from one nipple to the other. Even his cheeks turned pink.

"I, ah…"

"It's alright you know. I want this." Anything and everything he wanted to offer up was fair game at this point. I didn't care if this was a one-time thing. In this moment, if I didn't get Slade Lattimore inside of me, I felt like I'd die.

He licked his lips, slowly raising his hand. But instead of cupping my breasts like I figured he would, Slade took his time, slowly circling one finger around my hardened nipple. I gasped at the sensation, head tipping back in both lust and agony. The space between my legs began to throb worse than my knee.

"Beautiful," he whispered, his voice bringing my head back down. There was that half-smile on his lips again. It was my favorite kind of smile.

I rocked my hips against his bulging erection, desperate to relieve the pressure building. "Slade, please." Impatient, I took his free hand and settled it between my thighs, rubbing him against me. "Touch me *here*."

His lips curved up on both sides this time, and those dark eyes turned nearly black. "We got hours to play." He rolled over, pulling me down against him, then stopping when my nipple grazed his lips. One lick later, he whispered, "What's the rush?"

I squeezed my eyes shut and groaned. "I've waited too long for this."

One nip, a swirl across the tip, then one long slow suck later he said, "Don't you rush me, My."

My eyes rolled into the back of my head, frustration paired with lust taking hold of my body. Even as my knee began to throb more, the pain he suddenly elicited by the tug of my nipple between his teeth surpassed it all. Damn him for being so good at this.

I rolled off his body and onto my back once more, the covers twisted at my feet. That didn't stop me from sitting up and pulling at my leggings. The least he could do was get me naked.

"What are you doing?" He laughed, watching me. Such a sweet, silly un-biker kind of laugh it was.

"Getting naked so I can take advantage of you." I frowned, still struggling with my bad knee, only managing to get one leg out of my underwear and pants in the end. He tried to stop me, several times even offered to help, but I was determined to do this my way. Otherwise, he'd take over and go slow again. And slow was not what I wanted. Exposed, finally, my undies and leggings hanging on only one side, I rolled him over onto his back like before then straddled him. *Naked.*

"Maya, stop." His voice was a mix of angry pleasure and gritted teeth, fighting between what he wanted and what he knew was right.

Ignoring him, I shuddered, chin to my chest, rocking harder against him through his jeans. I took my time, feeling the length of him roll against me through the denim. Then I lowered my head, needing to be closer, nuzzling my mouth to his neck, kissing his skin until he was jerking his hips up in time with mine.

His hands slid around me, stroking my thighs, then lifting to cup my bare ass. He squeezed so hard I gasped, the pleasure outweighing the pain.

"Maya." My name was a moan as he tipped his head back and allowed my kisses to cross his throat to the other side.

"I need you," I whispered. Teeth found my earlobe, nibbling, sucking. "Please, I need the pain to go away."

He stopped. Froze in place, really. "You don't want this. You don't want *me*."

"How can you say that?" I pulled back, hands pressed against the pillow on either side of his face. My hair was like a curtain blocking the outside world. "I've *always* wanted you."

"You left." He blinked, as though he'd been drugged and was just coming awake.

Leaning forward, I nibbled on his chin, rubbing against him once more, desperate for my release—desperate to keep him with me too. "I'm here now."

He shook his head. "I can't be what you need me to be," he whispered, choking on his words. "Not anymore. I'm not who I used to be."

"I don't care." I rubbed harder, oblivious to everything but his body, the pleasure it gave me most of all. "I like you how you are." It wasn't a complete lie but enough of one that it had him shuddering beneath me as I increased the speed of my grinding hips.

Instead of stopping me, he urged me on again. Hips hard, jeans sliding against bare skin, his cock right there but not close enough yet. I panted heavily, loving his fast, rough hands as he grabbed at my breasts, my ass, every piece of skin he could get a hold of. Slade made me wild and unhinged. Worthy, even all these years later.

I was close already—so incredibly close to the release I craved. I knew I was wet, likely soaking his jeans, but it didn't matter.

Nothing did but him and me and everything we'd been robbed of. "Slade, I'm gonna…"

He growled, dropping his mouth to my neck, sucking so hard I saw stars. I took what I'd been dying to take for years right then, over and over, pleasure and pain and so many years lost… This, with my Sebastian, was the one place I was supposed to be so long ago, but was always too scared to find. Too terrified to lose. Too unsure to ever try to reach out for it, until it was too late.

"Oh, God," I cried out, coming hard, shaking.

"Fuck, My."

I chased the peak of my orgasm as he pushed me onto my back, hips seeking hips as I cried out his real name. And then his lips were against my lips once more: shuddering, violent kisses and breathy moans. Messy and wet and the best kisses ever. I curled my fingers into his hair as he screwed me relentlessly through his own jeans, reveling in the softness, comparing it to the hardening man he'd grown to be.

"Fuck, fuck, fuck," he chanted against my mouth, grabbing my hip, squeezing so hard I thought he might leave a bruise.

I moaned, needing more. Just minutes after coming, I wanted to come again.

"Condom. Get a condom. My purse. Please." I didn't care what this meant, not anymore. Life was too short to worry about anything but living for what you wanted in the here and now.

Slade kissed me again, shaking his head slowly as he continued the furious rubbing of his hips against mine.

"Please."

Blindly, I reached onto the floor, finding my purse, the lone condom in the side pocket. I kept it in my hands, scraped it slowly along his back beneath his shirt. "I need more," I begged again.

"Why?" He shocked me with that one breathless word, placing his hands on both sides of my head.

He looked so rough and sexy, hair messy and hanging over his forehead, dark, wild eyes seeking mine through the strands. How had I not remembered those midnight eyes?

"Do I need a good reason other than wanting you?" I giggled, thinking he was teasing me. But the longer I searched his face, the more my lips pulled down. The more my head spun too. "Hey, what's wrong?" I touched his cheek with my hand, holding it in place.

"I'm not…" He squeezed his eyes shut, blowing out a heavy breath. "I can't do this right now."

I shook my head, confused, feeling my insides churn as he rolled off my body and sat along the edge of the mattress.

Blinking, I studied his back, wondering what was happening. I thought we'd been on the same page. That this was mutual. That we could… I don't know, start over, maybe? But instead of questioning his behavior, clarifying with my words what I wanted, he jumped again.

"That was a mistake," he told the floor, not me. "You're Flick's niece, and my charge, and…" He lifted his head, empty eyes meeting mine over his shoulder. "We're not Sebastian and Maya anymore."

And then without further explanation, he left the room, leaving me stunned silent. And heartbroken all over again.

CHAPTER SIXTEEN

Maya

By noon that day, when we should have been close to arriving in Iowa, the train had stalled out in the middle of god-knows-where Nebraska, due to what the conductor over the intercom had said was an issue with the lead locomotive car.

Lovely.

So, what was supposed to be a fourteen-hour trip from Denver to Iowa, had fast turned into a nightmare and I was, officially, ready to bang my head into the wall.

Even after the announcement was made, Slade hadn't come back to our room, which angered me more than worried me. Stopped like we were in the open farm land left us susceptible to all things Red Dragon, and whatever dangers that were supposedly following them. I was familiar with the ways of a club, the trouble that came with it, and, in turn, my nerves were bringing back all the sour memories of my time with the Forsaken—memories I thought I'd long stowed away.

I knew my father was out of the picture, probably married with a new wife-slave who succumbed to his garbage ways. Yet for the first time in years, I was thinking, again, about what he put Mom and I through so long ago. It made me want to get messed-up-drunk like Slade had done.

Slade… Wonderful, lying, *asshole* Slade.

Screw him.

Not only was he refusing to communicate, but he was also refusing to keep me updated on what was happening. Some bodyguard he was. I knew the Story Boy I once knew and loved was truly gone, because there's no freaking way *Sebastian* would have left me alone in here for two solid hours. The thing I couldn't figure out was how did it happen? What made Sebastian turn into the hardened man he was today?

Done feeling sorry for myself, worrying about things I had no control of, I decided now would be as good a time as any to sketch some new tattoos. That was one stress reliever I could get behind, aside from popping sleep aids and pain pills… and getting shitfaced. By the time I finished, if he wasn't back yet, then I'd make the trek out of the room. Get myself a drink and, possibly, find the idiot while I was at it.

My sketchbook was tucked away in my bag. Using my trusty crutch, I pulled it over and found it in the zippered pouch right on top. A pencil, thankfully, was still pushed through the wire edge.

With my third bag of Cheez-Its, courtesy of my bodyguard again, tucked into bed with me, I sketched everything and nothing at all for two hours straight. By the time I was finished, my fingers itched to pick up a tattoo gun, to ink someone's untouched skin with one of the designs. Too bad that wouldn't be happening anytime soon, seeing as how I'd never been able to afford my own tattoo gun.

For years, I'd dreamed of opening my own shop, always one or one hundred thousand dollars too short to make it happen. No bank would loan me a dime and, because of that, I'd been stuck traveling from parlor to parlor, trying to find a place that accepted me: the girl who loved to ink but couldn't get any on her own skin.

The closest I'd ever gotten to success when it came to following my dreams was with this last job. Obviously I'd been wrong about that.

I felt like I was wrong about everything.

Maybe it was better this way, me coming back to Rockford temporarily to refocus on what I was going to do when I got back to San Diego. If anything, maybe Flick would take pity on me and offer me a cash loan to start my own business, though, like I'd told Slade back in San Diego, I wasn't necessarily one for handouts.

When the last page was filled, I decided enough was enough. I needed out of this box of a room, and off the bed that smelled like Slade, his gorgeous body, coated with memories of what we'd almost done.

Thankfully, the swelling in my knee had gone down a little so getting onto my crutches wasn't as hard as it had been. Putting shoes on though? That was a different story. I slipped a flip-flop onto my good leg's foot and was out of the room with all the speed I could manage.

The musty-smelling hallway was long and narrow, proving difficult to get down with crutches. Without the hum of the engine, and the tracks bumping beneath the train, it was oddly quiet. My skin prickled with nerves as I moved about, eyes darting this way and that. Even my breaths grew labored with worry, and if I hadn't known better, I could've sworn I felt someone watching me. Studying me.

As fast as my bum knee would let me, I hustled down one train car, then the next, until I found a sign that said "dining car." If Slade had to be somewhere, my guess was there.

Through the doors I made my way, finding several booths on either side of the train car. The room was filled with agitated faces, the tension thick, with passengers who were likely as angry about the delay as I was. Ignoring them the best I could, I focused on the back of the car, finding a tiny bar structure. Sure enough, there Slade sat, talking to a woman in a black skirt and a low-cut red blouse.

At the sight of the two of them so close, heads bowed together, my stomach twisted.

"You were a mistake, remember?" I berated myself in a whisper. Regardless, the truth tasted bitter on my tongue as I headed their way.

The woman's smile was wide as she looked at him, and the way she flipped her long, blonde ponytail made me incredibly self-conscious. My tar-colored hair, even with the bright splash of red, was dull and straight. Boring. I'd always been jealous of women who could rock out colors, though whenever I tried, I wound up looking like some sort of odd cartoon character. Short body, big boobs, pale skin… that was me. If there was one thing in life that my mom taught me, though, it was to be proud of who I was. What I looked like, most of all.

My heartbeat echoed loudly in my ears as I drew closer to them. Legs crossed and with a slit up the side of her skirt, the woman looked like a businesswoman—or a dominatrix.

To Slade's credit, he wasn't looking at her, or her legs for that matter. Instead, he nursed a small glass of brown liquid that was undoubtedly the same thing he'd been drinking the night before, and stared at the bar top.

He nodded occasionally at whatever the lady said, though. Proof that his listening skills were the same as they had always been. Even from a distance, I could see the murky lines under his eyes and the dark scar running the length of his beautiful, masculine face. He looked as exhausted as I felt.

Like he could feel my presence, Slade turned his head, spotting me halfway down the car. He shot to his feet, slapping a wad of cash on the bar top before walking my way.

I pulled his phone from my pocket and handed it over as he neared me, needing the conversation starter. "You forgot this."

With a solemn nod, he grabbed it with the hand not holding the drink, never once dropping his gaze from mine.

A tingle of awareness shot through my belly at the intensity of his stare. With one look, this man could melt me, make my insides curl with a need to lie bare before him, at his mercy, no matter how angry or frustrated he left me.

Out-of-control, thick, wild hair that I'd buried my hands in just hours ago, while I shamelessly rode him through his jeans, hung over one of his chocolate eyes. My fingers twitched with a need to brush that lock away, but I knew he wouldn't like it.

"Did you get on here?" He squinted, tapping the phone screen.

I finally let go of a heavy breath, refocusing on the conversation at hand. "No. All of your secrets are locked up by a four-digit code."

He scowled, likely from my attempt at a joke, ripping his gaze away. Briefly, he thumbed the screen before stuffing the phone into his jeans. "You good?"

"Just wondering what's going on with this train." I shrugged, tightening my hands along my crutches.

"Stalled lead car. Been told it's close to being fixed."

"Oh." I bit the corner of my lip, nervous for some reason. "Can we talk?"

His dark brows furrowed before he opened his mouth. But the lady who'd been sitting next to Slade approached his side, interrupting before he could respond.

"It was really nice talking to you, Sebastian." She held her hand out, barely sparing me a glance. Instead, she touched his forearm, holding it. "You sure you don't mind me stopping by later if I need you?"

My heart raced like a car engine in my chest at the woman's question—her casual use of his name most of all.

Do not get jealous. Do not get jealous. Do not get jealous.

Who was I kidding? I was totally jealous. And then when he flashed her that toothy, sweet smile I'd only ever seen, like, one time before, my stomach twisted with that ugly emotion I refused to feel—so much so I had to turn away.

"Sure, Sarah." His words were low and throaty.

Goosebumps traveled up and down my arms in turn.

Her heels clicked in her wake as she walked away, and I bit my lip even harder, watching her leave—giving Slade my back so I didn't have to see his reaction to her exit.

A second later, he slid in close behind me, his chest pressed to my back, his chin grazing my shoulder. "We'll talk. But not here."

"Alright," I nodded, too breathless for my own good.

Arguing was pointless. And from the shooting pain down the side of my leg, I wasn't opposed to the idea of going back to the room if *he* was with me. Not that I wanted to *be* with him. I just hated being alone right now. My skin was crawling with nerves, and everything about this delay was giving me the creeps. Weren't trains supposed to be a safe way to travel? I was having my doubts.

"Who was that woman?" I couldn't stop the question from slipping out as we headed through the dining car, then toward the door.

"Some lady. I helped her drunk husband to bed." He cleared his throat as we made it to a passenger car. "Why? You jealous?"

"Hardly." I rolled my eyes, chin high as I led us through the narrowed space.

"You sure about that?" He chuckled, and a flush of heat skimmed up my neck in turn. One minute he couldn't be in the same room as me, yet in the next, he was questioning my jealousy? *The freaking nerve of this man.*

"Positive." I huffed and quickened my pace.

We made it into the car which housed our room, finally. Just before I could open the door, Slade wrapped his fingers around my upper arm and pressed closer to my side.

"You don't fool me, hiding under all that couldn't-care-less attitude," he whispered into my ear. "I know you. And nothing about you has changed. Jealous girls turn into jealous women, am I right?"

I clenched my teeth together, eyes on the door latch. "You don't know *anything* about me."

"I know you like to be in control," he continued. "I know you love Cheez-Its, hate the snow and the cold, too."

I turned my head just enough to see his lips, but not his eyes. They would undo me emotionally if I looked into them. "So? Those things are trivial."

"Also know you've never been able to commit to anyone either."

"Lots of people don't commit, including you."

"You're so damn clueless." He shook his head, sounding almost stupefied at my denial.

I frowned, not in the mood to try and figure out what his comment meant. Instead, I decided on another path. The two-could-play-this-game kind. I could *easily* go toe to toe with men. Even the ugliest type with the dark, hideous souls.

"Well, I know you too, *Sebastian*."

His upper lip curled at my use of his real name, but he didn't take the bait… entirely.

"Don't think you do anymore."

I held my hand out, counting off my fingers as I spoke. "Let's see. You don't like crowds, and you prefer to be alone and suffer in silence rather than ask for advice or lean on someone for help."

He stiffened. "That's all RDs."

"True. But, I also know that you're afraid to admit defeat."

He lifted my chin with his forefinger, cutting my internal celebration short. In turn, our eyes met again, and another unwanted shiver raced down my spine at what I was seeing.

"Who cares about those things?" he hissed.

I toyed with my response, yet my tongue was too dry to react the way I should have. My silence, in turn, gave him some sort of power to continue his nastiness, and I took it because what other choice did I have now? We were alone in this dark hall, bodies close, breaths practically in sync. My vision swam with emotion, but to look away would be me giving up. And I refused to do so.

"You also sleep like shit. Always have," he barked. "Go to sleep crying, wake up crying, all because of those nightmares that you never told nobody about but me."

I flinched, hating how right he was. How he was able to call me out on all of my issues, get to me the way I'd been trying to get to him.

"And the only time in your life that you've been able to sleep without those fucking dreams is when you've got your head on *my* chest." He cocked his head to the side, lips twisting menacingly. "Isn't that what you told me once?"

Thankfully he let go of my chin. But that didn't stop my heart from throbbing, or my bottom lip from trembling either. Warm tears formed in the corners of my eyes, but I reached up, quickly wiping at them before they fell. My nightmares… they were awful. The worst kind of awful, actually. But I'd moved on from them, gotten better… or so I'd thought.

I rehashed the memories in my head that brought them about, pushing the pain right back to where it didn't belong. The thought of returning to Rockford, dealing with more death or bad men, dealing with things I'd been hiding away from for years, it did something to my subconscious. Brought about the memories of the things my father had done to my mom.

To me.

"That's not true." I jerked my head to the door, finally opening it, praying he didn't notice the pain in my face. He was winning at his game. And being the loser had never hurt so much.

He lingered in the doorway, but the space between us didn't stop his cruel words. "Sure as hell is, and you know it."

"I know what you're doing," I whispered, dropping the crutches to the floor and sitting on the bed. "And it's not working."

"You don't know shit." He growled.

"I do. You're being purposely cruel to me because…" I squeezed my eyes shut and blurted out the words, each syllable running together like word vomit. "You-want-me-like-I-want-you."

I released a long breath before lifting my gaze once more. His nostrils flared, eyes like fiery coals narrowing the longer he stared down at me. I'd hit the nail on the head, yet he stayed quiet, refusing to admit it out loud.

So freaking stubborn.

"I know what I felt on this bed, Slade." I patted the mattress, softening my voice. Arguing was so exhausting. "Don't try to deny it."

"That's nothing a couple of groupies won't fix when I get home." He lifted his chin, baring that cruel smile.

Nausea stirred in my belly, and I settled a palm against my closing throat. God, he'd changed, become what I despised about bikers most of all. He was now the epitome of dick, an Academy Award-winning asshole.

Even if it was an act, even if he was purposely trying to push me away because he was afraid of feeling too much, it still hurt knowing my Sebastian was that far gone. To the point where I'd never get him back, it seemed.

"The night before I left." I sucked in a heavy breath, taking another chance. If I was going for gut-wrenching chats, the sucker-punching kind, then I might as well let it all go. "In the club with those women. Why then? Why didn't you go earlier in the summer?" I wanted him to admit the truth. Get it out of his system once and for all. Even though the memory killed me, the only way *he* could get past that time in our lives was if he opened up. Told me the truth.

"Why'd I get drunk? Get with some chicks?" He rubbed a hand over his mouth, staring at me like I was nothing but the scum on the bottom of his boots.

"Yes. Was it because of...?" I pressed a hand to my chest, holding it there, hoping he would understand what I couldn't say.

"Because of you?"

I nodded again, holding my breath.

"Then you'll be stoked to hear that yes, it was because of you, Maya," he spat. "That what you wanna hear? You want me to admit that I waited around for you every day and night that summer, ready to fall to your feet and do anything you wanted of me, only for you to ignore me in the end?"

Tears dripped down my cheeks at his admission—an admission I'd wanted but suddenly hated at the same time.

"I waited for you that last night you were in town, ready to tell you the truth. Beg you to stay in Rockford, even. Yet what'd you do? You left with my cousin." He scrubbed both hands down the front of his face as he said, "You *always* left with Hawk."

"I looked everywhere for you that night. I was going to tell you everything. How I *really* felt." My excuse sounded weak, even to my own ears. But it's the only one I had left.

Bottom line was I *had* used him in a way that summer, and I hated myself for it. But I was young and stupid and mistakes happened, as did miscommunication. And Slade was no innocent here either.

"Yeah, well, excuse me if I was tired of being second best."

"That's not true," I argued. "I always went to you at night. Always slept in *your* arms."

"It wasn't enough," he said with a curled lip. "You treated me like a damn leper during the day, and that shit…?" Slade sighed and dropped his head back, eyes to the ceiling as he finished. "It ripped me raw, Maya. It ripped me so damn raw I've never been able to go back to the man I was. You made me bury him so deep in my gut that I have to kick his ass now every time he tries to come out. And you keep trying to bring him out, so do us both a favor and stay the hell away."

I sucked in a breath, blinking the tears away once more. He'd finally told me how he felt. Admitted the truth I deserved to suffer through. Now it wouldn't have to hang between us like an open, festering wound anymore.

"I don't know what else to say that I haven't said already." I sighed, frantically wiping my cheeks, embarrassed that I was so emotional.

He dropped his head back down, his expression blanketed in darkness once again. "Nothing else to say."

But there was. So much. This was our chance at starting over, even if all we ever could be was friends. I did want this man, sexually. But emotionally, I couldn't be anything but his friend. I would be going back to California after whatever was happening with the RDs calmed down. And he wouldn't leave the club.

Such was the way of two people who'd walked opposite paths in life.

The burn of his gaze followed me as I stood. "I'm going to…" I took in a slow breath, exhaling on a shudder, then pointed to the small bathroom. "To shower."

"Whatever."

My shoulders slumped as I headed into the tiny space. At this point in time, I was too emotionally and physically exhausted to speak anymore, let alone look at him. So, I did what I did best: I walked away.

CHAPTER SEVENTEEN

Slade

I'd been a dick. No doubt in my mind. But my intentions were good, even if they didn't seem like it to most. If I wasn't the asshole I was playing off to be, then I'd fall to her feet like a pussy. Give her the apology she deserved for my part in our fucked-up, broken past once and for all. The thing was, being a dick meant I could keep Maya safe. *That* was my job as an RD right now. Nothing else.

Maya could be my entire world, if I let her. But I was doing fine on my own. Had been for years. Now my number-one priority was keeping her safe, and that meant walking away at the end.

Even if we did get together, messed around a little bit, she'd just wind up leaving. Breaking me all over like before, and I couldn't stomach that shit.

Her life wasn't in Rockford no more. Mine always would be.

After she got into the shower, I left again to get her ice and a bottle of water. About that time, the train had started back up—which meant we'd be getting to Iowa in short order, thank God. Not only was I worked up about our fight, but I was also itchy with nerves, my entire body on edge for reasons I couldn't pinpoint.

It felt as if a storm was coming.

That everything was about to change in my life whether I wanted it to or not.

And the thought of possibly being blindsided scared the shit out of me.

It'd been a few hours since I'd last heard from anyone at the club, which in itself wasn't good. No texts or calls meant my brothers were likely keeping something from me. I'd tried to text Archer, but got no response. Then when I'd tried Hawk, it went straight to voicemail. Already, I was pissed I couldn't be the one to take down Carlos's killer, even though I was glad the guy was dead. Any other shitty news right now would probably send me over the edge—something I'm pretty sure Flick was well aware of. Hence the quiet, I feared.

I pushed through the door of our room about twenty minutes later, a bag of ice in hand, and a small sandwich for her to eat. But at the sight of Maya lying on the bed, I froze, nearly dropping it all to the floor.

Rolled over on her side, a bare shoulder exposed—even in the nearing dark—I gave myself a minute to study what I'd coveted for so long. I deserved to look at least, didn't I?

The view had my mouth going dry, my cock hardening in remembrance at how fucking amazing her lips had tasted earlier today. How her warm, wet pussy had been so dangerously close to the place I wanted it most of all.

I squeezed my eyes shut, gave my head a fast jerk to try and tone it down.

Things may have been different now that I was an RD, but watching her sleep… my damn heart struggled to get the memo my brain had put out about keeping my distance. Not when my cock and my heart tended to run together.

It'd be easy to slide under the covers next to her. Even easier to pull her close and kiss her neck and breathe her in most of all. But again, I could only be devoted to one thing in my life right now, and I'd made that choice. The club, my brothers—they were all that mattered. Keeping them all safe and ending the bad shit with Pops and now Maya's father, was my top priority.

I dropped my chin to my chest at the thought of Maya's old man.

That was a whole other hell I didn't wanna deal with right now. Because I knew what that'd do to her, knowing he was working against us. My hated him, yeah. But that wouldn't make the truth any easier to accept.

She'd called me out on my behavior before. It *was* easier to be a dick to her now—though I hated the idea of it. Because being a dick meant staying focused in the long run. Doing what needed to be done, no distractions.

She stirred in her sleep, a soft whimper sliding from between her lips. I knew that sound. Knew what would come next too. Sniffles, a sob, then a gasp…

Beside the bed, I dropped to my knees, shaking her shoulder enough to wake her. "Hey, My, wake up."

The train whistle began to blow, and her eyes popped wide at that. She didn't jerk away when she rolled over to face me; instead, she blinked back tears as her bottom lip began to shake. My chest burned at the view and I reached up, running a hand over my heart at the sight. God, her nightmares never went away. All these years later, the bullshit from her past still screwed with her. And I'd been such an ass about calling her out on them too.

"You alright?" I asked.

She shook her head.

Sighing under my breath, I sat beside her on the bed as I waited for something I wasn't even sure of anymore. Every day since we'd started out on this trip together felt scarier, and more unpredictable, than the next. And being scared and unsure was exhausting.

"Do you know why I left Rockford in the first place?" she asked softly, obviously nowhere near done with our earlier conversation.

"You wanted to start over." Just like I'd once wanted too.

"Kind of." She shrugged. "But it was more because I was free for the first time in my life when we arrived in Rockford. Free from my father, who no longer controlled my life. Free from taking care of my mother constantly, knowing Flick would help. I was free to be who I wanted and there was nobody around to tell me how to live or to stop me either. There were no expectations of me." She took a breath then slowly let go. "I lived eighteen years under the lock and key of my father's club. And even though the Red Dragons were different than the world I came from, staying there didn't feel right somehow."

Made sense, I suppose. In the beginning, before I even wanted to be an RD, I never felt like I fit in. Even when I prospected, then patched in, it'd been a different experience for me than the other guys. The brotherhood we shared in the club was unlike anything else, yeah, and being a part of it helped to erase the pain of Maya leaving, of not having a dad also. But even though I loved being an RD, I sometimes forgot who I was before.

"I hated all bikers before I got to Rockford. I hated them all so much. I tried to hate Hawk and Archer. Even my uncle. But being there, with them, and *you*... I felt like I was in a holding pattern. The worst and best kind. So, I convinced myself that it was meant to be the way it turned out and I'd find my freedom, even if it hurt to leave."

"You could've had that freedom in Rockford too." I frowned, but my chest felt lighter for some reason.

"Maybe, maybe not. But by the time I was ready to try and have the best of both worlds, it was too late."

A couple more minutes passed, minutes that were filled with questions I couldn't stop, even though I didn't want to talk about this anymore.

"Why the show?" I asked. "Why not just be real with me from the beginning if you liked me?"

"I told you. I was scared." She blinked, and the truth was there as plain as day. Maya never lied. She just didn't always know how to express herself, like me.

"Didn't mean you had to ignore me and run to Hawk like he was your damn hero every day," I muttered.

"I know." Slowly, she sat up, her chest hitting my shoulder, her lemony scent invading my senses. "*You* were the reason I became who I did. The reason I *left* in the first place. Not because I didn't like you, or wanted to leave you, but because you made me want to be a better and different person. You just… lived." She smiled, waiting another second. "And I wanted that too, by being a tattoo artist or any sort of artist, since the day I first picked up a pen. But for so long I was expected to be a VP's daughter; to marry into the world and basically become a baby-making vessel. By the time I got to Rockford, I didn't know who I was anymore."

"None of that would've happened with the RDs. Flick wouldn't have let it."

She shook her head. "Not all of it, no. But Flick's always been about control, making sure the women who surround him are a step below where they want to be. It's not intentional, it's just who he is."

I couldn't deny that. That didn't mean it was right. My pres lived with an old-school mindset because that's all he'd known. But if Maya had wanted to stay in Rockford, be her own person, I would've made that happen for her.

She lifted her hand and pressed it to my cheek, running her finger along my scar.

"Can we pretend that the past is the past? Forget it even?" She nibbled on her bottom lip, drawing my eyes to her mouth. "Maybe start over?"

"Won't ever be able to forget what happened, My," I said, pulling back enough to see her star eyes. "But if you want to start over, we can try that."

She nodded quickly. "Okay, yes. Let's… try."

I blew out a breath and rubbed both hands over my face. As hurt and pissed as I'd been about her treating me the way she had that summer, it was too tiring holding onto a grudge anymore. "We do this, there's one thing I gotta know first."

"Anything."

"Why'd you do it?"

She frowned. "Do what?"

"Fuck with my head. Be with me at night, then leave me during the day. I need to know the real reason. I mean, I get you were scared about something, but what the hell scared you so much that you had to pretend I didn't exist?"

A few seconds went by, but she didn't answer. I pulled my hands off my face, finding her sad eyes watching me. Only then did she answer.

"Because I didn't want anyone to know."

I flinched at her truth. But I'd wanted to know.

Before I got off the bed to go suffer in silence, she grabbed the back of my neck and sat up, leaning close, pressing her forehead to mine. "I didn't want anyone to know because I didn't want it to go away. I was selfish. And if it came out to the world that you'd stolen my heart, then I was worried it would end." She blew out a slow breath across my mouth. "You were the only good thing that had happened to me in years and I didn't know what to make of it, so I'm not going to apologize anymore for being selfish because I'm not the only one who made mistakes."

I groaned. "What'd I do?"

"You didn't tell me how you felt either. You were just as scared as I was."

My throat tightened, her truth hitting me like a punch to the neck. "I was a dumb, stupid kid in love with a woman I'd never be good enough for." I shrugged, hating the weakness in those words. But I did owe her some version of my truth, I guess.

"So, we were both wrong." She blinked back at me, searching my face.

"Guess so."

"So, what do we do now?"

I could think of a lot of things I wanted to do right then. Take her mouth, suck on that lower, pink lip… nibble it. Then touch her between her thighs, make her come on my hand. Then make her come on my dick too. But I was pretty damn sure that's not what she was angling at here.

"You tell me." I settled on that, urging her to move over on the bed. I lay down beside her, trying my best to keep distance between us. But the bed was small and our bodies were like damn magnets, even all these years later.

"We could sleep." She blinked, and it was there that I saw it. That look in her eyes. The one from earlier that said, *Take me, I'm yours.*

It would've been a good idea to get off the bed right then. Sebastian sure as hell would've. He was a good boy. Slade wasn't.

What happened on the damn train would stay on the train. And what I wanted right then was to feel and experience what I'd been missing out on for too long. There wasn't a club groupie alive who'd tame the beast inside of me that Maya created. Never had been. Never would be either.

More than air and water, food and a clear soul before God, I *needed* this woman. And if it all ended in a couple days, I wouldn't care. Maya was a dream and a storm and all the shit that'd been killing me for years, come to life in an explosion of perfection.

It was time to make her mine.

Growling, I climbed over the top of her, hands on her waist, tugging her shirt up with my greedy fingers. No more slow, no more pushing her away when it all got to be too much. Too emotional.

Her skin practically burned my palm raw. I kissed her hard, nibbling, tasting, *devouring* every inch of her mouth. Chest heaving as fast as mine, I knew she was on the verge of losing it too, and oh what a loss it'd be.

When I couldn't take it any longer, I leaned back and yanked her shirt up and over her head. She grabbed mine too, greedy fingers pulling at the hem. I hesitated, knowing what she'd probably see when I took it off. But we were long past the point of keeping secrets anymore.

I sat back a ways, watching her as I pulled it off my head. Then when I heard her gasp, I knew she'd spotted it.

"Is that...?" Fingertips pressed against her lips, Maya studied the long tattoo under my right arm. In the hall outside her apartment, she hadn't noticed; I hadn't lifted my arm enough to show her. Up close like this though, there was no avoiding the view.

"Yeah." I swallowed, the emotion in my throat making it impossible to speak coherently. "It is."

I lowered myself to my side, lifting my arm higher, watching her star eyes widen the closer she got. Her hand shook as she reached out to graze the tattoo centered along my side, just under my armpit, trailing down my ribs.

"How?" She blinked.

"You'd drawn it in Sharpie, remember? And the second I saw it in the mirror that next day, I knew I never wanted it gone."

Tears slipped out of her eyes when our stares locked. "This is really my design?"

"In the flesh." I smiled. "Just wish you could've been there to see it get inked on."

During our last night together, before everything had gone to shit, Maya'd asked if she could draw something on me. She'd called it practice for when she'd someday tattoo on real people, and I was so gone for her, I'd let her do anything to my body.

It had been the best, most torturous hour-long experience of my life. Her straddling my hip, her forearm and wrist on my ribs as she drew the arrow up and down my side. The letters N, S, E, and W, paired with a compass—it was simple and beautiful, more feminine than masculine, but I didn't give two shits. I loved it because she'd been the one to put it there. Never even thought of taking it off, not even after she left. To me, this bit of ink signified both pain and pleasure, a time in my life I wouldn't forget.

"Me too." She leaned forward, and before I could stop her, she kissed the tattoo, rising up to press those lips to mine again. Soft, thankful, and full of something so heavy I wished I could flask that shit and keep it in my pocket forever.

My leg hung off the side of the bed, and I struggled to keep my balance as our mouths grew hungrier, faster. I wasn't drunk or dazed on liquor, but alive and ready to have her the right way, as many damn times as she'd let me.

I slid down her body, kissing the spot between her breasts, pinching and grazing each nipple with my thumbs. She gasped and panted, hips bucking against mine, and I knew right then I needed to taste her.

She'd hidden me from the world because she hadn't wanted the world to take me away. Just like I'd hid Sebastian because he was hers and I didn't want anyone else to have him.

Fuck, *fuck*. Too much time had gone by. I should've gone after her. Told her my truth earlier. I should've, could've but didn't because I was dumb. Too prideful. But that all stopped now.

"Slade, what are you—"

"Sebastian." I dropped to my knees and pulled her around on the bed by her hips. With careful ease, I tugged her jeans down, followed by her panties, then finished with, "You'll call me Sebastian when I'm this close to your pussy, you hear me?"

Sebastian was the man who deserved this woman. And as much as I didn't want to be him anymore, I knew, with Maya, he'd never go away until he got what he wanted.

She nodded, lips parting as I lifted her bad knee and propped it over my shoulder. With my other hand, I pushed her good leg wide and to the side, making room for my body. The space was cramped at my back, and my thighs were pressed hard against the bed frame. But I didn't care. Nothing could stop me from licking the heavenly spot between this woman's thighs.

I kissed her belly, each hip, nibbled on her inner knee. Then I rose up a little higher and nuzzled my nose against the soft mound of curls covering her pussy. Sliding both hands beneath her tight little ass, I readied myself for what was to come. Then I squeezed, and she moaned, and soon I was sliding my tongue up and down her clit.

"Sl… Sebastian, oh God."

I shut my eyes, opened my mouth a little wider, and took my dear, sweet time devouring every inch of her pussy.

She moaned, bucked her hips. "Please, Sebastian," she panted. "I need you."

I shook my head, burrowing deeper, licking slower, the flicker of my tongue tasting every inch of her. Her thighs tightened around my head, fingers in my hair pulling tight. "Stop, I'm gonna come, Sebastian, I'm gonna…"

Her back arched, rising off the bed as she cried out, shook, her body gorgeous, her noise perfect. I pulled back, watching her breasts rise and fall as she tried to catch her breath.

Nervous for some dumb reason, I blew out a slow breath to try and keep myself in check, then grabbed the condom we'd not used earlier and set it next to Maya's hip as I stood. Pulling my pants down, I watched her lips twitch, wondering what was going through her mind.

"You okay?" I asked, grinning as the button of my jeans clicked against the floor.

"Mmm…" She eyed me up and down. "I could be better."

I lifted a brow. "You could be?"

She smiled, sitting up. "Uh, huh."

"How so?"

Slowly, she opened the condom wrapper, her lips curled in mischievousness as she handed it to me.

"You want me inside you?"

"More than anything," she whispered.

"Then put it on me."

Licking her lips, Maya leaned forward, giving my cock a slow stroke. But instead of doing as I said, she kissed the head of my cock, then took me in her mouth. I groaned, dropping my head back. "That's not…Jesus, My." Deeper she went, her throat making this vibrating noise that had me grabbing her hair, pulling. She reached around and took hold of my ass, her tiny hands grabbing and clawing.

I shuddered, allowing it. Loving it. For a long minute. Then two.

Just when I was ready to lose my shit, she pulled back and slid that condom right where it belonged. Then when she looked up at me, I knew I was a lost cause. Lost in my head. Lost in her.

Slowly, I urged her onto her back, taking my time to kiss her, savor her before she was beneath me, her good leg parted wide enough to where I settled easily between her thighs.

"Sweet, sweet, My." I kissed her chin, her cheek, her neck. "You ruin me. You always ruin me."

And then I lined my cock up against her pussy, and with the help of her hands against my ass, I slipped inside of her, my entire body stiffening at the feel. Beneath me, I felt her shudder, felt her breath on my neck, my chest. Fingers stroked down my back, between my shoulders too. And then the buzz of her words sounded against my ear. "I want you to ruin all men for me."

I shut my eyes, never wanting to leave this space. Her body was my temple. My worshipping place forever. Sweat slid down my spine from holding back, but I needed her to clarify what she'd just said. "What do you mean?"

Arching her hips against me, the space unforgivable, she whispered, "I want you to punish me for hurting you. I want this hard and I want this fast."

"No," I hissed. "Don't ask me to do that."

"Please."

"My." I lowered my forehead to hers, eyes shut, then kissed her lips, softer as I said, "You broke me bad. But the past is the past. So if I'm over it, you need to be too."

Then without another word, I began to move—eight damn years later.

"Christ, you feel good." I groaned, breathing hard, matching her breaths.

She wrapped her arms tight around my shoulder. "Don't hold back."

I nodded, all good intentions gone. Then what had started out as slow, fast changed into something I couldn't control. Merciless, angry fucking that made me think we were running out of time. The exact kind of fucking I never wanted with the woman beneath me.

But she'd told me things and made me feel and, fuck. *Fuck.*

I grabbed her hands and forced them above her head, holding them there. She cried out, loving it. And I loved the sound of my name on her lips. Loved that it was my body making her shake and shudder.

Over and over I fucked her, hips slapping hips, skin rubbing, the sound of the train whistle barely enough to cover up the violent growls in my throat and the whimpers in hers. I'd been with a lot of women in my time, but never like this. Never filled with so much hate and love combined.

I held her arms so she couldn't touch me anymore and gave her what she asked for, begged for, but in my own damn way. I wanted her to want me as bad as I wanted her, and yeah, I wanted to ruin all other men for her like she'd asked. But I was pretty sure I still loved her, and loving someone meant hurting yourself before ever hurting them.

I thrusted my hips harder, spread her legs wide, until I heard her pleasure turn into a whimper of pain.

Damn it, her knee.

I slowed the pace, kissed her forehead. "Tell me if I'm hurting you, okay?"

"N-No," she stammered. "I'm okay."

"Don't lie to me, My." One thrust, then another… my cock so deep inside, I could die like this. Buried in her tight little body, loving her in the only way I'd ever allow myself to.

"Am I hurting you?" I asked again.

"Please don't stop." She squeezed my hands, which I still held tight above her head, and I instantly regretted the fact that I hadn't let her go.

So, I did.

She sighed, contentment washing over her face. Tentative with her movements, she slid one hand into my hair and her other along the base of my spine. I shuddered at the soft touches, turning my face to kiss her wrist. Then I bit my bottom lip when I pulled away and began to move my hips again, this time taking care not to hurt her.

One jerk, then two, our eyes held, frozen on one another. She arched against me, matching me push for push. Shuddering, I drove in deeper, my balls slapping skin and tingling against her ass. Maya's lips parted, eyes hooded in pleasure as I loved her as hard and as soft as I could.

"Sebastian," she whispered, fingers tightening into my hair, nails digging deeper into my skin.

I watched her face as she came again, holding off on my own just long enough to see it all go down. Then a minute later, I pushed faster, harder, groaning. My heart raced, everything in me shaking with love and lust and all sorts of shit I couldn't identify but never wanted to lose.

"Maya." I shut my eyes, gritted my teeth, then rode the wave, coming hard inside of her, sweat on my brow and my back.

I'd made the woman who'd once been my past turn into my future… into my entire world. And I didn't have any regrets.

CHAPTER EIGHTEEN

Maya

Slade and I finally walked off the train in Iowa a few, short hours later. His hand was at my back the entire time, and though the winter air was brutal, and my crutches were unstable along the ice, his nearness settled me.

The shock of what I'd discovered under his arm had stuck with me for the remainder of our trip. Never in my life did I think he'd have that drawing tatted on his skin, especially if he hated me as much as he said. Everything was as I remembered it, down to the furry arrow that pointed north, the small words making up the center that said, "Not all who wander are lost."

Love and hate tended to stem from the same, deep-seated emotion, so perhaps Slade's utter hate for me fueled what we'd become.

He hadn't exactly grown distant on me the second we got off the train, but there was something new that seemed to haunt him. A quiet sort of torture I wanted to know all about so I could help soothe his aches away.

What we shared was as close to perfection as I'd ever experienced. But the fear of it not being enough for him made me second-guess everything I said and did from there on out.

"A friend of Hawk's should be coming," Slade told me as we approached the door that led to the parking lot. "An older guy. Summer's grandpa."

A few people bustled about inside, but otherwise the station was quiet and peaceful.

"Okay," I said, remembering how he'd mentioned this in passing. "A farm, right?"

He nodded, then continued with his silence once more.

I frowned, wishing I could touch his hand—cursing the crutches I would be ditching as soon as the doc gave me the okay. "Are you okay?"

Slade looked from one end of the station to the other once more before reaching for the door handle. "Yeah. Just ready to get home."

Deciding not to think too much about his bad mood, I continued to talk. "I'm kind of excited. I've never been to a farm before."

"We'll only be there for the night. Don't get too excited."

I rolled my eyes as he led me toward a set of stairs that emptied into a parking lot outside. It surprised me how patient he was with my slow movements, while there I was growing more irritated by the second with the entire crutch situation. At this rate, I was starting to feel like an old woman, especially when the cold only made the stupid thing ache more.

From the top of the steps, I noticed a maroon car running by the curb, alone and stationary. A man stood outside of it smoking a cigarette. The stranger seemed innocent-looking enough, wearing a dark pageboy cap and a pair of khakis, along with what looked like an argyle sweater vest. If anything, he reminded me of the preppy guys in high school I used to avoid, but with a large, protruding stomach.

"That's not our ride, is it?" I asked, marveling in the quiet of the night. The cold air was almost refreshing, despite what it did to my body. Yet at the same time, the stillness and peace of the parking lot was rather unnerving.

"No. We're looking for a truck."

The man waved us over, dropping his smoke and stomping it out with the toe of his shoe. As I started forward, Slade grabbed the back of his leather coat, the one I still wore, and pulled me to a stop. "Go back inside and wait till I figure this out. Something doesn't feel right."

"Absolutely not." I huffed, already heading for the stairs. It would take me a million years to get back in at this rate, and I wouldn't waste a lick of my energy on a hunch he seemed to be having.

He squeezed my shoulder this time, a warning in his low voice. "I *said* go back inside."

I rolled my eyes and ignored him still, making my way down the first few steps. Slow and steady always won the race, right?

"Race ya?" I taunted from over my shoulder.

"Christ," he growled in return.

Despite my taunting, he still beat me down the steps, of course, stopping a few feet from the man. The driver smiled and showed Slade something on his phone. Seeming annoyed but satisfied, Slade turned to me as I finished my stride toward them.

"What's up?" I looked between him and the driver, nodding my hello, watching as Slade typed on his own phone. A text message chimed through. I tried to look and see who it was, but I wasn't quick enough.

He grunted something like *bullshit,* under his breath, then shoved his phone into one of his pockets. "This guy's taking us to the farm."

Not looking at me, Slade opened the back door, urging me in with a hand before moving to stow our bags away inside the trunk. Once he packed them in, Slade moved to stand beside the door, cringing with an elbow on the roof as he leaned in to look at me.

"What is it?" I frowned.

"I forgot a bag inside." He shook his head and slipped in next to me regardless.

"Then go get it." I touched his arm. "I'll be fine here."

He looked toward the front doors of the station, not saying no… but not agreeing either.

"Excuse me, sir?" I said to the driver, taking matters into my own hands.

The guy glanced at me from over his shoulder, his mustache sticking against his lips. "Yeah?"

"Can you wait another few minutes, please? My friend forgot his bag on the train." Up close like this, I could see the wrinkles by his eyes, eyes which were a bright blue. A *safe* blue that made my decision even easier. Plus, he had his Uber credentials marked so clearly from his rearview, that it only made even more sense he was there. Summer's grandparents were likely both asleep, and coming to get us at this hour would be incredibly rude—hence our rider.

"Sure. Take your time. I got nowhere else to be." He tipped his hat toward Slade before refocusing out the front window.

I gave Slade a reassuring smile. "See? Now go."

Leaning forward, a hand pressed to the top of my thigh, Slade pressed his mouth against my ear and whispered, "Gonna keep the door unlocked. You get a bad feeling, you jump."

I shut my eyes, nodding, too distracted by the warmth of his breath to comprehend the grumbled fear of his words. Then without looking back, Slade slid out the door and strode toward the train station stairs, his feet fast and purposeful.

"You two newlyweds?" the driver asked a moment later.

"Oh, no. We're just friends."

The goofy smile on my face morphed to bashful as I followed Slade's body up the stairs with what I was sure were dreamy eyes.

That's when the driver started the car, clicking the locks at the same time.

I stiffened. Soon after, chills raced up my spine as he revved the engine.

I tugged on the handle, but it wouldn't budge. "Sir, please unlock the door."

"You ain't going nowhere, sweetheart." Then the driver put the car in gear and dropped his foot to the gas pedal.

Unlucky for him, the tires screeched and spun on the ice, keeping the car in place.

"Stop it!" I screamed.

Ignoring me, the man pressed the gas even harder, cussing when he couldn't get it to move. The smell of burnt rubber filled my nose, making me cough and gag.

"Let me out! Stop!" I yanked at the door again, but it wouldn't budge.

Panic filled my chest, and I turned to look out the window, finding Slade running back toward the car.

I reached a hand out and pressed it to the glass, slapping at it. "Slade. Help me!"

Half of his face was covered by shadows as he made it to the door. Then he began pounding hard on the glass and yelling, "Open this fucking door!"

The driver snarled then punched the gas even more, causing a cloud of smoke to fill the air behind us. The car skidded forward just a little, but the tires were no match for the snow and ice, thank God.

Still, I was trapped in here with this guy, no way out. My heart lurched into my throat at the thought, and tears formed in my eyes. I looked around, trying to find something to break the glass with. My crutches sat next to me. I picked one up and smacked at the window, but nothing happened.

"No, no, no!"

"Knock it off, bitch," the guy roared at me.

"Maya!" More pounding, more yelling… Slade jumped on the hood, kicking at the windshield now.

The driver turned on the wipers, sprayed the fluid, but nothing pushed Slade away—nothing worked in his favor either.

No second-guessing, I yanked my crutch back as far as it would go and slammed it into the driver's temple. The hat I'd admired earlier fell onto the console while the man curled over, covering his temple, momentarily stunned.

It didn't last long though.

"You'll pay for that," he roared, letting up on the gas, reaching his arm back to grab at me, or maybe my crutch. I threw it to the floor before he could get it and curled my body against the door as far from him as I could get.

Getaway long forgotten, vengeance now seemed to cloud the man's eyes. He reached over and grabbed something from the passenger seat, flicking it open. I gasped at the sight of the knife shining against the light.

"Should've killed you the second I saw ya." He started to climb into the back, his body slower due to his larger size. He grunted, heaving, until he landed on the floor of the backseat with a groan. "Screw the money."

It didn't take him but a second to pop up, and soon his knife flickered between us, shining against the lights outside.

"Please, please!" I lifted my arms over my face and kicked him with my good leg. My bad knee strained regardless, and I slid further down onto my back. The top of my head pressed against the door as I kicked and kicked some more.

Grunts sounded as he struggled against my foot, giving me the time I needed to grab my crutch and lift it, this time whacking him square in the nose. He screamed like a baby, dropping his knife to cover his face. Blood dripped down between his fingers, appearing black in the night.

Something cracked behind him, bits of glass shattering into the car. Slade was close to getting in, but not close enough.

Fueled by adrenaline, I searched for the knife my attacker had dropped. In an instant, I found it, grabbing the bladed end from the floor. It sliced my fingers and I hissed, but determination and survival urged me on.

Even more angry now, the guy finally made his way back to me, slamming his body against mine with a loud *oof.* I choked then gasped even more when he sat up and wrapped his beefy hands around my throat. Squeezing my neck, he cut off my air.

I nearly lost hold of the blade as my eyes began to blur.

My lips parted in a silent gasp. Still, somehow, I held that knife with all I had in me and raised it, slamming it into the side of his large gut.

"Fuuuuuck!" he screamed. His hold loosened enough that I could finally take in a heavy breath. The stench of his body odor filled my nostrils and vomit pooled in my stomach in turn.

Glass shattered throughout the car. I screamed, but it sounded more like a groan as my throat was raw from the man's hands.

"Maya!" Slade yelled.

My attacker struggled to sit up again, his fingers on my breasts, then my neck, ripping at my hair, yanking…

I pushed at him, struggled, cried… fought hard.

And then he was up and out the back door like he weighed nothing, though I could still feel him.

Everywhere.

A struggle sounded, followed by a loud thud, and then all went quiet. For a moment, I couldn't move, worry for Slade keeping me still. But then the door opened wider, and I blinked, taking in my savior. His mouth moved, but I couldn't understand any of what he said, until he was there, crawling across the backseat and pulling me against his chest.

"Hey, hey, shh. I've got you now. You're safe."

My face was wet, my eyes too, but my body… it was numb.

I wasn't sure how long we sat there. Seconds, minutes, hours… Too long, not long enough. The cops would be here soon, wouldn't they?

"Stay here," Slade whispered. "I need to tie him up and make a call."

I nodded, still not able to speak. Letting go of Slade was hard, but it had to be done. A minute after he got out, he was back in the car, a new shirt in hand. "Put this on, okay?"

Like a robot, I nodded, took the flannel from his hand, slid it on, then buttoned it slowly, unconsciously, methodically, emotionless. Nodding, Slade said something else, something I couldn't hear, then left the car again.

Somehow, the lot was still empty. How was that possible? This was a train station. Where were the people? How could it be this quiet? How could no one know what had just happened? I reached up, pressing a hand to my throat, feeling the man's blood on my skin, feeling his hands around my throat, squeezing.

"No, no, no." As quickly as I could, I wiped the remaining stickiness on my fingers against the seat then scooted to the other side, unable to catch my breath again as I stared out the window at the falling snow. A red light flickered on, a camera on a post focused solely on the car. Someone was bound to see us. See Slade and the man who'd tried to kill me, who I'd *stabbed*...

Slade crouched over him, a phone to his mouth, talking rapidly, animatedly. He looked left, right, then back at me, nodding once before he stood and began to pace.

For five minutes he did this, until flashing lights came on in the distance, approaching at a slow speed. I gasped, a hand to my mouth as a police officer pulled up next to Slade and got out of the car. He didn't reach for his gun, and there was no ambulance in sight either. Instead, the two men shook hands, then together, they carried the wiggling body to the trunk of the cop's car.

I winced as they slammed it shut, shuddering breaths flying from my mouth when Slade pointed at me. The officer nodded, just once, before looking away. I couldn't move. I couldn't even breathe. Instead, I sat there shivering even harder than before as I watched all the normality I'd been striving for since leaving the RDs suddenly explode right in front of my face.

Screw the money, he'd said. I blinked. What did that mean?

Before I could ponder it any longer, Slade strode toward me once more, whipping the door open. He stood there, staring, looking almost as helpless as I felt. But I couldn't find it in me to speak, tell him what the man had said, or stop crying and shaking.

Even after facing as much as I had in the past, with my father, I'd never had to stab a person before.

"Is he…?" I managed, not wanting to say the word.

Slade crouched beside me. "He'll be fine."

"He said something about wanting to kill me and…" I pulled in a breath then blew it out slowly. "Said *screw the money*." I waited a beat. "What does that mean?" My teeth chattered as I stared back at him, waiting for an answer. When all I got in return was a stoic expression, followed by a sigh, I knew I'd never get the answer I wanted. He was hiding something. More secrets. And because of his club rules, I wouldn't ever know what that meant—even if it had to do with my own survival.

I dropped my head, shook it. Looked at my still-shaking hands too.

Finally, he said, "I'm gonna put you up front next to me, that okay? We gotta go get a new car. Zeke's got one for us at his place." He jerked a thumb toward the cop car, whose brake lights had just flickered on.

"O-Okay," I managed with a jerky nod.

His warm arms pulled me from the backseat, and I clung to his neck, shuddering against him when we were upright. I settled my ear against his chest, wishing I could hear his heartbeat through his shirt.

Before he set me back in the car, Slade pressed his lips to my temple and sighed out another apology. One I couldn't even find in me to acknowledge.

He put on my seatbelt, his warm body hovering close as he continued to talk. "Zeke's one of the RD contacts. He's helping us."

My lips stuck together as I stared out the windshield.
"Maya." He leaned closer, hugging me again. "You alright?"
I shook my head. I wasn't okay right now.
But I would be.

CHAPTER NINETEEN

Slade

We'd driven in silence for almost an hour and a half, other than me on the phone with Flick. His voice echoed in my head even long after I'd hung up, his words rocking my already messed up mindset.

The hell were you thinking leaving her alone like that? Are you really that big of an idiot?

There was no denying it. It was my fault. A-fucking-gain.

I'd left her, even though I'd had a bad feeling about it. But the bag in the train station had all her shit, and I didn't want her being without it. Plus, Hawk had texted me right back after I'd asked about the new driver. Told me the dude was there because Summer's grandpa was sick. How was I supposed to know his number had been hacked, and it wasn't Hawk I'd spoken to, but someone connected to Pops? Someone who was trying to kidnap Maya at that? The guy had mentioned money, she'd heard it, asked about it too. It wouldn't take her long to figure out that there was a direct threat to her, a threat that might have something to do with her own father. That meant I needed to get her home so Flick could tell her the truth like he wanted to.

Thankfully Zeke was going to take care of things as far as the guy went. I didn't ask what that meant, knew it wasn't necessary. I trusted him: he was one of the hundreds of RD contacts we had across the country. Most were corrupt cops, or cops who did what they had to in order to keep the peace in their towns. Zeke was one of the bad guys turned semi-good, a former club member who'd chosen love over the life we lived. He wasn't an RD back in the day, not even sure what club he'd once been associated with. Not that it mattered. He was just the type who knew that some of the worst shit out there needed to be taken care of without getting the law involved.

Either way, it felt as if an army was gathering. That more things were happening. First Carlos's death, and now this. No matter their motivation, Pops and Maya's old man weren't standing down anymore, it seemed.

We crossed over the Iowa border into Illinois, the two separated by a bridge over the Mississippi river. The sun was starting to rise in the sky, shiny over the icy water below. I needed to stop somewhere. Take a piss. Get some food and pain meds into Maya. She'd been living on crackers for days, it seemed, while I'd taken up a steady diet of bourbon and whiskey and, well, her.

Seeing Maya this way now, like a zombie? It killed me. Made me want to punch something. She hadn't wanted to make this trip home in the first place. California made her happy, even with all her drama and lack of a job. Being with me, coming back to the RDs—that didn't. Which was why I'd do everything in my power to normalize her life once this entire nightmare with Pops, and now her father, was over and done.

Even if that meant pushing her away from me and sending her back to San Diego for good.

"Are you hungry? Thirsty?" My voice cracked when I asked. I noticed her eyelids flicker, squeezing then popping back open, then downcast, then half-lidded. Either she'd just woken up or she was fighting to go back to sleep.

"A little." She shrugged then slumped against the window, bad knee stretched out. Had to be uncomfortable for her. That knee of hers needed ice too. This tiny car Zeke had sent us away in was smaller than our rental. If I were any taller, I wouldn't have been able to fit.

At least there wasn't blood in the backseat or a broken window.

I wasn't sure what that guy had done to her before I'd managed to get in, before she'd stabbed him in the gut, but I sure as hell would do my best to find out.

"I gotta fuel up, so I'll grab something." I clicked on the blinker and sped across a few lanes.

She nodded, eyes shutting once more.

We continued on until I saw a sign for gas. I pulled off the interstate, following another road until a 7-Eleven popped up on my right, along with a crap ton of other stores and a movie theatre, as well as a tire place.

Tiny town, from what I could tell. Simple, happy, and oblivious—that was the kind of lifestyle people here led. What would it be like to live this way? To be clueless and normal? I knew Hawk was trying both ends out himself, what with Summer and all. It had me wondering if maybe, I could do it too.

"You okay in here while I pump gas?" I asked, hesitating, fingers on the handle. The last time I'd left her alone in a car, I'd nearly lost her.

She glanced out the window, away from me. "Yeah."

"I need to go in and pay with cash. I'll grab some waters."

"Yeah," she said again, her eyes meeting mine this time. Big and pretty and sparkling and… brown. God, not brown. I hated that pretty color in her eyes right then because it meant she was sad. So fucking sad.

Like ripping off a Band-Aid, I jumped out, hurrying to lock the door with the fob. I paid for the gas, some water, and a couple donuts, eyes on the car every other second through the glass door. It took me three minutes, if that. I hadn't been gone long. But the second I stepped outside and saw she wasn't in the passenger seat, I freaked.

"Maya?" I tossed our shit onto my seat, then slammed the door shut. Heart in my throat, I ran around the back of the car, then to the other side, but she wasn't there either.

"Maya?" I yelled again, louder this time.

That's when I saw her, off in a field of tall weeds along the side of the road. I stiffened at what I was seeing.

Her hands were in her hair, head back, and a loud yell left her mouth that sounded like a battle cry.

"Son of a bitch." I sighed, then began the jog toward her, cringing as the sound grew louder. *Angrier.* Eyes in the lot looked my way, then hers. I ignored them all, Maya my one focus.

To her left, I stopped and stared once again, waiting for her to get whatever was going on, out of her system.

"Go away, *Slade*," she yelled mockingly. "I'm fine."

She wasn't fine. But I wouldn't call her out on it. "Do what you gotta do. I'll be right here."

She whipped her head my way, her eyes wide, red... *wild.* "I don't need you."

"I know." I swallowed hard, wishing things were different. That our damn lives weren't tied into danger and bad memories. That we were just two people, who'd found each other on a train.

"I nearly killed that man," she hissed, leaning over to grab one of her dropped crutches.

"You did." I agreed with a shrug.

Pulling her arm back she tossed the crutch ahead of us and yelled, "I *wanted* to kill him."

I sighed, stuffing both hands into my pockets. *Me too,* I wanted to say, but didn't.

"I hate this." She turned to me then, her limp prominent, but not stopping her. I'm pretty sure she could handle anything. "I hate your stupid club and I hate the absolute bullshit that comes with it."

If this was her way of working through shit, I wouldn't stop her. I'd *help* her. Bending over, I grabbed the other crutch by her feet, handing it to her.

"Then show me how much."

She blinked, staring at it in my hand.

"Take it," I urged it closer. Her fingers shook as she grabbed it and put it above her head. "Throw it, Maya. Throw it far away, because I know that's exactly what you wish you could do to the club."

So she did, grunting as she tossed it even further than the other. When she was done, I reached down, finding a rock this time. I pointed at a sign then and said, "Hit that now."

Maya didn't question me. Just grabbed the rocked and tossed it. A ping sounded as it hit the post, and I reached down and grabbed another rock, and another, and another, until she'd thrown at least fifteen of them, each hitting the sign in some way or another.

She took out her anger, all her fears and frustrations, and threw those motherfucking stones like her life depended on it.

"I hate my father." A rock was thrown. "I hate his club." Another. "I hate what it did to my mother, and I hate that asshole who thought he could kill me."

Once she finished, she turned to me, her face red, breaths heaving. Her eyes were clearer than they had been, though, and I saw a thank you in her stare too. But I didn't deserve it. What happened should've been nothing more than a lesson for her to stay the hell away from me.

"I'm not gonna lie and say I won't let nothing happen to you again," I told her, because obviously I had no control over fate. "But I'm gonna tell you this, My. Whatever you go through, I'm gonna be there with you when it all goes down, okay?"

Slowly, she nodded, eyes locked with mine. I'm not sure if she believed me or not, but I wasn't gonna question it either. It was the most honest thing I'd told her since we'd reunited.

"You ready?" I stared over at the crutches, intending to grab them.

Maya looked there too. Then, as if knowing my thoughts, she snatched my hand up and shook her head. "I don't need them."

"You don't," I told her, not sure if I believed it. "But I'm still gonna grab them." There could be blood on the things. Evidence to a crime the RDs and Maya didn't want to delve more into—let alone rehash.

She seemed to understand, as her face paled a little, but she didn't stop me either. I hustled over, swiped them back up, stopping next to her again.

"I'll carry you." I tucked them under my arms, reaching to pull her up too, if necessary.

"No," she told me. Then she lifted her chin and grabbed my arm, urging us toward the car. "I'm gonna do this on my own."

I didn't fight her, though I wanted to. My heart jumped into my throat every time she hissed through her pain. Still, I led her back, being there if she needed me, even though she never asked me to.

CHAPTER TWENTY

Maya

Instead of heading straight to the Red Dragon clubhouse where my uncle was when we arrived in Rockford, Slade took me to my uncle's place. It was on the same land as the RD compound, like a little gated biker community, but instead of being surrounded by high brick walls, ponds, or fancy houses, his place was sealed off by an ugly, metal fence.

Unlike Hawk's house, which was apparently new and toward the back of the land, Flick's tiny place was toward the front of the compound, an eyesore you got to see before you noticed the ugly brick clubhouse directly behind it. As far as compounds went, though, the RD place was ritzy compared to the one I grew up in.

My mom was at Flick's place. It was where she'd been living for the last eight years. After everything, I honestly couldn't wait to see her, be pulled into her arms.

"You don't have to walk me in," I told Slade as he pulled up on the driveway. I wasn't ready for him to leave yet, but a separation would give us both clarity on what was going to happen between us from here on out.

Slade turned off the car, frowning at me, then the front door. "I'm gonna walk you in, My."

I looked the other way, swallowing the decent-sized lump in my throat. "Do what you think is right."

With a heavy sigh, he slipped out of the car and headed to the trunk, leaving me there with my thoughts. I trusted Slade, even though I was sure he was holding back secrets. His mood swings and possessive nature had to mean something. I didn't know exactly what was going on with the club, Pops, or anything for that matter right now. But I'd find out soon enough. I had to, for my own sanity.

Not bothering to wait for Slade, I opened the door to get out on my own.

"You sure you're good without crutches?" he asked, approaching my side.

I nodded, holding my chin up high, never wanting to touch the pair that sat in the back seat again. "Yes. Just gonna need some help up the sidewalk is all."

Before he could reach for my hand, the front door slammed shut and a familiar voice called my name. I looked around Slade and smiled at the sight of my mother barreling toward us.

Slade's phone rang from his pocket. He hesitated just enough that I knew it was more important for him to answer that call than it was for him to help me. I disliked the club world, yes, but I would, sadly, always understand it at the same time.

"It's fine." I spared him the guilt and nodded toward my mom. "She'll help me." His jaw clenched but in the end he stepped back and headed toward the house, the phone to his ear, his chin to his chest. My throat burned with strange emotions that I quickly pushed away the second my mom was in front of me. "Hey, Ma."

"Maya!" She lurched forward, hugging me while I was still in the seat. "I can't believe you're here."

I smiled and nodded, tears pooling in my eyes. Tears I couldn't decipher.

Mom and I were never as close as I wanted us to be growing up, but that was only because of my father. It was nice to feel her love, even if I sometimes didn't feel like I *knew* her.

She glanced down at my knee, eyes and cheeks damp. "Can you make it inside okay?"

"Yeah. Just moving slow." I tried to smile, tried to pretend like I was fine. Even as I reached for her, though, I hated that a part of me still hoped that Slade might come out and take over.

Arm's linked, Mom guided me toward the house. And just like that, she became my makeshift crutch.

She felt stronger than I remembered. Healthier. I hadn't seen her in several months. Not since our last Skype conversation. Even then she didn't look this good.

"Are you hungry? Tired? Do you need some ice?" she asked as we began the walk up the steps.

"I'd like to shower," I told her, face heating at the memory of my last shower, my inability to get out of the tub, and Slade's eyes when he found me with that curtain draped over my naked body. It seemed like so long ago when, really, it was a matter of days. "Might need a chair or something to sit on in there because of my knee though."

Mom nodded. "Sure." Then she opened the door with her right hand. "I've also called and set up an appointment for you with an orthopedist. The first available time is tomorrow afternoon. Hope that's okay."

"Thanks," I said, surprised by her sudden ability to parent, when for so long, I was the one who'd handled everything. "The doctor took X-rays in Colorado. He thinks something is torn." I cleared my throat. "Is Flick at the club?" I asked when we stepped inside.

"No. He's actually about an hour south on his way back from somewhere with Hawk. They had to follow up on something." She shook her head. "It's been a little hectic lately around these parts. Did Slade mention the brother who was killed about three weeks ago? Poor kid was so young. Shot in the head while he was out running to pick up some car parts."

I frowned. "Who was it? Do I know him?"

"Slade didn't tell you?" She glanced at me from out of the corner of her eye as we headed into the boxy living room. There was a feminine touch to it that hadn't been here eight years ago. Tan walls, brown leather couches. A man's home, with a lady's love.

"Um, we've been a little preoccupied." I winced as she settled me onto the love seat, my leg outstretched and achy from being bunched up in the car for so long.

Mom stood over me, hands on her hips. "It was Slade's prospect." She *tsked* then shook her head, lowering her voice. "According to Flick, they'd meant to get Slade, can you believe that?"

My chest squeezed and my face grew cold.

Flashes of a dead body shot through my mind like snapshots: dark hair, dimples, tan skin, midnight eyes…

Oh, God. That could've been Slade.

"He didn't tell…" I couldn't finish, my throat too tight to let it happen.

Was *this* why he'd been so agitated throughout the trip?

"Don't take offense, honey." Mom sat beside me on the couch and patted my shoulder. "Women know very little about what goes down in the club. You know that."

"Of course they don't," I grumbled, disgusted by the masochism of this life. Men weren't allowed to feel things, weren't allowed to show weaknesses or vulnerabilities either. And women in general were to know very little about the world—that much hadn't changed in my absence.

Five minutes later, Slade came tromping back into the room. Spotting me on the couch, he strode forward, scowled at my mother, and then, without question, scooped me up and into his arms.

"What are you doing?" I hissed.

"Putting you in bed." He headed down the hall, ignoring the noise of protest in my mom's throat.

"I was fine out there on the couch, damn it."

His jaw went rigid, proof that something else was wrong. I could see it in his eyes too. Feel it in his hold on me most of all. Still, he managed to set me down on the bed a little softer than how he'd picked me up. In turn, it made my chest go warm and fuzzy, made me feel everything I knew I shouldn't, when I should've been angry at his need to keep me in the dark.

Stupid heart. Stupid hormones.

"Gonna get some ice on that knee right away," he told me, voice all business. "You need to sleep."

"All I've done over the last few days is sleep," I argued, sitting up and swinging my legs around the side of the bed.

He walked out the door anyway.

I groaned, dropping my head back, putting both hands on my face. What I needed was a shower. To take as much time as I could to scrub my hands and nails. Being alone in the bed would mean thinking about what had happened, and I couldn't do that right now.

Pushing my fingers out in front of my face, I studied them, half expecting more of that man's blood to appear. After we'd left the train station, and after we'd gotten the new car, Slade had taken me to a rest stop, carried me into the ladies' room, and helped me wash—scald, really—my shaking, bloody hands under the water. My fingers burned from the superficial cuts, but it was nothing in comparison to the pain in my neck… and the pain in my soul.

It had been a wordless process, meticulous even. But I'd needed it. And Slade had seemed to sense that too, because he hadn't asked what was going through my head. The only time we'd argued was when he'd tried to set me in the backseat of the car. He'd told me he thought I'd be better there so I could stretch my leg out. But I'd refused, claiming the pills were doing their job of keeping the pain away, when really, I'd been too afraid to admit that there was no way I'd ever sit in the backseat of a car alone again.

I gave my head a fast jerk to rid it of the memory, only for Slade to come back into the room, arms full. "I've got meds, water, and ice, and your mom's bringing food." Methodic. Stoic. Like I was some sort of job to him—which I had been a few days ago. But now that I was home, he should have, by all rights, been done with me. Regardless, all hints of kindness and sweetness were gone. This was a Red Dragon standing before me now. The growly, asshole version at its best.

"You're gonna need to eat something before you pop the pills so your stomach doesn't mess with you," he said, pointing at them.

"You're being bossy." I rolled my eyes.

Ignoring me, he sat beside me on the bed. "Your appointment's tomorrow at two. Since your mom has to work, I'll take you. I've got places to be over the next few days. Not sure how much I'll be around, other than to drive you."

"Sure. Do what you gotta do. I'm not your keeper." Despite the nonchalant attitude, my heart thudded loudly in my chest. It was becoming apparent that what had happened between us was sex, nothing more. An itch that needed scratching.

Slade's brows pulled together. "I've got club business to take care of. Don't be pissed."

"Not pissed." I shrugged, though I most definitely was a tad bit on the irritated side. But I could mask my emotions just as well as he could.

Ignoring me, Slade continued, his voice almost growling now. "Also means I'll be out late. So, I'm gonna crash in one of the dorms at the compound tonight."

I froze at that.

I wanted space, but suddenly, it was hard to breathe, the air in my lungs almost suffocating. My eyes began to water. Every other second of my life, I was fine without him. But I'd forgotten nights were going to be a hell of a lot different.

With everything that had happened, the nightmares would undoubtedly come back, haunting me from dusk until dawn, and I couldn't, for the life of me, sleep alone.

Jesus, Maya. Stop this right now.

A heavy sigh filled the air, yet I couldn't look at Slade to see his expression. Not with the angry tears in my eyes, the ones seconds from streaming down my face. Weakness of any sort made life unbearable, and in order to survive the next few months, or however long I was stuck here, I needed to buck up. Be stronger. A survivor. A woman who did not need a man's heartbeat to keep her from falling apart.

"Maya." He lifted my chin, his voice a soft whisper. Calloused fingers stroked my cheekbone, nearly undoing me. "What's wrong?"

"Nothing. I'm fine." I shook my head, gathering my breaths. There was no other choice than to deal with this. Just like I should have done years ago when I'd stayed here. If I didn't, I'd no doubt become the last person I wanted to be. And a co-dependent, weakling version of Maya would *never* again exist in my world.

"You're lying." Slade sat down beside me on the bed, then took one of my hands between both of his.

I stiffened, still refusing to meet his gaze. "I'm not."

He sighed, but there was an edge to his voice. A finality even. "Fine then. I'll see you tomorrow."

The bed squeaked as he stood, and instead of watching him leave, I looked toward the window in the room. "Sure. Whatever."

Footsteps echoed against the floor. I heard him hesitate at the door, heard the light rap of his knuckles against the frame. If he was waiting for me to crack or break down, to beg him to come back, then he'd be waiting there a long, long time.

Eventually, he cleared his throat. "Maya?"

"Hmm?" I kept my gaze trained on the glass, watching tiny flakes of snow flutter to the ground. So pretty, yet so deadly at the same time. I rubbed my bad knee, hating snow even more now than ever.

"I've gotta leave in two days." He cleared his throat again.

At that, I slowly looked at him, pretending his words didn't affect me as much as they did—that there wasn't an instant zap inside my chest, threatening to take me down.

"Oh? Where are you headed?" I tried for casual, surprised by how smooth my voice stayed.

He rubbed a hand over his stubbled chin. "I have a run I can't get out of."

Was this about his prospect? I wondered. Obviously he hadn't told me what had happened for a reason, and I had no right to ask. Just because we'd had sex, spent some time together, gone through two severely crappy ordeals together, did not mean that we were going to actually *be* together. I had to get back to that mindset, stat. After all, I wouldn't be staying here forever; I still wanted to go back to my old life.

"South," he told me.

Despite my thoughts, I continued to fish. "Not too specific there."

"Just some club stuff going on I gotta take care of. Nothing you need to worry about."

"Club stuff as in…?"

Slade pursed his lips. "You're being nosy."

I stiffened. Then blinked. Then frowned, yanking the bag of ice off the table next to the bed, and putting it on my knee. "Never mind. Forget I asked."

"My—"

"Seriously. Just go do your club thing. I'm gonna sleep like a good girl." I forced a smile, feeling anything but chirpy. Feeling vulnerable, terrified, and, despite my best intentions, a little needy too. All three emotions were foreign to me, dangerous.

Slade continued to stand at the doorway staring at me. I could feel his gaze practically burning a hole into my face. Truth be told, I didn't want him to go on his run. I just wanted to cocoon our bodies in this bed, beneath the covers, and never leave this room again.

"Maya."

"Quit saying my name." I looked him dead in the eyes, and then did what I did best: I lied through my teeth. "I don't need you. Now, go do your club stuff so I can hang with my mom and not deal with your ridiculously, overprotective state."

He waited a beat. "This was planned before I even left to bring you home, just so you know." His dark brows furrowed in confusion, maybe anger too. I wasn't sure if it was toward me or what. "I can't get out—"

"It's fine. Seriously." I rolled my eyes for show. "I'm not your old lady, so you don't owe me explanations."

"But—"

"Seriously, Slade. I'm tired and have been through hell this week, so I... I just want to be alone right now."

My words made him flinch, but before he could respond, my mom was there at the door, a tray of something or another in hand as she pushed around him. "Knock, knock."

"Hey," I said with a smile, not feeling it in the least.

"I've got soup." She picked up the stuff that Slade had set down on my table, placing the tray there then putting the pills and water on the dresser. I watched her, missing the exact moment when Slade left... hating how my stomach churned with insecurity.

Most likely, Slade had probably missed the compound while he was gone. The endless stream of women and groupies and hang-abouts, the constant flow of drinks. Time with his *brothers* most of all. But those things didn't nearly bother me as much as I thought they would. It was more so the fact that he was still keeping secrets from me that did me in.

Once Mom left the room, I pulled the soup onto my lap, attempting to sip on spoonfuls, despite the fact that I wasn't even hungry. I was too spiteful and pissed to eat, and more than ready to rage hell until I got real answers about what was going on. Answers as to why I was even back here in the first place. If

Slade could have secrets, then I could too. We weren't a couple, probably never would be.

But the truth was always going to remain, no matter how hard I pushed it away.

I was falling hopelessly back in love with him.

With a biker.

Now I was going to have to force myself to ignore that fact until Flick let me leave and my feet touched the beaches of San Diego again.

CHAPTER TWENTY-ONE

Slade

"You look like shit," Archer said, his normal self in full force when I walked into the club forty minutes after leaving Flick's place. An arm loose around my shoulders, he led me to the bar, nodding at Tammy for a drink. She was one of the bartenders Flick had hired, a former groupie.

"I'm tired." And I wasn't really in the mood to talk either. It had taken me twenty minutes to pull out of Flick's driveway, yet I still felt detached from where I was supposed to be compared to where I wanted to be.

As a club, we had a hell of a lot of work to do when it came to Pops and Maya's old man. But there I was, thinking only about Maya again—and I'd just been with her. It was becoming a habit I was having trouble breaking. Her and those color-changing eyes, that smile and her full lips I would've done anything to kiss again. I knew she was hurting, despite her attitude. Not just physically, but her heart too. After what had happened outside the train station, how could she not?

God, I'd wanted to stay there with her. Hold her until she fell asleep. Even if that's all I'd ever get again. But duty called and the upcoming Church was just as much about her as it was about the club. I didn't have time to be distracted right now, but being around Maya for as long as I had made it impossible not to be.

And being around her also meant an inevitable ending. Something I couldn't deal with right now—or ever.

So after tonight, after going back to Flicks' place to check on her, I'd do what needed to be done, even if it killed me.

"Same." Archer sat on the stool beside mine. "Too many late nights trying to find the SOB who got Carlos."

"You did good." I nodded, throat tightening. "Thanks for taking care of that." As pissed as I'd been that I wasn't able to do the job, I was relieved knowing Archer had been the one to take care of things. There was no better man when it came to handing out revenge.

He nodded at me, his face stoic, fingers clasped on the bar. "We're brothers. It's what we do."

I cleared my throat. "Where's Flick, by the way? Thought we had Church."

Archer motioned for a drink from Tammy. "Last I saw, he was off with a couple ladies. Said he needed a break after listening to Hawk go on about Summer all day on their run."

I snorted. Life was falling apart around us, but our club pres always made time for pussy.

"How's Maya?" Archer asked, surprising me. I didn't think he even liked her, let alone cared enough to ask about her. Tammy set a couple of drinks in front of us, Archer a shot, me a Bud. She winked at me, then moved down to someone else.

"She's got a bum knee and a whole lotta shit on her mind." I took a drink of my beer, the cold burning my throat real good. "Happens when you almost off someone."

Arch nodded thoughtfully. "It was self-defense."

Wiping my lips with the back of my arm, I said, "Yeah. But it never should've happened in the first place. She's not an RD."

"You couldn't have known."

"I should have, is the thing." My instincts were always on. Except for when it came to Maya, apparently. Which is why the longer I was around her, the shittier things might get.

"You can't be the hero all the time." He downed his shot, tapping the bar for another one. Tammy held up a one-second finger, her eyes flitting back to my face.

I cringed, already knowing what she wanted. The two of us hooked up on and off—more than any other brother did with her. We'd never wanted a relationship, but for some reason, we always came back to one another. That shit wasn't happening tonight though, even if I didn't plan on committing to Maya.

Rubbing a hand over my forehead, I thought about something else. Something I hadn't for a while. "You remember what it was like? Your first kill?"

I'd grown so numb to offing someone that the thought of it didn't bother me as much as it once did. Or maybe if I remembered what that was like, I could relate to whatever My was going through, even if she didn't actually kill that guy.

"Yeah," Archer said, stroking his beard. He looked at something behind the bar, but he wasn't actually focused on anything. "I remember." He took a shot from another bartender, downing it with a loud sigh before she could even walk away. "My old man and I were on a run. I was sixteen, for fuck's sake."

I nodded, remembering that day all too well myself.

"You?" he asked, looking at me again. But I'd stirred something in my best friend right then. Something I was pretty sure he didn't want stirred. Could see it in his glassy eyes. The man was lit with a fire inside that burned angrier than any of us. I just didn't know why.

"I'd just turned eighteen. It was a dealer of Pops who'd stiffed him." Hawk had been with us, and when his dad had asked him to shoot the guy who was already half dead in a South Side alley, Hawk couldn't do it. Just… froze up. He was two years older than me, but he was soft, even when he wasn't trying to be. That was around the time he'd been fighting against his dad more. Before the dick-for-brains set him up. I hadn't wanted Pops to clock him upside the head, or worse, so I'd lifted my gun and done it for him.

I remembered crying that night. Puking too. It wasn't fun. None of this was. At least not when Pops was the pres. But things were different now. Or Flick was trying to make it that way.

A throaty, feminine voice piped up a minute later, breaking the strained silence of our thoughts. "Hey, Slade. Glad to see you back. This place was lonely without ya." Tammy touched the back of my wrist, scraping her nails up and down.

"Good to see you too, Tam." I pulled my arm out from under her hand because nothing about her touch felt right.

She frowned briefly, then said with a low purr, "I'm off in an hour."

I shook my head. "Sorry. Got club business tonight."

"After?" She cocked her head to one side.

"Nope." I looked down at the bar, too chickenshit to see her reaction.

She didn't move right away. And next to me, Archer stiffened. Both were likely wondering what the hell was going through my head, but I kept my gaze on my empty glass, waiting for it all to pass.

Slade never turned down a woman.

Sebastian, on the other hand…

"Alright then. Another time." Tammy sighed. I could tell she was disappointed, but we weren't together, like I said. Never would be.

Archer cleared his throat once she was gone. "After a week with that snooty bitch, Maya, I figured you'd be all about Tammy."

"Don't call her a bitch." I gritted my teeth, flashing him a warning.

"She is, though." He narrowed his eyes. "Miss *I'm too good for the club* and shit. The woman hasn't been back here for eight years, yet everyone is all 'Maya this' and 'Maya that'… First Hawk leaves for her, then Flick needs her back, and now you, of all people, are defending her."

I'd forgotten he knew what he did about her and me—her breaking me, her using me at nights, even if she had her reasons that I now understood. Arch would never get it though, and I wasn't in the mood to explain either. But he didn't need to be an ass.

"After *everything* she did to you, man."

I inhaled through my nose as steadily as I could, unable to speak.

"What're you gonna do when she decides it's time to run again?" He threw his hands up in the air, letting them slap against the bar. "Because once a runner, always a runner. That shit never changes."

"Fuck off." I stood, needing to walk away. If I didn't, I'd hit him.

I headed toward the back hallway of the clubhouse, which led to the dorms. I stayed in them now, hadn't been living with Flick for years.

"Oh, it's like that now, is it? You ignoring me? You runnin' like she did?" Archer called after me, his booted feet running across the tiled floor. A few prospects and a couple of the elders all watched me as I passed, but I didn't give a shit what any of them thought right now.

"She's a bitch, Slade," he continued, even as I stood in front of my room. "We both know it."

"No, asshole," I hissed, wrapping a hand around the knob but not heading in just yet. "She's not a bitch. She's a good person who never wanted to be a part of this shit in the first place." I waved a hand back toward the main bar, breathing heavy as I faced my friend again. "This life never leads you anywhere good, and because of that, it isn't the life for her."

For the first time in a long time, I believed in my words. Not because I didn't want to be part of this club, but because I knew this club wasn't the life Maya needed. She deserved better than this life, than me. She deserved the rich husband who'd love her hard, the kids, the fancy house, the dog or cat. Not me, damn it. I'd be an idiot to think otherwise.

And besides, Archer was right. She'd leave, and it was better I got on board with it than be broken like before when she did.

Archer dropped his head back and groaned. "Christ, it happened to you too, didn't it? Just like with Hawk."

I scowled, folding my arms. "What the hell do you mean?"

"You went and fell for a woman after being all trapped on the road together." His lip curled in annoyance. "But the difference between you and Hawk?" He shook his head, taking a step back. "You fell in love with the one woman you knew you shouldn't."

He wasn't wrong. Not exactly. I wouldn't fall back into the same pattern this time. If anything, I'd end it before it ever really began. But love? I'm pretty sure he was right about that.

"Did you fuck her? That why you turned Tam down? Feel an obligation toward Maya now or something?"

I frowned, the no on the end of my tongue. But for some reason, I wasn't ready to admit the fact that all my old feelings for her were coming back. Not yet. Maybe not ever, at this point.

"It was an itch I needed scratched." I settled with that instead, hating how wrong the words felt in my mouth.

"You get it outta your system, then?"

"Ain't gonna happen again." It wasn't the truth, but it also wasn't a lie either. I was gonna try my hardest to keep my hands off her tonight when I got back to Flick's. Even though she'd told me to stay away I was still going to check on her.

"You sure about that?" Archer slid up next to me, a shoulder to the wall and a sneer twisting his lips.

"I ain't in love with her, if that's what you think." Pushing the final lie out my mouth, I slipped into my tiny room and shut the door in Archer's face. What he didn't know wouldn't hurt him.

Three hours later, I was showered and dressed, sitting in Church. The shed-turned-office that sat behind the clubhouse was all dark wood. Wood walls, wood floors, wood table, wood signs hanging on the wall, most of which included the names of brothers lost throughout the years.

Flick had just gotten back from his little orgy, sitting at the front of the rectangular table, with Chop to his right and Archer to his left. Crazy, who'd been part of the club from the beginning, sat opposite him at the other end of the table. The guy was old as hell, but he knew more shit than any of us did. Talker and Mute were there as well, both standing; the two of them had only just recently been coming to Church. Good guys. Trustworthy. We needed them on our side.

My cousin, on the other hand, was nowhere to be found. Not that I was surprised. He was never on time anymore.

"You did it then. Got my girl back safe and sound." Flick leaned back in his chair, fingers stroking his beard.

"Not sure about the safe and sound part."

"She's alive and she's here. That's all I asked for." Flick shrugged.

"She's traumatized and doesn't wanna be here, Goddammit," I growled. "Soon as this shit's done with Pops, I'm gonna fly her back to San Diego where she belongs."

"No, you won't." Flick smirked.

My eyes narrowed. "What's your problem, huh? She was damn near killed, then stabbed that asshole. How can you be so calm about this?"

God, he was a good pres but a damn shitty human being sometimes.

His jaw twitched, and the smug look on his face fell away. "Fine. I'll talk to her tomorrow."

"You gonna tell her about her old man then too?"

He shrugged. Not a yes. Not a no either. Fucking asshole.

Hawk came barreling into the room before I could get a real answer. His face red, black hair messy. Knew right away where he'd been. We all did. Except for Flick, apparently.

"And you're late because?" he asked.

"Princess needed me." Hawk winked.

Archer groaned and rubbed both hands over his face. "Good Christ, I've lost both of you."

I kicked my buddy's leg under the table, which earned me a glare. Nobody else heard him, but I sure as hell did. He needed to keep his mouth shut until I could give our pres the PG version of what had gone down between me and his niece. Flick thought I loved her like a sister but didn't have a clue that I'd had her as a lover instead. Who knew what his response might be? I couldn't risk it.

"Tell us what we need to know, boy." Flick leaned forward and set his elbows on the rectangular table, zeroing in on Chop. The kid was our secretary, guess you could say. Twenty-one, prospected under Flick, former marine, injured leg at the hands of a landmine. A real badass in his own right. His smarts reminded me of myself.

"We've got the specs on Pops's locale." Chop sat up straight, eyes flickering across a sheet of paper. "Small town in New Mexico, brick house, no gates. Guarded well. All young guys surrounding him. He's got power, but not enough experience to go around."

"Except for the Forsaken," Flick added.

I flinched at the mention of that club, running a hand through my hair to try and keep them from shaking.

"How long he been back in the states, do you know?" Flick asked.

"About a week." Chop rattled off a bunch of shit from his papers: sightings, towns, names.

"Good. And Maya's old man, Satan? Inform the boys what else we got on him." Flick waved a hand toward the rest of the brothers, stopping on me.

My ears perked. This was what I'd been waiting for, the shit that might affect Maya the most. And even though she was safe on the compound now didn't mean I wasn't about to give up bodyguard duties. Not after what we'd been through, what may or may not be ahead.

"Your intel says he hasn't moved from Phoenix in weeks." Chop paused, narrowed eyes on Flick. "You sure that's a sign he's been working with Pops?"

I gritted my teeth and growled out, "Seeing as how Maya was almost kidnapped, I'd say that's enough of a *fucking sign* that the two of them have been working together, don't you think?"

Chop flinched, eyes downcast. The rest of the room went quiet too, knowing not to jump in. He was new to the table. I'd let this slide now. But if he ever questioned something so important again, I wouldn't be as nice next time.

Flick cleared his throat. "Arch and Slade are getting on a plane Friday. Flying to Texas and meeting with my intel to figure shit out."

Blowing out a slow breath, I rubbed a hand over my forehead. "How long we gonna be gone for?"

Flick shrugged. "A day or two."

I nodded, balling both hands on my lap under the table. Killed me that I'd be away from Maya. But if there was one place she was safe at, it was with the RDs on the compound. And now that I'd done my job with her, got her home, then it'd be someone else's job to take care of her.

Flick pushed away from the table then, signaling the end of Church. Yet all I could do was sit there and stare at the table, even as everyone left the room.

This was what I needed to do. What was necessary as road captain.

But why the hell did it feel like I was making a huge-ass mistake?

The door shut, but footsteps sounded, coming up beside me. Looking to my right, I found Flick lowering himself onto a chair, eyes narrowed.

"Wanna tell me what's going through your head right about now, boy?"

I winced, looking at my lap. "If I tell you no, you gonna let it be?"

"Nope."

Figured as much.

"This about my niece?"

I cringed but managed a nod.

"You love her."

"What makes you say that?" I lifted my chin, trying to keep a straight face.

"I'm not stupid."

All I could do was sigh.

"You gonna claim her?" He leaned back in his chair, a finger on his lips. But I couldn't read his face. Never really could.

Say no. Say no, asshole. But for some reason, a no felt too final, even if I'd already begun to let her go. "I don't know."

"It's a yes-or-no answer. Either you're gonna make her your old lady, or you're gonna walk. There ain't no in between."

I knew right then that I had to tell him the truth. He was the only person I'd tell what was really going on in my head. This man was the closest thing I had to a father.

"She distracts me. It's not safe."

"I get that." He nodded. "Takes a special kinda man to separate the two worlds."

He cleared his throat and stood, eyes on the dark window.

"Did you ever…?" This shit was weird. Too emotional. "Never mind."

"You asking me if I ever took an old lady, boy?"

"Guess I am." I shrugged.

"The answer's yeah. I did. Once. Didn't end well."

"You regret it?" I asked.

His answer cemented what I needed to hear. "If you're lucky to find that shit, then it's a good thing. But good ain't always what's best."

CHAPTER TWENTY-TWO

Maya

Even as the canned laughter on the television echoed throughout my uncle's living room, and Mom doted on me to the point of being obsessive, I still couldn't shake the feeling of that man's hands wrapped around my neck. According to Slade, he was put away—God only knew where—but that didn't mean the memories were erasable.

"You haven't eaten much." Mom pushed the mute button on the TV.

"I'm not that hungry." I stirred the second bowl of chicken noodle soup she'd given me today with my spoon and shrugged.

Five minutes after Slade had left, I'd made my way out into the living room, in no way ready for bed. I'd managed a shower, scrubbed my skin nearly raw to try and rid myself of the memory of blood, and now here I was, all but jumping out of my skin with every strange noise I heard, every movement of Mom on the couch next to me too.

Mom flicked off the television and grabbed both of our trays, taking them to the kitchen. It was black out but only seven o'clock. As much as I hated to admit it, I missed Slade. Not having him here made me uneasy and a little restless. But I knew we both needed space.

"Okay, two giant bowls of cookies and cream." Mom smiled wistfully as she returned a few minutes later. She placed one dish on my tray and held the other on her lap.

"Still your favorite flavor?" I grinned, feeling the tightness in my chest easing a little.

"Absolutely." She took a bite and shut her eyes, talking around it. "Still yours?"

I nodded, bringing a spoonful to my lips. It melted immediately against my tongue when I licked it off, and the flavors rushed over my taste buds in the best possible way. This wasn't a quick fix. But it was a good temporary distraction. And any time spent with my mom was a win right now.

"You know how that old saying goes? You can't be sad if you're eating ice cream." Mom winked at me, curling her legs up and under her. "I abide by that religiously." She shrugged. "Which is probably the reason for my love handles. But I've learned over the years that a little indulgence, even if it's a scoop of ice cream a day, is worth the extra weight on your hips if it makes you happy."

I nodded, wondering when she'd gotten to be so profound. The mom I remembered was closed off or crying constantly. Not this straightforward, eyes-to-the-sky woman I was sitting next to now. Though the mom I knew had also lied to me about Slade leaving.

That thought had me frowning.

Every so often, I studied her, trying to work up the nerve to ask about it. But things between us were so raw and new that I really didn't want to dampen the mood. Nevertheless, I had a right to know the truth about why she'd lied to me. And there was no better time like the present to ask for it.

"Mom?" I cleared my throat.

She placed her hand over the back of mine on my lap. "What is it?"

"Why did you tell me that Slade, I mean Sebastian, left?"

A beat passed. Then two. I lifted my head up, finding her face filled with regret, then finally, resolve. "Because he did leave."

"No, he didn't." I frowned.

"He did. The second you were gone, all traces of Sebastian disappeared, I guess you could say."

"I don't understand. You mean he changed, physically, right after I left?"

She hesitated, looking toward the front door like she expected someone to walk in at any second, and didn't want to get caught.

"It's… complicated. Obviously, the physical change didn't happen overnight. But the emotionally hardened man? That was immediate."

My Story Boy had basically disappeared overnight? That broke my heart.

Mom continued, unaware of the pain her confession was causing me. "Two days after you went to California, sweetie, he asked Flick if he could prospect for the club. He told him that Sebastian had died and that nobody was to ever mention his name again. Then he told me in private, later, that if you ever asked about him, I was to say exactly what I told you."

"Did he threaten you?"

"No, honey. He cried, actually. I think he might have had a crush on you or something. I'm not sure."

I shut my eyes at that innocent word: crush.

We were beyond the crush stage now, not that I'd admit it to Mom. She'd make a big fuss about it, indeed. Claiming I was home, finally, and embarking on the best decision of my life. The thing was, I didn't know what I was going to do tomorrow, let alone in a week or a month. I really, *really* liked Slade. Probably more than liked him. But Slade wasn't Sebastian. And I was no longer the Forsaken's VP's naive daughter.

Everything happened for a reason, I supposed, but that didn't mean I had to like that reasoning.

I waited a second, gathering the courage to admit it out loud. "I was in love with him, Mom."

"What?" Her eyes widened.

Secret friends in the night, my ass. God, how could I have been so selfish? "We got… close. He, um, used to come into my room at night."

"You two were having sex and I didn't know about it?" She gasped, a hand to her chest.

"God. Don't look so scandalized." I giggled, and it felt incredible to do so. "We never even *kissed.* But he used to tell me these stories…" I smiled wistfully, remembering how content I'd been. How *in love* I'd been, even before admitting it to myself. "We were friends. The night before I left I, um, realized I wanted more, but he was already with someone." Two someones, actually.

"I didn't know." Mom reached over and brushed a strand of hair from my face, eyes tender and filled with regret. "The only time you asked about him was when you moved away, and I thought that was you just being nice."

"Nobody knew." I looked to my lap, remembering that bus ride out of town.

How I'd cried so hard I could barely breathe.

How a woman had approached me and asked if I was okay.

How I'd told her my heart was broken.

How she'd sat beside me and said, *The first broken heart is the worst broken heart.*

She'd been right because I still wasn't over it. Probably never would be.

Slade and I had lost a lot of time together, and part of me had hoped we could make up for that. But now that we were back in the thick of things, no longer on the train, I wasn't sure if he wanted that anymore—or what *I* even wanted now, actually. He was hot with me one minute, cold the next… It was the kind of whiplash that burned the most.

Plus, he could have had another woman back here who I'd been unaware of. Or several women for that matter. The thought had my nails digging into my palms. Jealousy had no room in my life right now, especially since I wasn't sure where we stood or what I really wanted.

A few minutes of silence went by, Mom and I both likely thinking, remembering, reliving that first summer after my father. Back then, Mom had been as lost as me. The difference now was I'd stayed lost while she seemed to have found herself.

"Do you want to talk about it?" she asked me.

"What 'it' are you referring to, exactly?" I dropped my head to the side, studying her. "Because there are a lot of 'its' in question at the moment."

"Slade. You and him, together back then… Your trip…" She hesitated, letting go of a slow breath. "What happened to you?" She reached over and slid her fingers down my red braid—patient, sad.

At first, I waited, thinking this was some sort of joke. That she'd shut down like she used to, or maybe even fall asleep. But I tested the waters, let the beginning of my story fall out—from our nights when I was nineteen to the day I left, my time in California with my job, my crappy boss, and my apartment issue. Then I jumped to Slade showing up outside my door, and what happened on our trip, minus the intimacy shared. She listened to every single thing I said, never looking away. She even nodded and added her own two cents here and there.

By the time I finished, tears were streaming down my face, the ugly kind I struggled to control. But the thing that shocked me the most was the fact that I was in my mom's arms, pressed to her chest as she ran a soothing hand up and down the back of my head.

"It's okay," she cooed, kissing my temple. "Cry it all out, sweetie. I've got you."

Right then, I sobbed harder than I'd ever sobbed before. Not just because of the trip and the stuff that'd happened, but being back here, with her, like this, had my heart aching for all the time she and I had lost. Mom was like the third missing piece of a puzzle I hadn't been interested in putting together for years. Until now. Until Slade had found me and brought me home. Until he had unknowingly given me the gift of my mother as well as his heart—which I was fairly certain he wasn't aware of.

Maybe there was a benefit to this trip after all. One that went beyond mine and Slade's unfinished past. Maybe I was meant to come back because of my mom. The thought had my arms wrapping tighter around her waist. Had my throbbing chest easing too.

"Did I ever tell you about the time I met your father?" Mom whispered, stroking a slow, soft hand over the back of my head.

I cringed. "Mom, I don't want to know about—"

"Let me, honey. I need you to know."

So, I did let her—not happily, of course. Any conversation that focused on dear old Dad, appropriately named Satan in his club, did not end well.

"I was out with some friends from college. A bar in downtown Phoenix. There was this massive shooting inside. A massacre, really."

I shut my eyes. "Was is related to…?"

"The Forsaken?"

I nodded.

"No, it wasn't. Just some burned-out college kid with a false agenda."

"I'm sorry. That must've been awful for you."

"I'll never get over it." Her body shuddered against mine as though she were reliving that moment. "Anyways, your father was there that night. Wasn't his normal place, but he'd been doing a run in the back room when the gunman fired. He came out, found me and my girlfriends hiding in the corner, and sheltered us. He was even shot in the back shoulder protecting me."

I had no real emotions for my father, other than disgust or hate, but without him, Mom wouldn't be here. And neither would I. He was a sperm donor who'd apparently protected my mom just once. That didn't make me like him any more, but it did make me respect him for the tiniest of seconds. A blip in the radar of all the bad he'd done to us both.

"What happened after?" I asked.

"Once the gunman was shot down by police, I got your father into my car and started to take him to the hospital after he refused to go with the EMT." She laughed softly, stroking the back of my hair still. "When he insisted I drive him an hour and a half away to his compound, I should've known something was up." She shrugged. "But then nine months later, you were born."

Mom got pregnant with me on the scariest night of her life? The first night she even met my father? I wasn't sure how I felt about that.

"The point of my story, sweetie, is that sometimes we have to take a leap of faith. That night gave me the most wonderful gift in the world: you. And I wouldn't change that for anything."

"What do you mean by leap of faith?" I asked, a loud thump in my chest telling me to shut down the questions.

"Slade is a nice boy. One of the better ones. Now that you two are back home, and seem to be on the same page, don't push him away because you're scared of what could happen in the end. Go with your heart. It knows what it's doing."

I scoffed, not because I didn't believe her, but because it surprised me that she'd tied her story to mine. Still, I wasn't ready to admit to her, or even myself, that I may just want to take that leap of faith she mentioned, even though it went against all of my better judgement.

"With everything my father put you through, you think it was worth it?"

"Of course it was. How could I regret something that gave me you?"

More tears formed in my eyes, but I pushed them away, done with crying for a while. "But life with Dad was so awful."

"It was." She sighed. "And every day since we left Arizona, I've wished that I'd taken you from there sooner."

"Things with the Red Dragons weren't much different." Not then and definitely not now with Pops and the trouble he caused. At least they didn't beat and basically enslave women for the sport of it.

That I knew of.

"That's ridiculous." She scoffed. "The Red Dragons are nothing like the Forsaken. The problem is, you never even gave this place a chance. You judged it so quickly because… What was it that you used to say? You've seen one MC, you've seen them all?"

I looked down at my lap, trying not to cringe. She was right. I did judge. But she'd been so out of it when we left that it was impossible for her to see the bad in people until it was too late.

But here she was, alive and breathing and happier than she'd ever been. That had to count for something, I supposed.

"You're happy here, then? In this life you've got now?"

She nodded. "Absolutely. But that doesn't mean I wasn't once like you."

"How so?"

"Well…" She drew the word out. "When I was eighteen, I begged Flick to let me go to college. Since both of our parents were dead, and he was ten years older than me, he was my guardian, as you know. He'd just gotten in deep with the RDs around that time, so in a way, I think he was glad I wanted to go to Arizona for college. He could live his best Red Dragon life, and didn't have to worry about his baby sister anymore."

Flick didn't seem like the type of man to abandon what was important to him. But did I really even know him all that well? No. I didn't.

"But you wound up being a part of something worse."

"It happens," she said sadly, tucking hair behind my ear. "But this life now? Here? The brotherhood and Flick and the Red Dragons? It's a good one for me. They are decent human beings, even if they are a little rough around the edges, and not always law-abiding." We both laughed at that last part. Mom then finished with, "I feel safe here most of all. Loved and protected and so incredibly happy."

I blew out a slow breath, tightening my arms around her waist. "I'm sorry I didn't come back and visit."

"Don't be sorry. You like your life in California, don't you?"

"I do." For the first time, I finally felt as if I had a home in San Diego, even if it was a lonely one.

But the thing is, the demons of my father and his club never really went away with space from my mom. And that's all I'd ever wanted. Instead, I'd lost time and a shot at love. A realness that was possibly eight years too late.

The thought of going back to San Diego didn't pull at me like it had just days—or even hours—before. In fact, there wasn't anything left for me back in California at all, if I thought about it. No job, no apartment…

So, the question was, did I *want* to stay in Rockford? Live this life I'd been so adamantly against? I wasn't sure where things stood with Slade, or if we were meant to find our way back at all. But perhaps being here, with my mom, was the future I was meant to have. The one purpose I'd been missing for years. Maybe it wasn't club life I hated, maybe it was just my dad.

"Mom?"

"Yeah, honey?"

I took a breath and prepared the words we rarely shared, knowing I'd spent far too long keeping them locked away. I had time to make decisions. For now, I just wanted to be with my mom.

"I love you."

She didn't respond right away. Instead she sniffled and kissed the top of my head, her reply so soft I could barely hear it.

"I love you too, sweet Maya. So much."

A hard body slid into bed beside me sometime later that night. Knowing who it was, I didn't move right away, for fear he'd change his mind and leave. But at the same time, I couldn't help but speak.

"You came back," I whispered, keeping my eyes closed, wondering if this was a dream.

Slade's voice dropped to a growly whisper as he said, "Only place I wanna be right now is with you."

At that, I turned over and faced him, warmth burrowing in my chest. He was on top of the blanket, dressed in only his boxers, hands behind his neck, eyes shut. Right then, Slade looked so torn. So incredibly sad too.

I tucked both hands beneath my cheek as I spoke. "Are you okay?"

His eyes popped opened, and he let his head fall to the side, where our gazes met. "Yeah. Just a long night."

Inhaling, I took in the scent of soap and beer, studying his mouth and the whiskers surrounding those lips I wished were against mine. It's amazing what time and space did to the heart when it longed for something it didn't know it needed.

"Hey," he said, rolling over onto his side to face me too. Reaching out, he tucked a strand of hair behind my ear, then let his knuckles run down my cheek. "You okay?"

"Yeah. I think so." My throat still ached from the tears I'd shed earlier, but otherwise, I felt… good. Tired, but good.

I'd drifted in and out of sleep for the last four hours, waking, somehow, before the nightmares hit. Nighttime self-preservation. Who knew that was even a thing?

Moving even closer, his eyes dark in the night, Slade lowered his hand to my waist on the top of the blanket, hesitant as he began to speak. "I'm sorry for being a dick earlier."

He searched my face when I didn't reply right away, the acceptance of his apology easier said than done. Even in the night, I could see the fight there in his eyes He wanted me closer but feared something I could easily relate to. The fear of more; the fear of losing that more, most of all.

I scooted closer, despite my thoughts of holding a grudge, and made the decision for him. When our thighs touched, even with the blanket boundary between us, my body relaxed.

Slade, though, never did.

"I'm sorry too," I whispered, knowing he wasn't the only one in the wrong. We'd both acted like children.

Needing skin on skin contact, an affirmation that this was real, I wrapped my arms around his neck, feeling the stiffness in his body increase even more.

Let go, Slade. Please. Let go with me.

He pulled in a breath, holding it, then said, "Maya, you gotta know something."

My chest squeezed as I prepared for the worst. "What is it?"

"You…" He took another breath. "You scare the absolute shit outta me."

I shut my eyes, remembering my mom's earlier words about leaps of faith, taking chances, and having zero regrets. Maybe that was what stirred the fire in my chest and pushed the same words from between my own lips.

"You scare me too."

A beat past. I almost thought he'd fallen asleep. Up until I heard him chuckling, felt him drifting away from me, but only so he could crawl under the covers. And then he was against me even more, pulling me closer. My head was on his chest, his arm around my waist. Against my ear, his heart beat steadily. I didn't want to be disappointed; this was what I'd secretly wanted all night. But I was. If our time together was limited, which I'm fairly certain it was, I wanted to make the most of it. In all the ways we could.

"What's so funny?" I asked, despite the throb inside my chest.

Fingers stroked the spot just beneath the hem of my shirt and across my spine, testing my restraint. Internally, I wept for more, but I didn't push him. Even so, the movements, the grazing, the feel of it all was the best and worst torture.

How could he possibly be so clueless about the effect his touch had on me? Or maybe he wasn't, and just selfishly wanted to touch me too. I could relate.

"You remember that night when we heard Archer and that woman in the room next door?" He waited a second, tapping on the wall above our heads with his free hand. "I think it was the fourth night we spent together."

My mouth curled on one side when that memory came into focus. I'd just laid my head on his chest, like I was doing now, and was seconds from falling asleep when the giggles and moaning began.

Apparently, my uncle's spare bedroom was the go-to place for club members who didn't want an audience of bikers when it came to screwing. Sebastian—Slade—never slept in there because he feared what might be in the sheets. The thought had grossed me out and made me laugh at the same time when he'd spoken the words allowed, despite the fact that I was unnerved and a little freaked at the thought of random men coming in and out of this house I was supposed to be staying at.

Still, I'd trusted Story Boy. He made me feel safe. Assured me with his strong arms that it was just Archer, and there was nothing to worry about. There hadn't been either, regardless of the fact that it was a little awkward. At the time, I didn't know who Archer was, and Mom lived in the basement like she did now, so she didn't have to hear what went down. But Story Boy and I sure did.

"Yeah." I smiled, cheeks heating. "I remember alright."

"They were so damn loud." Slade chuckled.

Thump. Thump. Thump. Thump. Followed by long, drawn-out moans and over-the-top keening that had me wondering how any one man could be *that* good.

"I remember asking myself how a woman could moan that much but not lose her voice." I snorted out a bigger laugh.

"Yeah. She reminded me of Mania."

My heart leapt into my throat at his analogy. "You told me about her once." I smiled, proud of myself for remembering.

"I did?"

"Yes, if I remember right, she's the spirit goddess of insanity, madness, crazed frenzy, and…" I drew a blank.

"The dead," he finished for me, and I could hear the smile in his words.

"Yes, that's it." I pulled my lips between my teeth, wanting nothing more than to laugh right then. Not because it was funny, but because I felt, for the first time in years, pure, indescribable joy. He was still in there, my Story Boy. He was still alive and kicking beneath all of Slade's machoism. Regardless, I wouldn't call him out because I feared if I did, the memory, this happiness I was experiencing, would all go away.

"You really remember all that?"

I nodded. "I remember a lot more than you think I do."

He nodded, wordless once more.

I'd only been there for about a week when that night had gone down. Slade and I were new to the whole snuggling, getting-to-know-you thing. But then when *that* happened, it changed the game for me. Against him, my leg draped over his leg, my center pressed against his thigh through my sleep shorts, dampening as their noises increased—as the thundering of the headboard against the wall echoed like crackles of thunder in a storm…

It was the first night I'd realized that I could actually *want* a man, sexually. I'd wanted so bad to feel the way that woman had been feeling, and I'd wanted it with the boy who'd let me listen to his heart. The boy who'd made me feel safe and special at the same time.

Neither of us had spoken or moved while we'd listened to their fucking. But I remembered how his heartbeat had increased, how his breathing had grown more ragged against the top of my hair too. Such a gentleman he'd been, while I'd been like a woman practically in heat, needing something I didn't understand, but knew would be well worth it if it happened.

It had always left me wondering though…

I toyed with the light spackle of hair across his chest, shutting my eyes as I asked the question in my head. "If I had kissed you that night, would you have kissed me back?"

"Yeah," he whispered without hesitation. "Hell, My, I wanted to kiss you the second I first saw you in that mirror. Then with your body against mine like that, hearing Arch and that girl? God, I was so far gone," he whispered on a long breath. "so fucking far gone that it wasn't even funny."

Knowing what needed to be done now, despite our fears of what might come, I pulled away from his chest and pressed a hand to his whiskered cheek.

"Slade?"

He searched my face, his voice crackling. "Yeah?"

"I…" *I want you. All of you. Tonight, every night, or for however long I'm here.*

But the words wouldn't come; my tongue too tied up with fears and what-ifs. So, for the night, and the sake of my heart, I did what I was good at instead: used my body to do all the talking.

Ignoring the pain in my knee, I crawled over his hard stomach and straddled him.

He stiffened beneath me, hands on my bare thighs. "My," he whispered, watching me through shadowed eyes.

I kissed his cheek, his chin, his neck, where I nibbled and sucked and licked. My entire body shook with both nerves and unbridled lust, yet it felt so right. Every single second of it. He groaned, lazy fingers stroking my lower back now, then sliding beneath the silk of my panties. Squeezing my ass, his hips rose to meet mine as I continued my journey over his neck, to the center of his throat.

"Maya," he whispered my name with reverence. "We shouldn't…"

But we both knew we would.

"I wanted you to touch me that night," I admitted. "And I want you to touch me now like you would have if we hadn't been so scared."

His hands stilled. But because I was too frightened to see the expression on his face, I slid down his body even more, taking my seduction to the place I knew he couldn't resist. I kissed the tattoo across his chest and flicked my tongue around his nipples too. Tasting each bit of his flesh was like a trip to a winery, so delicious and decadent was his skin that I never wanted to stop sipping.

To my left, I reached over and scrambled through the drawer. There were condoms inside. A fresh box. I knew he didn't stay here anymore, so I had no idea whose they were, but when I'd snooped earlier, it had felt right finding them. Like fate.

I grabbed a lone condom, set it on his chest for safekeeping, then proceeded to inch lower, needing to taste him elsewhere before letting him inside of me.

Before I could tug down his boxers, his fingers tightened around my wrists, holding me in place. Wordlessly, Slade held the condom in his hands, staring at me from over the top when I lifted my gaze to meet his. There was something in his eyes that I hadn't seen before. A conundrum of sorts: honesty, fear, resolution all fighting for ultimate control. The sight of it terrified me but also pushed me to try harder. To make him realize that the two of us, together like this, was right.

"Maya, this isn't a good idea."

"Please." Because if I didn't, I'd feel too much, hurt too much, possibly make rash decision that would haunt me for days to come. And the last thing I wanted to do right now, was think too hard.

His lips sealed, and when I slipped his boxers down once and for all, grabbed his gorgeous cock, and lowered my lips to the head, he stopped trying to be the good guy and instead, let the lust take hold.

He watched with hooded eyes as I glided my tongue over the head to sample the saltiness of his pre-come. His taste gave me the bravery to move lower, taking him in as far down as I could go.

"Maya…" He groaned, fingers in my hair, gently pulling just seconds after the head touched the back of my throat. Up and down, I took my slow, sweet time, savoring his noises, the moment… until he reached his obvious last straw.

"Stop." He pulled my mouth away, hands on my cheeks. His eyes fought with something while he stared down at me—fighting even more as he toyed with the square packet in his shaking hands.

There were many ways I could take that one word. *Stop*, as in this couldn't happen. *Stop*, as in this wasn't right. *Stop*, as in this wasn't the way he wanted me.

I liked that last option the best and continued to hold his gaze and wait for further instructions.

Just when I thought I'd made a mistake, he dropped his hands and slid them beneath my arms, pulling me up his body like I weighed nothing, before kissing the space between my eyes.

"You're my dream." He kissed my nose, my cheek, my chin. "I never wanna wake up from you, even though I know it's inevitable."

Before I could tell him he was wrong and that this dream could be never-ending if we let it, he shoved his hands into the back of my panties once more and cupped my ass, the pads of his fingers digging into the skin even harder than he'd done earlier. As gently as he could, though, he urged my thighs wide, trailing the foil of the condom wrapper down the center of my backside. I shuddered at the thrill of something foreign there, not used to the intimacy of it all. Taking his time, he slid his other hand between us, cupping my sex with his palm, before kissing me—finally—on the lips.

"So wet for me…" A slide of his tongue, a shudder. Removing a hand from my ass, he tore the condom wrapper open with his teeth then whispered, "Your pussy drives me wild, My."

I groaned, my forehead on his, my arms trembling as they held me upright.

Using both hands, he slipped the condom over his cock then pulled my panties aside only so he could thrust his hardness inside of me.

"Sebastian," I moaned loudly, finally remembering his rule. Together like this, I was to call him by his real name.

My eyes rolled to the back of my head, a bead of sweat already sliding across my temple. Lips to my neck he nibbled again, dragging a moan out from my throat. And soon we were rolling, our bodies still connected, even as he hovered over me, even as his hips slapped with a frenzy against my own. I shuddered as he kissed me, played my body like he was fine-tuning a violin and was prepping me for the symphony between us. A stroke of his tongue here, a thrust of his hips there, followed by whispered *fucks* as well as *you're soaking me.* I was seconds from coming within only minutes, just like it was between us on the train. But he pulled out, taking his time before sliding back inside, hovering just on the edge of his own release, I was sure.

Hazy eyes searched my face as he rode my body. "You're so beautiful." Nuzzling his nose against my cheek, he whispered out the most untrue words I'd ever heard: "Don't deserve you."

I shut my eyes, shaking my head, but before I could tell him how it was the other way around, he kissed me again, harder this time. And I let him, lost in the euphoria of our bodies connected.

Using the tips of my fingers, I stroked his chest, his shoulders, his ribs, then, running my fingertip over that tattoo I knew was there beneath his arm.

Tenderness followed franticness as he began to love my body like no other man before him. With every gasp I released, he kissed me harder. With every arch of my back, he slowed his pace, tormenting me.

"God, I love this…" I groaned, loving how we fit so right together. Loving… him.

At the realization of my feelings, I wrapped my arms around his shoulders, unable to get close enough, barely able to breathe. Like he could feel my heart bursting, like maybe he felt that very same sensation, Sebastian hissed out a slow breath and started to drive deeper inside of me than before.

This wasn't like the train. This was slow, this was lovemaking, this was sex I could get used to, live for, for the rest of my life. Waking up like this, going to sleep like this…

The bed rocked beneath us, the headboard thumping against the wall…

I loved this man.

I loved him so much it hurt.

"Harder," I groaned. "More."

Our skin slapped together, the sweat on my temples dripping down my cheek now.

"Maya," he hissed, still soft, still slow.

Thud, thud, thud.

"Oh, God," I cried, legs shaking.

Slap, slap, slap.

And then I came so hard, so loudly, that the entire world could hear me.

As the tingles hit my belly, as his delicious cock rubbed me nearly into oblivion, I knew nothing mattered but this.

Him and me. Right here, right now.

Sebastian leaned up, grabbed the headboard, and finished on a low moan just seconds after me, his breathing ragged, hair hanging over his forehead, chest heaving like he'd just run a marathon instead of marking me as his own. It was stunning to watch. The most beautiful thing I'd ever seen. Sebastian's eyes were like beacons in the darkest of nights, and he'd just guided me home.

I sighed, content as I tugged him closer, letting him lay his head on my chest, over my shirt that I hadn't even bothered to take off. His cheek was on my breast, his breathing heavy.

Fingers in his hair, I stroked, never wanting this night to end.

CHAPTER TWENTY-THREE

I hated myself.

I shouldn't have given in and fucked her like I'd done.

Hell, I shouldn't have even come back here at all last night.

But I couldn't stay away if I tried.

No matter what feelings I had for her, though, I wouldn't let her in. Not anymore. Last night was the last time. For real. Because when this was all said and done, I promised myself I would take her home, no regrets. And I wouldn't go back on this promise, even though I was already trying to figure out a way to break that promise.

Maya deserved everything I couldn't give her here.

And I needed to let her go because of it.

I never managed to fall asleep. But at least Maya did. And when I couldn't take another second of her body against mine, I slid out of bed, dressed in only my jeans, and went to the kitchen. Now there I was, four in the morning, sitting with a cup of coffee at the kitchen table, trying to figure all this out. I didn't want to break her heart, but I didn't see any other way around it.

"Slade? What are you doing up?" a voice said from behind me. I turned, finding Maya's mom, June, coming up from the basement stairs.

"Got an early run today," I lied, then dipped my head toward the coffee pot. "Fresh pot if you want some."

"Hmm, don't mind if I do, thank you." She pulled it out and poured herself a cup, then sat at the table across from me.

"Why're you up?" I asked.

"Couldn't sleep." She shrugged, running a finger over the rim of her cup.

I half wondered if she knew her ex was currently conspiring against her and her daughter and all the RDs. I'd have to ask Flick in case she decided to tell Maya. I was still waiting on him to say something about it to her, but it'd only been a day. I'd give him until tomorrow before I broke the news myself.

An awkward tension filled the dark room. June pursed her lips and set her cup down, fingers still wrapped around the mug when she finally broke the silence. "Listen, I'm not going to beat around the bush here, Slade…"

I stiffened.

"My daughter is in love with you. And if you hurt her I *will* kill you."

Flinching, I rubbed a hand over the back of my neck, not real sure which part messed me up more. The love part, or the part where her mom threatened to end me.

"Do *you* love her?" She glared at me from over her cup. "Because if you don't, then you need to call this thing between the two of you off and let her go."

I folded my hands around my mug like she'd done, squeezing it. The answer was there, the truth on the tip of my tongue. I did love Maya, always had, but I would need to let her go. For both of our sakes. And if I didn't let her go, I'm guessing she'd let me go instead. It's who we were now. Two different people. Two different paths.

"Well?" She leaned forward, elbows on the table, waiting, eyes narrowed.

I shrugged, no real answer for her. Just like it'd been with Flick last night.

June shook her head. "Whatever is going on with you two was heightened by what she went through. To Maya, you're some sort of savior now. A hero. I dealt with similar issues when it came to her father, and all these years later, I hate myself for falling into what I did."

"There's a big fucking difference between me and Maya's dad." I curled my lip. "I'm *not* an asshole."

"No?" She batted her lashes at me. "You're not using her right now? Not taking what you can get just because it's there? "

"You ever think that maybe *she's* the one using *me*?" Just like she'd done all those years ago. Even knowing she'd fallen for me back then didn't change what had happened. She left. I broke. End of story.

"I've been through it, Slade Lattimore." She flashed her angry eyes at me. "And even if you think you love her, even if there *is* that pull in your chest, if you can't commit fully, then do her a favor and walk away before it's too late." Pushing back her chair, she stood and headed downstairs again, slamming the door in her wake.

I sighed, dropping my chin to my chest, *wishing* it was about an inability to commit. Because with Maya, that wouldn't be a problem, honestly. Hell, I'd make her my old lady in a heartbeat if I could. But she didn't want to be stuck here. She hated this place, these people. She wanted freedom. And I'd be the one to give it to her when I got back from Texas.

Even if it killed me.

A minute later, I looked to the left, movement catching my eye. Maya stood in the kitchen entryway, wearing one of my T-shirts and a pair of red yoga pants.

"Everything okay? I heard a door slam." She looked toward the basement. "And I thought I heard my mom too."

"You did." I looked to the table, ashamed. "She went back to bed."

"Oh. Well, if you can't sleep, I'll stay up with you." Maya limped over to me. Her bad knee was now covered with a brace June had found for her, making her steps a little easier.

"No. Go back to bed." I shut my eyes before she could see the regret in them, not wanting to do this here. "I'm gonna take off in a minute."

She frowned and stood between my knees, running her fingers through my hair. "This early?"

I nodded and grabbed her hips as I stood, then moved her to the side. "Got a run this morning." Avoiding her the best I could, I headed back to the bedroom.

It's better this way. She's safer, you're saner. Don't lead her on anymore. My inner voice knew shit my heart didn't, that was for sure.

"Where are you going?" Maya followed me down the hall, her movements slow but aggressive.

I stepped into the room. "Don't worry about it."

In my old dresser, I grabbed a new shirt from one of the drawers, not about to ask Maya to take the one she was wearing off.

"What kind of run is it?" She stood at the door behind me, still clueless. When I didn't answer, I heard her huff. "Sebastian. I'm talking to you. What kind of—"

"Slade," I hissed under my breath. "I'm Slade now, remember?"

She didn't say shit to that, but I heard the catch in her breath. God, did I hate being an asshole. But the seeds needed to be planted.

When I turned to leave, I nearly ran her down. She stood in front of me in the middle of the room, eyes narrowed and searching my face. "Did my mom say something to you?"

"No. She said nothing." *That I didn't already know.* "I just got places to go this morning, alright?" I stepped around her. "And I'm leaving Friday for a longer run, so you probably won't see me for a while."

"Oh," she said, and I didn't miss the disappointment in her voice. "How long will you be gone for that one?"

"I dunno, alright?" I ran a hand through my hair, frustrated with myself, with her.

Needing space, mostly so I didn't stop and kiss her gorgeous, pouty mouth, I moved around her and headed toward the door, then down the hall.

She growled, her feet thumping along the carpet as she kept up with me. I stopped to slide my feet into my boots, but that was a long enough time for her to catch up and stop behind me by the front door.

"Don't you *dare* do this, *Slade Lattimore.*"

I flinched, not meaning to. "Do what?"

Fight me, My. Fight me, Goddammit. Tell me to leave. Tell me to get outta your sight. That you can't stand the thought of me ever being close to you again.

Please. Please just fucking let me go.

But she did none of that. In fact, she did the opposite, walking around to my side with a fierceness in her voice that would make the strongest, bravest fools flinch.

"I know what the hell I felt last night." She poked at my shoulder with her finger. "Hell, Slade, I know what I've been feeling since you showed up at my apartment last Friday."

"You don't know a damn thing."

"Oh, I think I *do* know." She moved in front of me then, sliding between my chest and the front door.

I shook my head, but that didn't stop her from giving me hell once more.

"You feel things for me. A lot of things, in fact." She folded her arms. "Probably the exact same things I feel for you. But for some stupid reason, you're pushing me away, and I deserve to know why."

"I'm not gonna leave the club just to make you happy if that's what you think."

She jerked her head back and her lips pursed.

"This place is my home, those men my brothers." My hands shook with rage. Rage at myself for letting this happen, for not trying harder. But I was nothing more than a chicken who feared getting hurt when Maya inevitably left and went back to San Diego when the danger passed. When life for the Red Dragons got back to normal.

"Does this run today have to do with your prospect? The one who was killed? Do you worry that I'm gonna wind up like him because of you or something?"

I stiffened, her question making my head spin. "How'd you know about him?"

"My mom told me." She licked her lips and lifted her chin. "And in the ditch, back in Colorado, when you told me you felt like you kept fucking up. Being careless. I put two and two together…"

This was the exact out I needed. But I also didn't want to use my dead prospect as an excuse when this was all on me.

"I gotta go." I reached around her, grabbing the knob. But Maya wrapped her fingers around my wrist before I could twist it open.

"It wasn't your fault, you know." Her voice softened as she did that thing again. The one where she made up excuses for other people. For me. But I wouldn't call her out on it. Not this time.

"It was meant to be me, you know." I shrugged, wishing I felt as nonchalant as I sounded. "I was the fucking guy who should've been in that ditch with the bullets in my head. Carlos had been on *my* bike, his killer wanted *me* dead." But I'd been stupid and distracted and selfish and lazy and… careless. So. Fucking. Careless for letting him go alone.

"But it *wasn't* you." She rubbed her hand up and down my forearm.

I shook my head, selfishly and secretly glad it wasn't. Admitting that would make me a bad brother. An even worse RD. A real shitty man in general. Another reason I didn't really deserve to be the guy Maya wanted. I could protect *and* do runs. But I couldn't be her hero as well.

"I gotta go," I told her, looking everywhere but her face. "Don't go anywhere outside the compound without telling me or Hawk or Flick, you hear me?"

She shook her head, tears in her eyes, lips parted… her response lost in her mind.

Then I did what I'd become accustomed to. What I'd gotten real good at. I let it go. I let *her* go… Then I walked the fuck away.

CHAPTER TWENTY-FOUR

Maya

Instead of Slade taking me to my doctor's appointment that afternoon like he'd promised, it wound up being Summer who'd shown up at my uncle's front door instead, with two hot lattes in hand and a bright smile on her face that said, *Let's be besties*. I'd never felt more awkward in my life. But instead of insisting on taking an Uber like I'd wanted to, I got inside her fancy SUV and let her talk my ear off all the way into town. At least I got some decent coffee out of the deal. And Summer? Well, she wasn't terrible company. I was just in a rotten mood.

I wasn't sure if Summer noticed or not, but there'd been two bikers trailing us all afternoon. Watchdogs, I assumed, who'd sat in the parking lot of the doctor's office while we were inside. Maybe she did know and didn't care. Or maybe she was just that oblivious. I wondered what that might be like, to be so carefree. Not having to worry constantly, not having to fear the worst of everything and everyone, most of all. I knew she'd gone through her own version of hell last summer, but that was just a sliver of what could happen.

"I'm gonna cook tacos for Emily and me tonight," Summer said from the driver's seat on our way back to the compound. Emily was Hawk's sister and Summer's best friend. "You want to come over? Have a girls' night with us?"

I wanted to say no and just go back to Flick's place. But after my appointment, the results of my scan, I was in a piss-poor mood and wasn't in the frame of mind to be alone. Mom worked second shift, so she'd be late anyway.

Plus, the idea of hanging out in the space where my heart had been blown to smithereens this morning wasn't appealing in the least.

"Sure." I smiled, rubbing a hand over my knee, still a little shocked at what would be happening in a week. Major surgery for a torn ACL, followed by weeks upon weeks of therapy. I'd be housebound soon enough, so I might as well let myself live a little.

"Awesome." Summer smiled so wide, so happily, that I had to look away. Her peppiness was a lot to take in, and that was putting it nicely. I still wondered how it worked between her and Hawk, but to each their own, I supposed.

"We can make margaritas and watch rom-coms while the boys are out doing their club thing tonight."

"Club thing?" I frowned.

"Slade didn't tell you?"

"Uh, no." I laughed, though nothing about this was funny. At this point, I was lucky if Slade and I would even be talking come tomorrow.

"Oh, well, apparently they're celebrating some new patch-ins. A set of brothers who joined the club a while ago." She frowned. "Niyol said they haven't had a party yet, what with everything going on with his father and mom, and the prospect dying too." She frowned at that. Hearing her say stuff like *brothers* and *patch-ins* was… weird. Hearing her call Hawk, Niyol, was even weirder.

"You don't wanna go?" I asked.

She shook her head. "I don't do the club parties much. They're…"

"Disgusting? Chauvinistic?"

Her lips pulled into a side grin. "Ha. Yeah. That's a good way to put it."

My throat burned when I swallowed and stared out the window. The thought of Slade being at the club tonight made my skin itch. Did he have a favorite hang-about or groupie that he took too? A woman he slept with on a regular basis before I came along? As gorgeous as he was, there was no doubt in my mind that he had flocks of them.

That's nothing a couple of groupies won't fix when I get home... Slade's words on the train punched through my head like a nail gun. Still, I refused to think that he could be so cruel as to run and sleep with someone else when the two of us had just been intimate the night before—though I had no idea where we stood.

Summer continued to rattle on about something having to do with Flick, their spare bedroom, and a new couch she'd just bought for their basement.

"Oh! And I'll have Niyol run to the store and get us some stuff for ice-cream sundaes too, how does that sound?"

That actually sounded hideous. But it was better than being alone. I would much rather do some tattooing or drawing, but whatever. "Sounds good."

Fifteen minutes later, we pulled through the gates of the Red Dragon compound but didn't head to the actual club. We did pass by it, though, and I couldn't help but look for Slade's truck in the throng of bikes in the gravel parking lot. Now that his Harley was broken, he told me he'd taken to driving his dad's junker truck while Archer built him a new one.

"Oh, good, Niyol's still here." Summer nearly squealed as we approached a house, her eyes all but turning into hearts as she stared at their...

I blinked, taking in the place before me. Wow. It looked like perfection in an imperfect world: their home. Something suburbanized that made my chest ache with jealousy. I wasn't expecting their house to look like this, like it was real, and not a figment of someone's imagination.

Summer pointed at a smaller building to the left, referring to it as a set of in-law quarters. "That's where Emily lives, by the way. When she and her fiancé, Sam, broke up in the fall, I insisted she move closer. She did, which surprised me." Her shoulders drooped. "She hates the club life."

I could relate.

As I got out, my new prescription in hand as well as a list of exercises to do for my knee leading up to the surgery, Hawk came barreling toward us from their front door, a wide smile on his face as he all but ran to Summer.

"Hey, princess," he said with a gravelly growl. His arms went right around her waist and he swung her in circles.

I rolled my eyes, jealousy stabbing me in the ribs. I was happy for them, of course, but at the same time this was exactly what I wanted too.

But now...

"Hey, Maya," Hawk said, pulling back, grabbing Summer's hand. She whispered something into his ear, nodding her head back toward me before walking—no, *skipping*—over to Emily's place.

My oldest friend approached me then, a smaller smile on his mouth than he'd had for his girlfriend. I didn't share his happiness though, not when all I thought about was the fact that he'd spilled to the world that we'd slept together way back when.

"What's up?" He stuck his hands into his pockets, encouraging me to take his elbow. He knew I needed help inside, but he didn't call me out on it. I respected him for that, even if I was pissed at him.

"Nice place you have here," I said, meaning it.

Hawk held the door open for us, more prideful than I'd ever seen him. "Thanks. The guys did a damn good job, huh?"

I nodded, wondering if Slade had helped at all with the construction. Then I cursed myself for going there. Again.

It was odd to me that Hawk wanted to build a place on the compound itself. Even odder that my uncle had let him. But with nothing being secure when it came to Pops, I couldn't blame him. Not only were he and Summer constantly protected, they were both free to have their own space not constantly occupied by the club members.

There were bits of my friend scattered around the area from what I could see. Dark wood floors, black countertops in the kitchen. Cream-colored walls throughout, and black leather furniture. But it was lit up with Summer too. Yellow accents, flowers here and there. And pictures of Hawk and her on his bike, kissing at a park of some sort. It was the perfect blend of badass and sweet.

Jealousy still ate away at me for the entire tour. This was way better than the tiny dorm room on the Forsaken compound where Mom and I used to stay. Even as far back as ten years old, I remembered my mom begging me to keep quiet on the nights we couldn't make it home to our crappy apartment up the road. She'd curl up on a couch and sleep, letting me take the twin bed. Then at one or two in the morning, I'd hear my father walk heavy-footed into the room and force my mom onto her stomach on the couch so he could do things to her that no ten-year-old should have to witness.

I shuddered at the turn of my thoughts, then sat on the couch.

"You okay?" Hawk questioned, sitting down next to me.

I nodded, wishing I didn't have to lie. "Yep. Just tired." Then I scowled at him, remembering that I *did* have a bone to pick with the guy. "Hey. Why'd you tell everyone we slept together the night before I left for California?"

Hawk frowned at me, his expression saying, *Duh.* "Because we did."

I rolled my eyes and shoved him. "And what, you think it's cool to brag on the people you bag or something?"

"Jesus, Maya. Give me a little credit. I told Archer. That's it."

"Slade found out." I folded my arms and lifted my chin.

"Ahh, I see." Hawk leaned forward onto his knees, smirking as he eyed the front door.

"What's that supposed to mean?"

"Always wondered why he'd turned into an ass on me. Now I know."

"And why's that?"

"He loved you." He shrugged. "Guessing he still does and probably always will."

"Oh," I said, tears forming in my eyes.

Silence filled the room, an awkwardness between us that hadn't been there last summer. Then finally, like sticking salt into an open wound, he told me the last thing I ever expected to hear. "I asked Summer to marry me."

My eyes went wide. "Really? When?"

A smile lit up his entire face. "The other night, when you got home and I got back from a run."

I squeezed his shoulder. "I'm happy for you. So much."

He rubbed the back of his neck. "You think it's a dumb idea?"

I dropped my hand, not exactly the ideal person for this kind of conversation right now. Still, it's obvious he needed reassurance. "You love her, don't you?"

Though love wasn't always enough…

"Like nothing else." He lifted his chin, no hesitation in his eyes, or his words.

My throat burned when I swallowed, wishing things were different between Slade and I once more. But I put on a brave face, because that's what friends did for friends, and said, "Then that's the only thing you need to know, I'd say."

Hawk waited a beat, looking out the front window. Summer and Emily were walking through the yard, heads bowed as they laughed about something.

Neither of us spoke after that, but I knew our thoughts were running on the same wavelength: about love and living your best life, even if wasn't a traditional one. For years I'd tried to find myself as a woman outside of a motorcycle club, living in California, no longer surrounded by any sort of bikers. Yet there I was, full circle once more.

Nothing felt right. And everything just… *hurt*.

The front door opened and the women's laughter echoed throughout the home—a home that was real and happy. In a way, I wished Summer and Emily could stay away a little longer, but not because I didn't like them. This thing with Slade had been eating me up inside all day, and Hawk was the first—and possibly only—person who might understand what could be going through his cousin's head.

But like I figured he would, Hawk stood, disregarding me as his world shone bright for his fiancée. I rolled my eyes but didn't comment, knowing it would be completely pointless. A smitten Red Dragon was the most impressive Red Dragon there was.

CHAPTER TWENTY-FIVE

Slade

Around one in the morning, I finally made it back to the compound. I'd been driving in my old man's truck pretty much all day, wishing that I had my bike. I missed the rush of the air against my face, the adrenaline, the speed, the bumps under my tires too. Obviously, that wasn't happening until Archer could finish the rebuild on a Harley for me.

I shook my head at the thought, pulling through the gates. A prospect nodded me in, his face barely visible in the dark. From what I could see, he looked more like a soldier than a biker, eyes wide and alert and a hand on the gun in his belt.

I'd avoided my brothers at the club all day, the party going down at the clubhouse most of all. But there was no avoiding it anymore. Not if I wanted to actually sleep tonight. Everyone was celebrating the patch-in of Mute and Talker. Pre-California, that would've been a damn good time. But now it was the last place I wanted to be.

The alternative was worse though, but after a text from Flick came through just two minutes ago, the alternative was now a necessary order. I was to stop by his place before heading to the club, something about June not staying there tonight, and Flick worrying about leaving Maya home alone… I didn't like the thought of it either, but I'd begged him to get one of the other brothers to do it instead, not ready to admit that I'd put space between her and I. Seemed everyone else was either already fucked-up, or preoccupied, because he'd told me I was the only one available.

What-the-hell-ever. It's not like she'd be awake.

At least… I hoped she wasn't awake.

I pulled into his drive a couple minutes later, parking, but not getting out. The thought of seeing her in bed, asleep without me, was bad enough. I couldn't imagine what might happen if I walked in and found her awake, or worse yet, having one of her nightmares. But I needed to be strong, no matter what. I'd do my check-in, then I'd make my way to the club, get shitfaced, and pass out in my dorm.

The TV screen flickered when I walked into Flick's place, but nobody was around, which I thought was weird as shit. I shut it off, frowning as I made my way to my old room. Maya's room.

Holding my breath, I opened the door, the hinges barely squeaking, and stepped inside. But one look at the empty mattress and my entire world froze. Maya was gone.

I blinked, took a slow step back, my elbow slamming against the doorframe.

Déjà vu hit me hard, forcing my hands into my hair. I spun around in the middle of the hallway, thinking I was hallucinating, struggling to even breathe.

"Maya?" I yelled, hustling to the bathroom, gaze shooting left, right, left, right. The light was on, but she wasn't in there. I checked the basement, the kitchen, the back yard, but she was in none of those places. She wasn't here.

"Mayaaaa?" I yelled louder, still getting no response, knowing it was pointless, but not wanting to feel more helpless than I already did.

Racing out the front door as if my boots were on fire, I ran toward my truck, dizzy with worry, madness, fear, and guilt. If she left, or worse, if something had happened to her…

"Fuck!" I kicked a tire, then scrubbed both hands over my face, going into flight mode. Two seconds later, I opened the truck door and yanked out my phone. Two seconds after that, I had it to my ear.

"What?" Flick growled on the other end, a little breathless.

"Maya's gone." I squeezed my eyes shut, my chest burning as I crouched to the ground. There, I waited for my orders, needing to know what to do next.

Order and chaos.

Chaos and order.

My life revolved around both those things. But dealing with them at the same time, when it came to Maya. The woman I loved. The woman I'd pushed away. I couldn't.

"Fuck, fuck, fuck," I repeated, running a hand through my hair before getting to my feet again, only to kick the side of the truck this time.

Flick said something to someone on the other end, a murmur. A few seconds later, I heard a door slam, footsteps, then another door, screeching this time. "What's your problem, boy?" he asked. I heard his lighter kick on, the spark of his cigarette being lit.

How the hell could he be so calm right now?

"Maya's gone, damnit," I roared. "She's not here. She's fucking gone, Flick."

He sighed. "Oh, yeah, sorry about that. Apparently Maya's staying at Hawk's tonight with Summer."

I shut my eyes, knees going weak in relief, even as my heart still hammered against my chest. "Why the fuck didn't you call and tell me this then, huh?"

Flick laughed, but the sound was bitter. Annoyed even. "Christ, boy. I was getting head when I found out. Last thing I wanted was to stop to call you."

With another loud, *fuck*, I hung up on him and tossed my phone back in the cab of the truck before jumping inside. Gravel kicked up under my tires as I drove the lone road leading to the clubhouse.

In the parking lot, I slammed my foot on the brake and shut off the engine, pounding the wheel not once, but twice, as I struggled to catch my breath even still.

The music grew louder, even from inside the cab, the sound mixing with my jumbled thoughts. My messy mind. It was obvious the party was still going strong. And this really was the last place I wanted to be right now. But going to Maya at Hawk's place? Explaining that I've been a fucking dumbass because I'd been too chicken shit to lose her? That wasn't an option. Not at this time of night.

Tomorrow, though. I'd do it then. And this time, I would not go back on my word. I would be who she needed, for however long she wanted me to. And even if it did kill me in the end, at least I can say I was living my best life for a little while. A life I'd always wanted.

Decision made, I jumped out and pocketed my keys, trying like hell to tame the small smile on my mouth. God, I was an idiot. The biggest kind there was. And even if I was too late, come tomorrow, I knew this was a decision that I could at least live with this time.

"You're just in time."

I scowled at the sound of Archer's voice when I approached the steps leading to the door. He was stumbling down ahead of me, a girl on both arms.

"What're you talking about?" I sighed, not in the mood for girly drama tonight.

"Your woman's inside. Thinking Chop has got his eyes set on her."

My gut hardened at that. Every nerve ending inside of me seemed to burn hot at his words. Without my permission, a low growl sounded in my throat, proof I was more out of control than I thought.

Ignoring anything else my best friend had to say, I took off, chasing each step like they were leading me up to my own personal hell. Flinging open the front door of the club, I looked left, then right, and… there she was.

I couldn't breathe when I saw her. For fuck's sake, I could barely even blink.

She sat at a table in front of the bar, smiling, laughing, and… sitting next to Chop.

My palms began to sweat, my jaw ached from clenching my teeth so hard. His arm was draped around the back of her chair, fingers casually pressed to her shoulder. If I stopped to really look, I'd know there was nothing about it that looked bad. But with my nerves already frayed, and Archer's drunken babbles outside, I was falling down a canyon, no branch or rope in sight to catch me.

Another unintentional growl slipped up my throat, anger and greed fighting for control. With no thought for what I was about to do, no real reason other than jealousy and a dire need to claim her, I hustled to their table, stopping directly behind Chop, fists balled, eyes narrowed. A vision of both my hands wrapped around his neck from behind coming to the forefront of my mind.

Get it together, you son of a bitch. She's not yours.

But she would be.

Hell, she'd *always* been mine, hadn't she? And it was time that everyone knew it now.

Hawk was the first to notice me, the smug-looking bastard was all grins. I was so filled with fire I'd barely noticed he was there until he waved. Summer was on his lap. Empty beer bottles littered the table, and in front of Maya sat glasses of clear liquid, all filled with ice.

"Hey," I barked, not real sure what else to say. I'd lose my shit if I wasn't careful here.

Control. Stay. In. Control.

At the sound of my voice, Maya turned slowly in her chair. But instead of a drunken haze in her eyes, I saw… nothing. An empty stare, red-rimmed eyes that looked like the depths of the darkest pits, not the stars in the night sky. She looked like hell. Beautiful, still, but… broken.

And it was all my fault, no doubt.

For a second, I just closed my eyes, pushing through the guilt, yanking out the RD in me. He's the man I needed for what I was about to do here.

But then I heard her voice, even over the loud music, and I opened my eyes, finding her gaze locked with mine. "Hawk? Can you take me home, please? I suddenly don't feel so good."

My body began to shake. As did my hands, my knees, my entire world…

No, I mouthed.

"Well, seeing as how I'm not your old lady, *Slade*, you don't get to tell me what to do." Maya shook her head, snark in her words as she lifted the glass in her hands and took a drink.

"You don't wanna be nobody's old lady. You hate this club, and you hate the people in it, remember?" I goaded—definitely not the way to get on her good side. But I was pissed. Not at her, but at myself. This all could've been avoided if I hadn't been such an absolute dick.

Maya's upper lip curled. "Screw you, and the God damn horse you rode in on." Then she jumped to her feet, stumbling a little. I lurched forward, intending to catch her and pull her close to me. But motherfucking Chop was there, doing it for me.

"I'll get her home," he slurred, drunk off his ass.

"Absolutely not." I inhaled a shaky breath through my nose, taking another step closer. Maya was the only thing I could see right then. The only thing that mattered. "You keep your damn distance, Chop. She doesn't belong to you."

Something in my words must've gotten through to the guy because he put his hands up then sat back in his chair, muttering, *sorry man,* under his breath.

Maya lifted her chin, lowering her voice for only me to hear. "I don't belong to *anyone.*"

"That's a lie." Then, without giving her warning, I scooped her up and pulled her to my chest, fire burning like lava inside me.

"What are you doing?" she yipped.

Our eyes stayed locked, battling with need and want and hate and years of things we couldn't seem to connect the dots with. Not without hurting something or someone—each other—in the process.

It all ended now. Every single torment. Every single heartbreak. This was it. I was done fighting.

"Slade, stop this. You're insane," she hissed as I walked her around Chop, Hawk, and other tables filled with prospects and elders and everyone in between.

Ignoring her question and demand, I asked one of my own, inhaling her lemony scent as I pressed my lips to her ear. "You really wanna be an old lady, My?"

"Put me down, Slade. I swear to God, I'll—"

"So stubborn." I *tsked,* already knowing how wrong this was. Knowing I had no right to do what I was about to do without her permission. But I was captivated by the rage in my mind, the fear of not knowing where she was tonight. Then seeing her with Chop did my ass in, total nail-in-the-coffin-type shit.

"You're being an asshole." She shook her head, and when I looked down, the first thing I saw were her tits.

No bra, nipples pressed hard against her pink dress. A pink *lacy* dress, for fuck's sake. In a biker club. My nostrils flared, arms tightening around her body. This woman would be the death of me.

I carried her to the bar and set her on top of it, turning her to face me, spreading her legs to stand between them. There, I wrapped my arms around her waist, lips to her ear again as I whispered once more, "I went to Flick's. You weren't there." I took a deep breath. "So excuse my ass if I'm a little worked up right now."

She froze, other than the rising and falling of her heaving chest. "Wh-what are you talking about? Slade, I didn't leave. I told Flick where I was and—"

"Doesn't matter. Not anymore."

"But—"

"I *thought* you left again, damn it. Or that something happened to you," I repeated my fears, shutting my eyes as I continued. "But instead, you're here and I…" My words shook as my nerves snuck in. I shut them down before it was too late, knowing vulnerability wasn't welcomed in the club.

"I didn't leave." Fingers curled through the end of my hair, pulling. "I'm here."

"But you did once before," I hissed, pulling back, eyes locked with hers.

The room had gone dead silent. Everyone watched on, but nobody commented. I was thankful for that, but I also knew I'd catch shit down the road for being such a pussy.

If this is what fate had in mind when it came to us all these years later, then he was a seriously fickle bitch.

I wasn't this man. Swore I'd never be the person who'd do what I was about to do. But I didn't know what other choice I had that wouldn't make me crazy. I wanted Maya safe.

I tucked some hair behind her ear then let my fingers graze across her chin as I finished. "We're gonna do this the only way I know how."

Taking a step back, I pulled her dress down over her knees then whistled with two fingers.

"Listen up, everyone!" I yelled, gaze on hers even as I spoke to the brothers in the room. "Got some business to attend to here."

"Slade, what are you doing?" she asked again, her face going pale.

On a barstool directly in front of her, I sat down, my knees too damn weak to keep me upright.

Her beauty did that to a man.

"I'm just giving you what you want," I told her.

She frowned, her face pained, yet it was also filled with the kind of hope I didn't deserve, not with what I was about to do.

"Maya Davenport," I yelled, loud enough for everyone to hear, but I still never took my eyes off her face.

She blinked, her breath coming out even faster while her hands tightened on the end of her dress. If she knew what was happening, she never once tried to stop me.

"Right here, in front of everyone…" I took a breath, waiting for silence to come back as murmurs filled the space. Hawk called my name, I think, maybe even Chop, but I couldn't stop staring at the woman who'd ruined me for all other women, not even if I tried.

"I claim you as my old lady."

She stiffened, eyes widening in horror. But now that my mind was made up, it was too late for her to stop me.

"That means she's officially one of us now. An RD." My smirk was painful, the words making my throat nearly raw. A few guys whistled, there were even some slow claps, but nothing about the moment made me feel like it should have. "An RD old lady, I should say."

Maya dipped her chin, shoulders slumping in what I knew was disappointment.

"I hate you," she hissed beneath her breath when I picked her up off the bar and held her against my chest after the hollers in the club calmed.

Swallowing hard, the emotions making it hard to speak, I walked us toward the front door of the club instead of my dorm, down the steps, and toward my truck in the gravel lot.

When I stood next to the passenger door, staring at her wet cheeks, I managed a few words. The only ones that counted right then.

"I hate me too."

The two-minute ride back to Flick's was quiet. I didn't try to get rid of the tension, because I didn't regret what I'd done. Why? Because being an old lady meant a lot of things. But right now, in this moment, only two of those details mattered to me. And since Maya had grown up in a club world, that meant she likely knew exactly what those two details were.

Number one? No man could touch her besides me.

And two? She'd always have a bodyguard when I wasn't there. Which meant her privacy was gone.

My phone buzzed in my pocket, and I yanked it out, thankful for the distraction. I put it to my ear without bothering to look at the screen. "Yeah."

"Heard I missed out on all the fun."

I scowled at the sound of Flick's voice, knowing everything would've been different had he just told me she was at Hawk's. But at the same time, I didn't regret what happened. How the fuck could I when it made Maya mine, officially?

I set one hand on the wheel, holding my phone with the other. "You pissed?"

I quickly glanced at Maya. She was looking out the window, probably listening to everything I said.

"Nah. I knew it was coming. Just didn't expect you to do it the old-fashioned way." He chuckled. "She'll give you shit about it for the rest of your lives, you know."

"Yeah. I know." Even though I still wasn't planning on getting her for the rest of my life, but he didn't know that.

"I'll swing by in the morning," Flick told me. "Enjoy your night, boy."

Before I could say something back, he ended the call.

I swallowed hard and set the phone on the console as I pulled into Flick's drive. It was dark in the cab, but not enough that I couldn't see the pull of her eyebrows, the purse of her lips, the heat of her angry glare as she stared straight ahead.

"Do you plan on sitting there and staring at me all night?" she asked, her voice all but dead. When I couldn't get an answer out, she huffed and reached for the door handle, opening it. "I'm going to bed."

Even after she got out of the truck and headed inside, I wished like hell she'd turn around and at least yell at me. But she wouldn't give me the satisfaction.

I stepped out a few minutes later and walked into the house, hearing the door to her room—my room—slam shut. My gut tightened while I waited in the kitchen for her to get ready for bed. Five minutes, then I'd go to her. Apologize. Tell her I'd never hold her to it, that I was just jealous and stupid and… worried. Always worried. That something would happen to her. That she'd run again. Then I'd tell her the truth. That yeah, I wanted her, for as long as she'd have me.

After a while, I knocked a couple times on the bedroom door, but there was no answer. I twisted the knob, shoulders going stiff when I couldn't get it to turn. She'd locked me out.

CHAPTER TWENTY-SIX

Maya

Sometime after the sun rose the next morning, I stumbled into my uncle's kitchen. I'd tossed and turned all night, figuring out what to do, trying to clear my mind.

Hence why I now stood behind a counter, doing the one thing I sucked terribly at: cooking.

My skillsets were best with food when I picked up the phone for takeout, ordered off a menu, or drove through a drive-thru. But I needed something to keep me busy today, both my hands *and* my mind. I gathered pans and utensils, intending to make breakfast, though nobody was there to eat it. After locking Slade out last night, I hadn't heard from him.

As I collected ingredients and began, I got lost in my head, grew numb too—which was exactly my plan. It seemed there was something quite therapeutic about the idea of throwing random ingredients into a bowl and stirring them up. You didn't always succeed, but the ride to getting there, creating the final product, gave me reason to believe that even the crappiest of chefs could find their perfect recipe.

Eggs, sugar, milk, cinnamon. I mixed them in a bowl and stirred and stirred until I could barely see straight. I wasn't even hungry, but I cooked like it was my one and only task left in life. Hell, at this point, it kind of felt like it was.

Cheesy eggs, hash browns, French toast. It was a meal fit for an army. Had I been a little less stabby, I was pretty sure I would've called Hawk or Summer, maybe even Emily, and asked them to come over and eat with me. We'd sit around the table, eating and smiling and laughing and being normal. A family of friends. New and old.

But dreams were dreams for a reason, I supposed. And it was about time to start concentrating on new ones that stemmed beyond Slade. He'd gone and done the one single thing I despised the most and made me his old lady—made me into my mother.

Sometime later, I heard footsteps, the front door opening, followed by voices. Men. My uncle's voice was the first I recognized. Two days of me being back in town and he'd yet to even come see me. I should've been more disappointed than I was.

"Well, look at you, all domesticated and shit," Flick said from the kitchen door.

I didn't bother to turn and face him, too engrossed in digging the bread out of my French toast goop.

"Uncle. It's been a while." The bitterness definitely lit my words on fire, but that didn't stop him from coming closer, standing beside me. The man wasn't affected by much of anything it seemed.

"Yeah. Sorry I haven't come to see ya, kid. Been busy."

I shrugged, pulling out plates and silverware. I wasn't a kid, but that's what he called anyone younger than him.

"Hungry?" I asked.

He cleared his throat. "Nah. The boys might be though."

I turned to look at him, ready to say aloud what I thought about his *boys*, but his pale face distracted me. As did the hand on his chest, rubbing over his heart. I frowned.

"Listen, Maya. I'm sorry about the shit you went through."

More concerned about his current state than his half-assed apology, I set aside the plates and focused my attention on him.

He winced but kept going. "And there's somethin' I gotta tell you. It's about your old…"

Before he could get the words out, my uncle dropped to his knees, hissing in pain.

"Flick!" I shouted, my eyes going wide. Hands shaking, I attempted to slide to the floor beside him, falling on my butt in the process. Pain radiated up my back, the side of my bad knee too, but I ignored it, apprehension only for my uncle. "What is it? What's wrong?"

"Fuck, this shit hurts," he groaned. "Need to lie down. Get my boys in here."

Slowly, I rolled him onto his back, settling his head onto my lap. He shut his eyes, knees pulled up to his gut, wincing, groaning...

"Help!" I shouted. "Someone, help!"

"The hell?" I heard Archer say from above me first. The sound of his accented voice brought relieved tears to my eyes. He dropped down beside us, searching my uncle's face. "Flick, you alright?"

"Just got... pains," my uncle managed, then cursed loudly right after.

I rubbed his head and said, "Not pains. I think you're having a damn heart attack."

"Jesus," Archer hissed.

"What's going on?" Hawk asked next, rushing as he came into the kitchen.

"Call 911," I ordered.

"I'll call the doc who treats us." Hawk looked to Archer, who nodded, both of them ignoring me.

"No," I argued. "He needs to go to the hospital."

Ignoring me still, Hawk left the room while Archer laughed. "You dying on us, old man?"

"Maybe." My uncle coughed, hissing again through his teeth. "Good thing I got some ass last night, yeah?"

I blinked, disgusted and confused. How could they be so calm about this?

Footsteps sounded in the kitchen. I knew, without looking, who it was. Slade crouched down next to me, smelling like soap, wet hair dripping onto my forearm. His feet were bare, and he wore no shirt. I stiffened at the sight of him. Had he stayed here last night after all?

"What happened?" Unlike Archer and Hawk, he asked me the question, not my uncle.

"I think he's having a heart attack." My bottom lip trembled. My hands too. Every time I tried to breathe, my chest started to squeeze.

"Maya, hey." Arms wrapped around me, pulling me back as Archer and Hawk picked my uncle up off my lap and proceeded to carry him from the room. "Come here."

I shook my head but still found myself on Slade's lap despite my protest.

"Doc's coming," Hawk said, peering around the corner a minute later, looking down at Slade, not me. "Gonna get him to the clubhouse. Meet you there."

"No!" I hissed, turning to Slade. "He needs to go to the hospital."

"Our doc will take care of him at the club," Slade insisted. "I promise it's gonna be okay." Then he proceeded to rub both hands up and down my goosebump-covered arms, an obvious attempt to soothe me.

But I didn't want to be soothed. I needed space, and I needed to go with Flick, and I needed to call… "Mom." I blinked, a lightbulb flashing on in my head. "I need to call her."

"Let's wait till the doc gets to the club." Slade tucked a lock of hair behind my ear. "Don't want to worry her."

I pushed his hand away. "No. I need to call her now."

I attempted to stand but failed, nearly slipping on the tile, this time bumping my good knee against an open cupboard.

"Let me help you before you screw the other knee up." Slade was on his feet in no time, arms wrapped around my waist.

"Stop. I'll do it on my own." Pushing through the pain, I grabbed the counter and hauled myself away from him, standing upright at the same time. Then without looking back, I took off from the room.

"Hawk will call her, alright?" Slade caught up with me from behind, a hand on my elbow. "Then I'll take you to her later. I promise."

He just didn't get it, did he? I shook my head then pushed out of his hold when he jumped in front of me.

"For the love of freaking God, Slade. *I* will call her because she is *my* mom and that is *her* brother, not your blood, but *mine*."

He winced, jerking back as though I'd struck him. In turn, guilt hit me square in the chest, but I pushed it away, remembering how he'd hurt me just as badly over the last few days. An eye for an eye wasn't how I normally did things, but in this case, I'd live with it.

CHAPTER TWENTY-SEVEN

Slade

"You gotta be the one to tell her," Flick growled at me two hours later from a hospital bed in one of the dorms at the clubhouse.

Hawk was in a chair, eyes on the floor, while Archer stood at the window, looking outside.

It was a necessary setup for an MC to have an in-house doc and a room for sick brothers. Why? Because not all wounds could be seen by the authorities. In cases like Flick's, it was convenient, and a hell of a lot cheaper to do things this way. Especially since nothing was really even wrong with the guy.

"Tell who what?" I asked, eyes on the monitor as Flick's heartbeat continued to hold steady. He hadn't had a heart attack, but a panic attack instead. Doc had said he was under too much stress, that he needed a vacation. Hawk had laughed. Archer and I had shaken our heads. And Flick? Well, let's just say he wasn't amused.

"Maya, you idiot," he barked at me like I was the enemy. It was the first time I'd heard him snap in a long while.

My spine grew rigid, the air in the room thick. "That was on you."

"I know, but…" He winced. "She'll take it better if you tell her."

"You asshole," I snarled.

Ignoring me, he continued. "Satan has been in touch with my sister."

I stiffened. "Maya's old man? *That* Satan?"

He nodded. "The one and only."

"When?"

Flick coughed and shut his eyes. "Yesterday."

"What'd he say?"

"That he wanted to talk." He shrugged. "Other than that, I don't know."

I set my hands on the foot of the bed then bowed my head to try and breathe. This wasn't good.

"My dumb-ass sister," Flick kept going. "She didn't bother telling me about any of this until this morning, you believe that shit?" He shook his head. "Second I heard, I sent Talker her way. Swear to you that woman's got a damn death wish."

Hawk sat up straight in his seat, the natural leader in him coming out. "Want me to gather extra patrols? See if he's close?"

Flick nodded.

That was my job. But since I was leaving…

Shit. The Texas trip.

"We should call the trip off." I looked at Archer.

He nodded, adding, "Least for a while."

"Not happening. My contact down there ain't one for rescheduling. You two don't go, he won't be so gracious the next time I ask for help." He dropped his head back against the wall. "You'll both just stay a couple nights instead of a week. Guy said there was a rumor something was going down tomorrow afternoon so you'll get action the second you arrive."

I didn't like the idea of going at all, but opportunities couldn't be missed. Flick was right.

Everyone stayed quiet for a second, all our brains running through scenarios. Next steps and final ones.

Hawk knifed a hand through his hair. "I'm gonna head out. Go get Summer from work. She's got a half day."

The three of us nodded, not blaming the guy. Knowing Maya's old man could be out there—close and working with Pops at that—put us all on edge even more.

Once he was gone, Archer wasn't far behind, promising to stop back later, check in before we left for Texas, then telling me he'd swing by in the morning and pick me up.

I was ready to leave too, needing to go to Maya before her mom got home so I could tell her what Flick apparently couldn't. Still, I wanted to talk to my pres about something else for a minute. It was stupid, really, but I was kinda desperate right now, especially after last night.

After the door clicked shut behind Arch, I sat on the chair Hawk had been in. "I fucked up, Flick."

He laughed. "Figured when I saw Maya cooking this morning. What'd you do?"

"Besides claiming her as my old lady?" The list was endless. "Everything really."

"What do you want me to say about it, huh? I deal with bikers, not chicks."

"She's your niece. Can't you, I dunno, put in a good word for me?" Even to my own ears, that sounded stupid.

"We're blood, sure." He tugged at his beard. "That don't mean nothing if I don't actually know her."

I got to my feet, embarrassed I'd even asked, and headed toward the door.

"Hey, boy?" Flick called to my back just before I left the room. "Yeah?"

"Just… don't do anything I'd do, alright? I'm a shitty man when it comes to women. That's my answer for ya."

I patted the doorframe just once, then nodded. "I'd say that's the best damn advice you've ever given me, old man."

Maya was in the backyard of Flick's place, sitting on an old tree swing I didn't even know existed. Her good leg was rocking her body back and forth, and I couldn't help but stand there and watch. All that long hair swung in the cold breeze behind her, making it look like she was wearing a superhero cape. It was below zero, but surprisingly she didn't seem to be freezing her ass off.

"Hey," I told her back, my boots crunching over the icy snow as I got closer. Leaning in, I put my hands on the swing rope, holding her in place, but feeling far away at the same time. "You're not cold?"

She shook her head then started pushing back and forth again. I let go of the rope and let her—it obviously soothed her.

My heart slammed in my chest when I realized she was wearing my leather jacket. If this were any other time, I'd have called her out on it. Told her how damn happy it made me seeing it on her body. But there were issues that needed dealing with while Flick recovered. And with me leaving tomorrow, I figured giving Maya some space to think about what had gone down last night, that she'd maybe come around to the idea by the time I got back.

"What do you want, Slade?" she asked, not even looking at me.

"To tell you why I'm leaving tomorrow."

"Club stuff, I get it. You told me already."

I sighed and pinched the bridge of my nose. "Maya, I—"

"Don't, please." Using the rope, she pulled herself to her feet, facing me, finally looking me in the eye. "Like I told you this morning, I'm done with the excuses, and the back and forth. You go do your thing, I'll just keep doing mine." She twisted her lips before continuing. "What happened between us can't happen again if it means you want to trap me here though."

I stiffened. Is that what she thought I'd do?

"I'd never do that." I managed with a tight throat, a huge ball of something inside making it almost impossible to speak or even think. There'd be no trapping.

"I'm done talking about this." She held up her hand, and started to move around me. My gut was in knots watching her go, almost too damn distracted to get out what I'd come here to say.

"Maya, stop."

She did stop, just outside the back door. Her hand lingered over the knob, and her shoulders stiffened.

"There's shit going on," I continued. "Bad shit I gotta tell you about."

She hesitated, her voice stiff like her body as she asked, "What is it?"

I cleared my throat. "When's the last time you heard from your old man?"

She turned, facing me with narrowed eyes. "When I was twenty. Why?"

"We got reason to believe his club's been hooking up with Pops."

She folded her arms. "That's impossible. He wants nothing to do with me."

"No?" I lifted a brow, bothered that she was so clueless when it came to her old man. "Then why'd he call your mom yesterday, huh?"

"I-I… She didn't tell…" Her cheeks paled. "My mom wouldn't…"

"He called her yesterday, Maya. He said he wanted to talk. They talked. Not sure what about, but it's probably not good."

"He's just playing with her." She shook her head in denial. "It's a scare tactic. He won't follow through with it. He does this every so often." She lifted her chin in defiance. "Plus, Mom got a restraining order against him a long time ago."

"And you think that'll keep him away?" I shook my head, wondering when she'd gotten so lax about this life.

She looked at her hands, holding them out in front of her palm side up, wordless. She knew I was right.

"Flick said a buddy of his in Texas does business with the Forsaken. He saw them with Pops and his rogues a few times."

I waited for her to put two and two together, watching as it all seemed to circle in her head. "I don't understand. Why now? It's been over eight years since we left him." She paused for a second, then another. "Granted he's been in and out of prison over the years, but still…"

"We don't know why it's happening right now. That's why I gotta go with Arch tomorrow. Everything's just so… so fucked up." *For us.*

"I'll come too." Maya held her chin up even higher than before.

"And do what exactly?"

I watched her swallow, fidget with her hands some more, but her voice stayed strong, even though I saw the terror and panic growing in her eyes the longer she spoke. "I'll talk to him. Tell him that—"

"You're in no condition to deal with that shit right now, not with your knee." I growled.

"My knee is fine." She folded her arms, probably because they were shaking now. Goddamn My, and her goddamn need to be tough. "Just think about it. Maybe if I go, he'll listen—"

"The answer is no, Maya. Now leave it."

She stared at me for a long minute, then shook her head, but I didn't miss the wetness forming in her eyes before she turned away. "Whatever."

Then before I could stop her, she walked inside the house, leaving me trailing behind her like a lost puppy.

I was going to kill Flick. Why the hell did I always have to be the bad guy?

"Wanna know something?" She swirled around in the kitchen once I shut the door behind me.

I didn't speak, just looked her in the eye and waited. There was no point in saying no—not that I would. She'd always tell me what was on her mind. And right now, I'd take her fiery attitude over her fear and worry any day.

"I think it's stupid for you two to leave right now. A huge mistake, actually."

"Me too." I shrugged. "But if we don't try to figure out what's up now, then we might miss out on something big later."

"You're serious?" She nearly laughed, though nothing was funny when it came to her father, the club, and Pops, most of all. "The whole club needs to be smarter about this, Slade. Sending random guys off on hunts like this leaves the rest of the club and the people in it vulnerable, including me and my mom."

"No. You'll be here, protected. The compound's like an army base."

"I'm not going to stay on this stupid compound all day every day until this gets resolved, you hear me? I'm not a prisoner and neither is my mother."

"Please, My." I pushed a hand through my hair, frustrated that it wasn't simpler than this. "Just give it time. Least until I'm back and here to help. Two days, tops. That's all." Then I'd show her how much I regretted not loving her the way I should've been all along. The way she deserved to be loved by a man.

"You're not my bodyguard." She took a step closer. I did the same. And soon our chests were flush, and I could feel the rage in her body as she shook.

"I know I'm not." The pull to her was stronger than ever, my knees weakening each second longer I wasn't touching her. "But you're also my responsibility now."

"Why, because of some stupid club claim?"

"Yes, that's exactly why." I took a heavy breath, unable to stop myself from lying. Because I couldn't stop myself, I reached out and touched her cheek with my fingers, drinking in every beautiful feature on her face.

Her sad, brown eyes.

She blinked, and a tear fell down her cheek, over the back of my finger. "I'll never be able to trust you now."

My throat burned when I swallowed, regret making my chest blaze hot, my hands sweat. I dropped them both to my side and nodded again just once as I stepped away.

"Good." I wouldn't trust myself either.

For now, it was better this way.

CHAPTER TWENTY-EIGHT

Slade

We got to the Texas compound around noon the next day. Arch and I had the same feeling the second we stepped through the gates, and it took only a shared look for us to know that we weren't as welcomed here as Flick said we'd be. Dirty looks, people spitting at our feet, and a set of hulking fuckers who never left our side.

Ten minutes into our arrival, we met up with Flick's contact outside their main clubhouse. Ten of his guys stood around him. Most were older. Late forties, early fifties. But they looked deadly as hell, and making waves with them wasn't what we were after here.

"Morning, boys." The leader, who we'd come to know as Rodent, took a long drag of his smoke. He looked like he'd been plucked out of hell itself. Red-rimmed black eyes and stringy, gray hair down to the middle of his back. "Heard you're lookin' for a little intel."

"Yeah," Archer answered—the conversationalist, while I was the observer, the one who knew what to look for if shit went south.

Rodent pulled us inside the clubhouse after him with a wave. At the bar, he offered up whiskey, which even Archer refused, then proceeded to pull a couple young girls onto his lap at a round table.

"Good-lookin' girls you got in here."

I gritted my teeth the second those words left Archer's mouth, but not for the reason one would think.

"They are, ain't they?" Rodent winked then grabbed both of the girls' asses, causing them to giggle.

"Kinda young for my taste though." Archer rubbed at his short beard.

In my head, I counted the number of women in the room. Fifteen, from what I could see, all no older than eighteen, if that. This place was like a brothel with underage girls and perverted assholes. Most all of them probably had fake IDs and new names, if I had to guess, but it didn't make it right.

Had Flick known, I was pretty sure he wouldn't have sent us here. The authorities could come knocking on the door any second now if they got wind of this. Or maybe he did know and was turning a blind eye. It sure as hell wasn't how we ran things at home. The RDs weren't perfect, but compared to these guys, we looked like saints.

"They're good girls." Rodent winked again.

"Hmm." Archer managed to keep a straight face somehow, but the rage was buried deep in his eyes. I could see what no one else could, that he was already planning how to save them.

"We ready to roll yet?" I stepped up next to my buddy, arms folded. He was getting off track here and it was my job to keep him focused.

Rodent smiled at me. "I think we are." Then he lifted a chin at some of his buddies.

"Boys, get Flick's gentlemen here bikes."

Ten minutes later, Arch and I were standing in front of a couple new Harleys. Chrome wheels, untouched, and fresh off a lot. Archer looked ready to come in his pants at the sight. Freaking club shit or not, a set of new wheels always made the guy purr like a kitten.

Rodent stood between us, waving a couple of guys over that looked fresh out of high school. Young and inexperienced, like Carlos had been.

"Marco and Reggie will take you two out. They're the ones who spotted your people."

"Not our people," I clarified.

"Fine, fine." Rodent rolled his eyes and waved a hand in the air.

"What my brother here is saying," Archer slapped a hand against my back, playing up the part, "is we appreciate your hospitality."

Yeah, sure. Inexperienced bikers who weren't as important as the others. Expendable. Fucking award this douchebag a medal.

Rodent smiled wider, eating up Archer's words. "Once you find what you're looking for, y'all come back. We'll have ourselves a little welcoming party. How does that sound?" The dirty old dude winked at Archer. "I'll even let you try out one of my girls tonight, if you'd like."

Just barely, I held back a shudder, but Archer nodded, back to being the best of the best when it came to bullshitters. "Sure thing, boss," he told Rodent, hopping on his bike, revving the engine once it started. We wouldn't be back though. Least no longer than it took to drop off these bikes.

Five minutes later we were driving through skinny, gravel roads, one right after the other. Didn't take us long to get to the Texas–New Mexico border—an hour, tops.

It was nothing like I'd assumed it'd be. Just a hell of a lot of open ground separating the two states. We parked up on a cliff, hidden from everything below. Close enough to where we could see shit go down, but not close enough to be seen. According to the two guys we were with, this had been the locale for Pops and Maya's old man's once-a-week meetup. A meetup that was supposed to be happening again today.

"How'd you find out this was going down?" I asked. No one was there yet, but I was antsy. Something about this didn't feel right.

The guy at my right answered first. He was the younger of the two. Sixteen, if that. "We have business with the Arizona crew that we take care of around here. Found out the exchange was going down and let Rodent know. This is our trade point, no one else's."

"And, what, Rodent automatically knew to call our pres?" I could hear the distrust in Archer's voice, but they were questions we had to ask.

"Saw their patches, told Rodent. He knew right away who they were," the other guy said. "Red Dragons on the guy across the fence in New Mexico. Skulls on the ones closest—the Forsaken, who we do our trading business with."

"Anyway, the Forsaken cross our borders a time or two, with permission. The other club ain't allowed," the young one said, motioning a hand between him and his friend. "If the Forsaken club is working with another club, trading the same things that we trade with them, then we can't have it. Too many dicks in a pot, if you know what I mean."

I started to ask what kind of trading business they dealt in, but before I could, Archer interrupted. "This is too big for us." We locked eyes. "We're gonna have to get another crew down here."

I nodded. It'd been a mistake coming at all, we'd both known that, but we wouldn't fight Flick. A war was coming, and we needed to stop it before it came to our borders. That was what mattered right now. Which was why we'd get a flight home tonight, not Sunday.

A few minutes later, two guys on bikes rolled up to the fence, one on either side. I narrowed my eyes and stared through a pair of binoculars Archer had brought, my lungs squeezing. I'd know if it were Maya's old man, Flick had said. Apparently, he looked just like his daughter.

I focused, finding only a couple younger guys. The patches I saw on the back of their cuts were proof though, that this was really happening. One was a Red Dragon; one was a skull.

"Got one from each side." I handed the binoculars to Archer, rubbing my hands over my thighs as he looked. I hated seeing our patches on cuts that didn't deserve them. Especially ones run by Pops.

"Big guys will show at the end." The kid next to me motioned his chin a little ways up the road toward the New Mexico side. That was when I saw it. A car in the distance, waiting. Black with tinted windows.

Archer looked at me, eyes narrowed. "Maya's old man?"

"Likely." My palms started to sweat more.

"How do you think he and Pops hooked up?" Archer asked me.

I shrugged. "Wish I knew."

"Look," the kid said, pointing toward the Texas side this time. Two cars, five bikes. At the center of it all was probably my uncle.

"Shit. That's gotta be Pops, right?" Archer pressed the binoculars to his eyes, thinking the same.

I frowned and looked to where Archer was pointing, watched as a man stepped out. Long dark hair that hit him mid-back, huge muscles, no shirt, and only his cut. I couldn't see his face to know for sure, but he had the body and hair of Pops.

"Jesus, look at that shit," Archer whispered, dropping the binoculars.

I followed his finger, which was now pointed at three young women, all in motherfucking shackles, who stepped out of what we assumed was Pops's car.

Goosebumps broke out over my skin, and a sense of being watched ate away at the back of my mind. Slowly, I looked to the boys we'd ridden in with, narrowing my eyes at what I was seeing. They were snarling, looking almost greedy at the sight of the girls.

Teenage girls no older than fourteen or fifteen, being shoved into the arms of the Forsaken.

Son of a bitch.

The business they did was trading young girls.

And it seemed Pops had jumped in on it too.

I looked over the kids' heads, watching as my best friend put it all together too. His eyes met mine and I nodded, no longer caring about dealing with one thing at a time. With a nod, we turned toward our escorts and took them both down—me a foot to my kid's gut, Archer a fist to his kid's face. Once mine was pinned, I jumped on him then grabbed his gun and shoved it against his throat.

"Not a word," I hissed.

His eyes narrowed, but surprisingly, he didn't fight me. He was too young. They both were. The kid next to Archer was on his face, moaning but unmoving.

"Wanna put some bullets in their heads?" Archer grinned manically. "Fucking rapist pieces of shit."

I shook my head. "Not today."

"I'm the VP," Archer hissed. "And I say we kill these bastards." My best friend was seething, hands shaking, teeth gritted, his blond hair hanging over his eyes. Murder was at the forefront of his mind right then, but adding to our already huge-ass problems and list of enemies wasn't a good idea.

"Don't kill them," I repeated. "I want them buried in the ground as much as you do, buddy, but we have bigger shit to deal with right now and they're nothing but pawns."

I must've gotten through to him because his shoulders relaxed. The guy under me was damn near pissing his pants as I shoved the gun further into his throat. "Keep your mouth shut, ya hear me?" I told him.

He nodded fast, eyes bulging.

Archer and I moved in unison, wrapping their shirts over their mouths and tying their hands together with wire, then tying their bodies against two trees. When I finished with mine, I raced back over to the edge of the cliff with the binoculars, cussing when the cars started dispersing from the rogue RD side. Another dark-haired guy stood at the center of it all, though, eyes narrowed and looking my way. He was a hell of a lot shorter than Pops, but his mass was giant. And when I focused on his face, I nearly lost my shit, because the man looking through the trees, pointing in our direction, was the spitting image of my star-eyed girl.

I knew he couldn't see me through the brush of trees covering us, but I was guessing he'd heard us. We needed to move. Fast.

"We got problems," I told Archer.

"Figured as much. That's why we need to get the hell outta here."

I watched as Maya's old man waved his hand toward the trees, toward us, and felt the blood drain from my face. For a second, I couldn't do nothing but stand there and look at him, memories of Maya's stories and what he'd done to her and her mom hitting me in the head. Memories that weren't mine to avenge.

Maya wanted her father dead. Told me more times than I could count. And now, with a long-range pistol just inches behind me, I could do it for her.

More bikes roared in the distance. Archer hissed at me to move. He started his bike, yelling over the motor, all while I continued to focus on Maya's old man. He didn't look away from the trees, and I wondered what he was thinking. If only he knew that behind the thick brush was the man who would make Maya's world right again.

"Slade, let's go. *Now.*"

I shook my head, ignoring Archer's yelling, then turned around, grabbed the pistol, and aimed.

"Don't you fucking pull that trigger. You'll kill us both!" Archer yelled, jumping off his bike, grabbing my cut. He yanked, but I didn't budge. I didn't even breathe.

My hand shook, my finger too. I pulled, testing my strength, then seconds before I could do what I knew I shouldn't do, another shot went down, taking the job away from me.

Smoke filled the air, more gunfire sounded. Left, right, left, right.

The girls screamed, men roared, and when the smoke finally cleared away, when the rapid gunfire ended, all I could see was bodies.

Lots of them.

Including Maya's old man.

CHAPTER TWENTY-NINE

Maya

On Friday night I found myself sitting in the waiting room of the Red Dragons' soon-to-be body shop just a few miles outside of downtown Rockford. Flick needed to swing by so he could meet with a couple of guys about some car parts. Mom and I hadn't been off the compound for a few days, so we'd begged to go with and asked my uncle to take us out to dinner when he was done. He was fine with the idea, so long as we were patient and waited inside while he talked shop. Something about being sitting ducks if we stayed in the car.

Chop was there too, along with three other bikers I didn't know well but recognized from the clubhouse. The four of them were stationed outside somewhere, never seen, never heard, but constantly on our tails. They were our bodyguards, I was guessing.

"Is he almost done?" I leaned back against the plastic chair I was sitting in, listening to my stomach grumble. I'd taken my pain pills about three hours ago, expecting to get dinner not long after. Now that it was nearing ten at night, and I'd yet to eat, I felt like I was going to be sick.

Mom, on the other hand, fingered through a magazine on my left, completely at ease. "Your impatience hasn't changed one bit with your age, has it?"

"We've been sitting here for almost two and a half hours. My knee hurts and so does my head, and now I feel like I'm gonna puke." Plus, I was on edge. About the issue with my father. About Slade being all the way in Texas, and me being all the way… here. Where the two of us stood, most of all. I'd told him I was done with the push and pull. And I meant it. But that didn't mean I wasn't still crazy about him.

"Are you pregnant?" Mom asked, setting her magazine on her lap, peeking up at me.

I rolled my eyes. "No, Mother. I am *not* pregnant."

She shrugged then went back to reading, like this was normal life stuff. To her, it likely was. But not me. At least not anymore.

My thoughts went back to Slade again. It seemed he basically lived in my head twenty-four-seven now. I was still so angry at him—livid—about the old lady claim and his inability to make decisions when it came to me and him.

I was pretty sure he'd slept on the couch last night, despite our argument yesterday. The folded-up blanket at the end of it was my first clue. It had confused me and made my chest warm at the same time, knowing that even after I'd told him I didn't want him there, he'd stayed. If that made me a crazy masochist, then so be. I never claimed to be normal anyway.

The roar of a bike engine clicked to life in the garage, and I groaned when the hoots and hollers came seconds later. *Get parts my ass.* What were they doing out there, having a freaking kegger party?

Rubbing a hand over my knee, I looked at the glass door, frowning.

Chop wasn't down with the idea of us coming here. And every now and then, I could see his big, blond head pacing out front. He'd told Flick that Slade would be mad, and before my uncle could think twice about letting us go, I'd grinned and backed my uncle on the idea, willing to do just about anything to get under Slade's skin.

Plus, being away from the club kept me from thinking too much about things. My father, mostly, and what part of this entire thing with Pops he was in on. The sperm donor was an evil man, and if he got his hands on Slade, then I was more than positive he wouldn't let him go. At least not alive.

I shuddered at the thought, listening to the bike roar again, my mind drifting… until Mom piped in again.

"So, I heard your young man claimed you the other night."

I slapped both hands over my face and let go of yet another agonized groan. "I don't want to do this right now, Mother."

Giggling under her breath, Mom wrapped an arm around my shoulder and pulled me against her, kissing my temple. "Yeah. I figured as much. But just know: if he claimed you, it means he loves you."

In an ideal world, that's what I'd hoped, but when it came to Slade, I knew that was likely not the case. He'd had ample opportunity to come clean today, but instead, he'd chosen to talk about my old man and his role in all of this. A role I'd yet to really even broach with my mom, other than hearing her say it was *unpleasant*, something she didn't want to discuss just yet.

I settled in, my head on her shoulder, wondering if now would be an okay time to try again. "Did my father love you?"

"No." Mom shook her head, holding me a little tighter. His phone call had gotten to her, that much was true. "That man is not capable of love."

I sighed. "I hate him for what he did to us, Mom."

"I know, sweetie." She nuzzled her nose against my hair as she continued. "But I promise, I'll never let him hurt you again, alright? We're stronger now. We'll get through this, together."

I smiled, tears forming in my eyes, but for some reason, I couldn't believe her yet.

My stomach grumbled a little more. Mom apparently heard it this time because she said, "Let me get you something out of the vending machine, sweetheart."

"Thanks." I smiled, unsure of why I hadn't done that myself.

She squeezed my shoulder as she stood, her smile soft and motherly. Warming me from head to toe. Had I known what was coming next, I never would have let her walk away.

"Doritos or Cheez-Its?" she asked, looking at me from over her shoulder.

"Duh, you know the answer to that."

She laughed.

Put the money in.

Punched in a code.

Then before she could turn to face me, plaster exploded on the wall by her head, and one solitary bullet slammed through her skull.

I screamed. But it wasn't loud enough, because soon the entire room was engulfed in bullets, one shooting past another, zooming so close I could hear them. I dropped to the floor, covering my head, peeking out only to see Mom's lifeless body, blood beneath her head, and a bag of cheese crackers in her limp hands.

"Mom!" I screamed, no longer caring about anything other than getting to her. Hugging her. Holding her in my arms. I crawled and cried and crawled some more, my knee throbbing and burning the entire time.

"Mom!" I screamed again, making it to her side, shaking her shoulder. "Mom, please. Wake up. Wake up!"

I heard shouting, someone calling my name. But all I saw was her. Dead.

My heart burst in my chest, face soaked with tears. "Mom!" I tried again. "Mom, please, wake up."

But she wouldn't wake up. Her eyes were wide open but… blank. And there was so much blood.

So.

Much.

Blood.

The gunfire stopped then, but noises continued to whir in my ears. I couldn't save her this time. I couldn't. And I hated myself. So much.

"Mom, I'm sorry. I'm so, so sorry."

Voices grew louder around me. Doors opened, feet sounded by my head.

"Maya? Maya! Fuck, are you hurt?" I didn't look up at Chop's face. Not when Mom was all I could see. Every inch of me shook as I reached over to touch her cheek.

It was cold already.

Mom hated being cold, just like me. She would have liked the beach. She would have liked it so much.

"Oh, God, Mom," I sobbed.

"Don't look, kid." My uncle was there, pulling me up. Carrying me. And I lost it.

I hit his chest, I beat him until I was sure I'd left bruises. "Put me down, Flick! Put me down! I hate you. I hate you so much."

But he didn't put me down. He didn't try to stop me from hitting him either. He just whispered two words, over and over and over. *I'm sorry. I'm sorry. I'm sorry.*

"This is all your fault!" I screamed, hitting him with my words when I could no longer lift my fists.

And then when my throat was too raw from screaming, when he put me in a car and sat in the backseat with me, the numbness I craved finally came.

I embraced it with open arms, promising myself that it was the last thing I'd ever feel. Because the pain… it was too much.

CHAPTER THIRTY

Slade

We got off the plane at O'Hare around eleven that night, both of us turning on our cells as we made it through the crowded terminal. Reception was shit, and the number of people flying was a nightmare.

"You gettin' a lot of notifications?" Archer looked at me as he grabbed our duffels from the baggage claim.

I nodded, frowning when I saw that Hawk was calling. "Yeah, man?"

"You land yet?"

"Hello to you too, cousin." I smirked, thankful to be back on home soil.

Silence followed. Then finally, "June's dead."

I froze, thinking I'd misheard him. "The hell did you just say?"

"There was an attack on the garage in town tonight. Pops's guys, we're thinking."

"Where's Maya?" I broke out in a cold sweat, shaking.

"She's fine. At the club." He cleared his throat. "She's gonna need you though. Poor thing saw it all go down."

My head started spinning. This couldn't be happening.

Jesus, her mom wasn't really dead, was she?

Not bothering to wait for Archer, I took off toward the front of the airport, no idea where I was going, what I was doing, just knowing I had to do it fast because Maya needed me.

"Wait up, would you?" Archer grabbed my arm, yanking me back. His phone was to his ear, his face grim as he listened to someone on the other end.

He knew.

"We gotta go," I told him when he put his cell away. "I gotta get to Maya, man."

"Yeah. I get it. But you taking off like that? Shit ain't gonna help, brother."

I growled. "I'm trying to get the fuck out of here so I can go home."

"And I'm gonna take you there, but you've got to give me a damn minute to make it happen."

My chest hurt as I tried to breathe. Reaching up, I rubbed at the spot over my heart, wishing I could figure out a way to make it stop. Make it *all* stop. Everything. The world and all the bad shit it held, like death and heartbreak.

My old man once told me that there wasn't a simple way out of the life we led. That if there was, he would've found it a long time ago—for my sake. And for the first time in years, since I'd put on a cut, I thought about that life. What it would be like had I not patched in. Had I gone after Maya, to California. Had I become someone besides Slade.

I should've been there with her tonight. But by leaving, doing this pointless run, I'd nearly lost the one thing that mattered most to me.

When we finally pulled up to the front of the club, I raced up the stairs before Archer could even put my old man's truck in park. I hadn't been able to drive home, as my mind was messed up, and my stomach was in my feet.

Not thinking twice, I ran to the dorms inside, opening the door to each one but finding them all empty. Maya wasn't here.

A voice stopped me cold from behind. Hawk. "Church. Now."

I spun around. "Where's Maya?"

"Home safe. Summer and Emily are with her," was all he said.

"I need to see her."

I turned to leave, to head to Flick's, but Hawk barked at my back. "Church first. Got business to attend to."

"Fuck that, I need—"

"I know exactly what you're thinking, cousin." He dropped a hand to my shoulder from behind, squeezing. " But we gotta do this." A breath. "We *have* to do this."

I rubbed my face with both hands, breathing in, then out, then in, then out, until I forced Sebastian down once more.

"Alright." I nodded. "Let's go."

Archer came into the room just seconds after me, standing on my other side as Hawk took a seat at the table. I looked around, finding Mute and Talker there. Crazy too. Flick wasn't around though.

"Where's Flick?" I asked.

Chop spoke up from the corner. I hadn't even seen him until then. The guy looked like shit. Red eyes, dark circles, wild hair crazy-high on his head. "With the doc. He'll be here in a second. Just got grazed by a bullet." He motioned to Hawk with his chin. "Hawk's filling in."

No surprise there. Flick had wanted Hawk to take over the club since the guy got out of prison last year. Hawk wasn't willing back then, but things were changing apparently, now that there was a warning beating so close to our door.

"You got leads?" Archer asked, not second guessing the sudden role changes in the club, even as the VP. He knew Hawk was destined to run this club as much as I did. Plus, Arch never wanted the job either. He was just fine being VP.

Hawk's face looked grim, his gaze sliding to me, then back to Arch. "From what we can tell, tonight was planned a while ago.

Whatever guys Flick met up with at the shop were working for Pops. Had a crew outside, waiting in the shadows. Nobody had a damn clue until they just came at us."

"Jesus Christ," I hissed, dropping my head back. How could we all be so stupid?

"Luckily there weren't that many of them," Hawk continued. "But they had good weapons."

"They get anyone else?"

He shook his head. "Just grazes. Guys weren't experienced with the weapons they had, which is why…"

Why they'd gotten June.

I narrowed my eyes at Chop. "What the fuck were My and her mom even doing there, huh?"

"Slade," Hawk and Archer growled out together, yanking me toward the table to sit. It wasn't like I was gonna kill the kid or anything.

Archer jumped in with, "Ain't Chop's fault. He's the one who tried to keep 'em from going in the first place."

Chop looked down, not even fighting back with words. I could see how this shit tore him up inside. If I wasn't so damn pissed at the world, I might've felt sorry for the guy.

Hawk continued to tell us what he knew, pacing the room. "Maya's old man, the whole trade between Pops's rogues and the Texas and Arizona crew? It was a distraction. Apparently, Pops was going after Flick tonight. Got June instead. Thought it'd be best to divert our attention south. Away from where the real threat was."

Goddammit.

I dragged a hand through my hair and looked up to the ceiling. Maya was right. "We shouldn't have gone this morning," I said. By doing so, we'd left Maya and her mom, Flick, the entire compound less protected. Alone. Vulnerable.

"Not your fault," Hawk spoke low, an authority about him I hadn't heard or felt in a long while.

"One good thing is, Pops is weaker now that Maya's old man's dead," Archer added.

"No shit?" Chop sat up straighter, the rest of the brothers did too.

I nodded, recalling what had happened. How we'd seen Satan's body go down. Watched him lie lifeless on the ground, the blood running from the middle of his forehead…

There wasn't no coming back from a headshot like that.

"That's the best news we could have right now." Hawk nodded stroking his chin.

"Only real reason Satan wanted in, that we know of, is because of June and My. The rest of the Forsaken weren't part of it," Archer finished off, leaning back in his chair, feet kicked up on the table.

"How do you know?" Hawk's eyes narrowed.

I shrugged. "We don't know." As much as I knew I should've been worried, I couldn't find it in me to care right now. To me, all Satan's death meant was that there was one less piece of trash in Maya's life. "But we gotta have a reason to hope right now, don't you think?"

I kept my head bowed as plans were made, details set for what to do next. Wasn't in the mood to listen, or to join in anymore either, not when all I wanted was Maya.

Five minutes later, the doors opened. I stood, turned, walked toward Flick the second I saw him step into the room. He looked worse than Chop.

I could only imagine what Maya was like right now.

Arch and Hawk flanked my backside, but Flick's eyes were glued to me. "You good, boy?" he asked, voice cracking.

"Are you?" I nodded toward his shoulder, which was wrapped in a sling.

He waved me away, then coughed. "You been to see Maya yet?"

"On my way when I'm done here."

"She's alright. Tough girl, she is," Flick said.

"What about you?" Taking a breath, I moved closer, lowering my voice. "You lost a sister tonight."

I watched as his throat moved with a swallow. He didn't answer. I looked at my brothers, but they were all looking at him. I was sure their gazes held the same thoughts as mine did.

You're not okay. You can't come back from this.

None of us had the balls to say it though. For years and years, Flick had lived his life for June. Taking care of her. Doing whatever she needed. He lived for that woman. Would've died for that woman.

But now…

"Better this way," he managed, agreeing with all our earlier mindsets. "With Maya's old man down, that's one less threat."

The room went quiet again. All of us were likely thinking the same thing. We were officially going to war now. Pops attacking like that had shown his cards. The man would do anything and everything he could to take us down.

Flick looked at each of us, stopping on me again. "We don't tell Maya about her dad. Not tonight. Let her grieve for her mom. Be there for her." He cleared his throat. "As her man."

I nodded, hating that he accepted me as that person for his niece when I'd done nothing to protect her—when I'd hurt her on all other levels too. Now, more than ever, Maya would be hurting, in so many ways. Physically, emotionally. I'd die protecting her.

Even if she didn't want me anymore.

CHAPTER THIRTY-ONE

Maya

Lonely snowflakes fell from the sky, landing on the black casket sitting in front of my chair. It was impossible not to lose myself in the memories my mother and I once shared as I sat there mourning her: the bad ones, the good ones, and every single one in between.

"… but for those who know the Lord, as did June Davenport, it is a joyous occasion because she is now in His glorious presence." The preacher spoke words I didn't believe. Why? Because if God was good, he would've protected my mom instead of letting her die.

Movement caught my eye from the right. Flick. His gaze was laser-focused on the ground, angry brows drawn together in both hate and regret. Both of which I could relate to.

Besides my father—a man I would've gladly put in the ground instead of my mother—Flick was all I had now as far as family went.

Hawk squeezed my shoulder and stood to go after him. Slade, though, laid his hand on my knee, holding it there as he leaned over to kiss my temple for the fifteenth time this hour. He was waiting for me to crack. It should have confused me, but I welcomed it too much to question it right now.

Since the attack, I'd mostly stayed in bed, getting up just to use the bathroom, shower, and come here today. When I wasn't sleeping, I was listening to the voices coming in and out of Flick's house. The Red Dragon rage and fear that the walls were too thin to hide.

The tension was rising within the club. Everything seemed to be coming to a head with Pops.

Staying numb, pretending to be too traumatized, was easier than speaking. So, I chose not to talk, other than an occasional "yes," "no," or "I'm fine." It wasn't in my normal realm to play the weak card, but sometimes it was easier to be the person you didn't want to be than it was to be the real one that would eventually lose it.

I was the first person to lay a flower on my mother's coffin, the one who lingered next to it the longest once the service ended. I let the rose thorns prick my hand as I did, drawing blood before I let go of it. In death, now, Mom and I would always be connected.

A few people followed suit, women mostly. Groupies, hang-abouts, whatever they were called. Emily and Summer came up too. They cried. I didn't. Had I done so, I wouldn't have been able to stop.

"I'm so sorry for your loss." Summer hugged me, smelling like flowers. Emily did the same but didn't say anything, just wiped at her tears. Maybe she was thinking about her own mom during all of this.

I looked away from the rest of the people who tried to give me *condolences*. They didn't understand what I was going through. What I would be going through over the next several months… if not longer.

Slade kept his hand pressed to my back as I walked to the end of the casket after everyone had left the gravesite. Other than the club members standing at the edge of the cemetery, who were smoking and hanging around my uncle, we were finally alone.

"Do you want to say goodbye?" he asked me, his mouth close to my cheek, the smell of his minty breath cascading over my nose.

I blinked and lifted my chin, avoiding his gaze, and stared at the rose I'd placed on top of the coffin instead. "No."

Slade rubbed a hand up and down my spine, warming my chilled skin through my dress. I looked up at him, the first bit of emotion stirring inside of me from his hard yet gentle touch. I didn't know where we stood, but just being *next* to him made me feel *everything*, when I wanted to feel nothing at all.

"Are you sure?" he asked, his dark, beautiful eyes searching my face.

I nodded.

Through his shaggy hair, he continued to stare at me like I was his reason for living. In turn, I saw Sebastian Lattimore. I saw *all* of him. He held secrets and sadness that I no longer wanted a part of. Not because I couldn't handle it, not because I didn't love him. But because I just *knew* that whatever he'd been hiding from me since he'd returned from Texas wasn't good.

"Can we please go now?" I asked.

He pushed the strands off his face and nodded.

Not once did my gaze stray back toward the black coffin as we left. The woman inside wasn't my mom anymore.

Flick stared at me from across the road as we came up alongside Slade's bike. My uncle was readying to get on his, which sat behind Crazy's. I guessed he was going to head back to the club so he could drink and find a woman to let the pain go with.

Up until just a short time ago, he'd been numb like me. Sleeping in the dorms, not the house. I wondered if he'd be back there at all. I wouldn't leave that place though—had no plans to either. It was my mom's home more than it was my uncle's, and I liked feeling close to her spirit, her memories most of all.

Flick gave me a small head nod. I managed to give him one back. We would talk about what happened, someday, but it couldn't be now.

With as much strength as I could garner, I hoisted myself onto the back of Slade's bike, ignoring the burn of his hands against my waist, and even more determined not to let his touch make me feel anything.

Numbness was the only thing I wanted to encompass me right now.

My surgery was in four days, but it couldn't come fast enough. I was ready to be over this knee thing. Ready to do what needed to be done to put my life back together most of all.

As Slade stood in front of me on the ground, he tucked my hair behind my ears, the helmet I'd been wearing in his hand. "You okay?" He touched my chin, tilting my head up so our gazes locked.

"I'm fine." And I was. Or I would be. Someday.

He frowned, searching my face. "I wanna take you somewhere. You up for a drive?"

Part of me wanted to say no, not when all I wanted was to go back to Flick's house, lie in Slade's old bed, and sleep away the dull ache that had been creeping up on me since I'd laid that flower on Mom's casket. But he looked so hopeful, those dark eyes seeming to dig deep into my soul. In the end, I couldn't say no.

"Sure."

"Alright." He nodded and finally slid the helmet onto my head. I shivered when his fingers grazed my cheeks this time, when our eyes locked too. It'd been days since we'd last touched, and being this close reminded me how good we were when it came to intimacy. I missed his hands on my skin, his lips on my neck, the feeling of him inside of me, groaning against my throat as he came most of all.

"You sure you're up for this?" He leaned closer, his nose pressed to mine through the helmet. The heat of his breath washed over my mouth.

I shut my eyes, knowing it would be easy to let go of myself if he took me back to my uncle's place and undressed me. If he stripped me naked and kissed me and touched me. But I didn't know where we stood. And we hadn't taken the time to discuss it either.

"Take me for a ride, Slade," I murmured, a hand sliding across his neck.

He studied me for another beat, pulse beating faster against my thumb. Then before I could close the distance between us, Slade lowered the visor on my helmet. Without words, he straddled the seat in front of me, our bodies alive and electric, that familiar current running between us once more as I settled against him.

I liked his new bike. The one Archer had fixed up for him after his prospect's death. Slade did too, though he'd mentioned in passing that it was hard to get used to the smooth feel of the tires on the road when he'd been so used to the rough rattle of his old bike.

We drove away from the cemetery in a blustery cloud of smoke and snow, underlying sexual tension causing me to ache in the spot his body was now snuggling against. With my arms wrapped around his torso, and my helmeted head pressed against his back, I let myself remember what it was like to feel again. Feel, with Slade.

I didn't get the chance to ask where we were going, didn't necessarily want to know either. Instead, I simply watched the city go by as we drove closer to downtown and let myself live in the moment. It was what I needed to do now, because who knew what would come next?

The smoke in the air seemed to grow thicker the closer we got to downtown. Traffic was heavier, and there was an underlying smell of car grease and restaurant food in the air. The honks and the rush of inner-city traffic were nowhere near as bad as downtown Chicago, but I could feel the rush around me.

Slow and steady, world.

One day at a time.

I didn't mind the traffic when we were on this bike though. For some reason, it felt as if we could take on anything, riding as one on Slade's Harley. I smiled to myself, thinking of Mom right then. She loved bikes, but from a distance. Something about the fear of falling off them kept her from ever enjoying the ride itself.

Mom had never let go like I did. And I blamed my father for it. Since the day we'd run from Arizona, she'd always held an edge to her, only seeming to lose bits and pieces of her guard when it was too late.

At the thought, I shut my eyes and let the tears fall as each of my regrets and wishes warred inside of my head.

Mom would never see me get married—if that was my choice.

Mom would never meet any grandchildren—if I decided to have them.

She'd never give me advice again. Never eat ice cream with me again. She'd never kiss my temple or hold me against her chest, be a mom the way she'd always wanted to be but had never been able to. The way I'd always craved. We'd had a week together, finally just being us. A *week* damn it, which was robbed because of the Red Dragons and their stupid club and everything in it.

Inhaling through my nose, shuddering against Slade's back, I tried to reconcile the man he was now with who he was at seventeen. I'd loved him then. But I loved him more now. Yet with his life came death and destruction and loss. Drinks and women and a whole lot of awful, bad stuff. When I'd first come back, I'd thought to myself, *You're different now. Stronger. If you want to handle this, you can.*

Now I wasn't sure if I wanted to anymore.

Hell, I didn't know if Slade even wanted *me*, or if he just felt it was his duty to be by my side until I healed.

I knew he could feel me cry, because with each passing shake of my body, his hold on my leg grew tighter, his body tenser. Then when we arrived in an alley twenty minutes after pulling out of the cemetery, he finally parked next to a door beside a dumpster.

"Come here," he said, turning to straddle his bike so he now faced me. No hesitation, he all but ripped the helmet from my head before sliding his hands into my hair.

My bottom lip trembled as he searched my face. "It hurts," I managed.

"Baby," he whispered, his eyes filled with torment. This was Sebastian right here before me. Or at least part of him.

"I'm not gonna be alright," I blubbered, nuzzling my forehead against his chest.

He didn't respond. Probably because he knew I was right and didn't have words of encouragement for me. But that was okay, because it was true.

Minutes later, when I was sure I'd cried all possible tears away, Slade pulled back and took my face between his hands. "You're my Artemis today," he whispered against my hair. "Can you take a walk with me?"

My mind was too jumbled for me to ask which goddess that was, but I did manage a weak nod. Leaning forward, he pressed his lips to my forehead once before drawing back to slide off his bike. With an arm draped around my back, he helped me off too, his hand finding mine in a way that felt so natural and right that it nearly hurt my heart in the process. Why? Because this felt more like an ending than a new beginning for me. I just wasn't sure why.

We walked at a slow pace in front of a few storefronts, Slade helping to keep me steady the entire time. Families mixed in between us, people wearing suits and coming home from work, the sight making my chest hurt even more. None of them knew what was going on just miles from this spot. Or if they did, they turned a blind eye.

After a while, Slade drew me close and sat me on a small bench on the sidewalk, snow flurries stuck in his dark-brown hair as he kept me against his warm body. I didn't speak. Instead, I looked at our now intertwined hands, waiting for whatever he was about to say.

"Flick didn't want me to tell you this." He sighed.

I swallowed, waiting.

"Least not yet. But you deserve to know." He shook his head and leaned back, eyes to our hands like me. He squeezed tighter, as though he was afraid my fingers would disintegrate if he looked away or, worse yet, let go.

Shivers of unease raced over my skin, causing more goosebumps to join the ones already there because of the cold. "Tell me."

"Your father…" He paused, meeting my gaze then, cold eyes making me go still. "He's dead."

CHAPTER THIRTY-TWO

Slade

Maya's body grew stiff, no emotion on her face as she looked away. Either she was getting ready to run or she was getting ready to cry again. And it was all because of me and my inability to keep my trap shut.

"Fuck, My. I'm so sorry."

She didn't speak right away. Barely moved either. Her hand, though, surprisingly stayed in mine. Maybe so she wouldn't haul off and punch me? Wouldn't be surprised. I knew she hated her dad, but still…

I wasn't sure why I'd brought her to the city to tell her. Why I'd told her here, honestly. But something about showing her the normal lifestyles of everyone around us made it easier to tell her the truth. Made her understand that she did have a choice. Me or reality.

One thing I couldn't handle was her silence. Maybe karma was paying me back for being the same way with her for the last few weeks.

"Talk to me," I whispered, reaching up, using my free hand to brush a curl behind her ear.

She shook her head, voice empty. "I'm not mad."

For some reason, that shit made me feel better and worse at the same time.

"Wanna tell me what you're thinking at least?"

She shrugged. "I-I don't know anymore, honestly."

My chest squeezed, the tightness and the wind making it damn hard to breathe.

"How?" she asked, her words empty. "How did he die?" she clarified.

"Pops's rogues." Flick would kill me if he knew I was sharing secrets. But I didn't care anymore. Maya mattered right then. Nothing else. "It was a distraction, we're thinking. The whole thing in Texas a setup. Something to make us weaker here, leaving the club less protected." I gritted my teeth, hate burning through my veins even more than blood. Even out of the club, Pops was still trying to control things here. And we'd let him, even though it'd been unintentional.

"Like I told you…" She blinked but looked at the ground instead of me.

My throat burned as I swallowed. "Yeah. Like you told me."

"Hmm."

A few more minutes went by. Soon, Maya was shaking so bad her teeth were chattering. I needed to get her home. Get back to the club, too. Church was happening again. Some big announcement on Flick's end. Still, I'd wait until she told me she was ready.

And it wasn't long before she did.

"I think I'd like to go back to Flick's now, please."

Dead. She sounded dead. It tore me up inside thinking I was the cause. Now more than ever, I wanted to tell her that she didn't have to do this alone. That I was here, and I wasn't going anywhere. But the words wouldn't come yet.

"Alright." I pulled her up, and she still held onto my hand. This time when we got back onto my bike, that energy from our ride over was gone.

And deep down, I knew right then and there that she was done with me.

*

"Where's my niece?" Flick asked the second I walked into Church that night.

"With Summer at your place." For the first time since Hawk had brought his woman into our world, I was thankful she was there. Nothing against her, I just never saw how she fit in. But I did now. She'd be Maya's friend. And that to me was the biggest thing she could be.

Flick nodded, then looked to Hawk. "You wanna tell 'em or should I?"

My cousin leaned forward and shook his head, keeping it bowed as he set his elbows on the table. "Flick's taking off for a while," he told the room. "Means I'm taking the role of pres until he's back."

I stiffened. The rest of the room did too. The only person who spoke, besides Hawk, was Archer. And I was pretty sure he spoke for us all.

"You ain't going nowhere, you fuckwit."

Everyone started in at that point, everyone but me and Hawk. Instead, the two of us stared at one another across the table, the brothers who understood the truth. Flick was leaving because he wanted Pops dead more than any of us now. And because of that, he had a death wish himself.

"I'm going to Texas." Flick leaned forward onto the table. "Gonna stay with Rodent for a while."

"Dude, that place is a shitstorm," Archer hissed.

"Yeah, I know." Flick nodded. "But Rodent's not someone we want on our bad side, and after what you and Slade did to his boys, I got some redemption I need to do."

"Bullshit rapists," Archer growled.

"We'll take care of all that once shit with Pops is done. But I need to go there. See it all for myself." Flick lit a cigarette and put it between his lips.

"And what the hell does that mean for us, huh?" Chop barked, standing as he paced the room.

"Means you'll be better off without me." Flick shrugged, blowing out a stream of smoke. "I'm gonna do research. Get Rodent and his boys behind us. Form ourselves an army too."

"We don't need them." Archer sneered. "We got my stepbrother in Vegas. He'll work with us."

"We do need them. For now." Flick frowned. "Even the shady allies can be good."

"They're trading girls," Archer yelled. "*Teenage* girls."

More growls sounded. More angry bites and hisses with words that erupted into roars.

"This is the beginning of our in with that situation." Hawk shrugged. "We deal with Pops, then we go from there. Listen to Flick. He knows what's best."

I nodded then looked at Archer. "One thing at a time, brother, remember?"

He curled his lip at me but didn't fight. Why? Because he knew damn well we weren't big enough to take that empire down just yet.

Hawk's eyes narrowed as he spoke up again. "My first order as our new pres: we're done with the runs. We work, we take care of our men and families, and we fucking protect this club. Nothing else matters. We stay on the defense. Then when the time comes to protect ourselves against Pops again, we make that shit happen on *our* turf, in our way."

I nodded, letting his words sink in. So did everyone else in the room. Hawk as pres would be the best damn thing this club ever had.

Flick jumped back in this time. "Hawk's gonna make this club into something good. All of you are. Pops can't take that away, not anymore." His voice cracked, his words thick with emotion. He'd lost his sister, got shot in the process. If he wanted to get emotional, so be it. I wouldn't look down at him. None of the brothers would.

"For June, we'll make it all right." Hawk nodded. "And for our women and brothers and…" He waited a beat, blew out a breath, then finished with, "And for our future kids too."

I frowned at that, eyes narrowing toward my cousin. "Kids?"

He nodded, rubbing a hand over his smirking mouth.

Holy shit. My cousin was gonna be a dad?

"Babies?" Archer mirrored my word, but there wasn't awe in his voice like mine. He didn't see the club as anything other than what he used it for. Brotherhood, sex, and booze. I used to be the same.

Until Maya came back.

My stupid heart jumped in my chest at the thought of her. Go figure. Just when life got me in the gut, when I was thinking that maybe she and I might be able to have something after all, she'd decided to push me away.

I'd let her end it if that's what she wanted. Wouldn't blame her neither. Why? Because I loved her that damn much.

"We're a fucking family," Flick growled, standing, "and you can't rip family apart, Goddammit, am I right?"

"Hear, hear," Crazy said, nodding.

Mute and Talker both nodded too. Chop still looked like he wasn't a believer in Flick's words; neither, really, did Archer. But we'd make them that way if it was the last thing we did.

More plans were thrown out. More prospects would be taken in. More patch-ins too. Protection was the name of the game now. We wouldn't let anything touch us again.

Flick was gonna leave from O'Hare the morning of Maya's surgery—four days from now. He wanted me to be the one to take him to the airport for some reason. This was Flick, my old man's former best friend. A father to me when nobody else cared, so I'd take him, though part of me wanted to say no. I wouldn't be with Maya on surgery day. Then again, she hadn't asked me to be there with her either. So, I'd give her the space she needed until I couldn't give her space no more.

"Be safe, brothers," Flick said, dismissing everyone but me. "Slade, stay for a sec. We gotta talk."

I nodded, itching to get back to his house. I'd been sleeping on the couch, waiting for Maya's cries in the night. Cries that never came anymore. Another ache filled my chest at the thought. What if she didn't need me anymore?

"What's up?" I asked, shaking the thoughts away.

"You're all she's got." He stood in front of me. "Maya. After I leave, you're it."

"Not true." I shook my head.

"It is." He glared at me. "We both know she's not one for friends and you're her entire world. Don't be stupid about that and push her away, you get me?"

"I won't."

"Good." He nodded. "Because at this point, you never know when it'll be gone for good."

CHAPTER THIRTY-THREE

Maya

Days after mom's funeral, I could still feel the pain of her absence. It was like smog filling the air. Thick and painful when I breathed in. So close you could touch it, only to watch it dissipate in the air when you tried.

God, I missed her. So much I could barely breathe.

And Slade… I hated him and loved him even more with every exhale. He was there for me in all the ways a man should be. Stronger than ever before, almost as though he really wanted to be with me now. Only this time, I was the one pushing him away, the one creating distance, because the truth of the matter was this: I needed to heal before really focusing on the things I wanted with him.

Even if it was too late in the end.

I cried most nights still—waking up from wretched nightmares of my dead father coming back to life. The only difference now? I muffled those cries into my pillow so Slade couldn't hear me. Wouldn't feel guilted into coming in and being my savior. I was determined to be my own healer.

As I was being hooked up to an IV forty-five minutes after arriving for surgery just days after my mother's funeral, a revelation came into my mind.

Going back to California was completely pointless now. Like I'd thought once before, I had no job, no apartment to live in, and in that small storage unit were material things I no longer needed. A bed, a couch, and a kitchen table. Nothing of real importance to me. Nothing keeping me attached to the state, other than my love of the ocean and the beach.

"I'm just going to put a little something in your IV to make you sleep."

I nodded, watching the anesthesiologist, wondering—oddly enough—if she was happy. With her life, with her job.

When I worked at various parlors, I was always happy. Not because I liked the people or the location, but because I loved the work I did, the art I created, the smiles on people's faces when I was finished. I loved how busy it kept me, how it took every ounce of my concentration to make the perfect piece for someone. And though my getting a job close by would always mean, in some way, having my name attached to the Red Dragons, I didn't find myself caring as much as I once did. If my mom could see the good in their world, even if it got her killed in the end, then maybe my fate was to see the good in it too.

I'd also come to terms with the fact that everything that had happened between me and Slade didn't define our futures. And though I'd once run away from him and the RDs as a whole, I refused to do it again because I was stronger now. Better. Ready to have the best of both worlds, even if it still terrified me.

I would have Flick's place all to myself on the compound if I wanted it, though the ghostly memories of my mom would always be there to haunt me. But that meant I could start working somewhere close by to save money for my own parlor one day.

"That's the plan, Stan," I told myself, eyes heavy, drooping shut.

I'd move on… once I was recovered from my surgery of course. Save money, start fresh, for Mom's sake, and then see where it took me in the end.

For the first time since Mom died, I felt myself smile genuinely, just as the medicine pulled me under.

*

The screechy door woke me up sometime later that night once I was home in bed. I yawned and stretched my arms, thinking it was Summer. She'd been here since I'd returned from the hospital, in between bouts of running to the bathroom to puke. The poor girl looked green in the face, and I was pretty sure I didn't want whatever virus she was carrying.

Still, no matter how many times I told her to go home and sleep, she refused and proceeded to bring me more food, meds, movies, magazines. Everything I didn't want but quietly appreciated all the same.

"Summer, jeez, woman. Go home, would you? I told you I'm fine."

But Summer didn't answer me. Instead, loud feet sounded across the floor. Boots, in fact. I opened my eyes then, blinking through the dark at what I was seeing.

Slade was back.

I was dreaming. Had to be. Never had I seen a more beautiful sight. He looked so dark and perfect. So… mine, if I wanted him.

"Hey," I whispered, emotion heavy in my throat.

He didn't smile at me or ask if I was feeling okay. But the words he did manage cut straight through the broken pieces of my heart for good.

"You got room in that bed for two?"

CHAPTER THIRTY-FOUR

Slade

I love you. I'm sorry. I need you. Forever. Always.

Those were the words on my tongue that I couldn't get out. Not because I didn't want to say them, but because Maya took my damn breath away. Like always, the woman made me stupid with greed and lust—lost in my feelings as I stayed inside my head.

I closed my eyes and waited for her to say no or yes, moving to kneel beside her bed. My hands were pressed together, like I was readying to say a prayer. Hell, at this point I'd pray to whatever god or goddess existed just to hear her say yes.

She didn't say words right away was the thing. Instead, her fingers grazed the back of my arms, hesitant... until they weren't.

That was all it took for my emotions to get the better of me. It was as if she was saying, *Finally*, and I was saying, *I'm sorry it took me so long.*

I shuddered, laying my forehead onto the bed beside her arm, exhaling the nerves, taking her hand in both of mine.

Fingers grazed my hair, twisting and tangling in the strands. I shook my head, not deserving her acceptance. Her forgiveness most of all. A beat passed until she finally whispered out my salvation.

"I think I can make room for you."

Without hesitation, I crawled over her, careful of her propped-up knee, then shuddered out a huge sigh as I laid my ear over her heart this time. Eyes shut, I listened to the steady beats, letting it lull me, soothe me. That's when the words came.

"Can I tell you a story?"

Her breath caught at my question, then she laid her hand on top of mine, which now sat on her stomach. "Yeah. I'd like that."

Relief washed over me, and I shut my eyes, saying what I couldn't as Slade—letting Sebastian take over one final time.

"Once there was a god named Hades. He fell head over fucking heels for a woman who was too good for him."

"Her name was Persephone, wasn't it?"

I nodded. "The thing is, Hades was a bad dude. The god of the underworld. Secluded and cruel. Selfish. He didn't deserve Persephone, and he knew it too. But he had to have her, so he stole her away for months at a time, forcing her to be his wife."

"But out of all the gods," she whispered, "those two were some of the only ones who never cheated on one another, right? So, whether Hades knew it or not, Persephone loved him too."

I smiled, proud that she remembered. But that didn't change the truth of the story. "She was a dumb girl who could do a whole lot better though."

"Not true. He was devoted to her. And sometimes, that's all that matters."

I shut my eyes, deciding it was time to say what I'd been intending to all along. "I'm sorry, Maya. I'm so sorry for being an idiot. Pushing you away and shit when I did. But… I don't want to end this. I want you, and us. All the things I told you we couldn't have. The things I don't deserve after being such a gigantic asshole."

Five seconds passed, then ten. Then thirty. I counted in my head, sure she'd changed her mind. But I couldn't tear myself away and, instead, moved as close to her side as I could get, taking what she offered, until she told me goodbye.

I was too selfish to leave anymore.

"You're too good for me, My," I continued. "But I want you to know I'll *never* hurt you again if you give me another chance. I'll protect you and your heart until the day I die, and not a damn thing will ever stand in the way of us. Not even the club. I promise."

"You hurt me," she whispered.

I nodded, throat burning hot. "Which is why if you tell me to go away, I will."

Another ten seconds passed before she asked, "How do I know you're not going to do it again?"

"You don't," I choked out. "You have no reason to trust me." But fuck, did I want her to. I wanted her to want me the way I did her. *Always. Forever.*

I felt her breath in my hair as she exhaled. "I'm sorry for leaving you the way I did when we were younger."

I shook my head, lifting my chin to look into her eyes. "Don't ever apologize for that. We were both stubborn and young."

"I just… I want you to know that I won't leave you either. I'm not going to move back to California after everything settles. In fact, I've got plans already. Work plans. *Life* plans."

"Yeah?" I whispered, brushing a piece of hair from her eye then tucking it behind her ear. Just seeing her smile and feeling her excitement made me forget that nothing was right in the RD world. That there was a looming war and enemies around every corner, just waiting to end our club run. Maya made me feel like life went on, and stopping to fight back was only a small bump in our yet-to-be-traveled road.

"Yeah." She smiled. "I'm going to find a parlor to tattoo out of until I can afford to open my own place. Stay here at Flick's while he's gone and save money to do it with."

I tapped her chin, holding it between my thumb and forefinger. "I like that idea."

She nodded, smiling, obviously pleased with my response.

"Can you be my first client?" she asked, her voice softening—a sleepy rumble, really. "I'll make sure it's even better than the compass."

"I'd love for you to ink me." I squinted at her. "But don't you dare downplay the awesome piece I got under my arm, understood?"

She laughed. "Okay. I won't."

I laid my head back on her chest, just as Flick's words from the drive today ran through my ear again. *June had money saved up. It's in an account.* He'd handed me a key, talking about a safety deposit box or some shit at a bank in town. *Give this to her for me.*

I cleared my throat, nervous for some reason. "I, uh, I think I got a way to make things happen for you sooner. If you want."

Her heart thudded faster in my ear. "What do you mean?"

I swallowed, deciding I should sit up for this. When she tried to sit up too, I shook my head. "Rest." I touched her hand, squeezed it, then let go of a huge-ass breath when she interlocked our fingers.

"Slade. Talk to me here." She winced, trying to move, obviously still in pain from her surgery. Maybe I should've waited until tomorrow to do this. "Please, tell me what's going on."

Her eyes had tears in the corners, and I didn't like that at all. "No crying." I smiled. "This is a good thing. It's from your mom."

"My mom?" she whispered, watching as I pulled the key from my pocket. When I put it on her chest, she didn't move right away to take it. "What's this?"

"It's for a safety deposit box. Your mom left you a little something. Cash, I think." I slid a hand through my hair. "Apparently it's a lot. Enough for a building deposit."

Her eyes widened. "You're shitting me?"

I shook my head. "Wouldn't dream of it."

At that, she lifted her head, smiling at me, tears dripping down her cheeks at the same time. She didn't wipe them away. And I didn't either. It meant she was happy. I could see it in her now sparkling eyes. I could almost bet they were golden right then. Gold eyes meant happy.

"Eloquent boys become hard men." She grinned wider, searching my face.

"Huh?" I cocked a brow, confused.

"It's you. The eloquent boy with the soft words and stories. You've become a hard man, but an easy one to love."

"You still love me?"

"I never stopped."

I shut my eyes, then crawled over her with ease, damn careful not to touch her knee. "Maya, God…" I kissed her lips, just once. Loving her fingers in my hair—pulling with an emphasis that said, *Mine.*

"I love you so damn much." I parted her lips with my tongue, shuddering when her other hand wrapped around my back and tugged at the base of my shirt.

"Show me how much," she said.

I laughed. "Yeah, no. You should rest. We've got time."

"No. Time is something we might not have."

My throat burned when I tried to swallow, knowing exactly what she meant.

She was right. Time wasn't infinite. Nobody was safe. But I would make sure that the time we spent together was the best kind.

With shaking hands, she tugged my shirt up. I let her, grinning as she made short work of my clothes. She flicked at the buttons on my jeans after that, and I carefully maneuvered them off, along with my boxers.

I reached for her shirt next, a little crazed and hurried. Still, even as she lay naked beneath me, I had to ask. "Are you sure you're up for this?"

"It'd hurt me more if we didn't."

I took her mouth again, gentle, slow, tongues sliding, hands grazing. I took my time, determined to keep her comfortable, even though her nails dug into my back, and her hips arched, seeking my cock. Even in the dark, her body was a thing of beauty and perfection. Perfect tits, pink nipples, pert and ready for my tongue. I took one in, moaning as I sucked, loving the tiny hisses of appreciation coming out of her mouth. With my other hand, I slid my fingers beneath the waistband of her panties.

"Sebastian," she whimpered, shivering as I slid one finger between the lips of her pussy. "Feels so good."

I slowly slicked a finger across her wet and swollen clit, playing, pinching, flicking… She shivered, and my cock grew even harder.

"I need you," she pleaded and dropped her head to the side, allowing me to kiss her neck. While I did, she tugged out a condom from the bedside table's drawer.

My lips twitched. "Thought we went through those."

"I restocked."

I pulled back, smirking. "Insatiable."

She nodded. "For you, I always will be."

God, I didn't deserve her. Never would. But I'd be the best man I was capable of, for her. Forever. Ripping the condom wrapper with my teeth, I unwrapped the foil then slipped it over my cock, careful to keep my weight off her. Then between her legs, I settled in, spreading only her good one to the side.

"Sebastian," she groaned, fingers digging, playing with my hair. "I'm not gonna be too good at this tonight after all."

"That's okay." I kissed the space just to the left of her mouth and whispered, "I'm gonna love you enough for both of us."

She shivered, nodded, and then I licked her neck, nibbling, propping my hands up beside her head on the pillow as I pushed inside.

I froze, chest heaving, the world around me spinning.

"Fuck, I missed this." I kissed her nose, her eyes, every inch of her face. "I missed you."

Reaching around me, she ran her fingertips down my back, over my spine, her palms landing at my ass as she pulled me in even deeper.

"I missed you too." A kiss on my chin, my throat, my pulse. "So much."

Eyes shut, I shuddered at her words, her lips, nuzzling her chin to bring her gaze back to my eyes. "You mine, My?"

"Hmm," she murmured. "I've always been yours."

I smiled at that then pressed my forehead to hers, living in the moment. The feel of her wrapped around me, and her words sucked deep into my soul.

Slow and steady, I began to move, sweat slicking our skin, down my back. Over and over our bodies slapped together. Her fingers on my bare ass, in my hair, my spine, digging.

With one leg off the bed and on the floor, I slammed into her, keeping it slow, gentle, but still giving her everything I had left. Giving her not just my body but my heart, my world.

I was hers.

She was mine.

Connected as one, we were the only thing that mattered.

"I'm so close…" She panted harder.

I was close too. "Let go, baby."

Lips parted, she tossed her head back, the view so beautiful I couldn't see anything else. And then she moaned and shook, tremors pushing through her as she cried out my name once, then twice as she came.

I didn't make it long after, my cock pulsing as I finished, hot streams of cum shooting through me as I gritted my teeth together and finished with one last grunt.

Moving was impossible. I was tired. Sweaty. Well-loved most of all.

Maya sighed, feeling limp beneath me, sated in a way that needed no words.

"Stay with me," she murmured, the words meaning more than for the night.

And when I said, "Always," what I really meant to say was, *Forever.*

EPILOGUE

Maya

"Hold still. I'm nearly done."

Slade groaned and lowered his face to the back of the tattoo chair, small beads of sweat gathering across his temple. I couldn't help but grin at the view, careful though to keep my giggles inside.

My big, tough Story Boy was officially showing his wuss side.

He growled, slapping a hand over my thigh as I crawled a little higher onto his hip, adjusting this way, then that, to finish my shading. "This shit hurts."

I rolled my eyes and leaned down to get at his rib cage, only to drop a small kiss beside the outline of the final star. "There. All better."

His response was a grunt. And this time, I couldn't hold back my giggle if I tried.

Of all the tattoos I thought he would ask me for, I never imagined it would be three stars filled in with three boring colors. The first one was gold, but muted, which wasn't so bad, but the second was dark brown. Boring. Muddy. Now this last one I was getting ready to fill in was green. He wanted it to be the same shade as the grass, and was so specific about the color that he pulled up an example on his phone. I wasn't sure what the significance was behind his new tats, but I didn't ask, just appreciated the canvas I got to work on—and not just because it was insanely sexy either. Because it was Slade, and he was mine.

The building was empty now, just the two of us. Had been for the past two hours. The rest of the guys who'd been helping set up the shop all day had returned to the compound. Even my new, personally assigned bodyguards, Talker and his brother, Mute, were gone for the night—Slade's insistence, of course. I was pretty sure he thought we'd get to christen the parlor chair, but I wasn't down with bodily fluids on my brand-spankin'-new furniture.

"You going to stay with me tonight?" I asked, trying to distract him as the buzz of the gun slid across his skin.

He hissed but nodded, both eyes squeezed shut as I continued.

"I don't see why you won't let me move in," he hissed. "I'm there every night anyway."

I smiled and shook my head. "Because once Flick gets back, I don't want it to be weird."

"Then let me build something—ouch, damn it. You sure you're certified for this shit?"

"What'd you just say?" I stopped the tattoo gun, letting my hand fall to my lap.

"I asked if you were certified for this tattooing shit."

"No." I swallowed, failing to ignore the racing of my heart. "Before that."

His eyes narrowed, head turning at an awkward angle just to see my face. "What, about building something?"

"Yeah," I said, a little breathless. "That."

"I said I wanna build something for us. Like Hawk did for Summer."

"You do?" I blinked, tears filling my eyes. "Like, a real home?"

He grinned, one side of his mouth lifting higher than the other. "With soundproof walls."

"Slade…" My lips pressed tighter together as I tried to keep in my giddy sob. He wanted to give me a house. An actual *home*. For us.

"You good with that, I take it?"

Was I good with that? I was *more* than good with that. I was *great* with that. Ready for a step in my life that went beyond what I dreamed of.

"I am."

"Alright then." He reached over, grabbed my arm with the tat gun, and put it back on his ribs. "Finish me up first. One step at a time."

And just like that, he was going to build me a house. Granted it was on the compound, but... a house. A real house with a backyard and soundproof walls.

"Can I have a claw-foot tub?" I smiled, pressing the needle back against his skin. "Mom always wanted one of those."

He barely flinched after that, his voice taking on a little control. "Yeah, whatever you want. I'll make it happen, My."

I lowered my mouth to kiss the space between his shoulders, savoring each perfect second we shared.

This house thing wasn't something that would happen right away; that was an unspoken bit of knowledge. With so much going down with the club, and Pops, there were more important things to deal with right now. With Flick in Texas for another month, doing whatever he was doing down there, the guys were all about protecting home base. The people in it.

At first, the idea of buying and opening my parlor so quickly after the attack on the shop and Mom's death had made me nervous. But Slade had assured me we'd be fine. That we had to keep living, even if fear made it hard. Everyone else could believe his words, but I knew Slade well enough to understand that he was possibly more petrified than I was about things to come. Deep down, he just wanted to pretend like things could be normal for me, like I'd always craved growing up. But I'd come to the conclusion that there would be no sense of security or peace or normalcy in this world: the MC world. And for the first time in a lot of years, I was starting to accept that.

Thankfully, there hadn't been another attack on anybody in the club or on any club property for six weeks or so now.

Still, knowing it'd been so quiet made us all uneasy.

"Okay. I'm almost done." I dipped the end of my gun into the ink, swirling the green over the tip before pressing it to his skin. Using my left hand, I stroked a soft line at the base of his back, my urge to touch him stronger than ever before—even when it wasn't entirely the right time. I'd wasted too many years not doing what I wanted when it came to Slade.

"You okay down there?" I smiled.

"Hmm," he said, reaching around to rub at my bare thigh again. I'd chosen a skirt for the opening tonight, loving that the April air was no longer bitter cold. Plus, my scar had heeled incredibly well on my knee, so it was nice to be able to show some skin again.

As the stroking of his finger moved a little closer to the inside of my thigh, I paused. "You keep doing that, and I'm gonna mess this up." From the way my straddled thighs were now squeezing his leg, I could tell it wouldn't be long until my panties soaked his jeans.

God, what this man could do with his fingers.

"Sorry 'bout that." He smiled, so *not* sorry. He tipped his head back just enough to meet my eyes, and I couldn't help but zero in on his lips. So full, so pink. So… kissable.

"You're not sorry." I shook my head, and with one last drag of my gun, the green star was officially finished.

Leaning toward the tray I kept my equipment on, I grabbed the things I needed to clean him up, as well as the bandages he would need. "So, you're gonna wanna keep these dry."

He rolled onto his back, capturing both my hips beneath my skirt. "I know. Ain't my first rodeo, baby."

I lifted a brow. "From the way you went on about the pain, I never would've guessed."

He yanked me down on top of him, fingers in my hair. "There," he whispered, searching my eyes. *That's* the color I wanted."

My brows furrowed in confusion as our noses brushed. "What color?" I asked.

"The green in your eyes."

"Huh?" I scrunched up my nose, only for him to pull my mouth to his.

Slow kisses preceded his gentle tongue as he tasted my mouth, made me breathless. Maybe I was down for a little fun on this chair after all.

Lifting my head with both of his hands, he did that searching thing with my eyes like he always did. It was as though he was looking for answers to all of his questions inside of me.

"What are you looking at?" I asked, nuzzling against him, our foreheads flush.

"The tattoos, they represent your eyes," he whispered, kissing me again.

My stomach dipped, and tiny butterflies fluttered inside. "Oh."

He smiled and sat up, holding me astride his lap as he rubbed his hands up and down my thighs, beneath my skirt, dangerously close to my panties.

"Your eyes are my stars, Maya. Sparkling star eyes. Sometimes gold, but also green, and sometimes brown."

I blinked. "Like the colors of your tattoos."

His face grew pink, but he nodded, not looking away from me. "Yeah. Like my tattoos."

Breathless, I wrapped my arms around his neck, willing him to feel my love. Every piece of me was his, everything broken and bruised and battered; everything rebuilt or still untouched, too.

"I love you." I kissed his ear, tears falling. "Thank you for telling me that."

His big hands rubbed long lines up and down my back, over my spine, then back to my neck. "I love you too, My," he said into my ear, holding me close.

Who would've thought that the best tale Story Boy would ever tell me could actually become real?

A LETTER FROM HEATHER

I have a huge lump in my throat as I write this letter. Why? Because of you all getting to this point, reading this book. Whether you enjoyed it or not, I want to say thank you for giving Slade and Maya a chance. I don't write traditional MC stories, but I do write from the heart. And this book? It nearly wrecked me as I put my fingers to the keyboard—but in the best possible way.

If you enjoyed *Her Rough Ride*, I would be FOREVER grateful if you left a review somewhere in the universe. And if you'd like to be the first to learn about any of my books to come, be sure to sign up for my newsletter here:

www.bookouture.com/heather-van-fleet

Your email address will never be shared and you can unsubscribe at any time.

Thanks,
Heather

 authorheathervanfleet

 @HLVanFleet

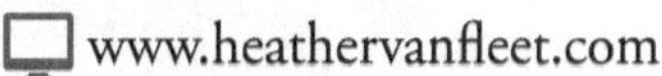 www.heathervanfleet.com